This book is dedicated to Clare, who changed my life; to my son, Hugh, whom I love more than I can say; to the memory of Sheila Keep (20 May 1937 – 13 November 1963); and to the Jewish woman from New York that I met at the Jewish Cemetery in Lodz on Tuesday 16 September 1997, 55 years after the 'Nightmarish Days'.

ACKNOWLEDGEMENTS

Terry Prone showed extraordinary kindness in agreeing to read the first decent draft of the book. (I thought the book was finished at that time but she showed me otherwise.) Her comments were clear, without exception correct and complete.

Jennifer Schweppe showed me the weaknesses of a later draft during two days in Prague. She also helped me with German translations. Anna Forstingerova held and gave me another key to the puzzle. I found the last of the clues in Slonim.

Josephine Bacon made translations from Hebrew, Yiddish and Polish.

Without Viki Williams, Paula McHugh, Amanda Bell, Jonathan Williams, Bernadette McHugh, Gundhild Lenz-Mulligan and Rachael Stock, the book would never have been published. Val Shortland did an extraordinarily sensitive job of editing the manuscript. I am grateful to the Bundesarchiv and the Zentrale Stélle der Landesjustizverwaltungen, both in Ludwigsburg, for their assistance.

'This fact of nature, so earthshaking in 1945, is an old story now. Still, it remains strange and frightening. We prefer not to think about it, as we prefer not to think much about the attempted murder of all the Jews in Europe by a modern government.'

Herman Wouk, War and Remembrance

Somewhere amid the forests of Bohemia a birch tree
*   bends its golden hair towards a reddish ruin.*
In mourning, hands clasped at its chest.
And yet the bluebells dance around its feet,
And coloured cow-wheat smiles upon the powerless dungeon
*   tower, while grasses idle mournfully on buried walks.*
Bright coppers flutter past the fallen, sunlit walls of
*   vanished generations.*

Gertrude Kolmar

'I have given orders to my Death Units to exterminate without mercy or pity men, women and children belonging to the Polish-speaking race. It is only in this manner that we can acquire the vital territory which we need. After all, who remembers today the extermination of the Armenians?'

Adolf Hitler, 22 August 1939

— PART ONE —

Chapter 1

The Polish country station appears deserted through the shimmering August heat haze that rises from the blackened cinders in the railway bed. Sunday. Late afternoon. The yellow harvest light beginning to steal amongst the buildings: the small waiting room; the signal box; the platform with its single wooden bench and small shelter, the stunted sunflowers growing in a trough against the red-brick wall. The last train to Lodz will be along in a bit, but for the moment there is just the heat and the silence; the occasional trill of a bird or cooing of a pigeon.

Ghosts come out at night. But ghosts can also emerge during the day. The older they are the longer it takes them to appear; the more difficult it is for them to appear. But appear they can.

Provided you try hard enough to see them.

There are plenty of ghosts here. Within living memory – if anyone still wanted to remember – there is the woman, a Jewess with false papers, who was discovered by the Gestapo in a random check on this very platform and shot on the spot. She had already lost her three children in round-ups. Mercifully, her ghost is sleeping this afternoon, the warm sunshine beaming through her atoms.

And that was 50 and more years ago. It is too nice an

1

afternoon to think about such things.

With a mechanical clank, the signal arm moves from the down to the up position. There is a dog sleeping under the bench, his dusty colour that of the platform itself, a natural camouflage. His tail gives a languid flick to show perhaps that he heard the signal change. Other than that he might as well be dead.

And now, faintly at first, comes the sound of hoof beats. It is so faint that it could equally be distant hammering or the knocking of a woodsman's axe, but at length the sound resolves itself into definite hoof beats. Somehow it is a comforting sound. The dog continues sleeping heavily. Unmoving.

A cart comes into view. It has four wheels and a worn canvas hood, which has been folded down. The driver sits in the front, bathed in sunshine, silent. He wears a flat cap and is deeply tanned. Apart from the driver, there are three other people squeezed into the back of the cart. A man and woman in their fifties and a girl of perhaps eighteen or nineteen. The cart comes to rest outside the door of the station. Almost as soon as it does a squadron of flies descends on the sweating, dust-coated horse. It begins to flick its head, ears and tail.

The three alight and walk into the station, through the shabby waiting room, and out onto the platform. The man has ambassadorial, silvery hair and round glasses. He points to the upraised signal and makes some remark. The woman is slightly too big for her white floral dress. It rounds and bulges in places where her body pushes against it. Despite the heat she wears stockings and shoes with heels. The man who drove the cart carries in a new suitcase. It is of brown leather with tan straps and reinforcements on the corners. He puts it down, removes his cap, shakes hands with the girl. He says something. They both smile, she especially. Her eyes smile. He goes back outside and lights a cigarette. Then he leads the horse to the shade of a tree and stands by its head, inhaling deeply and blowing the smoke at the hovering flies.

The train steams into the station, a small locomotive and a couple of battered carriages that railways seem to deliberately set aside for backwaters such as this. The man opens a carriage door, and lifts the suitcase inside. While he does this the woman talks to the girl. The woman is telling her things. Giving her instructions. The woman asks a question and the girl shakes her head. The woman then says something to the man, indicating with her finger and thumb that she wants money. The man hands over some notes from a leather wallet, but also reaches into his pocket for some change. In handing it to the girl, one of the smaller *zloty* coins falls, rolls off the platform and lodges amongst the cinders. It is still there to this day under layers of cinders.

Finally the girl hugs the woman, a hug which the girl is first to let go. She turns to the man, hugging him. He kisses her on the cheeks and then she climbs into the carriage. The door slams shut and the man and woman stand while the train slowly wheezes its way out of the station. They wave as does the girl, her shoulder-length dark hair blown round her face by the rushing air, until not just the train, but its plume of smoke has disappeared out of sight. There are tears on the woman's face.

The girl on the train has a broad face, olive-coloured eyes, high cheekbones and wide lips. She wears a white blouse, a summery skirt, sandals and sits by herself in the carriage, her suitcase touching the side of her leg. Gazing out of the window, she watches the flat countryside slip past. The soil is sandy and grey. It is the potato harvest. A horse-drawn plough moves solidly across the earth. Fires of dead foliage smoke. Whole families are busy in the fields. A kneeling woman in a headscarf picks up a bunch of potatoes in both hands, throws them into a bucket in front of her, moves the bucket and then shuffles forward to repeat the process. A farmer with a basket walks on the edge of some woods collecting mushrooms. The girl's eyes have a distant look as though she doesn't see these things. She rides alone for the duration of the journey.

The train pulls into the station at Lodz Fabryczna and the girl lifts off her suitcase. It appears to be heavy – occasionally she has to use two hands as she lugs it from the platform where she arrived. She goes into the station building, finds the notice board announcing the train timetables and spends a while trying to find her connection. Eventually she picks up the suitcase again and tramps back out to another platform.

She is early, but there are already some people waiting in the sunshine for the train to Warsaw. She finds an unoccupied end of a bench and sits down. There are a group of Chassidim, both young and old – caps, black and grey beards, black overcoats – in animated conversation on the bench. One of them, with round glasses, sideburns and a baby face, acknowledges her arrival with a casual glance and they shuffle to make some extra room for her on the bench.

As the time passes the benches fill up as does all the space around the gate leading to the platform. The girl continues to sit, glancing at the station clock, looking around her and checking that her suitcase is still there. Pigeons flutter in and out of a large circular hole set high up on one of the station's ornately moulded walls. At twenty minutes to the hour, a railway official comes along, unlocks the gate, closes it behind him and goes into the little cabin inside the gate. A ripple of expectancy runs through the crowd, causing several people to vacate their seats and move closer to the gate. However, the official sets his head firmly down, and begins to bustle with a sheaf of papers, occasionally licking a pencil and writing things on them.

Some commotion occurs near the entrance to the station and about twenty soldiers of the Polish Army carrying rifles and packs approach the gate. The girl checks her case again, pulling it closer to her. She crosses her legs and folds her arms, hunching forward. The soldiers' tunics are slung over their shoulders, or unbuttoned or tied to their packs. Many of them carry open bottles of beer. They are laughing. Singing. Joking. They gather in a group close to the seat upon which the girl and the Chassidim are seated. It isn't long before the soldiers notice the occupants of the bench.

'Bloody Jews should give up their seats to brave soldiers of the Polish Army.'

One of the Chassidim glances up and then looks away quickly, turning back into the conversation.

'Maybe we should just *take* the seats.'

'Their lady friend could keep her seat.'

The girl blushes and lowers her head over her folded arms.

'Or maybe she could come with us.'

'That would depend on whether she was a Yid or not.'

'Of course she's a Yid. Even a Polish whore wouldn't sit with Jews.'

'Well if she was a Yid, I wouldn't fuck her.'

The girl shuffles in her seat, unfolds her arms, clasps her hands and looks over her shoulder. In the same instant the nearest Chassid looks at her. Her eyes catch his. They exchange the minutest of expressions and an almost subliminal smile of acknowledgement.

'Maybe we should go ask her?'

'You ask her.'

There is a squeal as the platform gates are pulled open. The crowd eddies around the railway official's cabin. The Chassidim get up and the girl waits until they partially interpose themselves between her and the soldiers. The man who caught her eye offers to carry her bag but she smiles weakly and shakes her head. Her face is crimson. Using the Chassidim as a shield, she squeezes through the ticket check at the gate. She thanks the railway official who punches her ticket without looking up. Then she strides quickly, still blushing, away from the Chassidim towards the far end of the train. All the compartments are crowded but she finds one where she confirms that there is an empty seat. Despite her protestations, a young man helps her to put her case up on the luggage rack. Then she squeezes into the seat, one space from the window. Once the train pulls out, the man beside the window complains about the sun's brightness and asks the girl if she would change places with him. She agrees happily and slides into the space beside the window. There she spends the rest of the journey with her head resting against the dirty pane, staring out of the window. Once or twice there is hubbub in the corridor and the sounds of loud voices. The girl blushes whenever this happens and seems to press her head harder against the window. The journey to Warsaw is uneventful.

She joins the swarm of people leaving the train. However, alighting onto the platform, she steps to one side, out of the flow, and stands for several minutes, looking around. It doesn't look like she's expecting anybody, more that she's just catching her breath. By this time, the train has emptied and she is alone on the platform. Then, as if with great reluctance, she picks up the case and begins to haul it towards the exit.

Outside the station she queues at the taxi rank. One or two people jump the queue but eventually she finds herself in a car. She tells the taxi driver the address she wants and, sticking his arm out the window, he pulls savagely out into the flow of traffic.

An old man in a cap and black coat and carrying a chair on his shoulders so that his head lies between its legs, steps off the footpath with the intention of crossing the road. The taxi driver punches the horn and swerves theatrically.

'Stupid Jew,' he shouts, as he drives on, looking back in

6

the mirror.

They arrive at the address she gave him. It is a small hotel. The taxi driver pulls up, leans back and asks her for the fare. She seems surprised.

'Are you sure?' she asks.

'That's the fare.'

She reaches into the pocket of her skirt, extracts a purse and counts out the exact money. He looks at her when she reaches the end of the count. She hesitates, blushes and then counts out additional coins – several large ones. The driver says nothing, merely turning away when she has finished counting. She clicks the purse shut, opens the door and drags the suitcase awkwardly from the car as the driver races the engine. She closes the door behind her but it doesn't shut properly. The taxi driver glances round, an angry look on his face. She hears him mutter something. Then he pulls away from the hotel into the flow of traffic to the blaring of horns.

In the hotel the man in the small office under the stairs comes hurrying out from behind the desk, and shakes her hand.

'Miss Steinbaum. A pleasure to meet you. We've been expecting you. Your father said you'd be coming. Here, let me take that. Would you like some tea? Or coffee?' He is perhaps in his early forties, with a comprehensive paunch and a black moustache.

'No thank you, nothing thanks.'

The girl signs the register and the man carries her suitcase upstairs talking all the while. He knows her father. A fine gentleman. He can see the family resemblance. Dinner will be at seven. His wife does all the cooking. He hopes she will enjoy her stay. They may be able to help her find a permanent place to live. A cousin of a friend. When do her classes start? Tomorrow? So soon. No time to settle in and enjoy the delights of Warsaw.

He unlocks the room and gestures to her to enter. It is

7

bright and appears to have been recently painted. The room is stiflingly hot from sunlight streaming in through white net curtains. He puts down her suitcase and opens the door into the small bathroom, talking all the while. Finally, as he is leaving she proffers some coins. A genuine look of shock appears on the man's face.

'From Dr Steinbaum's daughter, no, I couldn't possibly. Save your money, my dear. You will need it once your classes begin.'

She tries to insist but he is adamant. Again the blushing. He reminds her that dinner is at seven and leaves.

Once he has gone, she pulls back the net curtains and opens the window with its four clean rectangular panes. A blast of fresh air and the sound of birdsong enter the room. She leans on the window sill and looks out. A narrow footpath. Striped sun awnings. A cobbled street. Some pedestrians. A thin tree with some dusty green foliage growing from a small disc of earth.

Leaving the window open and the curtains pulled back, the girl kicks off her sandals and bounces onto the bed, her skirt billowing before it falls. She puts her hands behind her head and looks up at the ceiling. Closing her eyes, she stretches a long, luxuriant stretch, which she holds until her arms begin to quiver. Then, hopping up from the bed, she opens her suitcase. She takes out two framed photographs. One is of the people who brought her to the train station. The other contains a man, a woman and a boy of about five. She places them on the small locker beside the head of the bed.

She goes to bed that night with the curtains open, and the street lights bathing the room in a white light. There is some desultory noise on the pavement but it doesn't appear to be this that keeps her awake, tossing and turning incessantly. Eventually, some time in the early hours of the morning, she drifts off into a deep but too short sleep.

It is the next day. Lunch time. In the crowded cafeteria of the Warsaw Conservatory of Music, the girl sits at a table eating. Her cheeks are flushed. There are others at the table but they are talking amongst themselves. She eats quickly and as soon as she finishes, gets up, leaves and goes for a walk outside until the lunch break is over.

The hotel room. The girl's name is Ariela. She is writing in her diary. *'I am an interesting and exciting person. How to let others know that? And how to not forget it myself? How I wish I were at Brzykow – where I don't have to justify myself to anybody.'*

It is winter. The streets of Warsaw are slushy as the girl goes up the steps of the Conservatory. She wears boots, a heavy coat and a fur hat. Passing by a notice board, leafy with paper, something catches Ariela's attention. She stops and reads intently. Then she opens her bag, takes out a music manuscript book and scribbles a note on its front cover.

Ariela walks along a city street. She counts off building numbers until finally she stops in front of what looks like a run-down bar. She takes a piece of paper from her pocket and checks the address. Then, somewhat tentatively, she enters.

She finds herself inside one large, long room, with a high ceiling. There is a bar near the front, a couple of dozen round tables and a small, low stage at the back. The stage is illuminated and on it, a four piece band – sax, piano, drums and bass – accompanies a female vocalist. All five people are young – in their early twenties. Ariela waits by the bar and listens to the performance.

The girl finishes, the band play the last few bars. There is some conversation and then the girl steps off the stage, gathers up her coat and hat, and comes towards the back of the hall. The sound of her feet on the wooden floor echoes in the empty room. When she reaches Ariela, she says:

'Good luck. They're a good band.'

'Thanks,' says Ariela.

She makes her way through the tables, unbuttoning her coat.

'You've come for the audition?' the saxophonist asks.

'Yes.'

'Leave your things there, and come up.'

Ariela removes her coat. She wears a white blouse and a blue-green skirt.

'What's your name?' they ask as she mounts the two steps onto the stage.

'Ella.'

'Like Ella Fitzgerald?' the saxophonist asks.

'If you like.'

'What are you going to sing?'

'Do you know *Stardust*?'

The pianist plays the opening bars. The saxophonist says 'we know it.'

'Could I get a glass of water?' asks the girl.

'I'll get it,' the pianist volunteers.

While he is gone, the girl waits on the edge of the stage, shins crossed, rolling back and forth on the outside edges of her feet. The musicians busy themselves with their instruments. Nobody says anything. The pianist returns with a beer glass of water. She drinks it all in one go. Then she says:

'Sorry to keep you waiting.'

She sings three songs with them, two slow, one upbeat. When she is finished, they tell her that they have two more singers to see, and that they'll be in contact with her. Can she leave her address? She writes it down and then asks if she can wait and listen to the other singers.

'I don't see why not,' says the saxophonist.

She steps down and goes to one of the tables furthest away from the stage, where she sits in the semi-darkness and listens to the other singers. As the second singer finishes, she gets up to go.

'Ella?' It is the saxophonist calling from the stage. 'Can you just wait a couple of minutes?'

When the other singer has gone, he asks 'Would you like to do a few more songs?'

It is later that night. From a public telephone she dials a number.

'David? ... No ... no ... there's nothing wrong ... listen... I did this audition with a jazz band ... I got it ... I'm going to start singing with them next week.'

In the nightclub where Ariela sings, the band has finished. Some girls are talking to the saxophonist and the bassist and drummer. The pianist is folding up sheet music. Ariela returns from back stage wearing her coat. She passes by the piano and he says as quietly as possible:

'What are you doing tomorrow, Ariela? Would you like to meet in the afternoon? Maybe go for a walk or a cup of coffee?'

'Oh thanks, Broni, but do you mind if I don't? These late nights are killing me. And I've got all this study to do. Maybe another time.'

'Yes,' he says, 'maybe another time.'

Winter. The four musicians and Ariela crowd into the steaming restaurant out of the frozen, slushy night. They order beers, choose from menus and chat animatedly while waiting for the food to come.

Tonight Ariela seems quite different from the girl who began her journey at the country station. Tonight she is laughing, lively, talkative. Two of the men, in particular, a rake-thin one and a taciturn, bear-like one, smile at her a lot and she returns both their smiles. However, there is a marked difference in the quality of the two smiles. To the bear her smile is warm, twinkling, friendly. Is there perhaps an expression of gratitude, that for once she is not the quietest one at the table? Gratitude but perhaps also sympathy that there has to be anyone at the table like this. To the thin one with the cigarette her smile is radiant and lingering. The bear is called Broni, short for Bronislaw, the other one Stefan. The pianist and the saxophonist.

It is late when they leave, breaking off to go in separate directions, except for Broni, Stefan and Ariela. They chat for a little while, stamping their feet and beating their arms against the cold. Eventually, Broni too departs and the other two walk off in a different direction.

'You're the best thing that's ever happened to this band,' says Stefan.

'I doubt it. You're all great musicians. Look at you. Look at Broni.'

'Yes, but up until now, I'd never seen how we might go forward. Okay, we're here and we're popular in Warsaw, but what does that mean? Nothing. It's in the west is where we need to be. Paris maybe, but eventually in America. Berlin was good, but not any longer, not with those stupid Nazis.'

'I have friends in Paris. A couple of girls who were with me in school.'

'So you'd come with me?'

'Well – what about the others?'

'They'll never leave Warsaw. Except for Broni, maybe. We've talked about it before. They reckon it's too risky. Especially now with the political situation. Anyway, you can find good musicians anywhere. No, I thought it would be you and me. We'll go to Paris, form our own band, and take it from there. What do you think?'

'When would we go?'

'As soon as we had enough money together. Next year. Early summer.'

'I have two more years of study.'

'That's the chance you'd have to take. If you didn't go you'd never know how it might have worked out.'

'Do the others know you're thinking like this?'

'I've talked about it with them a couple of times. I think they feel it's just talk, that I'll never actually do anything. But I have to. If I don't I'll never realise my full potential here.'

Ariela stops outside an apartment block.

'This is where I live.'

During the weeks that follow she is constantly in Stefan's company. On his arm. Holding his hand. Kissing him in public places. She sits at a kitchen table while Stefan scoops fillets of fish from a frying pan first onto her plate, then onto his.

'I've never cooked herring before,' he says.

She tastes it, grimaces and says laughing, 'Well, you can still say that.'

He looks at her.

'You're beautiful,' he says.

He leans down, frying pan still in hand, and she kisses him languorously.

Ariela calls cheerfully across the stage to Broni, who sits at his piano, fingering the keys. He plays snatches of tunes, which he breaks off as soon as they start to become vaguely recognisable. 'Coming for something to eat before we start, Broni?'

He shakes his head.

'Think I'll practice a little,' he says.

'Are you sure?'

'Yeah.'

'Okay, see you in a while.'

He nods and returns to his playing. As Ariela leaves the club with Stefan and the other two musicians she says:

'It's a pity he doesn't come with us as much as he used to.'

Chapter 2

Lodz, Poland. Mid-August, 1939.

David Steinbaum leant his head wearily against the door frame, surveyed his desk cleared and tidied for the first time in ages, then switched out the light. Holidays. Two long blissful weeks with Anna and Marek. He closed the door and went down the corridor.

'Another late night, Mr Steinbaum,' the porter remarked.

He was fat in the way of people who spend their life waiting while nothing in particular happens.

'The last one for a while,' said David. 'I'm going on holidays.'

He whispered the words, as though saying them too loud might cause someone to hear and abruptly cancel them.

'So?' said the porter. 'Any place nice?'

'No place special. The country maybe.'

'Lucky you,' said the porter, in a toneless way that David, in his tiredness, didn't notice.

'Well, good night,' said David.

'Good night, Mr Steinbaum. Enjoy your holiday.'

'I will,' called David over his shoulder as he disappeared out the door.

'While you still can, you dirty Jew,' muttered the porter, as he eased himself from behind his desk, and reaching for his bunch of keys, went to lock the front door.

Residual heat hung in the air, and the sky was coral blue after what had been an inordinately hot day. David could see a star. He slung his jacket over his shoulder, carrying his briefcase in the other hand. His face felt crackly with stubble and he was bare-headed, the lightly oiled black hair somewhat bedraggled from repeatedly pushing it back with his hand. He took a shortcut to get to Pomorska Street, passing apartments whose upstairs windows were open – yellow rectangles of light. Projections of these – angular parallelograms – carpeted the cobbled streets or dappled the leafy trees. He could smell coffee, and hear the sound of a phonograph playing Mozart.

A tram came careering round a corner, bell clanging, its overhead connection sizzling and sparking. A couple of other people were its only occupants, the mid-evening lull not having quite ended yet. David yawned and kneaded his eyes and cheekbones with the heels of his hands. He wished it could have been last year. That had been a holiday; the best ever, better even than their honeymoon. It had been the first year they had had any money for a holiday. Prior to that their house – first buying it and then the seemingly bottomless pit of renovation – had consumed all they had. But last year had seen the first light at the end of the tunnel.

They took two weeks in a small hotel in Krynica. Family-run. Jewish, but not very strict. The clientele mostly Jewish as well. David no longer practised the religion in which he had been brought up, yet he found it hard to think of himself as fully Polish. Three thousand years of Judaism wasn't shaken off so lightly. And though Anna didn't practice either, she had begun to talk about resuming for Marek's sake. At least to keep the Sabbath.

Marek was five. He was a solitary sort of kid but found some friends. David hoped that it might have marked a change in Marek, that he was starting to leave some of his shyness behind.

David played little scenes from the holiday in his mind. He and Marek at breakfast. Marek having made up a joke and saying 'Do you want to hear my joke again?' for the umpteenth time as they both laughed. Like all parents, David wondered what his son would be. Was he a poet or a writer? Because one evening Marek had asked:

'What two fruits can you make from the moon?'

The answer, it turned out, was an orange and a banana.

Or maybe he was going to study science like his father, since he had once asked 'Where does a sound go when it dies?'

David and Anna were sitting on the patio one evening when Marek called them from their second-floor window.

'Smile,' he said.

He had David's camera and snapped them as they turned simultaneously to look up.

David had gone up to the room one evening to check that the boy was asleep and found him crying, goodness knows for how long.

'I had a bad dream. Will you stay with me for a while?'

It was Anna's birthday while they were there. Over dinner that night they hummed 'happy birthday to you' quietly. Keeping it quiet so as not to attract attention to themselves was all part of the joke. When they had finished Marek came round the table and kissed Anna on one cheek while David kissed her on the other. He remembered how she had touched them both on the cheek. Later at the table, alone, while Anna was taking Marek up to bed, David gazed out at the still bright evening. A dancing band played some sentimental music. Life just didn't get any better than this. The thought crossed his mind that it would be better to die now than live to have it taken away. It was a morbid sentiment of a kind that he normally didn't engage in. But this evening as he looked out at a couple of birds hopping on the verandah and hovered his nose over some brandy, he felt he could just levitate into heaven.

He had met her in a Krakow hotel, he following his business as a salesman of scientific instruments, she teaching courses in how to operate a computator. It was rare – in fact, he had never done it, before or since – for him to 'pick up' somebody like that. But they had both been at separate tables and their eyes had met. (In truth, he'd been stealing glances at her whenever he could.) In a reflex action he had turned away, but while his head was in mid-turn she had smiled at him. His head had been moving too swiftly to stop, so he had failed to return the smile. He had to wait to catch her eyes a second time to smile at her. She smiled again. Did he really then just get up and walk across to her table and ask if she would like to join him? Even now he was staggered at his own daring. She had accepted and once it had turned out they were both from Lodz, then the evening was assured.

They married a little less than two years later. She gave up work when she was a few months pregnant. Even though she was a city girl, she wanted to live in the country. His parents had a place outside Lodz, which she said she would have liked – minus his parents! She made her own bread these days, she kept a small vegetable and herb garden, and it always struck David that she was preparing for that move out of the city. Some Jews talked of moving to Palestine, but Anna and David felt closer to Poland. What business would they have in a desert?

So much had happened since then. There had been all that business with the embassies. Innumerable letters and applications, trips to Warsaw, taxi rides to embassies, and always at the end, a bureaucrat, pleasant, content, telling them that the waiting list was a year, two years, five years. Days that had started out so full of hope and ended up with that awful,

17

silent train ride back to Lodz.

Looking back it was hard to imagine what it had all been for, since even if they had been granted a visa to some place, he wasn't sure if they would have gone. He might have, but he didn't think Anna would. Both of their parents were still alive and while David always talked about everyone having to be responsible for themselves, he wasn't sure, in the end, whether he would have gone off and just left them. Anyway, the question was academic now.

Kristallnacht was the thing that had really scared them, all of them, every Jew in Poland, even people who were only Jewish for their parents' sake like David and Anna. If the Germans could carry out a pogrom against their own Jews like this – before the eyes of the world – what would they do to Polish ones? The newspaper accounts still haunted David. He only had to be doing something in the house, to see Marek sleeping, or Anna knitting in her armchair, and they would be there: Nazis, booted, bull-necked, stentorian-voiced.

David had never imagined that he would have to deal with questions of military history and precedent, but now, as they entered high summer, he found himself wondering whether the Nazis would invade. This was the campaigning season. But then wasn't there something about bringing in the harvest before you invaded?

They had planned to go back to Krynica this year, but when all the uncertainty began they cancelled the holiday. Now that the days were actually upon him, David knew he didn't want to stay in Lodz. But neither did they want to be too far away in case something did happen. They would probably end up going to Brzykow, to his parent's house in the country, about an hour from Lodz. It wasn't the best. Given the situation there would probably be other members of the family there. That would be good for Marek – he would have cousins to play with – but he and Anna would have no time to themselves. Still that couldn't really be helped now.

Tomorrow was the Sabbath. Neither David nor Anna practised, but his parents were Orthodox, so he couldn't be seen to travel tomorrow. They would go on Sunday. Tomorrow would be the first day of his holidays. They spent most Saturdays working on the house, but tomorrow they would take off.

David wondered if his sister Ella would come down at all. It had been months since he had seen her. She came home every weekend when she first went to Warsaw, but then there was that night she rang, saying that she had joined a jazz band. They had hardly seen her since then. David's parents kept asking him about her. Was she safe? What kind of company was she keeping? They hoped she hadn't forgotten her religion. He knew little more than they did, other than that she was still singing with the jazz band. Very good too by all accounts. She had sent him a review from one of the Warsaw papers. He kept meaning to go up to Warsaw to see her perform, but it was so hard to give jazz any importance, what with everything else that was looming.

The tram reached his stop and he walked the short distance to his house. He opened the front door and stepped into the darkened hall. Anna had finished sanding it yesterday, and it was covered with newspaper, awaiting its first coat of varnish. That would have to wait until they got back now. He hung up his jacket and leant his briefcase next to the hallstand. Light showed under the living-room door.

She was knitting and reading. She read voraciously, the knitting was merely something to keep her hands busy. Looking up she offered her lips as he kissed her.

'I'll just finish this row,' she said. 'Did you eat?'

'Yes.'

When she had finished she got up and laid the knitting on

19

a small table beside her chair.

'I'll make some coffee,' she said, disappearing through the kitchen door. He followed her in.

'How was Marek today?'

'Fine. Fine. He spent most of the day in the garden. I hardly saw him.'

The kitchen was painted a bright yellow, with stripped floorboards and a large window that faced south east and looked out onto their small garden. The place had an almost country feel to it, something of an achievement in an industrial city like Lodz. He put his arms round her as she reached for the coffee tin. She squirmed and wriggled in his arms.

'Not now, David. I'm tired.'

'I thought tomorrow we might go into town – to the park maybe or the cinema. Have something to eat.'

'I was going to do the varnishing.'

'Leave it. We'll do it before the holidays are over. We haven't had a weekend off in ages.'

She said nothing, and he read the silence as agreement even though it felt more like she didn't care.

After she had gone to bed, he put a record on the phonogram. Smetana's *Ma Vlast*. He remembered the first time he had heard the second movement, *The Moldau*. He had felt like he was floating. He closed his eyes and had the same sensation now.

For nearly a year they had played the visa game, filling in forms, providing endless photographs, birth certificates and other documentation. Then they had phoned, written and badgered – insofar as this was possible – the embassies into giving them interviews. Anna had been behind this tactic.

'You should know yourself,' she said, 'you're the salesman. You have to get that first meeting. They won't take your calls. They'll throw your letters in the bin. Meet them face to face and you're halfway there.'

They had had three interviews, at the American, Canadian and Australian embassies. All it had needed was one of them to say yes. They would have been gone within a month. At least that's the way they had felt at the time.

David wore his best suit, dark blue with a white shirt, while Anna looked businesslike in a grey skirt and jacket from her training days. She had her hair done. They had agonised for a long time over whether or not to bring Marek with them and finally decided not to. The question had been whether they would have got a sympathy vote in having a child with them or whether, on the contrary, they would have looked like refugees. They finally agreed that the image they wanted to convey was of a successful professional couple. David carried his briefcase as though he were going on a business trip.

He felt optimistic as soon as he stepped past the two burly marines into the hall of the US Embassy. Even though it was here in Poland, this was a piece of American soil. Different laws operated here. An ocean separated it from the taint of Germany. Here was safety. Having given his name at the reception desk they waited in the cool marbled interior while tanned, well dressed men and pretty girls passed by carrying papers. David listened in fascination to their accents as they spoke English. He repeated some of the phrases in his head. Anna fussed with her hair, surreptitiously glancing in her compact to check her makeup. To his surprise, rather than feeling intimidated, David felt at ease – he could live amongst these people.

'Up the stairs and to the right,' the Polish receptionist said. 'The door marked "waiting room".'

In the crowded waiting room – there weren't enough seats even for the women – David and Anna were the only two who didn't look like refugees. This in itself was embarrassing. They also seemed to be the only two who weren't obviously Jewish. Everyone seemed to have dressed up for the occasion but most of the clothes were still poor. Fathers read Yiddish newspapers, while harassed mothers tried to control children. Several Jews with beards, side locks and dressed in black sat quietly, their minds elsewhere. Occasionally someone glanced at the clock on the wall and made some comment about the time. It was just after 9.30. Their appointment was for ten o'clock.

David quickly realised that the appointment time meant nothing. A secretary with a clipboard would look in at intervals and call somebody from the room. It appeared as if all the people in the room – there must have been nearly 30 – were ahead of David. New people arrived as fast as others left. It was like those arithmetic problems in school about filling a tank that has a hole in it. Sometimes the intervals were very short, sometimes longer. None was more than ten minutes.

It was 11.45 when they were called. The secretary led them into an adjacent room where a young man, thin, clean-shaven in a blue shirt with the sleeves rolled up on his forearms, invited them to sit. There were two columns of manilla folders, one high, one low. Other than these the desk was clear. David expected him to reach for a folder from one or other of the piles but he didn't. Instead he placed his elbows on the desk, interlaced his fingers and said in good Polish:

'As we would have explained to whoever arranged this interview, there is very little point in your coming here at this time. We have your application and we are processing it with all due speed. Once we get to a certain point in our procedures, then we will call you for interview. Until then I'm afraid it's just a question of sit tight and wait.'

He said the last few words with what sounded like genuine sympathy. He looked at them both in turn. David thought Anna was going to say something and he looked across at her. But she was staring at either the picture of

President Roosevelt or the American flag. David said:

'Er, we were anxious to check that we're in … that our application was being processed.'

The man smiled easily and placed a hand on each of the piles of folders.

'I can assure you it is, Mr Steinbaum. You just have to realise that we get such a lot of applications' – he paused – 'particularly from your co-religionists.'

'When can we expect to hear …?' David trailed off.

'About a year until we interview you. Then say, another six months if everything checks out, then you get your visa. With your qualifications – should I say, *both* of your qualifications – your case should be fairly straightforward.'

The man stood up. David and Anna followed suit. David hesitated, unsure whether or not to shake hands. The man smiled pleasantly and indicated the door. 'Mr and Mrs Steinbaum,' he said.

In a café afterwards they ate a sandwich and had some tea. David could feel a headache starting.

'Maybe we should have been more forceful? Pushed harder.'

'I thought you were going to.'

'It seemed to me that we shouldn't have been there at all. I'm surprised that a man as busy as that was as polite as he was.'

The Canadian embassy had the same large crowd in the waiting room – they might have been the same people from the American one – but here the appointment times seemed to have more meaning. They were still delayed though because the official they were meant to see was late back from lunch. Not that anyone said this but the fresh gravy stain on his tie when he eventually showed up told them as much. This time, as soon as they were ushered in, David took the initiative.

'You speak Polish, Mr – ?'

'Fennel. Ralph Fennel,' said the well-built man who filled his gleaming white shirt like wheat fills a sack. 'Sure I speak Polish.'

'Mr Fennel. We arranged this meeting for two reasons. Firstly we wanted to check that our application had been received and was being given attention. Secondly we wanted to ensure that it could be dealt with as quickly as possible, ideally before the end of the summer.'

Fennel looked at David steadily, saying nothing.

'We are both skilled, professional people, Mr Fennel. We believe that if we are allowed entry to Canada, we will very quickly become assets to your country and become wealth-producing members of your society. We would like to ask you to treat our application with special urgency.'

'Do you speak English?' asked Fennel, in English.

'No, Mr Fennel, we don't speak English,' David replied in Polish. 'German, both of us, yes, but not English. However, we are already enrolled in English classes for when we return from our summer vacation.'

'Good.' The voice was non-committal.

'We have looked carefully at your application, Mr and Mrs Steinbaum. Everything you say is true. You have impeccable credentials.' He paused.

'Unfortunately there is no fast path through any of this. We are a democracy after all, Mr Steinbaum. Which I presume is one of the reasons you applied for entry to Canada.'

He looked at each of them in turn as he said this and paused for some moments before continuing.

'We deal with applicants on a strictly first-come-first-served basis. I'd say we are about six to nine months away from dealing with your application. But after that things should go very quickly.'

'So how long do you think it would be altogether?'

24

asked Anna.

Fennel looked out the window as he spoke.

'Oh … from today to the day you walk out of here with a visa in hand – about twelve months.'

'But surely there are ways of speeding these things up?' asked David, trying to keep the desperation out of his voice. 'If we were famous or wealthy, there are … there are things that could be – '

His voice faltered as he saw a minute change in the expression on Fennel's face. Quickly David held up his hands palms outward. He continued:

'Please – don't get me wrong. I'm just trying to find out whether there is any way the time could be shortened.'

Fennel's voice took on an almost fraternal air.

'In other times, Mr and Mrs Steinbaum, maybe. I think it's fair to say you would have qualified easily. Now, in the current climate, it's not so easy. The sheer volume of applications and the relatively small quotas make our job extremely difficult. I'm sure you understand. We are doing everything we can. It is not for the want of willpower and effort on our part.'

When he had imagined these embassy trips they had always pictured a quick interview, success, followed by a day spent in Warsaw, shopping for Anna, a nice meal, perhaps an overnight stay before returning home. On their way to the Australian Embassy David remembered that they held hands tightly in the taxi.

They were ushered in quickly to a thin-faced man without an ounce of spare flesh. David started off as he had in the Canadian Embassy. When he had finished the man gave the usual platitudes, explaining why their application would take a year to eighteen months with no guarantee of success. This time it was Anna who responded. The man was polite, firm, more pessimistic than any of the others, using the same vague language that seemed to be the stock in trade of embassy

25

officials. Anna became more upset.

'Put yourself in our place, if you can. We have a little boy. He's five years old. If the Germans attack Poland what will happen to him?'

'I have explained that we are doing everything we can, as quickly as we can, Madam.'

'But surely you can do more. Your country is vast. And your people understand what it is to want to get away from oppression. Why will they not help?'

'We are helping in every way possible, I assure you.'

The man was becoming exasperated. David thought Anna had better stop. Her voice became pleading.

'Sir, we are only three people. What difference will three people make?'

The man went to speak but seemed to change his mind. He thought for a moment and then began.

'You must understand. Ours is a young country. Being young carries with it its own problems. And these problems we are doing our best to solve. However, there are some problems – happily – that we don't have; problems that might have made their way from the old world but, for one reason or another, have not. One of these is a racial problem. One that is rife throughout Europe. In Germany for sure, but also here in Poland. I must tell you that we Australians have no interest in importing such a problem. As a result our immigration procedures invariably take a long time.'

David was about to wind up the interview when he was startled to hear Anna say:

'I'm appalled to hear such offensive, anti-Semitic talk coming from a representative of your country. I'm sure this isn't your government's policy. Please, I wish to speak to somebody senior.'

No change came in the man's facial expression but when he spoke his voice was icy.

'I'm afraid that won't be possible without a prior appointment.'

He closed the file on his desk and stood up.

'As I have said already, we will be in touch in due course. Now please I have another appointment waiting. Good day to you both.'

As the door closed behind them, David imagined he heard something being dropped into a waste-paper bin.

He didn't sleep well and was awake early the next morning. For a long time he lay, listening to their house as it breathed. Water trickled in a pipe. A floorboard creaked. Finally, he went to the bathroom and lit the gas under the boiler, pouring steaming water into the sink. Then he reached into the bathroom cabinet and took out his shaving mug, brush, Samolin soap and razor.

The tools of civilisation. What happens to them when their owners die? Thrown out, most likely. Their functions are too intimate, the associations too close to their former owner, to be kept or passed on. So perhaps it is that millions of shaving mugs, brushes and razors find their ways into dustbins and hence onto rubbish heaps; pressed beneath the debris of each generation to become the archaeological treasures of those to come.

David Steinbaum's shaving brush had quite another ending. It ended up 300 kilometres south of where he last used it, and even though that was over 50 years ago it can still be seen today. Of course, you don't know that it is his. And anyone who might have been able to tell you is long since dead. David Steinbaum's shaving brush lies, with thousands of others, in a heap at the Museum in Auschwitz. Tiny crawling things inhabit its badger bristles, and tiny particles of soap cling to it from the last time it was used to lather David Steinbaum's face.

Chapter 3

A hot afternoon in late spring. Friday. The train bringing Lodzers home from Warsaw for the weekend pulls into Lodz Fabryczna. It is almost six months since David has seen his sister. She is wearing lipstick. When she sees him, she runs and they embrace. He smells a faint trace of lily of the valley. They hold each other, squeezing tight.

'It's great to see you,' he says.

They kiss on the lips.

'I've missed you, David. I missed you so much.'

He takes her rucksack and they stroll into town past the Savoy Hotel to Piotrkowska Street.

'Has anything changed?' she asks.

'What? Here in Lodz? Nothing ever changes here.'

They find a café and sit outside in the sunshine.

'I have a problem,' she says, after they have taken their first sip of beer.

'Don't tell me your pregnant.'

'I am not!'

'That's a relief. That was Father's big fear after you left home.'

'He said that?'

'Sure he did. Maybe not to Mama, but he said it to me.'

'No, I'm not pregnant. It's this band that I've been singing with. They're a good band. But two of them are particularly good – the saxophone player and the pianist. The saxophone player is moving to Paris. He wants me to go with him.'

'Why you?'

'He says that he and I are the ones with the real talent. That we don't have a future in Poland. That in the west, our careers could go anywhere.'

'What about the piano player? Is he any good?'

'Broni. Yes, he is. I don't know why Stefan – that's his name – hasn't included him.'

'Maybe he fancies you. Stefan, I mean.'

'I have gone out with him a few times.'

'Have you slept with him?'

'You know, that's what I like about having you as a brother. There's no pussy footing around the place. Yes, once or twice. Are you horrified at your little sister doing something like that?'

'No, not at all. Do you like him?'

'Yes, a lot.'

'So, where's the problem?'

'You know where the problem is. Mama and Papa. It would mean giving up my studies. I'd miss you and Anna and Marek.'

'We could come and visit. I've always wanted to see Paris. You could transfer your studies.'

'But going off with a guy. What would they say?'

'Is he Jewish?'

Ariela smiled, and shook her head.

Her brother said 'Ah, now, you've got a problem,' while, in the same instant, she said,' I've got a problem, haven't I?'

David grinned. 'Another beer?' he asked. 'I don't know what to advise you. It was hard enough convincing them that it was a good idea for you to go off to Warsaw. They'd never wear this. But then, in a way, that's their problem. It's your career, it's your life. You've got to decide. Transferring your studies would help a bit. It's this fellow, Stefan, is the problem. What's he like, anyway?'

'He's a bit like you. Maybe that's why I like him so much. I'd feel so selfish, though. They've done so much for me.'

'Could you wait until your studies are over? Of course, that's not going to make it any easier, is it? It's this Gentile saxophonist is the problem.'

Food smells fill the air as David and Ariela come in the front door. Marek is already in the hallway, running out to meet them.

'Ella! Ella!'

Ariela whisks Marek off his feet and hugs him.

Anna appears at the doorway and embraces her sister-in-law, kissing her on the cheeks.

'Marek was just saying that you're his favourite relation,' says Anna, as they go through to the living room.

'Why is that, Marek?'

'Because all the rest of them are so old. You're the only one who's about my age.'

Ariela laughs.

'I'm honoured,' she says. 'I've got a present for you, Marek. It's in my pack. Here, have a look.'

Marek rummages in the pack until he unearths a box of toy soldiers. Delighted he kisses her and tears open the box, setting the soldiers up on the table.

After Marek has gone to bed, David rehearses Ariela's problem for Anna.

'Are you going for your career, or because you love him?'

'Both, I think.'

'If it was only one, would you still want to go?'

'If it was my career, I think yes. If it was just him? Yes, definitely.'

'There's your answer.'

It is Sunday evening when David sees his sister off on the

train back to Warsaw.

'Have you decided what you're going to do?' he asks.

She shakes her head.

'When the time for the decision comes, I'll just make it. Fate has always been good to me. Whatever I decide to do will be the right thing. Remember, before I first went to Warsaw. Remember we talked. About my shyness. And I said how this would be a good thing for me. Despite all the fears everybody had. I'll tell you, nobody was more afraid than myself, but just look at all the good things that have come from it. This will be the same, however it turns out.'

Chapter 4

In the vegetable garden of his house near Brzykow, south-west of Lodz, David and Ariela Steinbaum's father, Aron is harvesting onions. It is the last day of August, 1939. A robin sits alertly on the low stone wall watching him. Aron has a few day's holidays and he is doing some cleaning up before returning to Lodz. Aron always works in the garden without his glasses, claiming that it both rests his eyes and allows them to draw energy from the sun. Whether there is any truth to this or not the result is that in high summer his tanned face coupled with the fish-white circles around his eyes give him the appearance of a man wearing goggles.

Sun and rain have pretty much uncovered the bulbs and the stalks are on their sides and starting to wither. He clicks them from the ground with a slight sideways movement and loads them into a wheelbarrow, his back warm from the sun as he works. In all he brings six barrow loads round to a chestnut tree which has a long overhead branch that runs parallel to the ground for about two metres before turning upwards. The tree had been growing there when they first came here. Surrounded by briars and nettles it had been stunted and scrawny; but once these had been cleared away it had flourished. Climbing onto a chair he reaches up, circles some string around the branch and ties it. Then he ties the first onion to the bottom of the string and begins to work his way upward, entwining the green crunchy stalks around the string. Soon his hands are wet with spittle-like sap.

When the bunch is about a metre and a half long, he wheels the wheelbarrow in under the dangling bundle and trims off the green stems. They fall in the barrow like lengths of green hose pipe. When he has finished, the narrow, heavy, sack-like pendulum rotates gently in the breeze. They are fine onions: shiny green and brown ellipses, earth still clinging to the stringy roots. He will let them dry in the sun for the next week or two. They will end up with six strings; four they will take back to Lodz and two will be left hanging here in the kitchen.

Aron loves this little plot of land. Often he will lean on his shovel and with his eyes, drink in the neat rows of vegetables, different sizes, shapes and hues of green; the chocolate brown soil made so by years of fearsome manuring so that the soil is so potent it will grow almost anything.

The moon at Brzykow is like he's never seen it anywhere. At night, if he walks a few hundred metres from the house, he can see immediately the immensity of the heavens. The starlit sky seems to climb up vertically, and as he walks back towards the house he gets a sensation of the stars being rolled up behind him and unrolling in his path.

Chapter 5

Berlin. Summer, 1938.

Rudolf Fest, briefcase in hand, and wearing a summer suit, stepped lightly up the steps of Gestapo headquarters in the Prinz Albrechtstrasse and past the two SS guards. In the cool but oppressive interior his documents were checked by another SS man, and he was directed to the second floor.

As he stepped onto the first flight of steps, Rudolf noticed a padlock on the lift doors, something that was repeated on the remaining floors. So this was how the prisoners travelled to and from the basement. On the second floor he followed the guard's directions, down long corridors painted in institutional shades of cream or pale green gloss. Without exception the varnished doors bearing their occupiers titles in Gothic lettering were shut. So too were the windows, grey with dust and looking like they hadn't been opened or cleaned for a long time. The air was stuffy.

He knocked on the door marked 'Inspector for Statistics to the Reichsfuhrer SS'. A female voice called 'Komm', and he entered. The girl, rather overweight and plain, greeted him by name, and asked him to wait a moment. Then he was ushered into the presence of Dr Korherr. They exchanged the Nazi salute.

'Herr Doktor Fest, how good to see you again. Welcome to the Department of Statistics.'

'It's good to be here, Doctor.'

'They're not too upset losing you over at the Foreign Office?'

Rudolf smiled thinly.

'They'll cope,' he said.

Dr Korherr beamed back.

'I'm sure they will,' he said. 'I'm sure they will. Would you like some coffee?'

Rudolf remembered the first time they had met. A job interview. Rudolf, vegetating in the Africa Section of the Foreign Office, had spotted the opportunity in the list of internal vacancies. There were in fact a number of different lists, and Rudolf should only have had access to the ones pertaining to the regular Civil Service. However, for the last year or so, he had been casting his net far and wide, and had spotted this particular one on an SS list, which he had managed to get his hands on. 'Statistical Specialist' was what they had been looking for. Since, in theory, Rudolf wasn't meant to have access to this list, he had written to the SS Head of Personnel, describing his skills and asking to be informed of any vacancies in his area. Incredibly – for the SS bureaucracy was immense and a standing joke in the ordinary Civil Service – 'they make us look like private industry' – a response had come very quickly, and the interview with Dr Korherr had followed. A few days later the letter came offering him the job, a substantially better salary and mention of expenses. Rudolf had been overjoyed.

Rudolf's briefing lasted about 45 minutes. Then he was given a tour of the Department of Statistics, introduced to everybody and finally shown to his own office. It was somewhat smaller than Korherr's with a more ordinary looking desk and chair. Still it was comfortable, and had a nice view out onto Prinz Albrechtstrasse. After Dr Korherr had left, Rudolf, with some difficulty, opened one of the windows and warm air and street noises drifted up from below. He sat down at his desk. From his window he could see a ledge opposite where a couple of pigeons cooed contentedly, their wings iridescent in the sunshine. In preparation for his arrival, somebody had placed a couple of fresh notepads, plenty of pens and pencils, and other stationary on the red leather-topped desk. A black telephone occupied the top right-hand corner. Other than these it was clear. He would keep it that way – he liked a tidy desk.

Dr Korherr had explained that over the next few years, big geographic and demographic shifts in the Jewish population of Europe were likely. Rudolf's mission was to set up a system which would track and report on all of this. There was more than just the population movements, though. He would have to monitor all sorts of trends – birth rates, death rates, types and levels of sickness had been some of the ones that Dr Korherr had instanced. And finally, and most important of all, there would be revenues flowing as a result of these movements. He would have to try and predict what these revenues would be and then track them as they happened. It was the family business all over again, Rudolf thought with a smile; except Rudolf's territory was not a small country town. Rather it was all of Europe, from Ireland to the Urals, from Scandinavia to the Mediterranean.

At the end of the day Rudolf left things in such a way that he could pick them up again in the morning. There was still detailed work to be done but the major pieces were there. Eventually, there would be maps on walls, tables of figures, weekly reports with coloured graphs, and all manner of data available in every conceivable format to whoever wanted it. There would be detailed reports for operational people and high level ones for 'Heini' – Heinrich Himmler – and even the

Fuhrer himself. There wouldn't be a Jew in Europe who wouldn't have been counted, tabulated, analysed and graphed. All of this would come very quickly in the plan that Rudolf had sketched out and which would, by the end of the week, be given to his boss as a statement of what he planned to do.

Lisa, his wife, was picking up toys and tidying magazines, as he came in the front door of their three-bedroomed apartment and deposited his briefcase. They kissed.

'So how was your first day?'

'Fine. It's a shame Father isn't alive. I think he'd have been impressed.'

'I'm sure he would. Dinner's nearly ready.'

Lisa disappeared into the kitchen. A smell of roast pork escaped as the door closed.

'We've got a surprise,' shouted his two children, Eva aged five and Viktor seven, as they came running from a bedroom to greet him.

'Auntie Ursula is coming to live with us,' said Viktor.

'I'm giving her my room,' said Eva.

'That's a nice surprise,' he said, looking up at Lisa who had come back in from the kitchen and was blushing.

'Now remember what we said, children. We said we would ask Papa if she could come and stay with us for a while. Just until she found her own place to live.'

'She's moving to Berlin?' asked Rudolf.

Ursula, Rudolf's unmarried sister-in-law, lived in Dresden where she worked as a personal secretary to a businessman. At 33, she was Lisa's older sister.

'The company she was working for closed down. She said she's never going to work for anyone else again. She's going to start her own business – here, in Berlin, where the opportunities are.'

'Good for her,' said Rudolf. 'So when is she coming?'

'Well, I told her I'd have to speak to you first.'

'Oh, it's fine by me,' said Rudolf. 'I'd be delighted to have her here for a while.'

'Are you sure you don't mind?'

'Not at all. Ring her up now and tell her to pack her things and come up here as soon as she can.'

'She'll probably come after our holiday,' said Lisa, her face showing relief and pleasure.

'That's fine,' said Rudolf.

She turned to go, and then stopped. Turning towards him again, she smiled, and tucked her blonde hair behind her ear with a movement of her finger. Looking happy and sweet and guilty all at once, she said 'thanks' and kissed him.

Later, as they lay in bed, Lisa said:

'I hope you're doing the right thing with this new job. I liked the old job. You had short hours, nothing much to do and plenty of time to spend with the children. I want them to grow up knowing their father.'

Rudolf lay with his hands under his head. He dismissed her suggestion.

'Don't worry. Nothing's going to change. You know I've always been good at managing my time.'

But he found Lisa's comment about having time for the children grated on him like a stone in his shoe. When she said 'spend time with the children' what she really meant was spend time with her. As long as he has known Lisa she had craved his company. And even before that any male company. Berlin in the late 1920s and early 1930s was a fairly wild place anyway, but Lisa had been as wild as the best of them. Shortly after they had met, they had quickly established that neither of them were virgins.

Lisa had lost her virginity when she was sixteen and the vast – in comparison to Rudolf – number of liaisons she had had since then was a reflection – in Lisa's own view – of a search for some kind of love. She had found it with Rudolf and the comfortable, middle class, two child family seemed for her to be the apogee of what she had set out to achieve in life.

Well, Rudolf wanted more than that. And today was the first move down that road. She would have her warm family setting, but there were other things to be achieved. And, by God, he would achieve them.

Ursula was scheduled to arrive on a chilly Thursday evening at the end of September. Since he was in town, Rudolf would meet her off the train. He came down the office steps just after six-thirty and decided he had enough time to walk to the station.

He was a month into his new job and it was going well. Three weeks ago he had given Korherr a presentation on how he proposed to do the first part of his task – count Europe's Jews. Rudolf had prepared meticulously, considering all the possible sources of information, how reliable they might be, what the best order in which to do things was, and how long it might all take. Then for the presentation, he used a large time chart pinned to a blackboard and built his presentation around that. The chart showed when he would have rough estimates, when Korherr could expect final figures and the statistical reliability that might be expected in each case. The plan was accepted without reservation.

Rudolf did Germany and Austria first, producing a preliminary report with a complete analysis by region, age group, and socio-economic category. This was easy, of course, since he now had complete access to all census information in these countries. While he was working on this data, he started his research on the other countries. All of these were either neutral to or hostile to Germany. In these cases, he would have to use resources beyond those of his graduate research assistants. Korherr had agreed with this obvious point, and arranged for him to meet Adolf Eichmann, in SD 'Jews' Office II 112. The 'Jews' office was engaged in building up a card index of all prominent Jews in the Reich and abroad. Rudolf 's work dovetailed nicely with this: Eichmann was concerned with the particular, Rudolf with the general.

Rudolf felt invigorated by the walk and was sweating slightly as he came in the entrance of the *Hauptbahnhof*. He checked the arrivals board, found the platform and waited at the gate. The train arrived punctually and as the hissing steam died away, she appeared wearing a heavy, dark red coat and carrying a single suitcase.

Ursula was about the same height and build as her sister. Under the lights of the station Rudolf saw bronze, brass and mahogany in her hair. Ursula also looked younger than Lisa, despite the fact that she was three years older. She waved when she saw him, gave the ticket collector a big smile and a '*Danke Schoen*', and then came over to Rudolf. They embraced and she proffered her lips for him to kiss. He was surprised by this - he would have expected her cheek - and afterwards, he could taste her lipstick on his own lips. Maybe his memory of her as distant, somewhat arrogant, was faulty or maybe the years had changed her. He took her suitcase as she began to talk excitedly, saying how good it was to be in Berlin at last, asking about Lisa and the kids and his new job. She linked him and he led her outside where they found a taxi and made their way home.

Ursula was asleep the next morning as he got ready to go to the office, but Lisa was up, looking exhausted, preparing breakfast and getting the children ready for school. He had left the pair of them at midnight last night, still talking about the family and their childhood and making plans to go looking for shop premises today. What kind of shop, Ursula wasn't prepared to tell yet – at least, not to Rudolf. He would find out eventually, and the two sisters had laughed, enjoying the mystery.

'What would you like to do for the weekend?' he asked as she fussed around in her dressing gown.

'Sleep?' she asked, smiling wearily.

'I was thinking I might cook dinner for us tomorrow night, you know, with Ursula being here and everything.'

'Mmmm, that'd be nice,' said Lisa, a bit distractedly, as she stirred porridge.

'If I made a list of what I needed maybe you would get it while you're out.'

'Yes, just leave it on the table. Where in heaven's name are those children? Viktor, Eva, come on. You'll be late.'

Rudolf was first home that evening. He came in and dropped his briefcase, pulling open his tie. He headed for the bedroom, throwing off his jacket and opening the wardrobe to look for comfortable slacks and a sweater. He would change first and then go to pick up the kids. He took his suit off and folded it neatly, standing there in his underpants. Then, on an impulse, he went out of his own room into Eva's. Ursula's suitcase was on the floor, half unpacked, its top thrown back against the wall. He opened the wardrobe. Eva's clothes and Ursula's dresses and coats shared the single rail. Rudolf leant close, catching Ursula's scent from the garments. Her shoes, three different pairs, stood on the floor of the wardrobe. He picked one up, running his fingers over the smooth leather, cradling it in his hands, one hand behind the heel, the other beneath it. He lifted it to his lips. Then he licked the leather. The material was still wet – it would dry off – when he replaced the shoe carefully in its place and looked around the room. On the floor beside the bed lay the knickers she had taken off that morning, an irregular figure of eight.

41

He retrieved them and held them over his nose and mouth. Again, her scent, mingled with other, bodily smells. Her smell. Ursula. His sister-in-law. His wife's sister. He inhaled deeply a few times and then put the garment back carefully on the floor. He went back to his own room to get dressed.

The next evening Rudolf was in the kitchen stirring gravy. He dipped his finger in it and tasted it. Some more pepper. Just then Ursula came in and stood beside him at the cooker.

'That smells good,' she said.

'Want a taste?'

'Mmmm, yes please.'

He dipped his finger in again, and lifted it out, coated in the thick gravy like glistening chocolate.

'Excuse my fingers,' he said, 'my mother always said that this was perfectly hygienic, and that it was the only way to taste food.'

Her mouth closed around his finger and drew back along it sucking the gravy. When her lips came away it was as though she had tried to peel his finger. She tasted it and smiling, said 'That's wonderful.'

Her eyes held his for a moment or two longer, and then the kitchen door opened. Lisa came in. Ursula moved away from the cooker and picked up an open bottle of wine from the kitchen table.

'That's a wonderful husband you've got there, Lisa, you never told me he could cook.'

On Monday, during his lunch break, taken at his desk, Rudolf drew an intimacy matrix for Ursula. The intimacy matrix was an invention of his own when he had been an undergraduate at university. He had subsequently shown it to a few of his pals, and it had caused huge amusement for a week or two but had then been forgotten. Since then Rudolf had continued to use it in private. As a statistician he liked the notion that you could measure sexual intimacy. It worked like this.

You drew a four by four matrix. Across the top were four headings each indicated by a letter - E(ye), F(inger), T(ongue), C(ock). Down the side were four other headings - M(outh), B(reast), P(ussy), A(ss). This then gave you sixteen possibilities. You then put an 'x' in each of the sixteen squares if that particular combination had occurred. Thus Ursula's looked like this

	E	F	T	C
M	x	x		
B				
P				
A				

It meant that with his eye he had seen her mouth. He hadn't seen any of her other parts. Also his finger had been in her mouth. None of his other parts had made contact with or been in any of her other parts. This gave an intimacy matrix of 2, or IM = 2. An IM = 16 was something he had never achieved, not even with Lisa.

One morning a few days later, he inadvertently walked in on Ursula while she was in the bathroom. The door had been unlocked – how could he have known, he declaimed afterwards at breakfast while the sisters chided him.

'It was my fault,' said Ursula. 'I just haven't got used to living with other people.'

Before he started work that morning, Rudolf updated the intimacy matrix to 4. He had seen her breasts – larger and heavier than Lisa's – and her pubic area.

Chapter 6

Normandy. The present

'Katya?'

'Come in, come in. It's so good to meet you after so long. She told me so much about you. Here, let me take your case. How was your journey? Such a long way. Do you need a sleep? A bath? A shower? No? Some tea, then. It'll just take a minute. As you can hear my Polish is pretty rusty.'

'It's better than my French.'

'We'll try Polish then. So then David, you found me through Broni? How on earth did you find *him*?'

'I went to Warsaw. Asked around the jazz scene. It's small. It wasn't too difficult.'

'So he's still playing, is he?'

'Do you have to ask? It's his life.'

'Yes, of course it is. The kitchen is through here.'

'So what about you, Katya – when did you leave Poland?'

'I left in 1938. I've been back there a bit since. Less and less as it gets further and further from the war. My plan was to head for America. I had this idea that the Americans were tolerant, liberal. Somebody once told me that they *worship* freedom. Maybe it's true. But I suppose I'm a European. And anyway, I found as much tolerance as I've wanted here in France. When the war started I slipped across the border into

44

Spain, but I came back after the Liberation. I've been in Normandy ever since. How long have you been travelling?'

'I left Israel about three weeks ago. I've been in Poland ever since. Poland and Belarus. I had planned to go home after that, but when Broni told me about you, I had to come and see you. It's my first time in France. It's so different here. In Poland I felt I was travelling through a graveyard.'

'Now, here we are. Tea and some pastries. The local baker still makes all his own. Please, help yourself. Yes, here in the West, they forget. They forget how it was then. There have been all these fiftieth anniversary celebrations – D-Day, Arnhem, VE Day. We get a lot of American and British veterans around here. Some of them have told me it was the best time of their lives. I think some of them see it all as a big movie with a Glen Miller soundtrack. It's so different from what you endured.'

'Yes, it wasn't like that for us in Eastern Europe. Those four years were the first four years of Hitler's New Order. I think the way the Nazis viewed it, a lot of the preliminary work was done during that time. The territory was captured – Poland, Russia and so on – and the races were stratified. Then most of the bottom stratum – the one that contained us, the Jews of Europe – disappeared. People say that the Nazis lost the war. Of course they did. But the war, what they know of in the West as the Second World War, was only one of the things the Nazis were engaged in at that time. For them the Second World War was nothing more than one part of a pro-gramme to set up their New Order. Other parts of the pro-gramme went ahead in parallel and – from *their* point of view – were highly successful. Anyway, I shouldn't be going on. I came here to listen, not to talk.'

'But I must also listen. I know so little of her early life. First you must tell me about that. Then I shall add what I know.'

'There were four of us – my parents, myself and Ariela –

45

except we always called her Ella. There were ten years between me and Ella. We lived in Lodz, on Zgierska Street, north of where they set up the ghetto in 1940. Our father was a doctor. We had a lovely house with a big garden at the back, with lots of foliage to play and hide in. Both my parents were great gardeners.

'Ella was born in 1919. December. I remember there was a lot of coming and going that lasted several days so I thought there had to be something wrong – otherwise why would these people be coming to our house through the snow? My father told me there was nothing to worry about, but the anxious look on his face made me worry even more. Then, a few days later, I was taken into our parent's bedroom. There was a smell of fresh flowers in the room – I can't imagine where my father could have got them at that time of year. Mother was sitting up in bed with a baby in her arms. I found out much later that they thought that Ella wasn't going to live. I think it had something to do with my mother's age – she was 42 when Ella was born. As a result of all this they doted on her – especially my mother.

'I'm told I was quiet as a child. Ella wasn't. She was wild. As soon as she could crawl she would speed up the stairs once your back was turned. Not that I was aware of her very much. I spent most of my time on the street with the other boys. There were Jews and Poles. Nobody seemed too bothered. At least not when we were children.

'Our parents were what I've always thought of as the best kind of Jews. They were strict in their observance and adherence to the law, but at the same time they had a very "modern" view of things. For instance, they never saw Ella as just having to grow up and get married. Their view – especially my father's – was that we should make the most of our lives and the talents we had been given. In this way, he said, we would truly praise God.

'Her singing? I honestly don't know how that started. It just seemed that from the time she could talk Ella was singing. She loved music. I would do anything rather than sing, but she hardly needed to be asked. She won some prizes in school, but it was only when she was chosen to sing on the radio that we started to realise she might have some talent. Our parents loved classical music. That was where she started but jazz became her real love. She talked about becoming a famous jazz singer, but I didn't realise then how committed she was to doing that.

'We became close around the time I started studying in university. She was ten, with all sorts of opinions and she had started listening to jazz. She would be hauled off with our parents to our place in the country and she would complain endlessly about how boring it was down there. She associated jazz with cities, and the country and Jewishness and our parents were all bundled together under the heading "old-fashioned". She wasn't obnoxious about it. She would talk to me about it, but with our parents she would usually do whatever she had to do to keep them happy. I think she kept them young. Not that it mattered much in the end. They hoped she would stay at home and study as I had done, but she wanted to go to Warsaw, to the Conservatory. I think in some ways she was biding her time for that. Waiting, because she knew that as soon as she got there, she could begin to do what she really wanted to do. Begin her life, really, I suppose. Our parents resisted the move to Warsaw. I did a lot of the persuading on her behalf.

'A couple of weeks before she left for Warsaw, I was in Brzykow – that was where our parents' country house was – and she spoke to me about her fears. Now that the way was cleared for her to go, she wondered what she would do if she didn't make a success of it. I told her it didn't matter. And it didn't. I think our parents would have been more than happy for her to fail and return to Lodz. But no, she was going to be a success and not just a small-scale success – a spectacular one. I told her to get her studies completed first and then she could see after that. We had to downplay the whole jazz thing in order to get our parents' permission. She was to train as a classical singer.

'She was lonely when she first arrived in Warsaw. But she told me she tried to make her apartment in Warsaw a place where she wanted to be rather than had to be.

'I could tell you more, Katya, but that's really her childhood. Happy and carefree. Her youth? Like all of us she was looking forward to a long and happy life. The worst that I could have imagined happening to her would have been that she might not have achieved her ambitions. How could we have known anything different? You cannot imagine it today, but you have to try. We were a world before Auschwitz. We could never have conceived of it. And Ariela – well now, you must tell me what you know.'

'Well, where shall I begin? I knew her for less than a year, and during that time I loved her as I've never loved anybody before or since. But there was no future in it, and so I left her and I never saw her again. I knew her first as Ella and she preferred that – she thought Ariela was too much of a mouthful. Amongst other things it perhaps made people think she wasn't Jewish. I don't have to tell *you* how it was then. The Poles reckoned that the Jews controlled the economy but from what I could see most of the Jews were poor. Sure there were some – ten per cent is a figure I have heard – who were well off. But no matter how rich you were, no matter what standing you had achieved in society, if you were a Jew you were a Jew, and nothing could change that. Even though I'm Polish, I guess I can take a clear view on this because I'm from another minority group, even if it is an almost invisible one … Ah, she never told you. I was … I am homosexual. When I say that I loved her, you need to be aware of what this

48

means. I hope you are not shocked by this. I felt I had to say it at the beginning of our acquaintance ... our friendship.'

'After the things I have witnessed in my life, something like this would hardly register as a shock.'

'Ah. I thought it might have been so.'

'So tell me what you remember. Tell me everything.'

'She might have been mistaken for a model, tall, with thick shoulder-length hair, high cheekbones – I guess there must be Slavic blood in your family somewhere. I remember her long eyelashes. And her eyes – they were green-brown – like olives. She tanned easily so she always looked healthy. She was so beautiful that sometimes when I saw her I wanted to cry. I could look at her endlessly and I loved to do it when maybe she was reading a book. Sooner or later she would become aware of me and laugh and say "what are you looking at?" It was the only time in my life that I wanted to be a man, that I might have been with her and loved her. Of course this is foolishness. I get the impression she was very serious as a child?'

'She was. Once the teacher kept her back after school. She told the teacher she couldn't do that "because my parents will be worried".'

'She was always singing or humming. When she first came to Warsaw, she was very lonely. It wasn't helped – well, you would know this – by her shyness and hesitancy which I think she never lost. In shops, for example, she would say hello to the sales assistant, but if she didn't get the same friendly greeting back, it threw her a little. You would see it in her face.

'Strange as it may seem, I think the shyness may have come about as a result of her beauty. At least this was what she said to me one time – that because of her looks, her classmates expected her to be snooty, haughty, to act like some kind of snob. And this was in a Jewish school. She said that irrespective of what she did they treated her accordingly. And

49

I remember she used to get so frustrated by the shyness. She told me how rather than diverting attention from the person it actually attracts attention to them; the very thing they are trying to avoid.

'She always struck me as being so vulnerable. I don't know whether this was because she was Jewish or for some other reason. Vulnerable but also private. She would smile at you – she was always smiling – but it was like the smile then stopped you from digging any deeper.'

'What used you do?'

'Oh, this and that. I've never been much of a one for a career, or even a steady job. My interests lie elsewhere. Books, art, music. You could describe me as a Sybarite, though not with the sexual connotations. I've only ever worked to get enough money to be able to afford these things. Provided I have a roof over my head and some food on the table, that's all I've ever wanted.

'Ella was less concerned about the purpose of life and more concerned about what she was going to do with hers. She was more concerned about her singing and she wanted to be famous, to have people come to listen to her. She kept a diary when she first came to Warsaw. Oh, you didn't know about this? Here let me go and get it – I don't think it's particularly detailed or well-written. It was just a small notebook she had where she jotted down how she felt about things. I think it was a companion during those first lonely months. Ella was very homesick. She dropped it after she met Stefan. You've come across Stefan? Oh, he's dead? Hmm. I can't say I'm upset. Anyway she gave me the diary when I left Poland, but I was only to read it if we failed to make contact again. I opened it after the war. Maybe you should have it now. Here, have a look. I want to finish making your bed.'

'I have booked into a hotel in Caen.'

'Well, we're not as palatial as the hotels of Caen here, but

50

I would be delighted if you would stay.'

'Thank you. I'd like that very much. You are the last person who … who knew her … I'm sorry, forgive my tears – it's been a long journey.'

'It is hard for all of us. There are some tissues on the table. I will leave you for a little while.'

I am feeling strong, like a warrior, self-sufficient, armoured against the world … Not feeling inadequate any more … If I do what my heart says … I'm going to have to talk to people, not be embarrassed and keep busy every day … What happens is that my image of myself slips away … I will just be interested in people but not caring what they think … Nothing but good happening since I arrived. Confidence begets confidence … Make peoples' encounter with you a bit outside the ordinary … This is an opportunity. Like a year spent in a foreign country. I must harvest from it all of the opportunities that I can … Letters from home are what I live for at the moment … How I would like to pack it all in … I must do more self-examination, look at the bad aspects of my character and see how to overcome them … The depression of youth and being away from home … I'm at last starting to find positive things about Warsaw … the breakthrough has been with people – my new friends, and one new friend in particular … Don't deserve all happiness and luck I've had this year

'So what do you think?'

'Well, I can see her in it. But she was hardly Anna Frank.'

'No. No. Writing wasn't Ella's thing. She loved to get letters, but replying to them was always hard for her. Still you get a feeling for what she was going through at that time. It just breaks off one day and never picks up again.

'I saw her the first time she sang jazz in public. I worked as a waitress in a club in Warsaw. There was this jazz band that had a residency there. A four piece. I don't remember much about them except for the sax player and the pianist. They were the two she left to go to Russia with. Broni was the pianist. But the saxophonist, Stefan, he was the one she fell for. Fell head over heels in love with him.

'Anyway, this jazz band was quite good. But they had decided they needed something new and had settled on a female singer. I'd seen their notices around the place, but apparently they had advertised in the Conservatory. And of course – she was studying singing there. They were holding auditions on the afternoon I was in. Nine or ten girls showed up during the day. Some were just plain awful. Most were alright but they just didn't light any kind of fire, if you know what I mean. You couldn't see them causing a stir.

'Within a few bars I knew the audition was over. Her voice, how can I describe it? Crystalline. Vulnerable. Breathy. And then at times so strong it was almost boyish. Broni joined in – he seemed to know every tune that had ever been written. She sang an American song – 'Stardust', it was called. She told me afterwards it got its name because a friend had told the composer it sounded like dust from stars drifting down through the summer sky. I remember during that song, Broni looked up and gazed at her while he continued to play. After a few moments she sensed him, turned slightly and smiled at him.

'She asked if she could stay behind while they auditioned with the remaining two singers. Then, when these had left, they asked her to do a few more songs with them. After that they all went off together. A few nights later she was on stage with them. By then I think there were at least three people in love with her.'

Chapter 7

Berlin. 27 November 1938.

By the time SS Scharfuhrer Otto Tauber made his entrance, the Jews were trembling. His assistant, Heinrich Katz, had done his work well. Of course they had had plenty of practice at this sort of thing since *Kristallnacht*.

Katz would have knocked on the apartment door first, appearing to be on his own. There was never a show of force. That would have defeated the purpose. The aim was to turn the heat up gradually. While not being *polite* – that would have been too demeaning – Katz was brusque and businesslike. There was a problem, Katz would explain. Then he would indicate with his hand, or more likely the baton he carried, that they should go inside. The fact that there was only Katz would have lulled the Jews into a false sense of security, made them believe that this was just some sort of official call about some bureaucratic mistake.

Once inside Katz would begin to give the impression that all he was really after was money, a bribe to make him go away. He would comment on the fine furnishings, the expensive looking china and paintings. Katz was quite a showman. The Jew would be frantically trying to find out the nature of the supposed 'problem', so that he could do something about it. Katz would be in no hurry to tell him. Finally, Katz would gradually begin to talk about foreign exchange, about financial instruments, about hoarding foreign currency, about a safe full of US dollars. It was hilarious to hear Katz talk like this. The man probably thought a financial instrument was an expensive piano, but he spoke like a man with intricate knowledge of international currency trading. If the Jew had anything like this lying around, there was a fair chance that he would bring it out now in the hope that he could buy off his tormentors. One way or the other it fairly quickly got down to what he would have to give them to leave. While all of this was going on, Otto was waiting outside the door.

At these times, he often found his mind drifting back to the events which had brought him to this point, and the day that had changed his life.

January, 1921. A grey, steely cold day. The new year only a few day's old, but already any hope that might have come with it, dissolved in beer and schnapps. It had begun in the damp flea-pit of an apartment that he shared with two other returned soldiers. He had come out of the single bedroom bleary-eyed, hung over and ravenous after a night's drinking. He smelt vaguely of urine and realised that he had probably pissed himself during the night. He remembered that there had been half a loaf of dark bread on the kitchen table. As he entered he saw that the grey-brown chunk of bread was still there, but there was a cord running out of it. It reminded him of booby traps he had seen in captured Tommie trenches during the Spring Offensive. It was only when he saw the loaf move that he realised the cord was actually a rat's tail, and that the rat, similar in colour to the bread, had burrowed into the loaf and was gnawing away at its insides.

Otto had served in the trenches of the German Army from 1917 right through to the 'stab in the back'. During that time they had lived, slept and eaten with rats. He loathed the animals; but they held no particular fear for him. Despite his hangover, the old reflexes were still there. He noticed that the bread knife lay on the floor, discarded there last night after some antagonism between his room mates. Otto squatted down slowly, keeping his eyes on the animal and groping for the knife. As he touched the blade and then found the handle, a strange thing happened. Otto began to cry. At his first whimper, the rat extracted itself, the two black beads of its eyes saw Otto, and it was gone, over the edge of the table and off through a hole eaten away between the skirting and floor boards. Otto collapsed onto the floor, back against the kitchen door, tears streaming down his face, his head buried in his hands.

Life had begun for him in a small village in Bavaria. His father was a labourer. They hadn't been particularly well off, but neither had they starved. He remembered walks with his father, fishing trips. The man loved nature, knew the names of all the trees and the wild flowers, the birds, their different songs and their habits. It was a love he passed onto his son. By the time Otto was twelve he was talking of becoming a vet. Even though this ambition, with its requirement of a university education, seemed way beyond the means of the Tauber family, the elder Tauber encouraged his son. Otto overheard them downstairs one evening after he had gone to bed, their voices murmuring about how they might find the money to do it. Could he get a scholarship? Perhaps, but so far he seemed only slightly better than average in school. Did you have to be clever to be a vet? His father wasn't sure. It seemed to him that a love of animals was what counted more than anything else. If Mother could get a job or take in washing or something, then they could save the extra money. They should really talk to the schoolmaster. He would know about these things.

Whether they did ever talk to the schoolmaster and whether anything he said would ever have made any difference, all became a bit academic in the end. The war, rationing, the disappearance of the older kids to the front, then the casualty lists and the realisation that some of them – kids with whom he had played – would never be coming back. Then, in 1917, there were suddenly no more 'older boys' and one day, Otto was driven away in a truck to begin his training as a soldier. The war was going badly for Germany just then and he arrived on the Western Front in the midst of the British offensive at Passchendaele.

He still had nightmares about it – a world devoid of sunlight and greenery and anything from the natural world. Beneath his feet, mud in seas, in pools, in every consistency and depth imaginable. They walked on slick log tracks and if they slipped off, they drowned, their lungs filling with the stuff. Overhead there was never blue or clouds, just the sound and smell and steel of projectiles ribbing the sky from horizon to horizon. At night a miasma of flares and rain and decaying flesh rose up and hovered over the holes they lived in.

Incredibly he survived without a wound until the 1918 Spring Offensive. It was Germany's last throw of the dice and for a time it looked like it might succeed. But in the end, American industry, controlled by Jews, had been the deciding factor. Not that he had had any chance to contemplate these things at the time. He had been blown up and buried by a shell. He remembered the explosion, its hot breath and the deafening noise which accompanied it. He had flown through the air, like an acrobat at a circus. He remembered feeling grateful to the shock wave which had lifted him, because it had been mercifully free of any pieces of shrapnel or shell splinters. But most of all he remembered the horror of being alive and buried underground; how he had clawed at the mud and tried to tunnel a way out, and how it had poured over his hands and into his mouth so that the more he dug the more he entombed himself. He was gibbering when they eventually pulled him out.

It had been the donkeys that saved him. After a couple of days in hospital, when they decided he had no physical damage, they were ready to return him to the front. Appalled at the prospect he had hunted around desperately for anything that would save him from going back to that troglodyte world. There was a chap on the mattress next to him – there had been no beds in the hospital – who was from the Transport. His face and head been carved up by a shell and he died within hours of being brought in. His papers fell from his pocket when his body was being taken out, and Otto retrieved them. When Otto was discharged, instead of returning to his old regiment, he sought out the Transport unit. He discovered that they handled donkeys, charged with bringing supplies and ammunition up the line. It took a bit of talking to get himself taken in, but he managed it. He soon showed an aptitude for working with these gentle creatures. It was one thing to send men up here – at least they had some sort of say in the matter – but to send these poor misfortunates was something he found totally unforgivable.

Then had come the surrender, the 'stab in the back'. The German Army, everywhere outside its own frontiers, with the Russians and Rumanians defeated in the East, betrayed by a bunch of Jewish politicians hungry for power.

Otto returned to a different world. His stupid fucking parents, behaving as if nothing in particular had happened, and that everything would just go back to the way it had been. Otto moved out of there within a week. He went to Munich. Vaguely, somewhere in the back of his mind, was the notion that he would earn enough money to study and become a vet. In his quieter moments he thought of it as paying back the animals who had saved his sanity during the War. But there were no openings anywhere for returned soldiers. The factories that had produced war materials were all closed, and those industries still operating were staffed by people who had stayed at home and hadn't ventured near the front. He took odd jobs, seasonal things, small snatches of work wherever he could find them, but the money he earned was just about enough to pay for his evenings with the old comrades. The vet idea quickly faded. It was replaced by days in bed and nights drinking with the *Frontkampfer*; a routine punctuated only by occasional street fights with Communists or roughing up the odd Jew or queer. He had been doing this for almost two years when he stumbled into the kitchen on that grave-like January morning for his encounter with the rat.

He had pulled himself together, washed and gone out. Miraculously he still had some money from last night. In a café he ate a good breakfast with plenty of scalding coffee. He stayed there until they asked him to move to make room for the lunch-time crowd. Then he spent the afternoon in the library reading the papers while he stood beside a radiator, a small pool of melted snow about his feet. He began to get more and more depressed as the afternoon wore on. The prospect of going home or of being with the comrades held no attractions.

It was dark when the library closed and he drifted out into the street. Bolsters of dirty slush lay along the pavements and in the gutters. The street lamps glowed yellow. People hurried home from work. Cars, trams, and carriages swished past throwing up spray off the wet cobblestones. He looked through condensation-soaked windows into the interiors of one or two of the larger cars, their occupants shrouded in deep rugs. Fucking profiteers. Fucking Jews. Even the *word* 'Jew' made him angry.

He wandered into the Kindl Keller. The place was crowded and noisy, its air opaque with tobacco smoke and steam from warm bodies. The bartender informed him that if he was looking for the meeting it was in the back room. Otto picked up his beer and followed the barman's direction. Any kind of novelty, no matter how slight, would be better than returning home.

In the back room, a number of benches had been arranged in rows. There was already a reasonable crowd there and Otto took a place near the back. A short moustachioed man, wearing a shabby brown trench coat was standing near the top of the room chatting with a couple of burly men. The room continued to fill up, cigarettes were lit and the conversation level rose. The air smelt of damp coats and smoke and beer. Finally the door at the back was closed and the conversation declined a little. Otto looked beyond the heads expectantly. The man with the moustache took off his coat and climbed up onto the low stage that occupied that end of the room. There was a ragged cheer. Somebody farted noisily and there was another cheer and laughter.

The man with the moustache said nothing, but held his hands together and began to scan the assembled faces.

'Get on with it,' somebody shouted.

The speaker narrowed his eyes and continued to survey the crowd. He stared at one section until it went silent. Then he moved his head and did the next section and the next. Finally, the room settled into an intense, expectant quiet. The man waited another good half minute before he began.

'My fellow Germans,' – the voice was soft, the words came slowly – 'like many of you, I am a returned soldier.'

'I can see why they returned you,' shouted a voice in front of Otto.

There were hoots of laughter. The moustache continued undeterred in the same soft, slow voice.

'Like many of you I fought for four years –'

'You couldn't fight your way out of a paper bag,' the voice interrupted again.

The man was sitting directly in front of Otto.

' – in the most unimaginable conditions, as our nation

59

was threatened with annihilation' – he said each syllable distinctly – 'by the enemies which surrounded it.'

A pause. The hands separated, the right one to form a clenched fist.

'We were undefeated in battle.'

The voice rose as he said these words.

'We were –'

'You were talking through your arse,' shouted the voice, 'and you still are.'

This time, there was a commotion along each end of the row in which Otto sat. The two burly men elbowed their way in from either side. The heckler, realising what was happening, went to get up but the two men were already upon him. One caught him round the neck, and pulled him backwards across the bench into Otto's row. The second man smashed ham-like fists into the heckler's face. Blood spurted from his lips and nose. Then he was punched in the abdomen, the blow coming low so that it connected with his groin. The heckler uttered a choking cry and was dragged out of the row and frog-marched out the door. The speaker waited until people regained their seats and silence returned before continuing.

It was a long speech; hard to follow and a bit incoherent at times. But, as it built to a tremendous climax, and as the man began to beat an imaginary lectern with both fists, there was no doubting the main message. It was the connection between everything that had happened: defeat in the War, the peace terms and the wealth transfer that had taken a place as a result. What did they all have in common? Jews. The Jews in America who had engineered the defeat of Germany. German Jews who had made vast profits from the War.

'The enemy within and the enemy without are the same enemy,' the man screamed, as he reached the crescendo.

He stopped abruptly, and the whole room fell silent. After another extended pause, he started once more in the same slow, quiet voice he had used at the beginning.

'You have seen even here tonight, even in our midst, there are people who would stop us from spreading our message. These people are everywhere, part of the Jewish plague, bacilli, germs who would poison and corrupt us. But –'

He raised the index finger of his right hand and moved it slowly from side to side. The gesture reminded Otto of a magician showing an audience that his hand is indeed empty. Heads moved slightly as they followed the finger.

'– you have seen how we deal with such people.'

He spoke the words slowly, singly, the finger turned now towards them, warning, admonishing.

'The National Socialist Movement in Munich will in future ruthlessly prevent – if necessary by force – all meetings or lectures that are likely to distract the minds of our fellow countrymen.'

The moustache dropped his arms to his side and lowered his head. His body seemed to shrink. He was like a man drained, exhausted. He wiped his dark hair off his forehead, and then brought his hands back together again. The room erupted in applause.

Otto joined the *Nationalsozialistes* that same night. Ashamed of his appearance, and with a nervousness that stemmed from two year's of very limited social interaction, he enlisted with one of the bouncers. As a result he missed the one and only opportunity he ever had to shake the hand of the Fuhrer.

After that he threw himself into the work of the Party. In 1932 he joined the SS, and at last opportunities began to open up to him. He got promotion, responsibility, men to command. What's more, he found that he was good at it and that this was recognised by both his superiors and those he led. He didn't know what all the fuss was about – all he did was to take an interest in the men, in their well being and their hopes and fears. It was a simple enough recipe – just doing the opposite of what had been done by *his* leaders in the War. The Obersturmfuhrer once remarked that he thought Otto's men would 'follow him through the fires of hell and out the other side'. It was one of the proudest moments of Otto's life.

Not only did his immediate circumstances and day to day life improve but now a plan began to form in Otto's mind. The Fuhrer said that Germany would have *Lebensraum*, room in the East. At first it had been nothing more than a political notion. Then for the SS it became a territorial goal that would be achieved, probably through war. But it was only slowly that the real significance of *Lebensraum* dawned on Otto. *He* would have a place in the East, some kind of farm or small estate. Here he could return to the things he had loved in his childhood, animals, nature, the countryside. As the vision became clearer it developed into a complete and detailed daydream, which Otto played like a film whenever he had a quiet moment. There was a house, surrounded by tall, dark green pine trees, growing in fertile, sandy soil. The house was set on a slight hill which ran down to a small stream or lake – he could never decide which – amply stocked with trout, or whatever fish they had in the East. A woman lived with him. She was a fine Aryan woman with all the domestic skills of the German female, a wife and a mother to his sons.

The result of his dream was that he longed for war; the war without which his dream could not happen. He waited impatiently for it and it was only the steady progress of Hitler's other measures, chiefly those against the Jews, that reassured him that the Fuhrer was keeping faith with the mission he had set himself in *Mein Kampf*. You only had to look at how the Jews had gone to ground to see how effective the Fuhrer's actions had been. Otto remembered a night in 1931 when he had gone into Munich to harass Jews. They had seen a bunch of Jewish women waiting at a tram stop. They were dressed in tracksuits and the like – athletes returning from a sports competition. The Jews had some organisation, Maccabi or something, which organised these things. He and his two comrades began to jeer at the women from across the street. One of the sows had called back, 'Go and fuck yourselves, you stupid Nazis'. Enraged, they had crossed the street to deal with the bitches, but then, Otto realised where their courage came from. In the shadow of a doorway half a dozen brawny Jews waited and now stepped into the light of a street lamp. On that occasion Otto and the other two had beaten a hasty retreat. You wouldn't find Jews behaving like that these days, that was for sure.

The first big victory against them had been the swimming pools. It was the district leader who had pointed out at a local Party meeting how outrageous it was that Aryans should have to share a swimming pool with Jews. Otto had gone down to the local pool with a group of men and youths to assess the problem for themselves and it was indeed completely unacceptable. Impudent Jewish women in scanty bathing suits, Jewish men passing close to Aryan women on the walkways and then, worst of all, Jews polluting the water in which Aryans were forced to swim. They went to the supervisor of the baths asking him to remove the Jews, but he said he was required to follow the rules of the bath's administration. Anyway he added, it wasn't easy to distinguish Jews from Aryans. At this one of the men had given voice to Otto's own thoughts:

'Line the men up and we'll tell you in two minutes!'

But of course this was unworkable. It would have been too humiliating for the Aryans. The best they'd been able to do had been to find any Jews that the group recognised and to expel them from the baths. That had been particularly entertaining with the women. They were not allowed to return to the dressing room but were escorted to the door and thrown out in their bathing suits. They stood outside, humiliated, jeered by Otto's group, clutching each other with nowhere to go. What were they going to do, walk down the main street? Eventually a car showed up driven by a Jew who had got wind of what was going on and they were taken away.

The apartment Otto entered was like so many other Jewish apartments that he had seen. Heavy furniture and curtains, deep chairs, paintings, all sorts of ornaments and bits of china and little statues, a seven-branched candlestick probably made from gold, bookshelves with books neatly arranged in series. The family huddled together on a sofa in front of a briskly burning fire. There were four of them, the parents and a boy and a girl, both in their teens. The children were in their night clothes and dressing gowns. The girl looked about seventeen, the mother in her late thirties. She might have been older – it was very hard to tell with these Jewish women. They lived lives of luxury and ease so that all they had to do was take care of their faces and their bodies. Mother and daughter looked very alike. When Otto entered, the husband went to get up, but Katz, who up until now would have been relatively soft-spoken, suddenly roared, 'Sit!' The four figures on the sofa, clutching one another, leaped in unison. Katz turned away to hide the grin which he flashed at Otto. Then he said:

'Doggy commands, Herr Scharfuhrer, that's all these Jews seem to understand.'

From the sofa, the Jew husband spoke.

'Herr Scharfuhrer, are you in command?'

Otto neither confirmed nor denied this, choosing instead to stare icily at the Jew. The man continued, with as much confidence as he could muster.

'We have no foreign currency here. We have already told your colleague this. You are welcome to look for yourself ...'

The Jew's voice trailed off in a pleading, whining tone.

Without saying anything, Otto motioned with his head, and Katz began to search the apartment again, this time more for effect than anything else. He opened drawers emptying out their contents; he knocked over bits of china smashing them on the floor; he pulled some paintings off the walls; when the door of a sideboard stuck slightly, he kicked it savagely so that his boot went through the wood. Then Katz disappeared into one of the bedrooms. He emerged a few minutes later carrying some white frilly knickers.

'Now, which one of you ladies would like to model these for us?'

The daughter buried her head in the mother's shoulder and began to cry. The Jew husband turned to Otto and said:

'Please, Herr Scharfuhrer ...'

Otto said nothing.

'Well?' roared Katz. 'I'm waiting. Which one of you Jew bitches is it going to be?'

All four sets of Jewish eyes were now on Otto. Turning slightly, he nodded to Katz who tossed Otto his rifle. Catching it deftly, he held it across his groin. Then he used his head and the barrel of the rifle to gesture to the wife.

'You,' he said.

Slowly the woman got to her feet. She extended her arm which was shaking violently. She took the small white bundle from Katz and went to go towards the bedroom. Katz blocked her with his baton.

'Here,' he said, indicating the rug immediately in front of the fire. She looked at Otto. The look he returned was blank, without interest.

'Do as he says,' he said.

'No, sir, please. Not this. Not in front of my children – '

'Do it, bitch!' roared Otto.

The woman stepped out of her slippers and began to slip one stockinged foot through the garment. As she did so, Katz

65

began to laugh. 'Excuse me. Excuse me. Haven't we forgotten something?'

The Jew husband stood up, and even though Katz motioned to him to sit, he took a step towards Otto. Otto levelled his rifle at the husband. The children screamed and the woman, dropping the knickers, made a move towards him. Otto stepped forward, placed his fingers on the man's chest and pushed him just hard enough to cause him to fall back onto the seat.

'You heard my assistant,' Otto said. 'Sit down. While we enjoy the fashion show.'

Otto liked to keep everybody – including Katz – guessing as to what he was going to do. Now, encouraged by his boss' support, Katz lifted up the knickers on his baton and held them towards the woman. He held the weapon low, pointed at her groin. The woman turned away but Katz said 'Uh, uh' and forced her to face them. 'Now,' he said, 'let's see what you're made of.'

The woman reached up under her skirt, trying to reduce as much as possible the way it rucked up, and pulled down the underwear she was wearing. She had fine legs, long and slender. Otto thought the children looked as much embarrassed as they were frightened. The Jew looked away, bowing his head in his hands. Katz spotted this and shouted at him to 'watch the fashion parade'. He complied. The woman pulled on the new knickers and drew them up. This time they saw more of her thighs, but somehow she managed not to show them anything else. When she had done this, she looked at them, a pleading expression on her face. Otto decided he saw defiance there too. The look infuriated Otto. Katz roared again.

'Well, they're no good there, you stupid sow. The Scharfuhrer can't see if they fit or not.'

Katz turned to Otto. 'I don't know, Herr Scharfuhrer, these Jews.'

The Jew watched with a sort of horrified fascination, as his wife undressed on the living room carpet in front of everybody. She undid her skirt and stepped out of it. They could see part of the white knickers, but the blouse she was wearing came down over them.

'Come on,' said Katz, his voice sounding as though he were tired of the whole game, 'and the rest of it.'

The woman unbuttoned her blouse, and took it off. Now she was left only with her brassiere, knickers, stockings and suspender belt.

'What do you think, Herr Scharfuhrer, is the size right?'

Otto said, 'I think they might suit the daughter better.'

At this a sound part way between a moan and a cry came from the daughter.

'On second thoughts,' said Otto, 'take the woman into the bedroom and I'll give her a private fitting myself.'

'Of course, Herr Scharfuhrer,' grinned Katz.

Katz caught the woman roughly by the arm and dragged her towards the bedroom. Strangely, the woman said nothing, and made no resistance. When Katz returned, Otto walked into the bedroom and shut the door. Ten minutes later he emerged, beckoned to Otto and both men left without another word.

As the sound of their boots receded on the stairs, the woman came out from the room. She had pulled a robe on over her underclothes and held the two sides of it tightly across her chest with her arms, as though they were locked into position. Her husband stood up and then faltered, unsure of what to do. The children sat on the sofa, staring at her. Her eye was bruised and her mouth was bleeding and swollen.

'He didn't do anything to me,' she said. 'He just beat me a bit. He didn't touch me.'

She burst into tears. Her voice became shrill. 'He didn't touch me. He didn't touch me.'

PART TWO

Chapter 1

Normandy. The Present.

'A little about my own background? Nothing like yours David. My mother died when I was four. I remember her vaguely. A great loving presence went out of my life. Very quickly – maybe it wasn't in actual fact, but it seemed that way to me – my father began to bring other women home. Some of them were nice, friendly to me, but most weren't. Maybe they didn't like the idea of a ready-made family. I was very lonely. I left home as soon as I could and began to fend for myself. I suppose I've never really had a direction in my life because it always seemed to centre on practical things – a job, a place to live, money, food. I think here is the closest I've come to happiness. This, and a handful of other times, like the six months or so that I knew Ella.

'The audition was on a Saturday, they opened the following Wednesday night. I drifted backstage – I suppose really to see if she was there – and I found her in the small room that passed for a dressing room. She was singing scales. Just like you hear opera singers doing. Well, I suppose she was classically trained. She was wearing a tight red dress with a square neckline. It wasn't particularly revealing, but it was

68

tight enough to show off her figure. The door was ajar – it never closed properly – and I think seeing me startled her because she suddenly stopped and blushed. I told her I was sorry, that I hadn't meant to interrupt her. She asked if she had been singing too loud, that she could be heard out in front. I told her no, and asked her if she'd like something to drink. She asked for mineral water, but I told her I could get her something stronger if she was nervous. I brought her back a bottle of mineral water and a brandy. She downed most of the water in one go – she got very dry when she was nervous. I introduced myself. She held out her hand and said "Ariel … Ella." I told her I knew. We shook hands. She had long fingers. Soft hands. Softer than mine anyway. It turned out we were the same age – nineteen. She was nervous because she was about to go on stage, and I was nervous just being in her company. She had that effect on you. And even to this day I don't know why. She had provincial written all over her and yet there was something about her self-assuredness, the way she carried herself – oh, I'm not describing it very well – that made you feel awkward. At least when you first met her and before you got to know her. Of course, maybe part of it was the way you feel when you're with anyone that you admire. That you don't want to give them any reason to be disappointed in you.

'She downed the brandy and it flushed her cheeks. Then she turned to the mirror and started to put on some lipstick. I told her she looked terrific and she turned to me and smiled and said "thanks". "Break a leg", I said and left her to it.

'It was a small jazz club in a minor European capital in a country that didn't really have much of a jazz tradition. There were a couple of big names in Warsaw at that time. Have you heard of Rosenbaum's jazz band? They used to play at the Bar Central nightclub. And there was Eddie Rosner's band. So when you use the word "sensation" you have to be careful. I mean, if a thing happens at La Scala, does that mean more than if it happens in a small smoky club in front of a few handfuls of people? I don't know. It seems to me that the same energy is involved, the same waves go out from that point on the planet.

'She was just sensational. The first few bars might have shown some nervousness, her voice a bit tremulous maybe, but after that it was like she had been doing it for years. She was a natural. It's my belief that she would have been great. She was like a professional, even though – you can correct me if I'm wrong – this was the first time she had done anything like this?

'Apart from the family things and that time on the radio. She called me the next day. She was so excited. It was the first time I heard mention of Stefan. She told me how several girls from the audience crowded round the band afterwards. Especially around him.'

'A few nights later – I don't think it was that night – there was some critic from one of the papers in the audience and he gave her a rave review. I used to have it but I burned all of that stuff a few years ago. The memories, you know, they were too upsetting. I didn't see her afterwards. The place got very busy and on the one occasion when I did manage to slip backstage to see her, she was with the rest of the band and Stefan was there.

'After that, pretty much every night she was in, we chatted. That was when I started to find out about her family and her background. She always left with Stefan, though. I think they were sleeping together by then. What did she see in him? I don't know, really. He was a great musician. I have to say that much about him. Maybe she saw a level of excellence in him that she felt she had to aspire to in her singing. I don't know why though. If the truth were told, she was in a different league entirely. Maybe it was that he was her first boyfriend, the one who took her virginity. Maybe it was nothing more than first love. Or maybe it was the intensity of the times. There was Germany and what was happening there. There was the threat of war all over Europe. And for her, in the midst of all of this, her career was starting to blossom. Maybe it was little wonder she fell in love – or thought she did – during those times.

'One night I managed to catch her after the show. The boys were out in front drinking, and I think she was changing before joining them. I went in and asked her if she'd like to come for something to eat some night neither of us was working. I was really scared she'd say no. Looking back on it now I was like a shy little girl asking for a favour. She accepted and we fixed a date for the following Tuesday night. We found lots to talk about. We never stopped talking.

'We became friends after that and would go out from time to time. Though not half enough as far as I was concerned. She was caught up in Stefan. I think she knew how I felt about him. Well, in fact, I made it pretty clear. She invited me to come out with them once or twice and when I had turned down the second invitation, she never asked again. Not that that affected how she felt about me. She was able to keep us both in separate compartments of her life. It was around that time she started talking about going to Paris. You knew about this?'

'Yes. She was going to finish her first year and then leave some time over the summer of 1939. I couldn't believe it. I'd had so much trouble persuading our parents that she should go to Warsaw in the first place. But once I had, at least they felt they knew where she would be for the next four years. Also I think they were starting to have vague feelings that maybe she was very talented; that maybe they would one day see her singing opera in some grand theatre somewhere. Now, here she was saying that she was going to pack it all in

71

and go off to try to make it in jazz. There was no way I was ever going to convince our parents of that. But at the same time, I felt she had to follow her star. Then, it seemed like the plan got delayed. I think it was lack of money. The new plan was that she was going to work the summer and then go round about October. She was going to come home to Lodz the first week of September to talk to them about it. That was the week the war broke out.'

'The best time we had was the time we went to Prague. Here, I have a picture of us.'

'You look so happy there.'

'We were. It was just a few weeks before the Nazis took over. I've always loved travelling. And I think there was a part of me that wanted to see it before the Germans overran it. Ariela said she'd come along. I was afraid she would want to bring Stefan, but no, she came alone. We left Warsaw on an early morning train. We were as excited as schoolgirls. I remember her looking out the compartment window and saying "Count the rails – the less there are the more we're leaving the city." It was a warm and sunny September afternoon when we arrived in Prague.

'We found a small, comfortable hotel and then went out to explore the city. It was so different from one of my usual trips. It was so nice having someone to share all of this with. I had done lots of reading in advance and she flipped through my Baedekker on the train, so that by the time we arrived we both knew what we wanted to see. Have you ever been to Prague? Before the war it was regarded as one of the finest and most cultured cities in Europe. I think it's perhaps returning to that now since the communists left. We spent the whole afternoon wandering around. We bought some food and climbed the hill to the Strahov Monastery. We didn't go in – just lay on the grass in the sunshine and ate what we had brought and talked.

'I often tried to understand what made that day so special. I finally came to the conclusion that it was special because it was so ordinary. We did nothing earth shattering. It was just a day when we had sunshine on our bodies, and enough food to eat, and plenty to drink and each of us was with someone we really cared about. That was all. It was a day when you ask "why can't every day be like this?" Coming back down, someone handed us a notice about a concert that was on in some church or other. I remember the program included Vivaldi, Handel and Telemann. We looked at it for a moment. We looked at each other. Then we both said at the same time "Naw!" and handed it back to him, laughing. I'm sure he didn't know what to make of us.

'By late afternoon we were ready for a drink and ravenous. We found a café in Old Town Square, ordered two beers, and sat watching people coming home from work; men with briefcases, women with cardigans over their arms, cyclists and vehicles all hurrying past. I can still see the Square as it was that evening, bathed in a dusty yellow light from the sun.

'I don't know if I've told you but I don't believe in an afterlife. I lost any faith in that during the war. But you shouldn't get the impression that I don't believe in some form of other power or energy. I believe this thing they say, that we only use a fraction of our brain power. And I believe that if we could use other parts of our brains we could tap in to all kinds of strange forces and levels of energy.

'Why am I telling you all of this? Well, it's about this sunny evening in Old Town Square. The Square is still there. The café may be still there for all I know. But other people pass by or sit there now. The people who sat there that sunny evening in 1938, well, most of them are dead now, dead or grown old. But she and I sat there that evening. We talked and laughed and commented on small things that happened and sometimes we were just silent. In the silences I thought about the afternoon we had had, the things we had seen, her excitement. Remember that this was her first time outside of Poland. And in the silences we seemed to draw closer to one another. It was a rare joining, a closeness of two people. And I wonder where that intensity, that concentration of energy, that touching of two people, has gone. Because I don't believe it can have died. I believe that if only we could work out how, there must be a way to tap back into that moment.

'We were just getting up to leave when a man approached threading his way through the tables and chairs. He was obviously Jewish with wispy sideburns, a bushy beard and a battered black hat. Despite the warmth of the evening he wore a heavy herringbone coat which had seen better days. He carried a battered cardboard suitcase. The man wasn't old, probably in his late forties or early fifties, but with his tramp-like appearance, he could have been any age. He was working the tables. Begging, I mean. I tried not to look at him but he was already making his way towards us. His voice was croaky as though he hadn't spoken in a while.

'"*I'm sorry to trouble you ladies, but I wonder if you could spare some change so that I could buy a bowl of soup.*"'

'His accent was cultivated, refined, not at all what I had expected from his appearance. We were the last table and he'd had no success at any of the others. We were his last hope.

'"*I'm not a beggar, you understand, even though you may say I'm begging from you now. I'm a refugee ... from Vienna. The Germans, they have taken everything we own. I was once well to do. Look at me now. It's two days since I last ate.*"

'Ariela asked him to sit down with us, and we ordered him some food. After initially wolfing some of the meat and bread and fried potatoes, he slowed down and said:

'"You must excuse me. I neglected to introduce myself. My name is Moritz Friedell My wife and I lived in Vienna where I practised as a lawyer. We lived there all our lives. We were both Austrian. I was born in Vienna as was my father.

"Six months ago, as you know, the Nazis came. The Anschluss it is called now. Overnight they took away all our rights. We couldn't own houses, we couldn't work, we couldn't eat in restaurants, we couldn't even walk in the park. One day about a month after they came, it was the Sabbath. My wife and I had been to the synagogue and were walking home when the Stormtroopers caught us. They put us in a lorry – I thought we were to be killed – and they took us to the Prater. It is an amusement park in Vienna. They made us kneel on the ground like cattle and ordered us to eat grass. They stamped on our hands or kicked us. Then forced us to climb the trees and pretend we were birds. We had to make bird sounds and they laughed and jeered and threw things at us as we squatted there. They made the women – they made the women excrete into their underwear.

"They beat them if they couldn't. They made us all run round and round in circles. Old people, even pregnant women. We had to do this until we fainted or collapsed. Then they beat us and kicked us again. It was during this that my wife suffered a heart attack. She died soon after the Nazis left."'

'Later, as he was getting up to leave, she asked him if he had money and a place to stay.

'"Please, you have done more than enough for me already. I will be fine. With a full stomach' – he patted the coat where it folded over his stomach, and smiled broadly – "everything is possible. May God bless you beautiful young ladies and keep you safe. Thank you from the bottom of my heart. I will think of you in my prayers.

That night she asked me about how the Poles saw the Jews.

'When you Poles talk about us Jews – "the Jewish problem" – what does it mean?'

'Well, I can only tell what I've picked up along the way. And what they taught us in school.'

'What they *taught* you?'

'What they taught us. They teach us that the Jews are different and that for the Jews the word "different" means better. They say that this sense of superiority has been handed down over hundreds of years. You are the "Chosen People" after all. You have your own Sabbath, your own food, your own schools, your own places of worship, your own way of doing things. So you live amongst the Christians but you are different. So now the Christians say: "You say that you are Jews, not Poles. Very well, we have no objections to that, but you'll have to get out. You can't live amongst us." We had a teacher who used to describe the Jews as "undigested and undigestible".'

'And what was the problem with having a group of different people in a country?'

'Well – and you've got to remember he was teaching these things to children – the problem arose, according to him, when the percentage of Jews to non-Jews rose above a certain point.'

'What point?'

'Ah, you see, that was the catch. The non-Jewish population determined that point. When it rose above that point, anti-Semitism made its appearance. I still remember the expression the teacher used to use. He used to say "Anti-semitism makes its appearance and finds its expression in ways varying from social ostracism to massacre. When there are two or three Jews in a village, things go well and there is a living for everybody. But when more Jews come, things go badly.'

'But he was one of the liberal ones, Ariela. While he felt

that Poland had far too many of this "non-Polish element", and that Poland should get rid of a good part of it, he didn't agree with the way the Nazis were going about it. He felt that such brutalities would shatter Polish self-respect and demean us in the eyes of the world. We used to have to recite this stuff – that's how I remember it so well. The last line went like this: "Only as a last resort, when all other ways and means have proved fruitless, might some kind of drastic action be entertained as policy".'

'This reminds me of my first week in Warsaw,' Ariela said. 'You know there are moments you look back on, and you realise they were really important. My first week in Warsaw was one of those. As a child I was very sure of myself. Unselfconscious. Confident. Cocky, even. Then, somehow, and I don't know where it changed or how it happened or what caused it, I became totally shy. Maybe it was puberty, though I think it happened before that. I felt inadequate and inferior for most of my teens. There are times when I feel it now. I have to be careful. My confidence is a very delicate shell.

'When I was about seventeen – in fact it was my seventeenth birthday, I decided this was no good, that I would have to do something about it. I imagined the way I wanted myself to be, the way I wanted other people to see me, then I tried to behave like that. It was a bit of a struggle. Every day there were all sorts of little tests. I would try to see how many continuous days I could get without faltering. Eventually I seemed to have got the hang of it. People began to remark on what a different person I had become.

'That was why I came to Warsaw as much as anything. I had two really close friends in school, Sophia and Rebecca. There was a saying that I used to quote to them. "What doesn't destroy me makes me stronger." I told them that going to Warsaw to study at the Conservatory was the

77

biggest challenge I could take on in my life. My idea was that it was important to put yourself in stressful situations because only in that way could you grow and tap into your hidden reserves of strength and achieve your potential. I had overcome this thing in a sort of sheltered environment, with my family and friends around me. Now I wanted to see if I had strength enough to withstand a big shock. Go to a place where I didn't know anybody and see if I could fend for myself. I used to think of my self-confidence as a sort of force inside me that I had to keep topped up. For days before I left, I was doing everything I could to keep the force there or make it a bit stronger. It was there on the train from Lodz. But it was so fragile. I remember seeing a flock of birds and thinking how simple their lives were and wondering why ours had to be so complicated.

'When I stepped out on the platform in Warsaw, all my courage just seemed to drain away into the ground, and by the time I got outside the station and into the taxi, it was gone. I tried to restore it in the taxi, but the driver cheated me, and I felt lonely and tiny and frightened by the time I shut the door of the hotel room behind me.

'I was like that for the first few days. If the hotel owner and his wife hadn't helped me to find a place to stay, I don't know what I would have done. My power was gone. I remember I sat on the bed for ages wondering what I was going to do. It was no good. When I looked in the mirror, all I could see was a shy country girl, a hick from the provinces.'

'So what did you do?'

'Well, I decided the problem was that the image of me in my head and what I saw in the mirror didn't tally. So I would have to do something about the me in the mirror. One possible me was the girl come up from the provinces to the big city. But there was a different me possible – self-confident, relaxed, happy in my own company.

'I had some emergency money with me. I know Papa had intended it in case I got robbed or something like that, but this seemed like an emergency to me. I went to a department store. It was the first one I found – and ferociously expensive. A woman asked me if she could help and I blushed to my roots. I decided I would have to buy something, so I told her I was looking for lipstick. She accompanied me to the cosmetics counter and I chose the first one I saw, a deep red colour. I fled that shop. Then I found another, more reasonable place on Marsalkowska Street. I went to the clothes section, and – I'll always remember it – there was this Jewish girl there. She helped me to pick out a dress. She was so helpful. Oh, I know they're trained to sell, but it was like she really cared that I made the right choices. I was floundering. I had never particularly cared how I looked, so I hadn't a clue how to match things. She guided me very gently, explaining what things would suit my colouring and my build. She asked if I was trying to match anything in particular, and without thinking I pulled out the lipstick, and said "this". I felt so stupid, but she looked at it and said that the colour was perfect for me. When she said that, I felt the first hint of my confidence returning. I began to enjoy it. We picked a dress and matching shoes. She asked about underwear – now she really was selling – and said they had a sale and I could get really nice things very cheaply. She asked somebody else to mind her post and came with me while we chose underwear and stockings. The shop was closing by the time we had finished, and she asked if I was going out straight away and would like to wear the things out. It hadn't occurred to me, but I thought that if I put these things on, they might act like a magic cloak and restore my confidence. I changed everything, and put on the lipstick in the changing room. When I came out, with my old clothes on my arm, the Jewish girl clapped her hands, and said "Bravo".

'I came out of that department store a different person. I felt like I belonged in Warsaw, that nothing bad could touch me. I found a restaurant – it wasn't too expensive – and asked for a table. It was empty at that early hour. The man hesitated for a moment - maybe he thought I was a pick-up or something. Then I said to him, "Look, I'm hungry, I want to eat, I'm on my own. Just give me a table where I can eat undisturbed." I couldn't believe I was the same person who had arrived in Warsaw just a few days previous. They had a couple of musicians there. A guitar and a piano. I remember they played a soft, jazzy version of some of the Songs of the Auvergne by Canteloube – do you know them?'

'That sounds like an important moment to me, alright.'

'Maybe. Maybe it was just a happy evening. Like this one.'

'It's nice to remember times when you were truly, unconditionally happy. Maybe they don't come that often.'

It was late when we left the restaurant and walked back to the hotel. We felt warm and cosy. Whatever about the situation in Vienna, in Prague the prospect of war might have been on another planet. The evening was still warm and people were out with thin jackets and light clothes. Shop windows blazed with lights and were packed with goods. People strolled on the pavements or the cobbled streets, coming from the theatre, going to restaurants or clubs. There was conversation and laughter and gaiety, and the smell of a dozen different perfumes in the air. Once we had to get through a large crowd that had gathered to watch a street entertainer. Ariela led the way, but she put her hand back and I held it, feeling a warm sparkle-like electricity at the sensation of her skin upon mine. When we got to the hotel, I remember we took off our shoes in the lift and raced down the corridor to our room.'

Chapter 2

The room has two single beds in it. Katya locks the door, throws her shoes on the floor and falls back onto the bed. Ariela goes into the bathroom. The toilet flushes and the door opens. Then the bed springs twang as Ariela collapses onto her own bed.

'It was a great day,' says Katya.

'Except for the poor little man,' Ariela says quietly.

'Try not to think about him,' says Katya, rolling off the bed, and kneeling beside Ariela's. She lies with one foot sticking out over the end of the bed, and the other flat on it, her knee in the air. Her arms shield her eyes from the bedside light.

'I'm too tired, even to undress,' she says.

Katya looks along Ariela's legs, across her breasts to her face. 'Ariela. You have such a beautiful name.'

Ariela lifts her hands from her eyes, opens them and looks back at Katya.

'There's an Ariel in one of Shakespeare's play,' says Ariela. There is a tipsy giggle in her voice.

Her lips move as if to say something else – there is still some faded lipstick on them from earlier – and then Katya lowers her face and kisses Ariela on the mouth. Katya may have intended it to be hardly more than a good night kiss, a kiss of affection, but whether it is the wine or the moment, she kisses Ariela hard. Katya lifts her head. A momentary look of confusion steals across Ariela's face. It is replaced by a soft smile as Ariela puts her hand behind Katya's head and

81

guides her face towards her.

They undress each other in the lamplight.

'Do you know what I think is the sexiest part of the body?' Ariela says softly.

Katya shakes her head.

'Here,' she says, tracing Katya's skin with her index finger. 'Under the arm and down a bit where it curves and turns into breasts.

'Your nipples are like the erasers on pencils,' says Katya.

Ariela laughs. Katya teases Ariela's nipples with her own.

In the lamplight, the two friends play with one another's bodies.

The next time Ariela will undress naked in front of anybody will be more than three years from now. It will be under very different circumstances. But tonight – mercifully – that lies in the future.

'You're so wet,' Ariela smiles. 'Where does it come from?'

'I don't know.'

'It's like tears. It's hard to understand where they all come from either.'

'Hush,' Katya says, as though to a baby, 'don't talk about tears.'

Later, they lie on their sides, thighs intertwined. Occasionally one of them moves an entangled leg slowly, languorously, stroking the other's limbs.

'I can smell us,' Ariela says, her smile weary.

Katya pushes Ariela's hair behind her ear, and caresses her cheek. With feather touches, butterfly touches, she runs the tip of her finger down the other girl's nose, across her lips, across her eyelids. Ariela's eyes close to receive the touch.

'You look radiant,' says Katya. 'What are you thinking?'

'I was thinking we live such sheltered lives at home.'

Some time during the night Katya reaches over in the darkness. She can feel Ariela's long legs. Her thighs are cold where the blankets have slipped. Katya pulls them over to cover Ariela and leaves her hand on her friend's thigh.

The bed is empty when Katya wakes the next morning. Looking over at Ariela's bed she sees that it has not been slept in. Then she becomes aware of water running in the bathroom. She gets up, pulls on her dressing gown, and opens the bathroom door. Ariela is in the bath, her breasts surrounded by soapy water, her hair wet. She looks up.

'Morning,' she says, brightly.

'I think I owe you an explanation,' says Katya, leaning her head against the door jamb.

'There's nothing to explain. I was part of it too.'

Ariela lifts her hand to her nose. 'I can still smell you on my fingers.'

Katya sniffs her own fingers. 'Sticky fingers,' she smiles feebly.

'I was wrong – to do that to you.'

'It was wrong of me. It was leading you on when I knew it couldn't go any further. I'm really sorry Katya. You're the dearest friend. You really, really are. But I can't feel any more than that.'

'I knew that last night.'

'We're lucky we're not in Germany,' says Katya. 'This kind of thing is illegal there.'

Ariela suddenly picks up a wet, soapy sponge and throws it at Katya.

'At least you're not Jewish,' she laughs.

Chapter 3

Normandy. The present.

'I was in love with her – I freely admit it. And there was no future in it. It would have broken my heart to stay around her. I told her the last night of our stay in Prague.'

'I'm leaving Poland soon after we get back.'

'What ... Where will you go?'

'France first I think. Though the Germans will probably invade there after they've finished with us. Then England, Ireland, America eventually, if I can get in. The further away from these Nazi bastards the better. It isn't just the Nazis though. Poland is no country for people like me. I need to go somewhere where you can be whatever you want to be.'

Then I took the plunge.

'Will you come with me? Oh, I don't mean as a lover or anything like that. It's just that you won't be safe in Poland once the Nazis invade. You heard what that old man said. We could catch a train and be in Paris within a week. With a voice like yours you'd have no problem getting into any school you liked over there ... There are your other friends there.'

'There's my parents, Katya. And the rest of my family.'

'Tell me you'll think about it. I don't think you realise the danger you're in.'

'I have to stay. You know I do.'

'It's not Stefan, is it?'

'No, it's not Stefan. Too many other reasons – my studies, but mainly my family. We all came together last year and talked about it and said we would stay put.'

There was nothing else I could say. Then she said:

'Would you like to make love again tonight?'

'You're too sweet. But probably not. Let's just share the same bed and hold each other.'

The next day we caught the train back to Warsaw.'

'I left Poland early in 1939. Her plan was to leave later in the year after the term finished. She had suggested I wait for her and Stefan, but I wanted to go and get my own life established. Anyway it wasn't clear to me how much I wanted to be involved with her when Stefan was on the scene. We arranged to write. Around April she wrote to say they'd decided to delay it a few months in order to get some extra money together. As I understood it she still hadn't told her parents at that stage. Her letters stopped at the end of August.'

Chapter 4

West of Breslau, Lower Silesia, Germany. 31 August 1939

Otto Tauber spent the last day of peace in a sunny meadow. Lying on the fragrant grass, he picked an occasional wildflower and pressed them between the pages of his copy of *Mein Kampf* which he kept in his pack. In a few weeks he would be 39, and now at last, within sight of 40, but still on the right side of it, he felt that things were moving his way.

The men were in high spirits and played football on some green space at the edge of the vehicle park. Others, like Otto, lounged in the sun or read or wrote letters while they waited. Around five the field kitchens served a hot meal – pork, potatoes, cabbage, freshly-baked bread, a beer – and when it began to grow dark, the order was given to prepare to move forward.

In the gathering gloom, they heard the sound of many engines being started and revved. Diesel and gasoline fumes caught at their throats. Aircraft could be heard overhead. Soon they were on the road, their mechanised column joining a line of tanks, motor cycles, staff cars, trucks and artillery, both motorised and horse-drawn, which pushed past columns of marching infantry, their steel helmets like a bobbing sea in the semi-darkness. It had started.

Some time after midnight they arrived at their jumping off positions, and settled down to wait. This wasn't like 1917. This time they were dry, warm, comfortable. There was food in their bellies and they carried the best of weaponry. A million and a half men, the Hauptsturmfuhrer had told them, would be crossing the Polish frontier at dawn. It would be over within a couple of weeks.

Otto was not with the first line troops. Rather, his regiment had been assigned to mopping up operations, once the push began. The stormtroops would surge forward, breaking through the enemy. His outfit would take care of saboteurs, isolated pockets of resistance and pacifying captured towns and villages. Their ultimate objective was the encirclement of Lodz, 150 kilometres to the north east.

In comparison to the last war, the next few days turned out to be like a driving tour. Indeed, a couple of the young guys began to jeer him, saying that they couldn't understand what all the fuss from the last war had been about – if this was war it was a picnic. It was a measure of Otto's good humour that he laughed off their comments – in the past he had nearly killed people for less.

The first troops crossed the border just after 4:45 on Friday, 1 September. Otto's regiment crossed a couple of hours later. By then, the sun was hot, the column was enveloped in dust, and ahead the horizon boiled with rolling clouds of black smoke, spattered occasionally with orange explosions and red fire. They had already exceeded their first day's objectives by early afternoon, but they pressed on. Initially they had approached villages or clusters of houses with some caution, but – incredibly – there had been absolutely no resistance. Otto had yet to see a Polish soldier – a live one, at any rate. The dive bombers, tanks and artillery had done their work well.

Towards evening, with the sun warm on their backs, they approached the outskirts of a shattered Polish village. Word was passed back that they were going to stop here. The street they were travelling down was lined with trees in full bloom.

The leaves were grey and dusty. They were the only thing that were still intact. Behind them the roofless shells of houses were stacked with rubble and scorched beams. Above the windows and doors the white paint was blackened where fire had raged. Much of the wreckage still smouldered and an acrid smell hung in the sir. They turned a corner. A sign, leaning drunkenly, read 'Piotrkow 26 Km', pointing upwards. Otto nudged the man next to him and pointed at the sign.

'Up in smoke – that's where it is,' he yelled, above the roaring of the engine.

His companion laughed. On the pavement, standing on the rubble, a woman in a black shawl held a young boy in a cap by the hand. They looked on with taut, frightened faces. So these were Poles.

The column pulled to a halt in the main square. Engines died, dust began to settle and orders were shouted. Otto swung himself over the side of the troop carrier and motioned to a couple of men.

'Come on, let's see if we can find some food and a decent place to stay.'

They strode out of the square and down a side street that seemed to have been left all but unscathed by the bombardment. Stone-built houses with shoulder-high window sills lined the street. Many of the windows were open, their glass still intact. A heavy wooden door led through to a sunlit courtyard where rugs hung on frames. A carpet beater lay on the cobbles, abandoned. A quick inspection of the cool interiors showed that all the apartments were deserted. They were untidy, showing signs of a rapid departure, but had not been looted. He sent one of the men back to bring on the rest of the squad.

When the men arrived, he ordered Rottenfuhrer Bauer to allocate beds. 'We'll go and find some food,' grinned Otto, 'and some Jews to cook it.'

'We'll need some bedding as well,' one of the men said.

'Just leave it to me.'

Otto and a couple of men wandered back towards the square. The brass were already installing themselves in the large, undamaged buildings, but their own place would be fine.

'This place is too fancy for the Jews,' said Private Eberle, a fresh-faced nineteen year old who looked younger. 'We need to find the rattiest part of town.'

'Either of you good at sniffing out Jews?' smiled Otto.

'Over there, I'd say,' answered the other youngster, Private Fritsch, the helmet, which he never seemed to take off, perched above a tanned face.

Otto followed them good-humouredly. The cobbled street was deserted. Not a dog barked.

Eberle kicked open the first front door he saw, and went inside, his rifle at the ready. There was the sound of more doors being kicked, some objects smashing, and he emerged, shaking his head.

'Mustn't have the nose for it,' grinned Fritsch to Otto.

They hit lucky on the sixth house. They knew even before they entered – the smell of cooking wafted out of an open window. This time Otto led the way, clumping across a threadbare mat that lay on a bare wooden floor, and bursting into a kitchen that smelled of boiled vegetables and boiled clothes. In the kitchen were two women and three children – girls of various ages. They had all been sitting at the table upon which lay plates of half-eaten food. When they had heard the intruders, the three girls had run to huddle with what Otto assumed were their mothers. Five terrified faces looked at the men.

Eberle began to turn out the cupboards, stacking food carefully on the counter top. Fritsch kept them covered while Otto sauntered over the pot on the range, helping himself to a ladleful of some kind of stew. It wasn't bad – for Jew swill. Otto dipped the ladle again. One of the women got slowly to her feet. Fritsch levelled his rifle, but the woman, terror in her eyes and shaking badly, tried to smile and indicated the pot with her hand. She said something in Polish.

'Ja, ja,' said Fritsch, jerking his rifle to indicate that she should get plates.

She took plates from the dresser, barely able to hold them, her hands were shaking so much. Large helpings were ladled onto each plate. The other four withdrew into the corner of the room. The three men laid their rifles against the table, straddled the chairs and began to eat hungrily. There was bread on the table and they divided the loaf between them. The woman emptied the pot giving them seconds.

Otto, Eberle and Fritsch arrived back at their billet about an hour after they had left.

'Good old Otto!' the men cheered as they made their way through the gate. With them were the two women, the eldest of the three daughters, and a handcart full of food, cooking utensils and bedding commandeered from the house they had eaten in and some of its neighbours. There had been a bit of a scene when the other two daughters hadn't wanted to be separated, and had begun to cry. Eventually they locked the kids in the cellar, and with lots of Polish wailing the convoy had set off. The woman who had served the soup was set to cooking the food while the other woman and the daughter were sent to make up beds.

'Make sure those dirty bitches wash their hands, especially the one doing the cooking,' Otto shouted as he went off to relax in the courtyard. Later, as he sat reading the chapter entitled *Germany's Policy in Eastern Europe*, he heard shouts and cheers and womens' screams coming from inside: the boys were letting off some steam. They were a good bunch of lads. There would probably be tough days ahead – let them relax while they could. Hey, that food smelt good. That Jewish cunt could cook.

Chapter 5

Brzykow. The first week of September, 1939

The breeze fans the dog's grey fur, making it stand porcupine-like. In the slanting, late afternoon sun, each individual hair seems to stand out. The air, smelling chokingly of burning, wafts past the dog's nose. But the black snout is dry and unsensing.

Flames are already consuming the house. They also destroy a long-forgotten tree house that Aron built for Ariela when she was five. The Germans discovered it while they were searching the grounds and lobbed hand grenades into it.

The two bodies hang narrow, heavy, sack-like from a tree, swinging gently in the breeze. Beneath them discarded, trampled and crushed onions, cut down to make room for the bodies, ooze juice onto the grass. The soft air blows flakes of onion skin away over the manicured lawn.

Chapter 6

Lodz, Poland. September, 1939

David continued to report to work during the first week of the German invasion, even though by then there was hardly any work to be done. Lodz was still unoccupied. Throughout the city, however, rumours and counter-rumours were born, circulated and died. Ella was missing, whereabouts unknown. So too were his parents, though he assumed they must be in Brzykow.

David and Anna agonised over what they should do. David was prepared to stick by their decision to stay put until the evening when they first heard artillery fire booming and saw – from an upstairs window – a fiery glow towards the south. Thankfully, Marek was asleep while this was going on. As they came downstairs, David said:

'Maybe we're doing the wrong thing. Maybe we should be fleeing.'

'Fleeing where?'

'East.'

'What, just walking out and leaving? On the road? Like gypsies?'

'Better a live gypsy than a dead Jew.'

At the look in her face, he said:

'I'm sorry, I shouldn't have said that. I don't know what to do. Part of me is saying that once the Germans have what they want they'll leave us alone. Or they'll turn their attentions to the West. Then, there's another part that says we should just get out. At least we'd be in control of our own destiny. I remember once when I was eleven or twelve, a policeman came to our school. He gave us a talk on strange men trying to take us away. Most of us were so young that we were all a bit baffled as to what he could mean. He said that if somebody tried to do it we should kick and scream and shout and do everything possible not to go with them. Looking back on it, I see his reasoning. Somebody like that would have prepared a place. If he got you there you would have no chance. The thing was to avoid being taken there.'

'At least here we have food and a roof over our heads,' she said.

'We'll have to decide,' he said. 'If we're going to go, we can't leave it any later.'

'What if they catch us on the road? We could be bombed or machine gunned. We'll be prisoners, we'll have no home. No, there's too much uncertainty if we leave. Let's stay here and see it through.'

'Okay,' he said, embracing her. 'That's what we'll do.'

Chapter 7

Lodz, Poland. Winter, 1939

The gloved hand swung the door knocker so vigorously that Otto thought the Pole would wrench it from its mounting. His slushy boots kicked the door a couple of times for good measure, as though anxious to show his enthusiasm for the job. Otto stood a pace or two behind the two Polish policemen, stamping his feet and blowing on his hands. Jesus, it got cold in this country in winter. They heard the sound of bolts being unlocked and then the door opened a fraction to reveal two frightened Jewish faces.

'We've come for your telephone,' said one of the Poles.

'It's already been disconnected,' the man blurted out, anxious to please.

'Don't you think we know that, you Jewish moron? We've come for the fucking telephone itself.'

The woman had already disappeared, and now the door opened a little further as she returned and passed the telephone out. The Pole snatched it from her and the three of them turned away, the door closing quickly, so that Otto just had time to see a child of about seven, with a confused look on his face, in the hall. There was a black car on the pavement and the Pole opened the door and threw the unit onto the back seat. The other Pole consulted his list, and indicated a house three doors away.

'Jesus, I'm cold,' said Otto. 'Let's see if we can get a cup of coffee in here.'

When the next door opened they barged their way in and one of the Poles ordered the woman to prepare coffee – 'real coffee', he emphasised. There seemed to be no man around, just a woman in her thirties and a child of about four. The house was a wreck and only marginally warmer than the street outside. The signs of neglect were everywhere. A curtain rail had come away from the wall leaving two big holes in the plaster, and the curtain had been put back by nailing it into place. The floorboards creaked and in some places there were holes in the floor under the carpet. The carpet on the stairs was half up, with most of the risers missing, making it more like a slide than a set of steps. A Jew could break his neck on that!

Otto went into the kitchen, where the two Poles sat at the round kitchen table in the centre of the room. They stood up hastily as he came in. The woman stood at the stove with her back to them, the child by her side. She glanced nervously over her shoulder as Otto entered, before returning to her work. On the table was a half-cut loaf of dark bread and some marmalade. The woman wiped the table with a cloth, trying to keep herself between the child and the three men. Suddenly though, the child came round her and walked straight over to Otto, a big smile on her face.

'What's your name?' she asked in Polish.

She had dark eyes, and long hair which was dull and tangled. Her sharp little nose was running, and her clothes were shabby, the colours long-faded from them.

'Riwka, Riwka, come here,' the mother said, her face fearful.

The child ignored her, and continued to look up at Otto. She still had that smile on her face, disobedient, sly, coy, wilful. When she got older he could imagine her being coquettish, flirting, teasing, a slut like all Jewish sows.

'Riwka.' The mother's eyes filled with tears. Otto knew very little Polish, but he could hear the fear in her voice. She began to come round the table towards her child.

'Go to your mother now,' said Otto in German in a reasonable tone. He put out his gloved hand and pressed the child's shoulder gently. But instead of moving away, the child came closer to him, putting her dirty hands clumsily around the skirts of his coat as though to embrace him. He noticed the particles of food on her fingers – they were sticky with marmalade and snot.

Well, he had warned her. The mother was still a pace or two away when he pulled his right hand back almost to shoulder height, and lashed down at the child. He could feel his knuckles connect with her cheek and he was pretty sure he heard something crack, as she was carried across the room by the force of the blow. The mother ran to the screaming bundle against the wall.

'What about our coffee?' roared Otto.

She had been about to crouch down to lift the child, and now she froze in her stoop.

'My child,' she pleaded.

With her hands she indicated the crumpled form against the wall. The two Poles had now turned and were also looking at Otto. The child continued to shriek, her crying becoming wild and animal-like as she found nobody was coming to comfort her. Otto shook his head.

'Coffee, first,' he said, in the same reasonable tone in which he had originally spoken. He sat down, and gestured to his comrades to do the same. Her hand shaking, the woman poured the coffee into three cups.

'We have no sugar,' she said in Polish, 'and only a little milk.'

'We'll take the milk,' one of the Poles answered.

However, Otto had already lifted the cup to his lips. The child sucked in great gulps of air amidst hysterical crying which continued unabated. She lay where she had landed, her legs tucked in under her body and her shoulder and head against the wall. A small trail of blood began to seep out onto the fabric of the wallpaper. Now that the coffee had been poured the woman made a second attempt to reach her child, and this time she was unhindered. She knelt on the floor, and taking the little girl by the shoulders, prised her away from the wall with difficulty. The child's face was obscured by hair that was wet with blood. Beneath the mask of hair, the crying was ear-piercing.

'This coffee is like piss,' shouted Otto above the noise.

Than, after a pause, he shouted to one of the Poles: 'You – tell her to get that little bitch to shut up.'

The mother was trying to wipe the hair off the child's face to gauge the extent of her injuries, when the Pole translated this for her.

She darted an anxious look up at Otto and then began to half pick up, half soothe the child.

'Riwka, shhh ... please Riwka ... the soldiers will get very angry if you don't stop ... please Riwka, shhh ...'

It was as though the child didn't hear any longer. The hysterical crying and gulping for air continued. Her mother was now trying to pull her to her feet so that she could get her out of the room. The child clung deliberately to the floor, flailing her arms and legs.

Otto shouted once more. 'I asked you to stop that crying. This coffee is bad enough without having to put up with this.'

'Riwka,' screamed the mother, with panic in her voice.

No response. The crying continued.

'Jesus Christ!' Otto roared.

There was the sound of crockery shattering as he flung

the cup against the wall above the little girl's head.

The hot coffee splashed out over the child's head and bare neck and the resulting screams were louder than anything she had achieved up to now. Otto pulled up the skirts of his coat and reached inside, unbuttoning his holster. The mother saw the movement and shrieked at her daughter:

'RIWKA!'

This time she managed to scoop the girl up off the floor, and embracing her in her arms, she turned so that her body was between Otto and her daughter. Otto's pistol was out and levelled. Frozen to the spot, the woman tried to keep her child turned away, at the same time twisting her neck to see what Otto was doing. The pistol cracked twice, then again and again and again. Both mother and daughter screamed. The window shattered, then the sink. Plaster drizzled from the ceiling. Some dishes shattered on the dresser. Otto emptied his Luger into any inanimate object he could see.

Then suddenly he began to laugh. He stepped towards the woman and delivered a tremendous booted kick to the back of her knees. Then, as she collapsed onto the ground he kicked her savagely at the base of her spine. Still grasping the child she rolled onto the floor, trying to protect the child's body with her own. The resulting foetal position gave him a target area that included her buttocks, and the undersides of her thighs. He kicked again, aiming deliberately for the rear of her groin, and with satisfaction he felt his boot sink in through the material of her dress and connect with the softness within.

'Come on,' he said, catching the edge of the table and upending it in her general direction.

'And don't forget the fucking phone.'

Chapter 8

Lodz, Poland – David Steinbaum's diary

THURSDAY, 2 NOVEMBER 1939
*I have decided to keep a diary. After all these are historic
events going on around us, and since I am not working now,
I need to find something to satisfy whatever creativity I have.
I need to go back a little, to bring things up to date.*

*It was September, early September when we first heard
the gunfire in the south west. Of course, there had been
bombing before that, but that had seemed remote, imperson-
al. That all ended when the first Germans appeared on
Pabianicka Street. Anna had been stocking up with food for
several months – tins and bottles and dried things – and it
looks like we have enough in the cupboards and under the
bed to keep us going until the end of the year.*

*It wasn't long before there were the first measures against
the Jews. The Germans started seizing people for digging. It
became dangerous to go into town or be on the streets or to
travel on public transport. We took all of our savings in cash
– it wasn't that much, probably no more than two month's
salary, three if we really tightened our belts – out of the bank
and stashed it here. (I must also stash this diary in case anyone finds it.)*

*Within a few days things had deteriorated even further.
There were incidents of Germans walking into shops and*

helping themselves. A working party of Jews were apparently told to stop working, take off their clothes and they were faced against a wall and told they'd be shot. Shots were fired in their direction several times. Thankfully, nobody was hurt. At the same time I stopped going to work, Marek stopped going to school, and so the three of us started spending all day around the house. Lots of work was getting done in the garden! I've never seen it so spotless.

After a week or so of this, I had had enough. I said to Anna that we couldn't just go on living like this. I was going out on a shopping expedition, to see if there was any fresh food to be had. Anyway, we couldn't keep eating into our supplies – there's a long winter ahead. The first expedition was a huge success. I was away for most of the day, but I had told Anna to expect that, and came back with some milk, potatoes, meat and leafy greens. The next time I did it a few days later, I got a nasty fright. People – Poles – started pulling people from the queue. I never thought I looked particularly Jewish – Ella and I are alike in that respect – but this guy came up to me and said something like 'here's one', and then 'come on, out you'. I fled the queue and even though I should have tried to find another one some place else, I was so shocked that I just went home. Anna said that it looked like I had seen a ghost. I didn't step outside for a few days. Anna was going to go, but I wouldn't let her. Eventually, there was nothing for it but to go out and take our chances.

I had been in touch with work every day by phone, and eventually we all (them, Anna, me) felt that things had settled down enough that I could return to work. Anyway, we needed the money to stock up our little pile. Anna started doing the shopping – queuing would be a better expression – with Marek, and I went back to work. Luckily we had no more incidents. Even though they seemed to be grabbing Jews left, right and centre, I wasn't seized for any manual labour. Anna did have a queuing incident similar to mine. She has black hair, high cheekbones and a thin sharp nose, and that combination is perhaps what singled her out. I think it scared the life out of her. (She had calmed down by the time I got home. And somehow or other, another woman in the queue had got her some food or given her things, I'm not sure which.) Marek kept asking why Mummy was pulled out of the queue. What could we tell him? There are some bad men running the country at the moment. But they'd soon be gone. Once the British and French came over to fight them. Of course this was a stupid thing to say, because ever since then he's been asking when they're coming. I had to tell him it could be a few months – it takes a long time to get a big army ready.

At the end of October, a German officer and two Polish policeman came and took away our phone

I'm coping (I think) and Marek is oblivious. He's always enjoyed his own company, and he spends hours in his room lost in his own imaginary world. Occasionally he goes to one of the neighbours' houses or their kids come here, but not very often. Firstly, there aren't too many Jewish families around here, and now, all the parents are anxious to know where their children are at all times.

It's starting to get cold now. We've put off lighting the fire and instead camp around the stove in the kitchen. Again, we have a small stockpile of timber and coal, but it won't last long once we start using it. Better to hold off for as long as possible.

I'm still going to work every day, but now a new thing has happened. They have started throwing people out of their apartments so that Germans can come and live in them. A whole lot of new anti-Jewish orders have been issued. Jews are not allowed to walk on Piotrkowska Street because it's the main street; Jews and Poles are to yield everywhere to Germans in uniform; Jewish stores are to be marked

'Judisches Geschaft' next to a yellow star of David with the word *'Jude'*.

This is where we've come so far. And so tonight, we are here the three of us. It is late. Tomorrow I will go to work, but only I think to complete the week. Next week, I don't know what to do. Anna managed to get some food today, and that will be enough to keep us over the weekend without eating into our other supplies. Marek is asleep. Anna has gone to bed, and I will go now. Who knows what tomorrow will bring? Perhaps we should have left, but it is too late now. Would we have been better off in Brzykow? It's all idle speculation now, I suppose. I wish it were tomorrow night, and then I would know that at least we are all together for the weekend.

FRIDAY, 3 NOVEMBER 1939

The streets were almost deserted on the way home this evening - so different from a normal Friday night. In places the gutters are full of drifts of leaves, crackling like dry paper and swishing if you kick through them. I walked home by back streets. I had been in two minds whether or not to take a tram, but there are problems with that now too. Just a few days ago, while walking along the pavement, I saw two German soldiers and a Polish policeman stop a tram, climb on and order all Jews off. By the window nearest to me there was an old man. From the way he was behaving he seemed too embarrassed to get up. After the Jews had got off, the Germans then went round and checked everybody's papers. Of course, they caught him. They dragged him from his seat, one soldier taking each of his arms, and threw him out the door of the tram. You would have thought they might have left it at that, but no, they came down after him, kicking him with their boots and roaring at him to get up. Their anger was terrible – 'Jew pig', 'Jewish piece of shit'. Somehow he struggled to his feet and then they drove him ahead of them down the street to where a truck was waiting. He was man-handled into the back of the truck and they drove off with him. I fear for what may have happened to him.

Anyway I stuck to the back streets. There were a few points where I had to break cover and cross a main street or walk a short distance on an open pavement. I took it slowly and carefully, spying out the terrain before making a move and got home without incident. In fact, I have to admit, for a while I was almost enjoying it. It was like a real-life game of cowboys and Indians.

I have always liked November. (I like all the months if the truth be known. Each has its own special appeal.) November I like the leaves, the cold, or rather being able to come in out of the cold to hot food and drink. Or the opposite, going out in it for a bracing walk. I like November in Lodz. The feel-ing that the year is coming to an end. For me it has always been the beginning of the time when I recap on the year that is now ending; to see what has been achieved and what has been left undone; and then to prepare myself for the new year, to make plans, to set goals, to dream dreams. I have often done this, walking home from work, through busy streets on chilly November evenings. Now the Germans have turned my city into a place of fear and I hate them for this.

Marek normally stays up late on a Friday night and that's what he did tonight. He read and played with his toys and we played a game together. Now he is gone to bed. Anna is knit-ting and I am writing this. She asked me tonight what I was doing and made some remark about what the point was now that all of this was happening. She is very depressed and makes no secret of the fact. We are all unhappy but what can we do about it except put a brave face on things. Our week-end looks like being long and – I was going to say boring, but in a sense boring is the best we can hope for. Our door is bolted, we lit a little fire tonight, and we had some food and wine. It was almost like old times. We will probably stay indoors all weekend. We'll go out in the garden, but at this time of year there's not much you can do. We've dug up a lot of the lawn and prepared the ground for vegetables, so that next year our food problems shouldn't be so severe. I will probably write some more in this, and read and play with Marek. Perhaps Anna will cheer up a bit. I hope so. If she does and nobody comes near us over the weekend, then that is all we ask. On Sunday I will decide about work on Monday.

SUNDAY, 26 NOVEMBER 1939

It has been over three weeks since I have written in this. Many things have happened – every day is now disconcertingly devoid of any kind of routine. Or rather there is a routine, but it is like the way one carries out a routine in the aftermath of the death of a loved one. You go through the motions, but you are constantly aware of something huge looming over you, something which never allows your mind to rest or slide easily into the mind-soothing groove of a routine.

The biggest thing that has happened is that we must now wear a yellow star. It is a return to the Middle Ages. Nothing could have prepared us for this.

I have focused so far in this diary on our own little family, but what of the others that we love. Anna's parents are well, and we try to make contact with them at least once a week. Though this contact is becoming increasingly difficult to make, with no phone. There is no news of my family. My parents' whereabouts are unknown. Again I fear the worst. Also there is no news of Ella. We have no way of getting in touch with Warsaw, and so if she is there we cannot know. For about a week after the arrival of the Germans, every time there was a knock at the door, my heart would leap and I *would hope that I would go out there and she would be standing there, smiling like she always does. When I am not thinking about the three of us I think about her.*

I don't know how any of this will go, but presumably, soon the Germans will settle down into their role as occupiers, we Poles as the defeated people, and we Jews as the particular butt of any of their measures. Then, hopefully, it will be possible to get back to something approaching normal life. It will be possible to work and travel and buy food. As soon as that happens, I have resolved to travel to Warsaw and see if I can find her. Despite what my mother may think about Ella being her baby, in ways Ella is the most resourceful of all of us – she was only nineteen when she left home – and I'm sure she is safe and well. I pray that she is.

Usually, at this time of year, we take a trip down to Brzykow. Sometimes, if we are lucky, we have some of those cold, clear-skied, sunny days of late Autumn. More than anything else I miss the trees – red, yellow, orange, brown – the colours of fire.

PART THREE

Chapter 1

Normandy. The present.

'Katya, was Stefan … was he good for her? What was she like around him?'

'Very different from when he wasn't there. It was as though all her independence and free spiritedness disappeared; as if she was playing a kind of submissive role that she thought girlfriends should play. She used to hang on his words. Relate stories of things he had done or said. It wasn't nice to see. If he was happy he expected everyone else to be. And if he wasn't, then he wasn't a particularly nice guy. He complained a lot. Sometimes he did nothing but stay at home and play the sax. For a long time she pandered to him. When he was in good form, she was happy and when he was being a shit, she fussed over him and tried to coax him out of it. It was like she was married to him: he was the great artist and she was there to cater to his every whim. It didn't seem to matter that she was probably much more talented than he was.'

'I never told her any of this. I kept my thoughts to myself and said nothing. I don't know if it would have made a difference. Maybe she wouldn't have gone east. But would that have made a difference? I don't know. By the way, I've been meaning to ask, how did she get into jazz in the first place?'

'I don't know. The first anybody knew about it was she wrote to a radio programme asking if they would play a particular song. They did and read out her name, saying that she had written in and how surprised and delighted they were to receive a letter from a fifteen year old. What was her singing like? When she sang jazz, I mean.'

'Well, it was like she could have different personalities within the same song. There was one she used to sing, a how-could-I-have-been-so-foolish-to-have-fallen-in-love-with-you sort of song. She would begin sounding fragile, weary, as though on the edge of tears. Then there was a part in the song where she remembered how the love affair used to be. At that point she became warm and passionate. Then all of that faded and she returned to the present, alone, deserted. The song always reminded me a bit of Sibelius' *Valse Triste*. Her natural shyness somehow came across in her songs. She gave an aura of being easily broken and some of the songs – like this one – gave you the impression she had been hurt a lot. Of course, with her, all of the hurt was still to come. But, in some ways, I thought the hurt she projected stood for the hurt of all the Jews.'

Chapter 2

Lodz, Poland – David Steinbaum's diary

1 MARCH 1940 (BUT WRITTEN A FEW DAYS LATER)
Some day, when this is over, when sanity has returned, the Nazis, the Germans, somebody, is going to pay for all of this. Somebody is going to pay for the uprooted families, the devastated homes, the children whose childhoods have been shattered. If it takes me the rest of my life I am going to work to ensure that this happens. When the world finds out what the Germans did, there is going to be hell to pay. Poland after the war is not going to be a nice place for the Poles. At least not for those who assisted in this. And as for the Germans, if they thought the Versailles Treaty was bad, they haven't seen anything yet.

It is evening as I write this. We are in our new abode, of which I will say more in a while, but first I must relate the events of the last 24 hours.

Some days ago the Germans announced they were setting up a Jewish 'residential area' into which all the Jews in Lodz must move. They call it a residential area. We Jews have a much older name for such an area – the ghetto. It had been our intention that Anna's family and ourselves would move together, and try to find living space near to one another. As it turned out, however, this proved impossible. The 'relocation', as it was called, started off in a relatively well-organised sort of way. But then the Germans decided they wanted things completed in a few days and so the rest of the people were just uprooted at short notice and herded into the ghetto. We came sort of in the middle, so it ended up that we had some notice and had about a day to get organised. That was yesterday.

Yesterday morning at breakfast, the three of us sat down to our meagre meal and we told Marek we would be moving. At first he was excited, but then we explained that the new place we would be living in would probably not be as nice as the one we had now. 'Will I have my own room?' he asked, and we told him not. Then he started to cry. We told him he should get his little case – the one we got for the holiday we took in 1938 – and pack his favourite toys and books and things into it. He wanted to bring all his toys, but we told him no, we could only take a little, so he should take his favourite ones. Again the crying. It was heartbreaking. We told him we would pack all the rest of his things and leave them safe in the attic.

Children are wonderful. He was gone for a while, and then he returned, crying stopped, eyes red. 'Which books do you think I should bring?' he asked, and he had a whole heap of them in his hands. He dumped them on the kitchen table, and Anna sat down with him and asked which was better than which and what he thought of this particular one and at last he made a selection. At one point she looked up at me while he was thumbing through the pages of a particular book and I thought my heart would break when I saw the expression on her face. When Marek was finished, he gathered up the books he wouldn't be taking and, as he was leaving he said, 'Maybe I'll take just one more out of this pile as well'. After that, periodically during the day, he would come down to discuss a particular selection with Anna or me. He was ready by lunch time but re-packed several times during the afternoon, as he thought more about his choices.

We had inherited a handcart with the house when we bought it, and we loaded it with as much as we could. It didn't take much to fill it. A couple of mattresses, all the food we had, cooking utensils, pots and pans, bedding, clothes and shoes, a few tools. Each item was carefully considered, weighed against others and then accepted or rejected depending on space in the handcart or what we could carry. Apart from this we were leaving everything else behind us. My beloved books. I spent ages agonising over which ones to take and finally decided against any of them - the presence of a handful would only make me long for the absent ones. In the end though, I did take one, mainly because it was fat and had plenty of reading in it – Three Cities by Sholem Asch. That, my diary – it is also a fat, empty book – and every pen and pencil I could lay my hands on. Writing the story of our existence, rather than reading will be my main mental activity in our new life. When it is all over, somebody must know that these things happened. All of the things with which Anna had filled the house – things she had gone to such trouble to find – we left behind. Anna's father had been able to find storage space for his things, but this was at a premium now and we had had no such luck. We would be walking out the door and leaving the house to whoever might lay their hands on it.

We were ready by dinner time and then there was nothing much for us to do, but eat another small meal, and sleep a last night in our bed. Next morning, we put on all the clothes each of us possibly could, winter boots, and as soon as it was light, we opened the front door and pushed the handcart down the step onto the pavement. Marek and I took a last look around and wondered when we would be back. Anna just walked out. She wanted to get away early. She wanted the least possible to do with the neighbours.

It was warm for March, and in the gutters the dirty banks

110

*of piled up snow were melting. Our street was quiet, but as
soon as we left it, we found that there seemed to be more
people than usual about for a Sunday morning. Nor were
they Jews because none of the people we saw were carrying
bundles or looked like anything other than people out for a
Sunday morning stroll. When we reached Piotrkowska Street
and stopped, we realised the reason – they were going down
to watch the Jews going into the ghetto.*

*On Piotrkowska it seemed like the whole city was on the
move. Looking down the canyon of buildings there were people with bundles, cases and knapsacks; people pushing hand-
carts; people with furniture on their shoulders, their heads,
their backs. They were like looters returning from having
raided a rather second-rate department store. Horse-drawn
conveyances, droshkies, carts, wagons, threaded their way
through the streaming people. The men seemed to be pre-
dominantly bearded in shabby coats and battered hats or
caps. Most of the women wore scarves or shawls. On the
pavements, in doorways or from windows and balconies
overhead, Polish men, women and children as well as the
occasional clutch of Polish policemen, in all attitudes – smiling, expressionless, laughing, jeering, sorrowful, chatting,
spitting, indifferent – watched the endless procession. There
wasn't a German in sight.*

*The Jews looked grim, straining from heavy loads. The
unhappy faces of children. There was the occasional person
– incredibly – cheerful, whistling, as though they didn't care,
but mostly there was just emptiness, depression, weariness,
sorrow. Looking over their heads the grey sky hung over the
fine buildings of Piotrkowska Street. What I found hardest to
believe was that this was happening on the main street of one
of the principle cities of a European country. It seemed to
belong to not just another place but another age. I found all
three of us were blushing – we were embarrassed and*

111

ashamed to be here.

My first reaction was that these were poor Jews – not our class. But then as I looked more closely, I could see middle-class people amongst them. They were dressed more for a day's hiking in the country. The most bizarre sight I saw was a man carrying two small violin cases and flanked by two little girls. I pulled our cart into the main street and we joined the throng and the steady forward movement. A sweater or something slipped from a mound-shaped bundle on a wooden handcart in front and fell on the wet street. Marek picked it up and ran to hand it to the man pulling the cart. He thanked Marek, and turned to us, his eyes looking like he was going to cry. As we continued on, though, the street became spattered with things that people had dropped, and these were now being walked into the mud by the continuing flood of people. Piotrkowska turned slightly to the left and became Zgierska. The road was a lot sloppier now. Great puddles of melted snow and mud lay on the street and people splashed through these oblivious to wet shoes and trousers. A driver urged a wagon through and was cursed by the people upon whom he splashed liquid mud. Up ahead we could see the buildings of Baluty.

As an aside let me explain to anyone who might come to read this about Baluty. Baluty is the most famous slum in Poland. It rivals Kercelak in Warsaw or Sukharevka in Moscow. Very few of the houses have proper sewage or plumbing. Indoor toilets are a rarity, as is running water. The only form of heating is open fires. Even the brightest summer's day seems to bring no joy to Baluty. The place is like something out of the last century. Entering it is like passing through a time warp and finding yourself back in a time when Eastern Europe's Jews were the poorest people on the continent. In the main its Jews are unassimilated and Orthodox; the lowest of the lower working class or else with

112

no jobs at all. There is a sizeable criminal element.

All non-Jews living there were being moved out and the Jews herded in. The elegant three- and four-storey stone buildings of Lodz gave way to a landscape of squat buildings made of mixtures of bricks, wood or corrugated iron. Nettles and scrawny bushes grew out of gutters and many of the walls were of cracked plaster or else green and slimy with mould. Barefoot children ran in and out of open front doors. The streets were paved with cobbles and were awash with mud and slush.

If there was a saving grace in all of this it was that at least in the ghetto the Germans would probably leave us alone. Having been impoverished and put out of the way, we Jews could then carry on and live our own lives. It was some consolation, albeit a small one.

Again we were 'lucky', relatively speaking, in that we had an address to go to. During the following days, when the Germans were driving people into the ghetto, they were just pushed in and had to find some place, any place. Families already ensconced had to try and make room for friends, relatives, acquaintances, and those that had nobody already there were left to fend for themselves. Many families ended up sleeping outside, until the Jewish ghetto authorities found some place for them.

Our new abode is on the third floor at the rear of a building in a street called Grabinka Street. I cannot describe the growing sense of dread we felt as we pulled our cart through a maze of broken down back streets, occasionally stopping to take a rest or to ask for directions. Finally, we found the correct number, a building where the plaster on the façade was chipped and flaking and downstairs, shutters were closed inside the windows. The entrance hall smelled of urine – human, cat and rat. Anna and Marek waited with the cart, while I went up the rickety wooden stairs to find our apartment.

'Apartment' is not the right word to describe what I found. Right at the top, in an annex at the rear of the building, I found the single room that is to be our home. Now that my anger, my horror, my frustration, my sense of powerlessness, my shame, have calmed somewhat I can and must give a clear description of this room.

A plank door leads into it. The bottom of the planks has been eaten away so that a gale blows under them. I had to shake and kick the door before it would open. The room is 5 metres by 4 metres, and is colder than the grave. As I have said, it is the topmost room in an extension that juts out at right angles to the main building. As a result, the shape of the ceiling follows the shape of the roof. Thus, the walls rise about two metres, then turn in at an angle for about a metre and then meet the ceiling. There is a single window at one end of the room whose sill is about half a metre off the ground. As a result of the positioning of the window, there is a reasonable amount of light at that end of the room, but then the rest of it is gloomy. The window is divided into four panes, two of which are broken, the others almost opaque with dust and dead flies held in spider's webs. I have since found a couple of pieces of wood and boarded the broken ones over.

The floor was unswept when we arrived, covered in a mixture of fallen plaster, dust and rat droppings. The stench in the place, again of rat's piss as well as dampness, was overpowering. There had once been a fireplace there, but it has been ripped out – recently it would appear – and now the empty hole sits there reminding one of a skull. There are numerous holes in the plaster on the walls and ceiling, where the laths show through. A single electric light bulb hangs from the ceiling, with a switch by the door. A wire runs from the switch vertically up the wall to which it is stapled, and then hangs in an arc across the ceiling to the bulb, like a

114

washing line. For the moment the electricity works. The floorboards either never fitted properly, or else have warped, resulting in mouse-size gaps between the edges of the boards and the wall. There is no skirting board. The floor reverberates when we walk across it. Both Marek and Anna cried when they saw the place. Marek said over and over again 'I don't like this place'.

That first day Anna cleaned it as best she could while I blocked up the big holes with whatever materials I could find. For cooking we must use the open fire. There is no toilet. We must use a chamber pot – Anna thought to bring one – and empty it in the cess pit out the back. On the second floor there are four Jewish families, each in a room not much bigger than ours. We are all in the same predicament. Since we came here, Marek has had to sleep with us due to the cold. He sleeps in the middle. Anna spent that whole first night with her back turned to us shivering. Marek wet the bed – something he hasn't done in years – and Anna lost her temper. (She apologised to him afterwards, but the incident only added to the awfulness that we are all experiencing.) It was impossible to wash the mattress because there is no way of drying it until the weather improves. In the end we just turned it over and slept on the dry side.

Now, a few days later, as people continue to seep into the ghetto, they are going through the same shock we went through some days ago. We are still adjusting, but I think we are over the worst of it. Maybe now that they can take no more from us the Germans will leave us alone. Maybe now, apart from the difficulties imposed by the war, our troubles are at an end.

Chapter 3

Early spring, 1940

The map of Poland on Rudolf Fest's desk had been drawn up by Paul, his first, and still his best, research assistant. It showed Polish towns and cities with 12,000 or more inhabitants. A black circle represented the position of the town, then in neat black characters was its name and total population. The Jewish population, both numerically and as a percentage, was written in a yellowy-brown colour. The figures were taken from the 1931 census. His statistician's eye and curiosity caught a couple of interesting facts. There were three towns that were over 70 per cent Jew. Warsaw and Lodz between them had over half a million. The phone rang peremptorily. It was Inge, his new secretary. 'Fraulein Ursula Grabner on the line for you, Herr Fest.'

'Rudolf, I'm so sorry I haven't called sooner, but everything has just been crazy.'

'How lovely to hear from you Ursula. How's business?'

'Booming.'

'Excellent. You must really come round for dinner or for a weekend. The children are always asking about you. It's ages since we've seen you.'

'I know, but it's been hectic. Sundays are the only days I have to myself and I need those just to catch up on lost sleep and to do the books. Soon now, I promise.' After a pause, she said: 'I was hoping I could meet you. I have an idea, a business idea, and I wanted to hear what you thought of it.'

'Of course, when?'

'That's the problem. I'm tied up all day, and I know you like to get home to Lisa and the kids in the evenings, but perhaps we could have an early dinner or something?'

'What about this evening?' suggested Rudolf.

'It's fine by me, but are you sure it's not too short notice?'

'No, it'll be fine.'

'Then why don't you come by the shop as soon as you finish?'

'Can you tell me your idea, so that I can be thinking about it?'

'No,' she said cheerily, 'I'll tell you when I see you. Bye.'

As soon as she was gone, Rudolf hesitated a minute before phoning Lisa. What she had predicted had happened. He was indeed spending much more time at the office, leaving first thing in the morning and usually not home until 7.00 or 7.30 in the evening. And even when he was home she accused him – and he knew it was true – of being distracted, his mind elsewhere, so that often when she or the children were speaking to him, he answered in an absent way that told them he wasn't listening. The only thing about this phone call was that it was about helping Ursula. Lisa would have no difficulty with that.

'Sounds intriguing,' Lisa said. 'Anyway, that's fine. I won't keep dinner for you. Arrange with her to come over and stay some night soon, won't you?'

He was just back into things when the phone rang again. It was Korherr. Could Rudolf do a presentation on his findings to date? Of course. What time? 10.30? It wasn't much notice, but yes, he could put something together – as long as the audience wasn't too fussy. Rudolf heard Korherr make a sort of gobbling noise at the far end of the line. Then, stammering somewhat he said:

'I'll try to explain as much. But – I should tell you – it's for the Reichsfuhrer-SS himself.'

Rudolf was nervous but he wasn't overawed. At least this is what he kept telling himself, as he waited in the conference room. Finally, he heard a bustle in the corridor and Heinrich Himmler swept into the room surrounded by his SS entourage. Korherr made a rambling introduction to a stony-faced Himmler.

It was over in half an hour, and the great man had departed, leaving Rudolf glowing in the warmth of unrestrained praise and Korherr still trying to recover from the whole affair. Rudolf's exposition had been punchy and to the point. Various charts – pie charts, histograms, neatly drawn in pens filled with coloured inks by his research staff – had illustrated the figures better than any speech. Having given a high level overview, Rudolf had then explained that he was working on much more detailed analyses and even though these were incomplete, the Reichsfuhrer was welcome to see them if he wished. Himmler nodded, a light catching his thick spectacles momentarily so that for an instant his eyes couldn't be seen.

These new analyses were ones that Rudolf had begun to work on in odd idle hours. He had done them only for Germany, but he had found the results fascinating. What he had done had been to take financial and economic data from the census before the Nurnberg Laws were passed and try to use them to predict the wealth transfer that would take place as the Laws gradually removed Jews from the economic life of the country. The work was far from complete, but he explained the model and the Reichsfuhrer seemed to grasp what he was driving at. At that point Rudolf had asked if they wanted him to continue, but a black uniformed officer sitting behind Himmler had tapped him on the shoulder, whispered something and pointed to his watch. Himmler nodded, stood up, shook Rudolf's hand and congratulated him on his work, saying that if he needed any further assistance he merely had to request it. Then, with a brusque 'Dr Korherr', Himmler strode out of the room.

Rudolf left his office in Prinz Albrechtstrasse just before 6pm and made his way through the chill winter evening to Ursula's shop. The new business had turned out to be a lingerie shop. Lingerie. When he thought of the word, it was in a suggestive, oozy sort of voice that Lisa used and which he found intensely irritating. It had opened just before Christmas last year around the same time that Ursula had moved out into her own place.

On the way he passed a shop which had been a men's clothes shop, but now the window was empty apart from a couple of scattered clothes hangers and a dummy's arm. On the plate glass of the window was daubed a six-pointed star, and the word 'Jud'. Above it the proprieter's name had been painted over and replaced with the words 'Gone for a holiday in Dachau'.

'Ursula's Secrets', the shop was called. An amusing name. On the glass of the door a large sign read 'Jews not welcome'. Above it a smaller sign with the Party emblem said 'German businessman'. A bell jingled as he opened the door. Inside, Ursula was selling something to a woman of about 40, a little on the plump side, with a deep tan. Ursula held up the scanty white lace while the woman fingered it.

'I'll be with you in just a moment, sir,' said Ursula, winking at Rudolf.

'No hurry.'

'I think this will go wonderfully well with your complexion, Madam.'

'Are you sure about the size?' the woman asked in an assured voice.

'Absolutely, Madam. They stretch so as to become totally

figure hugging.'

'Very well, I'll take it.'

When the woman had gone, Rudolf said: 'You don't look much like a German businessman to me.'

She was mystified for a moment and then laughed: 'Oh, the sign on the door. A lot of my customers like to see that. Now, I'm ready.'

They went out into the cold night air, she linking him as before.

'You look well,' he said, 'and prosperous. Business must be good indeed.'

'Not bad,' she smiled. 'And you, how's work?'

'Guess who I did a presentation for just before I came here?'

'I can't imagine,' she said, 'the Fuhrer?'

'Almost,' he said. 'The next best thing – the Reichsfuhrer-SS – Himmler.'

She whistled – genuinely impressed. She had changed since he had first met her. She had always been self-confident, but this was more than just self-assurance. This was an aura of competence and sophistication that was almost masculine in its presence. It was refreshing to see it. The regime seemed intent on confining women to child bearing and the kitchen, and most of them were happy to go along with this – Lisa was a case in point. It was nice to see someone who wasn't.

At the restaurant she shed her coat. She was a study in primary colours – red lipstick, white teeth, blue eyes. Her suit looked expensive.

'Apart from just wanting to see you today,' – she smiled as she said it – a warm, interested smile; he didn't know how good she was at selling lingerie to women, but he thought that she must hardly ever fail when selling to a man - 'I wanted to meet you to ask you a favour'.

'Anything, if I can,' he said.

She lowered her voice and moved her aperitif a little to one side.

'My business is going reasonably well. I've managed to build it up - it's been a bit of a struggle – but now that it's on some kind of a sound footing, I want to try and expand, to do more.'

'Are you going to open more shops?'

'No, not more shops. I want to keep the personal touch, and I don't think I could find anyone who could run one as well as I could – I'm a bit of a perfectionist,' she grinned apologetically. 'No, maybe I'll carry more stock, but what I really want to do is to differentiate my shop from its competitors. I want to be the most exclusive, specialist, carrying only the best.'

'And the most expensive?' he ventured.

'Of course,' she laughed.

'So where do I come in?'

'The people with the money are the men in the Party. You're pretty high up – you know who's who. Oh, I don't mean the Goebbels and the Goerings, but the senior civil servants, the police, the SS. How do I reach these people? Where should I advertise? Could I send them individual letters or a catalogue? If you could think about this and we could talk about it maybe at the weekend. What do you think? Can you help?'

Her eyes opened a fraction wider as she finished, and there was an uncertainty, almost a vulnerability in her look that belied the earlier assurance.

'I can think of one thing straight away,' he said. 'Move the shop. It's the most obvious thing to do. Try and get a place near the Wilhelmstrasse.'

'I thought about that,' she said, 'but the rents are crazy over there.'

'I passed a place tonight and I think it would suit you just fine. *And* I think you could get it cheap.'

'We must go over there.'

'Dinner first,' he said, 'I'm starving.'

When they left the restaurant there was frost on the roofs of the cars parked beside the pavement. They walked in the direction of the shop on Voss Strasse. They went slowly, meandering, stopping to look in the shop windows. Rudolf thought they looked like a couple of lovers.

'It's in the same street as Party headquarters,' he said, pointing, when they got there. 'There, number eleven. What could be better than that?'

'It's perfect,' she said, when she saw it, 'just the right size. But how do I find out about the rent? Who owns it?'

'Let me check on that,' he said, 'I have some friends' – he was thinking of his Gestapo contact – 'who should be able to find out for me.'

A month later 'Ursula's Secrets' opened on Voss Strasse, Ursula having not just rented, but bought the shop from its previous owner at a knockdown price. There was champagne for customers on opening day and a small party that evening to which Lisa and Rudolf were invited.

'I owe it all to your husband,' said Ursula to her sister, as the party rolled on into the late hours. 'Without him I never would have found this lovely place.'

'And without this opening, I probably wouldn't have seen him at all.' There was no lightness or humour in Lisa's voice as she said this, then adding: 'It's the first night we've been out together in as long as I can remember.'

Chapter 4

Poland.

Cigarette tips bobbed around in the darkness as the men climbed onto the trucks. Stars still shone overhead, though in the east, a low pillow of pale sky marked the onset of dawn. It looked like being a fine day. Otto sat down heavily on the wooden bench. He settled the butt of the rifle between his boots, and pressed the barrel between his knees. He always felt awkward and ungainly clambering onto these trucks, not like the young bucks who vaulted easily onto them With luck the war would end this year. Time was moving on for him.

It was still dark when the convoy of trucks passed through the outskirts of Ozorkow and into the countryside. Otto drifted between waking and dozing, the jolting of the truck acting like the rocking of some giant cradle. He glanced at his watch. Just after 5.00. Another hour or more before they reached their destination. He didn't even know the name of this one, just another Polish village in what seemed like an endless series that they had been working their way through since last October. He could feel the anger building. Another infestation of Jews to be rooted out. Was there no end to them? If the SS crossed all of Europe 100 times would they find them all? Get rid of them all? And in the meantime what about Otto's house and piece of land?

123

If there was a consolation in all of this, it was that one of the pieces of his vision had fallen into place. Her name was Helga and he met her at a dance for so-called 'heroes on leave'. She was 35, a teacher, somewhat overweight with fat calves, though with a pretty face. They hit it off immediately. She had pets, a cat and a dog and lived alone, her parents having died some years previously. They went for a meal and afterwards he walked her to the train. He offered to see her home but she was reluctant and he didn't press it. They kissed and arranged to meet again the next day. He had been afraid that she wouldn't show up but she came after school, freshly made-up, thin, dark hair brushed to a shine and a happy smile on her face.

He had three days left in his leave when she brought him back to her house and they slept together. It turned out she was a virgin, but what she lacked in experience she made up for in eagerness and consideration and lack of inhibition. That was a Friday night. The weekend went by in a blur of walks, meals and lovemaking. He told her about his family and the last war and how things were different this time around. When she told her story, she related it in terms of the relationships she had had, as though she was anxious to explain why she had never married and at 35, didn't have a steady man-friend. Otto didn't care. He was overjoyed to discover there was nobody else in her life.

The following Monday was terrible. She was going to take the morning off and come to the station to say goodbye, but they both agreed it was better to do it at her place.

'Please be careful,' she said. 'I don't want you taking any risks or getting into any danger.'

'I'm a soldier,' he smiled.

'Yes, but you're my soldier,' she said, holding him.

He hugged her fiercely and left, shouldering his pack and rifle and walking slowly down the street, his boots echoing on the pavement. She stood at the door and waved. He took one last look, blew her a kiss and turned the corner, with no enthusiasm to return to Poland and wondering when he might be able to get his next leave.

They pulled in by the side of the road on the edge of the village. The earlier promise of a clear day had faded. Now the sky was cloudy and overcast. It was still very cold. A wooden fence marked the edge of the village and beyond that a tall, bare tree loomed out of the darkness. The gables and ridges of some single-storey houses were faintly visible. A dog barked somewhere, soft, distant. Invisible birds twittered.

Like a well-oiled machine, the soldiers went into their routine. A squad went off in each of two directions to link up at the rear of the village, throwing a cordon around it. While this was going on, and the remaining men stood blowing on their hands and stamping their feet, the sky brightened so that features started to take some concrete outline. A telegraph pole, its wires still invisible. Some low, wooded hills beyond the village. A cock crowed and as if in reply some geese honked. The Obersturmfuhrer nodded and the men began to move forward down both sides of the dirt road that constituted the village's main street.

It was all over by mid-morning. Of course the fact that it was pretty much an all-Jewish village helped. With the mixed ones, even though the Jews generally lived in their own quarter, there were parts where you sometimes couldn't be sure. Then, if you couldn't tell from their appearance, you had to check the house for the things they used in their worship or, in the case of totally assimilated ones, check papers, occupant's names, even get them to say the Christian prayers sometimes. This time there had been none of that. Very quickly the long-noses were tumbling out of their houses, shepherded along by a line of men, while others went on ahead, blowing open doors, routing

125

out occupants and giving them five minutes to pack what they needed. Otto stayed behind the line of men, occasionally diving into houses to make sure they hadn't missed anybody. He always caught people – the CO said he was better than any Doberman – and today was no exception. They were generally the younger ones, in their twenties or teenagers or even infants. How could the Yids do that, leaving their children behind like that? They were a different race, they really were. This morning he hustled out a number of young men, having found them in the most ridiculous hiding places – under beds, in cupboards, behind furniture. What did they think it was? A game of hide and seek?

It was an easy day – in the sense that there was no resistance to speak of and so very little shooting. Otto did hear some firing which sounded like it was out on the perimeter somewhere, and he fired himself once or twice just to make a couple of stay-behinds jump. He did it more out of mischief than anything else. Today they were particularly passive and made their way to the square with only the mildest of prompting from the guards.

Of course it didn't depend on the Jews. You could decide in advance whether you wanted a quiet one or make a bit of a party of it. Wednesdays always seemed kind of quiet. Mondays could be rough with everyone a bit surly after the weekend whilst Tuesdays were hardly much better. Wednesdays tended to reflect a midweek calm and then, if there were wild ones with lots of shooting and games of 'beards' and things like that, they generally happened on Thursdays or especially on Fridays. Today, being Wednesday, everyone had been fairly happy to just go through the motions, get the job done and get back to base, a fire and a good lunch.

A trestle table had been set up in the square, and at it two policemen were registering people. The Jews, with their hands up, and trying to move their belongings along at the same time, queued at the table and were processed two at a time. Then they were moved to the square where they lay face down in ranks. A couple of times people raised their heads or moaned and the guards fired, but they deliberately aimed high. Nobody wanted to waste time clearing up bodies afterwards.

Later the trucks moved into the square, the Jews – about a hundred of them – were loaded and the convoy drove back to Ozorkow. There they were dumped at the entrance to the ghetto, the gates were opened and they flooded inside as if they had been cattle being brought back from the fair by a new owner. Otto was sitting down to lunch by two o'clock, his mind full of Helga and the prospect of a lazy afternoon.

Chapter 5

There has been a fresh snowfall in the ghetto. About fifteen centimetres; enough to put a thick white coat on every surface that is even minutely horizontal. Streets and pavements are as though carpeted, roofs look shaggy and wires resemble delicate candy ropes. Even though it is not yet daylight, David is up. He has gone to join a queue for bread, despite the fact that the shop will not open for several hours. He has always been an early riser and this has become even more true in the ghetto. Despite his tiredness, despite the weakness caused by an inadequate diet, the urge to be by himself, to walk, to think, to have some privacy is so strong that it overcomes even the cold, and he is abroad before most living souls. He is indistinguishable from those few people he does pass in the grey gloom – swathed as he is in coat, scarf, boots, hat. He swishes through the snow and enjoys briefly the childish feeling of kicking it into spray. He only does one or two kicks. Any more is to waste energy.

He is reminded of the last winter before the war. They had gone down to Brzykow and it had snowed heavily, weighing down the branches of the trees. Marek had stood under the trees and asked David to shake the snow down on him. The snow had lodged on Marek's shoulders and the peak of his cap with the result that it looked like he had been out in it all night. Of the small number of photographs they have been able to bring with them, this is one of them, Marek standing grinning and looking like a fixture in the snow.

It is midwinter's day. The shortest day of the year. Only a few days to go and it will be 1941. They will have survived nearly a year of this. The new year may not hold any great promise at the present time, but if they can survive one year, they can survive another and another until the Nazis are defeated. Although he tries not to think too much about this. The French and the British armies never materialised. France is now as occupied as Poland, while Britain declared war and seems to have decided to leave it at that. Russia is happily digesting Eastern Poland, and it looks like this situation could stand for many years. It is something not to be dwelt on.

David is a natural optimist, and today the snow, gradually becoming white in the gathering light, has come as something of an omen. Better days ahead, cleaner days, brighter days. Just like animals, armies hibernate for the winter too. In the spring there will be movement. He is sure of it.

It has not been an easy year. In a time when just to survive has been an achievement, they have done as well as could be expected. Soon after they moved into the ghetto, David managed to get a job. This was quite something because the only people who seemed in demand were those who had a trade – cobblers, tailors, hat makers, seamstresses. For a while it was Anna who earned the money stitching shirts while he stayed at home and minded Marek. But then he succeeded in getting work as a clerk in the Address Registration Bureau. The work was boring beyond belief but at least it was work; he would be paid and could buy food. His wages were slightly better than Anna's and so she went back to taking care of Marek. David was now one of the people who maintained a card index of the ghetto's occupants and their addresses. The population was in a constant state of flux. On the one hand, there was the high death rate from illness, cold or – for those too poor to buy enough food – starvation. On the other hand there was a constant flow of people into the ghetto from the small towns in the environs of Lodz.

Daylight has finally emerged, as though from the streets and alleys of the ghetto. Smoky and wan it hangs over the dull white of the snow. Despite this there is a cleanliness, a certain picturesque quality, a beauty almost to the cityscape, that David's eyes drink in. It is all very deceptive. He knows it is a deception. But he savours it nonetheless as he approaches the short line of people gathered at the bread shop, where the snow has already turned to slush.

Of the three of them, Marek has adapted most easily to their changed circumstances. But isn't this always the way with children? David maintains his own calm and – well, sanity, really – through an iron-willed mental attitude not to let the whole thing grind him down. It is Anna who has really changed. She is morose, silent. David feels she is blaming him. He remembers again the remark she made after their first failed embassy visit. He had wondered whether they should have been more forceful and pushed harder. 'I thought you were going to' was what she said. The remark, throwaway as it had seemed to him at the time, now takes on a whole new significance. Somehow, she seems to think, he should have anticipated all of this or, failing that, that he should have resisted, fought. But when he asks her she says it isn't so, that then she might have lost much more than just the house. She sometimes seems to brighten up a bit after such conversation, but soon lapses into her silence. It is as though she makes an effort but cannot sustain it. David finds her moods bring him down and make the effort required of himself to keep his own head above water even greater. She is a constant drain on the fragile confidence, self-respect and optimism with which he tries to surround himself. Occasionally he finds himself wishing he had married someone more like Ella. His kid sister, but so much older than him in some ways. She would have been so much more positive in the current circumstances. He wonders for the umpteenth time where she is, whether she is alive. She must be alive. He cannot countenance the possibility that anything might have happened to her.

Lost in his reverie, David has been unaware until now that the sun has come out. A patch of blue has found a place for itself in the leaden sky and through this a bright sun has emerged. The effect on the snow is immediate and wonderful. The places where nobody has yet walked glisten and the ghetto is beautiful in a way he would not have thought possible. In the shadows, the snow goes through varying tints of blue, while where the sun bathes the snow, there is a glow of pink. The air feels pure, as though on a mountaintop. David notices that all the people in the now much-longer line are staring at it in a sort of wonderment. He realises what it is. Their senses have been starved of colour, so that this small scene, which would normally be so mundane, is like a banquet for their eyes. He tries to record its every detail, to find the right words, so that he can write about it in his diary tonight.

Even though he arrived early it takes him nearly three hours to get to the head of the queue and purchase his two loaves of the grey, heavy bread that tastes like plaster. By that time, the sun has gone in, the clouds have closed over and the snow has been defiled so that only muddy pools, piles of dirty snow and a scattered field of slush remains. He is frozen through and can no longer feel one of his feet, the one in the boot which leaks. David remembers, within weeks of moving into the ghetto, seeing yellow sunrises with smiling faces chalked by children on the sidewalks. They are long gone now. He makes his way home clutching his purchases, his mind far away.

Chapter 6

Ursula came to stay with Rudolf and Lisa for Christmas. On Christmas Eve, Ursula, Lisa, Rudolf and the children went to a carol service in the local church. It was a cold night. Snow had already fallen and more was threatened, and their breaths hung in big clouds in front of their muffled faces. Rudolf held the children's gloved hands in his own as they marched along on either side of him.

Rudolf loved Christmas. The English seemed to think they had invented it, what with Charles Dickens and Scrooge and everything, but a German Christmas was the only *real* Christmas. Pine trees. Snow. Silent Night. Santa Claus himself. All of these came from Central Europe. The singing was beautiful. Voices that were as chill and clear as the night itself sang all the popular songs, including Rudolf's favourite, *Still*.

He loved Christmas and even more than that, he loved the days which followed it, the dying days of the year. They were a time for retrospection. Whatever about the war, 1940 had been good for him – one of the best he could remember. A dozen people now worked for him, with probably more to come in the new year. A happy, healthy family – and too young, thankfully, to be involved in the war. His friendship with Ursula, and the growing success of her shop, something that wouldn't have happened without him.

The pastor called on the congregation to sing *Silent Night*. Everyone stood and the kids grasped his hands tighter, sensing that the service was nearly over. Rudolf glanced at

Ursula, noticing her fine skin and long eyelashes. Her hair, caught inside her scarf, looked shiny and silky. She must have sensed him looking at her because she turned and smiled. He felt a glow of pleasure.

They had dinner late on Christmas Day, Lisa having spent most of the day in the kitchen. Later, after the children had gone to bed, Rudolf volunteered to go into the kitchen to wash the dishes. They all had a lot to drink and Lisa was ensconced in an armchair and looking like she wasn't going to move for anybody.

'I'll help,' volunteered Ursula, and she went out into the kitchen with Rudolf.

'I've had a wonderful Christmas,' she said once they were alone.

Her eyes fixed his. Then she moved towards him and embraced him.

'I could love you,' she said. 'I could so love you.'

He held her, conscious that if Lisa walked in, he could pretend Ursula had had too much wine. Then, however, he kissed her deeply on the lips. She responded and he felt her tongue pressing into his mouth.

'Dishes,' she said, suddenly, brushing back her hair with her hands.

'Dishes,' he said, half relieved, half disappointed.

Later that night, Rudolf realised he had notched up two more points on the intimacy matrix: tongue in her mouth and fingers on her breasts – admittedly fully clothed breasts.

PART FOUR

Chapter 1

Normandy. The present.

'I tried to patch it together after the war. I took a train from Paris to Warsaw in the early 1950s. When Poland was invaded, she went east with Broni and Stefan. As it turns out it was the right thing to do. Had she tried to link up with her family she wouldn't have lasted any time at all. Lodz. Well, you were in the ghetto. East was the only way for her to go. Sure, it was dangerous, but west was almost certainly fatal.

'It was Stefan I found first. I tracked him down in Warsaw – it was easy enough – like you – asking around the clubs. He couldn't tell me much. He was strange – he acted sort of defensive ... guilty. Yes, she was with him but they got separated. Some story about being in a column of refugees and being strafed by German planes. He got separated from both of them, he told me, and never saw them again.'

'Did you believe him, Katya?'

'I wasn't sure. It sounded too vague. Too convenient. But then the war was like that. Things just happened. Quirks of fate. A chance incident went one way and you survived; it went against you and you died. There wasn't much I could do, though. I tried the Red Cross and all of the various places that dealt with displaced persons. In the West people were sometimes successful in tracking down missing people; in the East hardly ever – especially if they were Jewish. Too often the answer was the same. The problem really was that apart from Stefan there were no other witnesses.

'He told me that the three of them had been heading for Brest Litovsk. These days it's in Belarus, but after the invasion of Poland, when Stalin's soldiers came to pick up the piece of Poland that Hitler had given them, Brest was on the border of the territory incorporated into the USSR. So, when he told me this, my reckoning was that if they managed to get that far, they would have survived at least until the summer of the following year when the Nazis invaded Russia.'

'Hello, Stefan.'

'Do I know you?'

'Before the war you did.'

'I'm sorry. Maybe it's the light. But your face isn't familiar.'

He pushed the glasses up his nose and squinted.

'I'm Katya Halecki.' Katya paused. 'You might have known me just as Katya. I waitressed in the club where you played before the war. I was a friend of Ella's. Ella Steinbaum.'

The expression on his face didn't change. If she'd been trying to surprise him by the mention of her name, it had had no effect. 'I think I do remember you. Katya. Yes. Katya.' He was holding a saxophone in his left hand and a cigarette in his right. He put the cigarette between his lips, and extended his hand. 'How are you? Yes, I remember. It's great to see you after all this time. Where have you been? Come on over and we'll have a drink.'

They took a table near one end of the bar and he ordered a bottle of vodka.

'I've come back to look for Ella, to find out if she's alive or what happened to her.'

Stefan downed his vodka and refilled the glass. He lit a fresh cigarette off the old one. 'We went east when the bombing of Warsaw started. She and Broni – the pianist, do you remember? – and I. We were in a column of refugees that got shot up by German airplanes. I lost them both in that and never found them again.'

She continued to look into his eyes. He blinked. Looked away.

'Broni didn't come back?'

Stefan shook his head. 'It doesn't look like it. I would have met him on the scene. Jesus, what a waste, he was such a good pianist. Anyway, tell me what you've been doing with yourself. I remember you now, I really do. It's amazing to meet someone from that time.'

'How long more are you in Warsaw for?' he asked after she had briefly filled him in.

'A while,' she shrugged. 'I'm in no great rush. I was hoping we might meet again and talk about the old times. And I'd like to hear some more of your playing. I got here too late tonight. Are you here tomorrow night?'

He nodded.

'OK, I'll come along. Maybe we could have dinner or something afterwards.'

'Tell me about yourself and Ella.'

'She was so pretty, Katya. So pretty. That afternoon after she'd passed the audition, we played a few more songs as a band. I remember I was studying her from behind. Her thick hair. The press of her bum against her skirt. Her calves – they were really athletic looking.

'We went for a meal afterwards to celebrate. I remember she did something odd. There was a thing for grinding pepper on the table and she ground a little pile of it into her hand. Then she held it under each of our noses and asked us to say what it reminded us of. I remember Broni saying it reminded him of an old trunk when you open it, full of musty old clothes and stuff like that.'

'What did she say?'

'It reminded her of Morocco. Mysterious exotic things. "Dark scented alleyways" was a phrase she used. I remember that because afterwards Broni wrote a tune that he called 'Black Pepper'. She used to write poems – they weren't very good – but she came up with some words to go with Broni's music and the phrase "dark scented alleyways" was in it.'

'What did you say – about the smell of the pepper, I mean?'

'I just said it reminded me of pepper.'

'Why did you say her poems weren't very good?'

He seemed surprised by the question, because he shifted in his chair, and seemed to take ages to come up with any kind of an answer. Finally, he just shrugged and said:

'I don't know really, I don't know why I said it.'

'Was it that night you first slept with her?'

Stefan stopped in his tracks. 'How did you know I –? That's none of your fucking business, is it?'

'Don't be like that, Stefan,' said Katya, in a soothing, almost fawning voice. 'I want to find her. Anything she said, or did. Any hint she might have given. You must tell me everything you can remember.' She noticed that he wasn't listening.

His eyes had assumed a vacant, distant stare. In a dreamlike tone, he said: 'You won't find her.'

'Why not? What do you know? What happened?'

He jerked back out of his reverie. 'Sorry,' he said, with an agitated smile. 'I was just thinking about her. I loved her. Do you know that, Katya, I loved her.'

'Yes, I'm sure you did,' said Katya.

Her voice sounded so off-hand to herself that she said the

words again, trying to instil a bit more feeling into them: 'I'm sure you did. But how do you know I won't find her. Is she dead? What do you know?'

'Aren't all the Jews dead? Or nearly all of them. I'm sure she went the same way as the rest of them. I didn't know when I first met her that she was a Jewess.'

His body seemed to slump in his chair. He joined his hands and held them in front of his mouth as though he were chewing on them. His eyes fixed on the table.

'That was all bullshit about being strafed by the Germans, Stefan, wasn't it? What really happened?'

'I told you the truth.'

'My ass, you did. Where did you get to? Do you know if she's alive? Is she in Russia?'

Slowly, Stefan began to speak.

'We were going to Brest. The three of us. But we split up on the road. It was after the plane shot us up. I decided to come back here.'

'You left her?'

'She wouldn't see sense. She wouldn't come back.'

'She couldn't come back. She was Jewish. The Nazis had her under sentence of death.' Katya looked at him balefully, accusingly. 'You said you loved her.'

'Look, I did everything I could.'

'Everything you could,' repeated Katya.

Chapter 2

January 1941.

There is at least another hour to go before dawn when David Steinbaum is woken by the cold. He has a headache. It is due to having the place almost hermetically sealed in an attempt to conserve whatever heat there is. Despite this he can still feel the bitter cold around the small piece of his face that is not covered by the blankets. He lies in bed for a few minutes savouring the warmth and steeling himself to get out. Finally he does, stepping into his unyielding, freezing shoes and pulling on his overcoat which lies on a chair beside the mattress. In the corner of the room he finds the chamber pot and removes the cloth that covers it. Kneeling down he urinates into it first, and then sitting on it, he excretes. While he sits he massages his forehead and eyes with the palms of his hands, trying to ease the pain somewhat. It is a bad headache. In the past, a headache like this would have driven him to bed.

His shit is tiny and hard. This is good because it means he can get away with a quick, clean wipe. Toilet paper disappeared within a couple of weeks of their arrival in the ghetto. Newspaper and wrapping paper sustained them for the summer, but now paper is something of a rarity and used primarily for writing on. These days they use cloths. He, Anna and Marek each have their own cloth, that lie on a sheet of brown paper beside the chamber pot. In the darkness he finds his – the one nearest the wall – and, having wiped himself, folds it with the dirty side inwards. The cloths will be washed this evening in the remains of the dishwater. The runny, splattery shits are the worst, a nightmare to clean up; and they all suffer from them from time to time what with the poor quality food. At least so far, no one has been really sick.

He gathers his clothes from the chair and gropes his way to the end of the room beside the fire. The ashes are cold, the meagre fire they had last night long out. He could turn the light on now, but that would wake the others. Better to grope around in the darkness like he is doing at the moment. The ghetto isn't allowed electricity between eight in the evening and six in the morning. Even this is somewhat unreliable. Often there is no electricity when he leaves in the morning. He begins work at eight and finishes at eight. Thus, by the time he gets home, there is only a flickering candle for light. He still tries to write in his diary but finds the strain on his eyes too much at times.

A bowl and two buckets of water stand on the floor by the fire. They didn't bring buckets with them when they came and had to sell a gold necklace belonging to Anna in order to buy two. With the cold weather, water has been freezing in the pipes and would certainly be frozen at this time of the morning; so they always try to have a couple of buckets on hand just in case. There is a thin screen of ice on top of the buckets. He breaks it and pours water through the smashed ice-pane into the bowl. Then he washes – hands, face, under his arms, privates – and shaves by touch with a blunt blade in the bitterly cold water. Inevitably, he cuts himself. He has thought of growing a beard and even tried for a few days, but just ended up looking and feeling dirty. Some day, when all this is over, he will shave and bathe in piping hot water. He has begun to keep a mental list of the things he will do again when they return to civilisation. This is top of the list.

Second on David's list is coffee, or tea, or any hot drink first thing in the morning. The fire that is their only means of cooking and heating is voracious for fuel which has become increasingly scarce over the winter. Now, Anna lights the fire at about 6.00 or when she can stand the cold no longer, whichever comes first, prepares the evening meal, and tries to keep it going so that David can have a bit of warmth when he comes in. Once they stop feeding it, it burns down in a matter of minutes, and is almost always out before they are asleep. Then, they lie for long periods, Marek between them, and try to keep warm. They brought all the blankets they could carry when they moved here, but it seems to take ages for the bed to heat up. The blankets are permanently damp, and this means that they spend longer and longer shivering together every night before warmth begins to seep into their bodies. Marek has wet the bed a couple of times, but they have become used to the smell of urine in the air. In the morning, without a fire, the only drink available is icy water.

The food situation has gradually become tighter over the winter. As city dwellers who, in the past, have had a wide selection of food to choose from, David realises they have forgotten how closely food production is tied to the seasons. Now, with food scarce, a scarcity that has gradually increased over the summer and autumn of last year, they realise what winter used to mean to their ancestors. Winter was a time when nothing grew. It was a time when you had to fall back on whatever food reserves you had put aside. The quality of the food coming into the ghetto, poor last year, became appalling with the onset of winter. Vegetables that aren't rotten or bruised or damaged become something of a rarity. The bread is more and more chewy and tasteless, and now, apart from occupying space in your stomach, has little else to recommend it. Meat, when it comes, is fatty or fibrous or beginning to smell or has maggots in it; and their diet seems to have become an endless round of minute quantities of chalky bread, rotten potatoes and mouldy vegetables.

Food is strictly controlled by the ghetto authorities and allocated using ration books and coupons. David has built a low plank shelf beside the fire, and their food is kept on this. Their bread is wrapped in three separate pieces of threadbare muslin, the three small mounds positioned in the same way that they sleep, so that each of them will know their own bread. David takes his own – the left hand one – and cuts two slices of it. One he wraps in another piece of muslin that he will take to work. The second he begins to chew. He loathes this flavourless bread and its dark brown crust, hard and dull. After he leaves here he vows he will only ever eat white crusty rolls again. He pours some water into a cup, and chews his bread slowly. Moist gobbets of chewed dough slide down his throat.

It is still dark when he emerges into the piercing cold, but already people are on the streets hurrying to their places of work. Since there are no street lights, they pass in the murk like huddled ghosts. The crowd of people gradually thickens as they approach the Zgierska street footbridge, and here David joins a long, shuffling queue. Coughs, snuffling and the occasional brief murmur of conversation are the only sounds. David had hoped the fresh air would improve his headache, but the cold stabbing at his nostrils and throat serves, if any-thing, to intensify it. Now, as he becomes part of the crowd moving slowly towards the bridge, the mingled smells of bad breath, old cooked food, body odour, urine and faeces, close around him, make him feel weak and unsteady.

He has been getting a lot of headaches recently. If they're not caused by the fuggy atmosphere in the room, they're caused by hunger. Before the war, missing meals had always

142

caused him to get headaches. Now, he never feels full after he has eaten and he gets headaches with monotonous regularity. The line reaches the foot of the stairs and begins to climb. David has always been impatient with queues, always squeezing as close as decency will allow to the person in front of him. He finds himself doing this now. His foot is on the first of the wooden steps before the woman in front has her foot on it. He wonders how long more all this is going to last. This is endurable, if only just. But what really depresses him is that the best years of his life are being frittered away here. He feels like a man imprisoned for a crime he did not commit. They have been in the ghetto for nearly a year now; a year stolen from him, that he will never get back. Marek is suffering too. His schooling is way behind. David's relationship with Anna has settled into an almost sullen, practical living arrangement.

Somehow David gets through the day. He spends it preparing lists of apartments that have less than four people per room. His own address is on the list. The headache throbs away with the result that when he finally makes his way home, he is nauseous and goes straight to bed. As he dissolves into a merciful sleep, his last conscious thought is that at least Anna and David will have the rest of his rations.

Anna is woken by Marek just as the first pallid light is starting to creep into the room. The temperature inside is still below freezing. There is no curtain on the window. Given a choice between putting a blanket on the window or on the bed, Anna has opted for the bed. The window panes are opaque with beautiful patterns of ice. Marek dresses himself rapidly. Anna pulls on her coat, its twin yellow stars of David, front and back, making her shiver when she sees them. She pushes back her hair, and wipes sleep from the corners of her eyes. She takes both her and Marek's rations from the shelf and prepares a breakfast of one slice of bread each, spread with beet marmalade. Marek no longer complains about the meagre slice of bread. At least in school he will get some hot soup at lunch time.

When they have eaten, Anna puts on a scarf, picks up a shopping bag and goes out with Marek into the morning. Having left him to school, Anna goes to the local food distribution centre, where she joins a long line that stretches for 600 or 700 metres, and which people are still joining like birds flocking to a telegraph wire in autumn. They settle down, first to wait for the line to start moving, and then to follow it through its various stages; first getting to the beginning of the building that houses the distribution centre, then to its corner, then along its front, then through the door and finally to the counter where they hand in their ration cards, their coupons are removed and small quantities of food are weighed, measured and handed over. As usual there are complaints, recriminations and arguments about the weighing out of the food and this slows the process down even further.

The Jewishness all around Anna is starting to do strange things to her, make her think thoughts which appal her. With all this squalor, and all these Jews around her, the phrase 'dirty Jews' starts to take hold in her mind. Her rational mind tells her it isn't their fault. In similar circumstances any group of people would have begun to smell, would have begun to let things slip as they wondered what sense it made to bother about cleanliness and tidiness in the nightmare of the ghetto.

Then there is the unspeakable drabness which has become their daily grind: that dreadful room that she hates with a passion. After the war she will buy that building and stand there while it is torn down in front of her eyes. The ghetto is like some vast, uncared-for gypsy encampment with its muddy, slushy streets and decaying buildings; its people in their uniforms of poverty, the once-fine coats, the caps, the shawls; the people with their gaunt faces that rarely smile or show any kind of life. Maybe it is just the winter weather that is making her feel this way; the terrible cold, the leaden skies, the mud-logged streets. She has never felt this bad, even after her arrival in the ghetto when it seemed like her whole world had fallen apart. Perhaps the arrival of spring will make a difference.

She has come to the conclusion that the best thing to do with David is to put her whole relationship with him into a kind of suspended animation until this thing is over. Then, on that bright day, when the barbed-wire fence is no longer guarded, when the gates hang open and there are no Germans, when they walk back out into the real world, *then* she will try to pick things up again. Now it is all just too wearying after the daily grind of trying to stay alive.

She thinks about Marek. From the day of his birth, over the short years of his life, Anna has experienced emotions she never knew she had. Marek is the most important person in her life. Heartbreak doesn't even begin to describe what she feels now when she sees how his life has been ruined by all of this. It never crossed her mind that he might be denied a decent place to live, warmth, enough food to eat; that somebody somewhere in the world would see him as a threat, would want to endanger his innocent life. These things are beyond the bounds of her comprehension, yet every day when she wakes up they are with her. What will happen to him if anything happens to her and David?

Because now people are dying in the ghetto. Some have been shot by German guards because they supposedly approached too close to the wire. Others are dying of disease. But now, people are dying of starvation. Anna knows they sometimes get some extra rations through David's job. She knows that those who were dying are the most powerless ones, those who have no way of getting that extra bowl of soup or chunk of bread or few potatoes. They are those who have perhaps always been malnourished, before the war started at all; those who have used up whatever reserves of resistance and strength they had, a long time ago, so that ghetto rations have finally cast them over the edge.

All along Anna has felt that they have limitless time, if necessary, to wait out the war and begin life again. Now she, along with everyone else, is never satisfied with what there is to eat. She is losing weight. It had been imperceptible at first, but her clothes have became looser and more ill-fitting as the months have passed. Marek too has lost any kiddy fat and looks scrawny now, with bags under his eyes. For the first time, a doubt has entered her mind and is starting to bore like a worm. Even if the three of them stray nowhere near the wire, even if they give the widest possible berth to the merest sniff of a German, is it possible that they might just run out of strength themselves?

Chapter 3

The train from Poznan shot out of the tunnel into sunshine. When it had entered the long tunnel, the weather had been cloudy, overcast, April weather that smacked of showers. Now, as it emerged, the cloud cover had suddenly begun to break up; the blue skin of the sky was starting to show through, and a watery sunlight drenched the landscape.

Rudolf Fest noted these things and then returned to his papers. He was alone in the first-class compartment. On his lap was a series of index cards containing notes that accompanied the slides he intended to use during his presentation tomorrow. The notes were brief, a major heading written in red on each card, followed by between three and five points each, represented by a few key words written in black. Most people at these conferences *read* their papers. The result was that it sounded like it wasn't their work they were presenting at all. Rudolf's presentation wouldn't be like that. He would deliver it as though he were extemporising, hardly referring to his notes and using coloured slides as his focus. The phrases were all there in his head, and he knew he would be able to string them together when the time came. After all, he had been rehearsing for weeks and was doing so again now, mentally going through what he would say in connection with each chart and graph. He even had a couple of witty remarks, enough to lighten the message but not too many to trivialise it.

His paper was entitled *A Model for Projected Wealth Transfers in the Eastern Territories*. In it he described a layered

147

approach to the transfer of money and property from Jews to Aryans in what had been Poland. There were three layers. In the first, a certain wealth transfer took place when Jews were excluded from particular careers and public offices, and when Jewish businesses passed into Aryan hands. His model predicted what this would be, and was most accurate here because it had actual data from the German experience.

The second layer involved Jews being removed from their homes into ghettos or other accommodation. As well as houses, much additional Jewish property was confiscated at this stage. Here, to a large extent, he was guessing, since little if any data had yet become available from Germany or Poland. Still he would show what his predictions were for the Eastern Territories as a whole, and also broken down by geographic area.

The third layer generated the least revenue but was included for completeness. In this, as Jews died, there was some final wealth that could be extracted. First there was their accommodation, though often this was little more than a slum and fit only for whatever it might bring through demolition. Then there were clothes, cooking and eating utensils, furniture, that sort of thing. Finally, there were body by-products: gold from teeth, organs that could be used in the medical area, hair and so on. His model contained parameters which tried to put a price on each of these as well as trying to predict mortality rates. Here the guesswork and the potential for error were greatest. He would need some actual data to calibrate the model in this area.

The final element was a tentative cashflow forecast presented as a bar graph showing the monthly revenues and profits accruing to the Reich. In all, the conference would see only a fraction of his work since his department had, or was engaged in similar models for the countries Germany had occupied and those it had yet to conquer. The conference was scheduled to last two days, and would involve SS, military and civilian government officials from all over the Occupied Territories. The venue chosen was Bad Krynica, a spa town in the foothills of the Tatra Mountains. He would have been happy just to have attended, but to have been asked to give a paper had astonished and delighted him. It was more evidence of the advance of his career, and he could feel the excitement and nervousness churning together inside him. He declared himself happy with his presentation and returned the file of papers to his briefcase.

He gazed out the window. The clouds had completely broken up now and were scudding before a fresh wind. The sky had turned a Prussian blue and this shade mingled with ochre light from the sun which had begun to set. The flat landscape of farms, freshly ploughed fields, hedges and villages rushed by. Rudolf let his mind wander. He was excited for another reason.

Since 'Ursula's Secrets' had opened at its new address, he managed to meet his sister-in-law about once a month, despite their busy schedules. Occasionally, if Lisa could find somebody to pick the children up from school, she would join them for lunch; but more often it was just Rudolf and Ursula. Last week he had told her about being invited down here. He had been describing the old world charm of Krynica, and out of the blue she had decided that she needed a break. She would come to Bad Krynica for the weekend, but would come early so that part of her stay overlapped with his. He had been simultaneously surprised and thrilled. The arrangements had been quickly made – despite the conference she was able to book a room in the hotel – and she arranged to arrive tomorrow night, Thursday, and would stay the weekend. The conference ended at lunch time on Friday so that they would have Thursday night and a half day on Friday before he caught the evening train. Rudolf told

Lisa, who lamented the fact that she couldn't get away. She toyed with the idea of them all coming down and staying the weekend, but what with wartime travel arrangements and the cost, they eventually decided against it.

Rudolf was quite uncertain what all this meant. He and his sister-in-law were the best of friends, and she was certainly an attractive woman. He was attracted to her himself despite his marriage, and she seemed to enjoy his company. But was there anything more to it than that? There was the hug and kiss and what she had said at Christmas. But maybe that had just been the alcohol. Still, why fret? It was enough that with the most stressful part of the conference over, he would have the pleasure of her company and they could stroll around and look like lovers even if they were not.

He was easily the best speaker of the day. Where the others wandered on through endless statistics, stodgy or rambling ideas and stilted phrases, Rudolf's speech had been light, utterly clear, and completely to the point. They had given him the toughest slot of the day, after a large lunch replete with wine, when everybody had just wanted to sleep. The atmosphere in the room, darkened for the slide projector, had been oppressive, yet even in the semi-darkness, he had sensed the interest as his model unfolded to the final slide, the punch line – how it all translated into cash. He was the only speaker to get a real round of applause – the rest had either had none at all or else a smattering of clapping. There was a coffee break immediately afterwards and people kept coming up to congratulate and compliment him. The adrenaline was still pumping when he returned to the conference room and spent the rest of the afternoon replaying bits of his own speech in his head. There were two other speakers that afternoon, and when the conference closed for the day, he hadn't the faintest idea what either of them had spoken about.

Several people asked him to join them for dinner, but he

made his excuses and left. He asked the concierge for the name of a good restaurant – not too far, good food, quiet – and then hurried upstairs to his room. A bath, clean clothes and then he pulled on his overcoat and hurried to the station. They took a taxi to the hotel and he was relieved to find nobody from the conference in reception while she checked in. He carried her bag up to her room and she told him to wait while she freshened up. He sat on the bed and thumbed through a magazine, aware of the sounds of water coming from the bathroom. In the restaurant they ordered food, a heavy red wine and smoked while they drank an aperitif. He told her about the conference and his presentation.

Changing the subject, and still feeling some lingering adrenaline burning there, Rudolf said: 'Do you know, you are probably the woman I admire most in the world?'

She laughed. A flash of white teeth against red lipstick.

'Me? Don't be silly. Anyway, what about Lisa?'

'Yes, of course, Lisa is my wife, and I love her, but I said "admire". I admire what you're doing with your life. Making something of yourself.'

'So are you.'

'It's different with men. Men do that. Or if they don't they ought to. But most women just seem to let life happen to them. You've taken it by the scruff of the neck and made it be what you want it to be.'

'I just want to make every day count,' she said simply, 'pack it full of as much as I can. Look back at the end of a day or a week, and say "yes, that was worth living through".'

'That's exactly what I mean,' he said, 'about admiring you.'

'Well, all right,' she said, raising her glass and smiling broadly, 'I accept the compliment. Thank you.'

He nodded, raising his own glass.

'Tell me about your marriage,' she said later. They had

opened a second bottle of wine and were smoking a cigarette before dessert.

'What do you want to know?' he asked

'Everything,' she said. 'I know what Lisa thinks of it. What do you think?'

'What *does* Lisa think?'

'You mean you've never asked her?'

It was the kind of trap he might have prepared himself. Before he had a chance to think of anything, she laughed and said, 'Come on. I asked first.'

He shrugged, throwing the palms of his hands upwards. 'We've been married nearly ten years. Lisa is a wonderful person and a wonderful mother. We have two great kids. It's a good marriage.'

'Is that all?'

'What more is there?'

'Are you happy – both of you?'

'Sure. Did she say otherwise?'

'Not at all. She's crazy about you. Always has been.'

'I know,' Rudolf smiled.

'And are you crazy about her?' asked Ursula.

'I love her.'

Ursula leaned back in her seat. 'Love,' she mused. 'Now that's a funny word, isn't it?'

'I suppose it is,' he agreed.

'I don't think I've ever been in love. And I don't know how I'd know if I were.'

'Are you lonely?' asked Rudolf suddenly.

'Yes, I think I am. It would be nice to have somebody to share one's success with.'

'You have me,' he ventured, 'and Lisa. Your other friends.'

'I don't really have any other friends. They're more just business contacts. I think it's not so much that I *am* lonely but rather that I'm afraid of ending up alone.'

Then, stubbing out the half-smoked cigarette, she said, 'Enough of this mournful talk. What are we going to have for dessert?'

They didn't finish the wine, but had two cognacs each before taking a taxi back to the hotel. They huddled together for warmth as it sped through the deserted streets.

'A night-cap?' she suggested, as they came up the front steps. There was a large crowd of conference goers in the bar.

'Not here,' he said, 'we'd have to join this lot.'

'In my room, then,' she said. 'Ask someone at reception to bring them up.'

In the room she peeled off her coat and threw it over the back of a chair. She bounced onto the bed and asked him if he would take off her boots. He knelt down and began to untie the laces on one of the boots. He felt quite tipsy and the smell of the leather and the sight of her stockings pulled tense across her shin and calf made an erection grow in his trousers. A not unpleasant smell wafted up when he removed the boot. Just then there was a knock on the door.

'That must be our drinks,' he said.

'Don't be long,' she called up from the bed where she now lay back, her arms sprawled and eyes closed.

Rudolf took the tray from the waiter, tipped him and closed the door. He could feel the erection awkwardly positioned in his trousers.

'I think I've had a bit too much to drink,' she sighed

'Don't worry,' said Rudolf, 'we'll soon get you into bed.'

He returned to the other boot. If she heard his last remark she didn't acknowledge it and, looking up, he thought she might be asleep. When he had finished he stood up, not quite sure what to do. She opened one eye.

'If you get in under the blankets I'll cover you up.'

'No, I can't go to sleep like this. I have to undress.' Her

153

s's were slurred.

'Do you want me to help you?'

Her other eye opened.

'If you want to,' she said, in a tired voice.

'You'll have to sit up.'

She extended her arms and he sat her up. Then rather unceremoniously, he managed to pull her out of the jacket of her suit.

'S-s-skirt,' she said.

Catching her under her arms, he hoisted her into a standing position. She leant against him while he reached behind for the buttons. He could smell her as she lolled heavily in his arms, her eyes shut.

His erection had subsided somewhat. Despite the drink, he felt clear headed – at least clear headed enough to know that she was drunk, and that he needed to be careful about what happened next. The buttons of the skirt popped open, it slid down a little and rested there. She wiggled her hips, but failed to move it. He slipped his hands inside the waist band of the skirt and slid it down. It fell in a crumpled heap on the floor and she stood on top of it. Underneath the skirt she was wearing a slip.

Her eyes were closed again. He undid the buttons of her blouse and again with difficulty, slipped it off her shoulders. It joined her coat on the chair. He held her with one hand while he turned back the covers on the bed. Then he sat her down onto the bed, this time on the edge. Her eyes were closed and her head lolled.

'Are you asleep, Ursula?' he asked softly.

There was no reply. He kissed her on the cheek, but she failed to respond. He stood for several minutes looking down at her. Her chest was rising and falling gently. Then he walked to the door, switched off the light and went out, taking one of the drinks with him.

Chapter 4

Lodz, Poland. Spring 1941.

Even though he had been reading and re-reading bits of *Mein Kampf* for nearly ten years, Otto Tauber had to admit that he found much of it hard going. He had never been much of a reader, and he assumed that it was his unfamiliarity with books that was the problem. Here though, in Poland, at least some of its abstract concepts had become clearer. You could read indefinitely, for instance, about how the Jews were subhuman, but it was always a bit hard to imagine what that actually meant. Any Jews he had seen in Germany had usually been quite the opposite – wealthy, well-dressed, driving around in big cars, eating out in the best places. Now, here, he realised what a veneer all that had been. You could dress up a monkey and make him look like a prince, but that still didn't stop him being a monkey.

Here the subhuman nature of the Jews really emerged. You only had to stand at any of the arteries of the ghetto to see this for yourself. Inside the wire the buildings were colourless, shabby, their façades crumbling and decayed. Where glass was broken in windows, the Yids, instead of replacing it, had merely boarded them up. The people themselves were a shambling mass of drabness. Even in summer, everyone seemed to wear musty old coats, often tied with string, and head scarves or hats. The kids looked out through the wire with the same bovine stare of cows in a field or animals at the zoo. Indeed, all of them were more like animals than people. Rather than walking around puddles they just seemed to splash through them as some beast of burden might have done. They didn't need those yellow stars on their coats to show that they were different. You only had to look inside the wire and see them staring blankly back at you to see that they were.

Then there were the ones who played what Otto called 'the game of manners'. These were the ones who supposedly rose above their brethren and tried to pretend they were on a par with the Germans. Otto had seen an example of this only recently when he had had to escort Herr Biebow, the ghetto's German administrator, into the ghetto for a meeting with Rumkowski, the head Jew. Two cars had gone into the ghetto, Otto and a driver in the first car, Biebow behind. At the Jewish so-called offices in Balut Market, the cars pulled up, and Otto got out first. He carried a Schmeisser machine pistol and quickly scanned the area for any signs of trouble. Not that he expected any. By and large, there were very few security problems here. The main Jew-related problems were administrative ones, associated with having to corral and feed and care for such a large herd of people. And of course epidemics from this pestilential horde.

Even before he had completed his scan, the Jews were scurrying out of their hole. First came Rumkowski, with his shock of white hair, then a Jewish sow, her features unmistakable. The Jews had obviously dressed up for the big occasion. Rumkowski wore his best suit. The sow wore make-up and had her hair tied back. She wore a dark suit and blouse exactly as if she had been a secretary in Berlin. She held her hands together while Rumkowski introduced her. For a second Otto thought she was going to reach out and shake hands with Biebow. However, Biebow just indicated impatiently that he wanted to go inside. He went in first and they followed him in, with Otto bringing up the rear.

The game of manners. The Jews trying to behave as though this was a meeting between representatives of two companies to do some piece of business. Did they really think this was a game of equals? Did they not realise that it wasn't *even* a meeting of employers and employees? Rumkowski, like some petty manager who invites his boss home, so that the boss can see the man's pretty wife and family. And maybe the pretty wife will make a big impression on the boss; soften him up so that the man can then get a rise or promotion. Otto could imagine Rumkowski and the sow talking beforehand, planning all of this. She wasn't even pretty what with her prominent jaw and nose. Did the stupid whore really think she could please Germans? It was like a pet dog, thinking that by sticking up its tail and cocking its ass it could charm its owner. It might charm another dog, but the owner certainly wouldn't notice.

In April Otto got three days leave and spent it with Helga. It was during this time that he told her about his house in the East. Sleeping with her had been the first big test of whether or not she cared for him. For Otto this was an even bigger one. He explained all about *Lebensraum* and how, after Russia was conquered, that Germany would send colonists into the Eastern Territories. Then he painted the picture of the house, the land, the pool or river – she said she would prefer a river – and the children. When he had finished, she said:

'They'll need teachers in a new land like that, won't they?'

The thought hadn't occurred to him before.

'I suppose they will. Yes, of course they will.'

He hadn't thought of his wife working, but now that he did, it added an agreeable new dimension to his daydream. They would be part of a community. She would drive their car every day to the schoolhouse and here she would teach the local children while he worked the land. The Fuhrer discouraged wives who worked anywhere other than in the home, but here Otto would have to disagree with him. Anyway, it was quite possible that the Fuhrer was talking about suburban Germany. It would be different out on this new frontier.

'Can you drive?' asked Otto suddenly.

'No,' she said, looking puzzled.

'It's alright,' he said, 'I'll teach you when the time comes.'

In bed that night, Otto realised that now only one element of his plan remained to fall into place.

When he heard that they were looking for volunteers for special duty in Russia, Otto asked for, and was given, a transfer straightaway. It had been nearly two years since the invasion of Poland, and much of the time it had seemed to Otto that the German Army had done nothing except sit on its arse. Yes, there had been the campaigns in the West, but that was only a side-show. Over here was where the real business would be done. Now, at last, the rumours were flying: the invasion of Russia, the final campaign, the achievement of *Lebensraum*. They had been told that the special duty would speed the eventual victory. Added to that was the fact that it was behind the lines, which would keep Helga happy that he wasn't in too much danger. The rumours said that the invasion would take place at the beginning of the summer. If it went at the same rate as the Polish invasion, even allowing for the vastly bigger size of Russia, then he could be leaving the military by the beginning of 1942, to begin life as a colonist.

Otto's transfer took him to the Police Academy at Pretsch on the Elbe near Leipzig. Here, for three weeks, they did terrain exercises and the occasional night march. Then, the evening they finished their training, and just before they were due to go out on the town, they were addressed by

Brigadefuhrer Nebe, their commanding officer.

'You men come from many different backgrounds. Some of you are from universities and have spent much of your time working behind desks. There you have served the Fatherland with your ideas, with your intellect. Others have already served with great gallantry during the campaign in Poland. Perhaps you have been wondering what we have been waiting for since 1939.'

A murmur of agreement rose from the packed briefing room.

'Perhaps you have been wondering whether the German Army had any plans to make a move again, or whether you would be spending the rest of your military careers guarding ghettos here in Poland.'

The approving murmur became louder.

'Well, gentlemen, permit me to put your minds at ease. Within a few weeks, you will be going east on your new mission. At the moment, I cannot give too much away, but there are a few things I can say. First of all, you can forget anything you have been involved with in the past. This mission is, first and foremost, a war mission. So for those of you who are new to it, this mission will be one of both military and national security. In a few weeks, the Fuhrer's heroic Panzers and mighty divisions of the Wehrmacht will be going on their summer holiday.'

A laugh and a cheer went up.

'This year, for a change, they are going east.'

He paused for effect.

'*We* will also be going east, gentlemen.'

There was another cheer.

'As our combat divisions move forward into the heart of Communist Russia, we will begin our work behind the front. It will be our mission to pacify rear areas, to put down resistance behind the lines, to keep the rear area clear –'

'Like toilet paper,' muttered a man beside Otto.

The group of people within earshot began to giggle and stifle laughter.

'– and to protect and pacify the army's rear.'

'Like a thick pair of underpants,' muttered the same man.

This time, they roared with laughter, the noise merging into the general high spirits. Nebe held up his arms, palms outwards to calm things down enough for his words to be heard.

'Pacification. That will be our role.' He began to speak softly, and the noise subsided as men strained to hear what was being said. 'While you are in Russia,' he continued seriously, 'I fear you will be exposed to a great many temptations. As well as normal temptations that beset all soldiers, I fear you will be tempted with weakness. Yes, gentlemen, weakness.

'The task ahead requires tough men, men who are willing to obey orders, men who will push through and get the job done. You will need to be strong in mind and body. We can train you to be strong in body, and this is what we have tried to do here during your training. But the real strength, mental strength, can only come from yourselves. That is why I must say the following to you gentlemen. If any of you thinks you are not up to the task ahead, if you are not up to the stress and psychological strain, then you should report to me afterwards. For you we will make alternate arrangements. I can assure you that, should you choose this route, there will be no negative impact whatsoever on your careers.

'But to those of you who feel you have the strength, I would say, enjoy your night out tonight. Enjoy the leave that has been granted to you. And be ready, when you return, to take up your mission in the east. Thank you gentlemen.'

Nebe sat down to spontaneous applause and wild drumming of boots on the wooden floor.

A few weeks later, early in June, Otto was on his way by train to Eastern Galicia.

Chapter 5

Once the invasion of Russia began all military leave was cancelled. For civilians like Rudolf the concept didn't really arise, but nonetheless he cancelled his holidays. Lisa and the kids went; he stayed put. With so much happening it wasn't a good idea to be away just now.

Rudolf was surprised at how well Lisa took this news. In fact, ever since Christmas, he had been pleasantly surprised by the fact that she seemed to be adapting – and about time too - to his new job. Now at last he could get on with things and know he could come home in the evening to a decent, relaxing, family life free of angst.

With the war in the east at last underway, Rudolf put a second map of Europe up on his wall so that he could keep touch with the unfolding situation. He needed this anyway now because a vast amount of statistical data was starting to flow into his office. Amongst these were Operational Situation Reports from the USSR. According to the distribution information, only 30 or so copies of these were made and he was one of the chosen recipients. It appeared to Rudolf as if the Fuhrer himself might be one of the potential recipients. He was indeed in heady company.

Apart from the distribution list, though, these reports were not the kind of reports that Rudolf felt were particularly good. While they did give a good *general* feel to the situation, there were some tantalising gaps, particularly in the statistical area. Sifting through a sheaf of them for July he re-read the bits he had highlighted.

The Jewish armies massed in the east were clear: *'During the last 3 days Lithuanian partisan groups have already killed several thousand Jews'. 'In Garsden, the Jewish population had supported the Russian border guards repulsing the German attack'.*

Nor would the Jews be able to operate with impunity. They were all being rounded up. *'Fort VII in Kaunas will be organised as a Jewish concentration camp with two sections:*

1. male Jews

2. female Jews and children'

But the women were also fighting. *'... on 2 July, 133 persons were shot in Tauroggen; on 3 July, 322 persons (among them 5 women) in Georgenburg; in Augustowo 316 persons (among them 10 women); and in Mariampol 68 persons'* What kind of women were these?

Paul did the statistical analyses of these reports. Even so, he wasn't allowed to take them from the room. Not when they were marked *Geheime Reichsfache!*, 'Secret Affair of the Reich'. Instead he sat at a small table specially set aside for the purpose in Rudolf's room and extracted from the reports the data he needed. These data were marked in green ink, to differentiate them from Rudolf's own jottings, which were in red.

The initial, relatively small numbers hadn't been long in going up. By 11 July, less than three weeks from the start of the invasion, the numbers were in four digits. *' ... a total of 1,743 persons have been shot'. 'After the retreat of the Red Army, the population of Kaunas killed about 2,500 Jews during a spontaneous uprising' ' ... a total of 7,800 Jews have been liquidated'.*

This was part of his problem with the information contained in these reports. It was very hard to tell which totals related to which individual incidents. Some incidents might be already counted and would be counted again if he included the totals. On the other hand, some incidents didn't get an individual mention and so, the only way they were counted was in the totals. He and Paul tried to manage as best they could. They cross-referenced data which was already in their files about Jewish populations in the particular area. They correlated current reports with previous ones and tried to ensure that where they used figures from particular incidents, that these figures weren't already included in total figures upon which they tended to rely fairly heavily. The result was that what should have taken Paul a few minutes tended to take up most of the morning. It was their first job every day now. While Paul worked on it Rudolf cleared his desk and in-basket, and discussed queries with the younger man.

No, the reports weren't ideal. If Rudolf had had his way he would have sent them all off a memo, pointing out the difficulties with their current reporting style and asking them to fill in what would have been for them, as well as for he and Paul, a simple tabular form. However, this was not something that was within his personal sphere of influence. However, he might talk to Korherr about it.

By mid-July, he could see from the reports, things were settling into a routine.

'The liquidations, in particular, are in full swing and usually take place daily. The carrying out of the necessary liquidations is assured in every instance under any circumstances.' Given that these reports were coming every day, there was a real feeling of history in the making, of seeing the unfolding of events while they were still fresh in the participants' minds.

Another problem with the reports, another inaccuracy with the way things were reported, was that sometimes it wasn't clear which executions were Jews and which weren't. *'I personally had dealings with 6 officers in the area who were undoubtedly Jews'*. Things like this were obviously subordinates saying what they thought their superiors wanted to hear.

He had marked a lengthy piece in the next report as an example to anyone who might ever question Hitler's approach to the Jewish Problem. *'As early as 1939, a large number of Ukrainians were shot, and 1,500 Ukrainians as well as 500 Poles were deported to the east'*

'Russians and Jews committed these murders in very cruel ways. Bestial mutilations were daily occurrences. Breasts of women and genitals of men were cut off. Jews have also nailed children to the wall and then murdered them. Killing was carried out by shots in the back of the neck. Hand grenades were frequently used for these murders.'

'In Dobromil, women and men were killed with blows by a hammer used to stun cattle before slaughter.'

'In many cases, the prisoners must have been tortured cruelly: bones were broken, etc. In Sambor, the prisoners were gagged and thus prevented from screaming during torture and murder. The Jews, some of whom also held official positions, in addition to their economic supremacy, and who served in the entire Bolshevik police, were always partners in these atrocities.'

'Approximately 7,000 Jews were rounded up and shot by the Security police in retaliation for the inhuman atrocities.'

It was lunch time he and Paul had finished. By then Paul had extracted the necessary figures and agreed their derivation with Rudolf. He would now go off and accumulate these into his overall totals, which would then be put into a daily report go to Korherr. Once approved, these would be submitted to Himmler. Rudolf went out into the sunshine, bought a sandwich, an apple and a bottle of mineral water and headed for the Tiergarten. He would be meeting Ursula this evening. He would go round to the shop after work. Lisa was away on holiday with the kids. Tonight he might reach sixteen on the intimacy matrix.

Because he had been attending the conference, he hadn't seen her for most of the Friday after she had fallen asleep drunk. It wasn't that it was the conference was particularly interesting but it was good to be circulating. Several more people congratulated him about his talk the previous day.

Part of him was avoiding her out of embarrassment; part of him desperately wanted to see her. Finally, when the conference had ended and the delegates were starting to depart, Rudolf slipped away and upstairs to her room. He knocked softly, half wishing she might not be there. Then he heard movement, the door was opened and he realised his heart was racing.

'Rudolf,' she said, brightly, 'come in.'

As soon as she had closed the door, and before he had a chance to say anything, she said: 'I must apologise for my dreadful behaviour last night.'

'You were just tired,' he said, with exaggerated understanding, ' after all your travels.'

'Drunk more like it. You know, Lisa is very lucky,' said Ursula, as though brushing his comment aside. 'You did a very comprehensive job of putting me to bed.' She smiled.

Rudolf felt himself blush. Was she angry? Humiliated? He had no idea what to say or do next. She said nothing either, letting the silence between them deepen. Her smile remained fixed, her eyes held his.

'I thought you'd be more comfortable ...' he began, falteringly.

'I was comfortable, alright,' she said, and now it seemed that there was mockery in her voice.

'You've got a beautiful body,' he blurted out. Not knowing anything polite or tactful to say, no excuse which he could realistically make, the words had formed themselves and seemed to have issued of their own accord.

The words hung there. Their eyes held one another. Then

he said, 'I want to see all of you.'

'Are you sure?' she asked. It was asked using that tone which implies that the question is a formality, that the decision is already long past.

'No,' he said. 'But I want to do it anyway.'

'Then, come here,' she said.

With that first strong kiss, he thought that he would burst through his pants. Her hand reached down, stroking him.

'Mmmm,' she said, 'I think you like this.'

His hands were in her hair, and she eased his coat and jacket off. He felt no guilt, no worry that tomorrow remorse would come thundering down on him like an avalanche. Indeed, he realised that he had wanted to do this from the first day she had come to live with them, all that time ago.

He took his lips away from hers, and pulled back, looking at her beaming face. In the silence, he heard laughter from somewhere downstairs – a world away. She unbuttoned her skirt and blouse and stepped out of her shoes.

'Have you really had nobody in all this time?' asked Rudolf.

'Nobody,' she said.

She held his eyes as she reached behind to undo her brassiere. Then the smile was gone from her face.

He was awake before her next morning. It was early. He could feel the curve and heat of her naked buttocks and legs beside him. There was a feral smell in the room. They had stayed in the room for the rest of the evening and night, ordering some food somewhere in the gaps between their lovemaking.

He tried to analyse what he felt. Certainly, as he had expected, there was no guilt, no remorse. Nor did he feel any revulsion towards her. Everything often looked different in the light of day. Yet he felt the same affection for her that he had felt for the last two years; and he realised that this must be the sign of true friendship, that a relationship remained unchanged despite everything that happened. Now, for the first time in his life, he was puzzled by the word 'love'. Maybe this was love. Maybe friendship was love, and marriage was something else, a different form of relationship.

She stirred. 'Been awake long?' she asked, sleepily.

'A little.'

'What were you thinking?' she asked, rolling over onto her back.

'About friendship,' he said, 'yours and mine. I love the relationship we have together. It's unlike anything I've ever experienced.' Then he ventured, 'I hope nothing ever happens to spoil it.' He turned his head and looked at her.

She looked back, her face beautiful and deadly earnest. '*I'll* never do anything,' she said.

Later that day, sitting on the toilet, he updated the intimacy matrix. He realised that it was the biggest single jump in an intimacy matrix that he had ever experienced.

Chapter 6

Poland.

Eva Frank reads the letter again, checking for any spelling or punctuation mistakes. SS-Sturmbannfuhrer Rolf-Heinz Hoppner is very particular about such things, especially if the letter is going to no less a person than an SS-Obersturmbannfuhrer, in this case, Adolf Eichmann. She will get this ready for signing and then go to lunch.

16 JULY , 1941

During discussions held in the governor's office, various agencies looked at the solution of the Jewish question in the Reichsgau Wartheland. The following solution was proposed:

(1) All the Jews in the Warthegau will be taken to a camp for 300,000 people, to be constructed as near the main coal railroad as possible. The camp will be constructed in the form of barracks, in which there will be workshops equipped for tailoring, shoemaking, etc.

(2) All the Jews in the Warthegau will be assembled in this camp. Those who are fit for work could be grouped into working parties as required and detached from the camp.

(3) According to SS-Brigadefuhrer Albert, a camp of this kind could be guarded with fewer police than is at present the case. Moreover, the danger of epidemic, which threatens the

population in the vicinity of the ghetto in Litzmannstadt and in other places, will be reduced to a minimum.

She smarts as she always does when she sees the word 'Litzmannstadt'. She once called it by its Polish name, Lodz, in a memo which was inadvertently sent. Hoppner hit the roof.

(4) This winter there is a danger that it will not be possible to feed all the Jews. It should therefore seriously be considered whether the most humane solution would not be to eliminate those Jews unfit for work by some fast-working method. That would in any case be more agreeable than leaving them to die of starvation.

(5) It has also been proposed that all Jewish women of childbearing age in the camp should be sterilised, so that the Jewish problem would in fact be resolved with this generation.

(6) The Reichstatthalter has not yet given his opinion on this matter. It would seem that Regierungsprasident Ubelhor does not wish to see the ghetto in Litzmannstadt disappear, as he makes quite a bit of money out of it. As an example of how money can be made from the Jews, I have been informed that the Reich Ministry of Labour pays 6 RM from a special fund for every Jew put to work, but in fact the Jew costs only 0.80 RM.

Chapter 7

It is summer in the ghetto. David has never liked cities in summer – a trait he shares with Ariela. In the past they had both been grateful for the refuge offered by their parents house at Brzykow, a place of cool greenness, air that you could drink, streams and swimming holes, and a landscape that fades off onto a blue horizon. Now, such memories are so distant that they seem like lives lived by somebody else, or read about in a book.

David tries not to think about such things. He tries to focus on his job, petty and mind-numbing as it is. He tries to forget the humiliation and shame and degradation he feels every time he crosses the Zgierska Street bridge and his eyes meet with those of a Pole passing underneath. (He would never catch the eye of a German – people have been shot for less.) He is David Steinbaum, he reminds himself. He had a career, a life, a future. People once knew and respected him. Now, he is just part of a shambling mass of humanity, subject, like so many cattle, to arbitrary rules that make no sense, rules that have been made up by other people, rules whose only aim seems to be to cause suffering and death and to tear families apart.

He tries to focus on the important things. He has a wife and child to ... to what? Once he would have said 'support'. Now it is more like 'protect', 'defend'. Yet how can he protect them? What power does he have? They are subject to the same capricious dictates as he. The powers-that-be have already – with almost effortless ease – taken away their home and all their possessions. It was done with hardly a whimper on anyone's part. Now, for over a year, they have been taking away peoples' lives. The ghetto streets are thronged. Beggars, people with hollow eyes who seem to have withdrawn into themselves; children, orphans, often with younger children in tow or even carrying infants in their arms. There is no day that goes by that David doesn't see dead bodies on the street. Dear God. Dead bodies on the street of one of Europe's major cities. And these are not victims of war in the conventional sense. These have not been accidentally shot, or bombed or blown up. They have been *starved to death*. Starvation. This is something that happens far away – in Africa, somewhere in the depths of Russia. This is not something that happens in Europe in the twentieth century.

It is amazing how quickly the body deteriorates. Collars that once squeezed necks now encircle them without touching skin. The waistbands of skirts and trousers have ballooned, so much so that at first it had been something of a joke. Now, even with whatever supplementary rations they can gather from their various sources, they are starving. They suffer from weaknesses and shaky legs. During the winter there were days when David thought that the cold would break him. Some days, even in summer, he feels so weak that he thinks he is going to die. Then he wonders what would become of Anna and Marek. Climbing the stairs to the apartment or the steps of the ghetto bridges becomes a slow, laboured experience. All three of them get pains in their shoulder blades, toenails and coccyx, so that it is uncomfortable to sit down. Everyone has begun to move in a slow, shuffling sort of way, designed to conserve energy. The shuffling seems to add immeasurably to the greyness of their situation. The ghetto. The word beats down on them like a hammer on an anvil.

How David has let Marek down. How he has betrayed

his son. They should have gone to America. As soon as Hitler came to power – way back in 1933 when there weren't any obstacles – they should have left. The Steinbaums have enough relations over there. If they had, then Marek would be eating breakfast in a sun-bathed kitchen. Fresh orange juice, cereal, fresh bread, butter, fruit, jam. He would probably speak with an American accent – he would know English better than either of his parents. The boy would be confident, athletic, talented – like his aunt.

How different the reality is. Every night when Marek is washing and getting ready for bed, David has to turn away when he sees Marek's matchstick figure. His tummy is hollow, his legs and arms bony and spindly, his buttocks almost indistinguishable from his back and thighs. Marek is tall for his age and this seems to exaggerate the effect. He reminds David of a small dog amongst a group of boys, constantly searching with his eyes, looking upwards, sideways, and cowering when anybody approaches him. Marek says very little, not even complaining of hunger much any more, and is an almost ghost-like presence around the apartment. He plays by himself most of the time, often lost in a world of his own. David likes to watch him, particularly when Marek is unaware of him, and often his lips move as he talks to some imaginary friend. According to his teacher he is good in school but everything has to be coaxed out of him. His class had a school photograph taken. Amidst the childish posing, smiling, laughter, funny faces, shyness, arms around one another, faces so serious they looked sullen, he sits on the floor in the front of the group with crossed legs and a wide-eyed, distant look of sadness on his face.

At times David feels as though the guilt will crush him. Even more than the lack of food it weighs on him night and day, with sleep his only respite. He feels it when he sees Anna, quiet now, with most of her old fieriness gone. It was hard to imagine she is the same woman with whom he fell in love. He remembers the first night they slept together. It was a couple of months before the wedding and they had gone to Warsaw for the weekend to do some shopping. There, in an expensive hotel room, they had undressed one another, and David had felt as though they were alone in the world and that the night would last forever. A moment in time when their future life and stability had seemed assured. A lifetime ago now. Who could have thought it would have come to this?

There are suicides every day in the ghetto, and David has wondered briefly about it, but has dismissed the thought. He might have had the courage, but this takes more courage, to live through this hell into which he has brought them and to see if they can rebuild their lives afterwards. At night with Anna and Marek asleep in the room, he pulls aside the curtain and looks out on the desolate houses opposite, the empty streets, the occasional dim yellow of a street light. After the war, he wonders, when it is all over, what will become of the ghetto? If he has anything to do with it, these buildings, the entire ghetto, will be levelled. Nobody should ever have to live in these rooms again. An occasional German vehicle can be heard going past beyond the houses. Further again, the city sleeps. People live normal lives over there, eat, sleep, go about their daily routine. Do they ever wonder about the people in the ghetto? Is there somebody over there now wondering what life must be like over here? He thinks it unlikely. The thin veneer of tolerance that the Poles had felt for the Jews has been easily broken. Over the rooftops, an almost full moon plays hide and seek amongst the scudding clouds. David can see dark shadings on its face. Craters? Dry seas? He doesn't know or can't remember. For ages he gazes while the shining white disc sails through a patch of open sky. He longs for its remoteness and serenity.

Chapter 8

Russia. Summer, 1941.

The truck carrying Otto and his detachment sped out of town in the direction in which the Jews had gone. Even at this early hour, the heat was intense, and a trail of discarded coats, bags and bundles marked their progress. Soon a distant dust cloud showed where they were and in another few minutes the truck had pulled level with the tail end of the straggling column. The truck pulled off the dusty road onto the grass verge and made its way past the line of people. Otto timed how long it took them to pass the group and used that to estimate that the column was less than a kilometre long. A couple of thousand. The guards accompanying them would have the exact number. They would take a solid day's work to get through. It was three or four more kilometres to the site, so it would be another hour at least before the Jews arrived. Time to set up, get ready and have some coffee.

The truck pulled off the road and bounced along a dirt track spattered with dust-filled potholes. Ahead stood a grove of thick pine trees on a sandy hillock. It was the only feature for miles around, and it reminded Otto of what the British had called Hill 60 near Ypres in the last war, '60' because this was its height in feet. As they approached they saw that the track actually cut through the hillock like a railway cutting. The truck pulled in just under the shade of the trees. The two men at the back released the tailboard and the squad jumped down.

'Somebody get the coffee on,' said Otto. 'Erwin, you come with me. The rest of you unload the ammunition, check your weapons and make sure everything's in order. You know the routine.'

Erwin, a young man with a face like a film star, walked with Otto out from under the shade of the trees to the far side of the hillock. The soil was sandy and dotted with tufts of coarse grass. On the left were more trees, shielding them on that side. Over to the right the terrain ran level for about twenty metres and then formed a lip. They walked to the edge of the lip looking down about seven metres into what appeared to be a dry river bed. Rocky soil, grass and stunted thorn bushes covered the base and sides of the small ravine. Looking beyond the ravine the steppe stretched off towards a shimmering horizon where the biscuit-coloured ground met the cloudless blue sky. There were birds singing in the trees.

The smell of coffee came to them as they returned to the truck. Somebody handed Otto an enamel mugful, which he drank as he walked out to the far side of the trees with Erwin at his side.

'We'll block most of the track with the truck. Just leave a small passageway where they can get through. Marshal them on this side, out in the open. That way if any of them try to make a run for it, we'll see them. Anyway, they'll get a better sun tan that way.'

Erwin laughed.

'Queue them from here in past the lorry and bring them forward in fives. We'll keep five shooters and five resting at any given time. I reckon we should be able to do five to ten a minute, that'd be somewhere between 300 and 600 an hour. That includes time for reloading. We'll rotate the teams every hour. Four to eight hours should see us through. We should have a better feel after the first hour or so. Depending on how we're doing, we'll break for an hour for lunch. It's just after ten now. Hopefully we should be going by eleven. That means we'll be finishing up this evening about seven or eight.'

'A long day,' mused Erwin.

'It is,' agreed Otto, 'but it's Friday. We've got the week-end coming up. The men can get a good rest then. And of course Friday is the Jews' big day of rest. We'll give a few of them a good rest today.'

Erwin grinned. Otto finished his coffee and threw the dregs onto the dust.

'Right,' he said, 'let's get organised.'

The men arranged five positions on the lip of the ravine. These were indicated by a stack of ammunition boxes three high. The top box was opened with a crowbar, and the rows of shining brass bullet cases uncovered. Then a pair of rifles, their mechanisms oiled, were loaded and placed at each position leaning against the cases. With this done, the men sat down on the ground under the trees and smoked cigarettes while they waited for the Jews to arrive.

There were 2,530, the police officer commanding the column told Otto when they arrived. Otto was pleased that his rough calculations hadn't been too far off. The truck was reversed into position, while Otto explained his plan to the police officer.

'As long as all we have to do is provide a cordon,' said the pasty-faced officer, 'you can run the show any way you like.'

'That's all I want,' said Otto, amicably. 'Make sure nobody escapes, keep them quiet and I'll do the rest. Oh, there's coffee if you want some.'

They had been right in Pretsch. Not everybody was up to this kind of work.

Otto watched while the policeman briefed his men and they spread out to take up positions around the crowd of Jews who were now seated silently on the dust. They were a sorry looking lot of *Untermenschen*, streaked with dust and grime, their clothes shabby and dirty, their bundles scattered untidily around them. The policemen stood, their rifles at the ready. Otto's men took off their jackets and he turned his back to take a piss on the sandy soil. Otto counted off the first five shooters and ordered them across to the far side of the mound to their shooting positions. Then he nodded to the police officer. The man prodded the nearest Jews to their feet and indicated that they should begin to move in a line towards the opening beside the truck. More Jews got up and joined the queue, shading their eyes from the hot sun and jostling to get closer to the shade. Soon, like a partially unwound ball of string, they snaked in past the front of the truck, and then, thanks to a small rise and dip in the ground, they passed out of sight of their compatriots in the sun. It would be hard to imagine a more suitable place.

Two of Otto's squad who weren't shooting sat on the rising ground near the rear of the truck, their rifles slung lazily across their laps. Erwin, his second in command, who was also there, lowered the tailboard. For the men this was the best spot. The first ones came on and Erwin shouted to them in Polish to halt and undress. He also knew the Russian words, but there seemed to be no need. The people got the message. These first ones were mainly old men and women, with a young buck scattered here and there. White skin, pot bellies and figures ruined by childbirth. The women tried to cover their breasts with one arm and their cunts with the other. Erwin indicated that they should flip their clothes up onto the back of the truck.

'This will make their breasts bob up and down,' Erwin said in German to the men, miming the action with cupped hands.

177

The men laughed.

The undressing complete, Erwin extended his arm and index finger and pointed in the direction of the ravine. The Jews, head bowed and still trying to cover their privates as best they could, scurried over the dusty soil and out into the sunshine.

The bodies seemed even more white now. Bucholz, of Otto's squad, stood like a commissionaire in a bank, directing people to the next available teller. As the Jews came towards him he used his arms as a traffic policeman would and pointed them towards a vacant shooting position. Bucholz carried a short whip. If there was any momentary hesitation on the part of the Yids, he lashed at them, urging them in the direction he had indicated.

The shooters used their rifles to nudge the Jews into position at the lip of the ravine. The Jews stood facing the ravine, their shoulders hunched. Then the shooter raised his rifle and fired. Nine times out of ten they tumbled straight in. Occasionally one fell awkwardly or hadn't stood close enough to the edge, and failed to fall in. When this happened the shooter just kicked the body, tumbling it over the edge.

Otto had stayed back where the Jews were corralled while the first shots were fired. This was a tricky time because exactly like a herd of cattle they might bolt at the first rifle shot. As the first cracks were heard, there were screams and a sort of wailing sound went up. Children began to cry. A figure stood up from amongst the sitting crowd, and was downed immediately by a shot from one of the policemen. Good, thought Otto, these fellows know their stuff. This end should be all right.

He turned away and walked past the queue of Jews up the slight slope to the back of the truck. One of the men had jumped into the truck and was kicking an untidy mound of clothes towards the cab. Erwin was shouting orders and his voice became more stentorian as Otto approached. He smiled at Otto amidst the shouting and Otto smiled back. The thread of naked Jews towards the ravine continued. White bottoms on the older ones, pink bottoms on the younger, they scampered to where Bucholz, the traffic cop, took care of them.

Otto stood a few metres behind the shooters and watched as they took care of a few clients. They all seemed to have the hang of it now and most of their shots were accurately aimed. Even so, it was still something of an inexact science. In theory, a shot at the base of the neck should have severed the spinal column causing instant death. In practice, particularly with so many, it was hard to get the spot right all the time. Having them naked helped, but sometimes hair obscured the aiming point, or the shooters arm was just plain tired. When this happened, heads exploded. Ah, it happened there, he noted, as some mush and fragments of skull like pieces of a broken plate, went flying through the air.

At noon, there was a five-minute break, while the shooters were changed. According to Bucholz, they had done just under 300. This should pick up now – that was the usual pattern. Otto took his place, loaded his rifle, and indicated to Probst, the new traffic cop, that he was ready. Probst checked with the other four and then began to bring them on again.

Otto's first few were sloppy and he had to kick a couple over the edge but he soon settled into it. He began to count the number of clean ones versus wet ones, as they called them. The necks came past, thin ones, fleshy ones, male, female, bald, obscured by long hair, tanned, white; an endless cavalcade of necks. One after the other they disappeared over the edge like ducks in a fairground. Otto's score had reached 99 clean, seventeen wet when he heard someone calling a break. They had done over 500. That was more like it. A few more good hours like this and they would be finished long before eight o'clock. They deserved a lunch break.

The police stopped the flow of Jews and made them all sit down again. There were some already naked and these were just made to sit at the back of the truck, the bed of which was now a good half-metre deep in shoes and clothing. Food – cheese, sausage, bread, pickles and vodka – was brought out and Otto's men sat on the bank in the shade, chatting. The police could make their own arrangements, Otto reckoned. Afterwards his people smoked or lay down on the soft sandy soil, eyes closed, half asleep.

At two o'clock exactly, the first team of shooters went back to the lip, but this time to a new spot, further along from the original position, and with an empty section of ravine beneath them. Otto went round to the front where the diminished crowd of Jews still sat patiently. They were incredible. Just sitting there. No resistance. No fight. Jesus, cattle going to an abattoir made more fuss. They were crying for water. Water, for Christ's sake, when in a while they would be dead. Strange the way the mind worked. Well, the Jewish mind at least.

He walked up the line as they waited patiently. There were some good-looking women amongst them and along with a number of others, he dallied at the undressing place, to see what they were like. What a world! Where you could do this as part of your daily work. One of the women was blonde, not dark-haired like the others. Her hair was the colour of straw, and her pubic hair had a sandy tinge to it. Her nipples were tiny. Maybe that was what happened to women the same way that men's cocks shrivelled.

In that hour they again exceeded 500 so that now they were more than halfway through. Only about 1,000 left to go. The shooters changed again and Otto took his place once more at the ravine. This time there were a lot more children. The kids and teenagers were no problem. They came up, skinny bodies, arms and legs, their sex sometimes almost

180

indistinguishable, and were quickly dealt with. Infants in their mother's arms were more problematic. Originally Otto had tried to make the mother stand so that he could hit both with the one bullet. This was too time-consuming though. Shooting the child first and then the mother was worse. Eventually he had settled on shooting the mother and assuming that the child, if it wasn't hit by the bullet, would be killed in the fall, or crushed, or buried when they eventually covered all the bodies. In terms of time it was the most efficient way. The Fuhrer said that it was the Jewish children who were the most dangerous, but there was no danger from these little ones.

By the time he had finished, Otto's trigger finger was aching. He exercised it flexing and unflexing it. At this point there were only about 600 left. Another hour and a bit would finish it. The squads changed again, and the well-oiled machine ran.

The sun was in the west now and was shining on the right cheeks of the shooters. It was just as well they were nearly finished. Another couple of hours and the sun would have been right in their eyes and that wouldn't have helped. Otto sat in shirtsleeves in the welcome shade of the trees. Then he lay back and watched the frond-like upper branches of the trees waving in a gentle breeze. The birds had stopped singing, frightened off by the gunshots.

At five o'clock, Otto went out to check the corral. There were less than 50 left now, all standing. They were embracing and kissing and speaking to one another. Parents lifted their children into their arms. Most of them were crying. Not long now, Otto thought, and you'll be out of your misery.

He returned to the ravine where the previous shift and the incoming one were sharing a cigarette. As they finished, they stubbed the butts into the ground and the new shift took up positions. The others walked back towards the truck to begin tidying up.

The orange sun was now full in Otto's face and he could feel sweat on his brow and in his armpits. He was aware of droplets of sweat on his eyelids which occasionally, when he blinked, went into his eyes, stinging them. He wiped his face with his sleeve which came away streaked with grey dust. The traffic policeman checked with the shooters and the remainder of today's naked Jews came on.

Almost the last of Otto's Jews were a girl and her young daughter. They came forward together. The girl was beautiful, there was no other word for it. Chestnut hair, the same colour on her head as on her pubes, luscious breasts like grapefruits, columnar thighs. He caught a brief glimpse of her tear-stained face. As they came to the edge of the ravine, they turned their backs and stood together hand in hand. Jesus, she had a beautiful bum. He was momentarily tempted to spare her for the weekend, take her back to the barracks and have some fun with her. He could always include her in Monday's lot. But she was Jewish; and there was Helga – he would never be disloyal to her. He lifted his rifle and shot the child. It was a wet one. Her head disintegrated. The body fell but the girl kept holding the kid's hand so that the corpse failed to tumble into the ravine.

Lowering his rifle, he took a step forward and caught the girl's hair, moving it to one side as though it were a curtain. Inexplicably, he did it gently, as though conscious of her beauty. Then he flipped it with his hand so that it fell in front of her left shoulder. The hair felt heavy and silky. He saw a shudder pass through her body. Her neck and shoulders were visible now. She hunched them, her right shoulder dragged down by the weight of the child's body. He lifted his rifle, took aim and fired. A clean shot. Then, as the body fell, he kicked it so that both girl and child tumbled together over the edge. He turned as the next Jew came towards him.

In another few minutes they were finished. Otto leant his hot rifle against the ammunition boxes, and turned his back to the ravine. He flexed his fingers. Then he shook his hands as though he had touched something hot. Finally he stretched his arms skywards, his fingers extended fan-like. The sun felt luxurious on his back. Around him, the other shooters were doing the same, stretching limbs or lighting up.

A groan behind him from the ravine, reminded Otto that there was still some work to be done. Turning round, he picked up his rifle again and walked to the edge of the lip. Below him the bodies carpeted the bottom of the ravine, in a long, even mound. It was as though they had been sown there by a giant hand. In the morning bulldozers or Jews would be out to complete the sowing and cover them up with earth. In the meantime, however, there were still some signs of life and it was to these that the men now turned their attention. Sitting on the edge of the ravine, with their legs dangling over the edge and cigarettes hanging from their lips, the men scanned the white, blood-splashed heap. Whenever there was a sound or a sign of movement they fired, and bodies twitched and jumped with the impact of bullets. Movements were the easier to deal with. A head or a hand raised, a leg or a backside moving – these were quickly dispatched. Sounds were more difficult. It was hard to know exactly where they came from. And some of them just wouldn't stay quiet. It became a bit of a game, and the five shooters took turns to see whose shot would finally silence the most persistent ones.

Eventually they tired of it, and leaving one man to take care of any last-minute moaning and moving, the others began to tidy up. Empty ammunition boxes were pitched into the ravine. The remainder were carried back to where a second truck, recently arrived and stinking of hot diesel, waited beside the first one, now packed with clothes. This truck pulled out to where the Jews had been corralled and some of the men collected up any remaining bundles and items of clothing and threw them into the back. Meanwhile, the weapons, ammunition and cooking equipment were loaded into the second truck. One of the men pissed on the fire to put it out and a bottle of vodka was passed around. As they lounged around, occasional shots came from the ravine. Finally, they were ready. The man at the ravine returned to announce that all the Jews were sleeping peacefully. They clambered up onto the bed of the truck, the engine was started and they followed the clothes truck back to barracks through a green and purple summer evening.

Because it was Friday the cook seemed to have pulled out all the stops. There was tomato soup, baked fish, salad, freshly baked bread and plenty of fruit for dessert. To drink they had beer, schnapps and vodka. It was a loud, boisterous meal, which developed into something of a party afterwards. Somebody turned the radio on and the romantic, sad music made Otto long for Helga. The evening wore on. They sang and lamented the lack of women with which to dance. They told jokes, one or two people passed out, and as it got later and later, the surviving group got smaller and smaller. Finally, when light was breaking in the sky outside, Otto tottered off to bed to sleep the sleep of the dead.

Chapter 9

Lodz Ghetto. 6 September 1941.

The rattle of a tram resonates off the underside of the wooden footbridge and then slowly dies away as the vehicle trundles up Zgierska Street. It is a warm evening, though not so warm that David and Anna have been able to leave their coats behind. Years ago they would have but now, their lack of body fat makes them wear several layers of clothing on all but the hottest days. After nearly two years wear the coats are frayed to the point of being threadbare. They descend from the Zgierska Street bridge and continue up the pavement of Brzezinska Street in silence. They are coming from Bazarna Square where Anna has just sold a watch David gave her as a present to mark the first anniversary of their meeting. The money will help them to buy a little extra food. This evening they are going to a concert.

Almost since the inception of the ghetto, concerts have been run in a building which has been named the House of Culture on Krawiecka Street. These have mainly been concerts of classical or light classical music conducted by Theodore Ryder, who prior to the war was conductor of the Lodz Symphony Orchestra as well as symphony music conductor for Radio Poland. David has steadfastly refused to go to these concerts for reasons which he is feeling acutely tonight as they make their way along the crowded pavements.

Before the war they *did* go to concerts. In those days, they would often arrange a babysitter and go to listen to the local orchestra or a visiting one. Evenings such as this one, with summer not quite faded, they would make their way – he in a light suit, she in a summer dress – to the symphony hall for a concert, followed by dinner, often at some sidewalk restaurant.

Tonight is like a parody of that time. The milling crowds on the streets are all dressed like beggars and tramps. David can only assume that he and Anna look like that too, or even worse, that in trying to look their best, they have ended up looking like comic tramps trying to dress up as gentry. They walk slowly, a walk developed over the long months of hunger. Tonight there will be no supper after the concert, just an exhausted walk home in the dark. David has avoided these concerts because he is afraid that they will not lift his morale as they have been intended to do. Rather, he fears that they will break his heart. That they will do what the hunger, the humiliation, the degradation, the suffering, the destruction of his family's life have all failed to do. That these concerts will be the straw that finally causes his frail resolve to snap completely.

He is more aware than normal of these feelings tonight. Last Wednesday evening he was queuing up at the Zgierska Street bridge. Just after he had put his foot on the first rung, and was looking down at his feet waiting for the next step to become free, he heard a shout. Startled he looked up to see a man clambering onto the rail of the bridge. His right foot went onto the first rail, then his left foot. Meantime, with his hands he pulled himself up onto the top rail, and hesitating there for a moment, he leapt off the bridge, arms upraised. It is common knowledge in the ghetto – at least David thought it was common knowledge – that that fall is not enough to kill anybody. So, it was in this case. As the man lay groaning on the cobbles, the Germans – through the barbed wire –

ordered the Order Service man who stood at the foot of the stairs to go and get an ambulance. Then they hauled the man to one side so that traffic wouldn't be disrupted and left him lying there. Every time he groaned they kicked him and shouted at him to be quiet.

It is his resolve David fears for. If this snaps – and it now hangs by the slenderest of threads – he can see himself going the same way as the man on the bridge. Tonight, however, he must go to the concert – because Marek is appearing in it.

Marek has been attending a sort of summer school in Marysin, the part of the ghetto that has the most open space and greenery. Tonight, the students who have been at the Marysin schools are presenting a show entitled *A Summer Holiday*. Marek is in a choir, and as parents, David and Anna have been invited.

The show comes close to realising David's fears. He manages to maintain his composure for the first hour or so. Different groups of children work their way through choral singing, recitations, little vignettes of the children's lives in Marysin, or sketches of life in the ghetto – there is an hilarious one centring around queuing for food. There are dances and little farces and songs by individual contributors. The whole show runs like clockwork. One act finishes and hurries off, and is replaced quickly and professionally by the next one. Older children and adults help the smaller children off the high stage or off benches.

Despite himself, David is transported. It is identical to similar concerts before the war, or even to ones David himself took part in when he was a kid. Two children get into a shoving match over the same spot and narrowly miss knocking each other off a bench at the back row of the choir. A small kid at the front of a group yawns wildly. The music teacher, the sleeves of her shabby dress pulled up, conducts a group of smaller children, mouthing the words of the song with huge lip movements.

When Marek comes in, David can hardly bear to watch and feels pinpricks in his eyes and tears surging into them. Marek is nervous, and keeps his face rigid and unsmiling while he sings the words. David hardly hears what they are singing because he is thinking of all the potential and promise there on stage. All those lives and what the future should have held for them. In normal childhoods, scope is narrow but the potential is awesome. Then it seems like in adult-hood, the scope is widened, but just at that point for many people the potential is narrowed, whether through choice, through circumstance, by design, by accident.

Here, there has been none of that. The children's lives have been narrowed from the beginning. Yet, despite that ,here they are singing of flowers and animals and heroines and imaginary lands and living happily ever after. Ordinarily, for a few of these kids, the magic of tonight might never have ended – they might have gone on to do something creative with their lives. To make a mark. To do something meaningful. David looks at Anna but she is engrossed in what is happening on stage. He holds his hand over his eyes to cover the tears.

At the end of the show everyone comes on stage for the finale. Some children hug one another, and even Marek is some-what more animated. When they are finished, Rumkowski, or 'the Chairman' as he likes to be known, comes on stage. He thanks and congratulates everybody involved in the production. He reminds everybody of his five priorities: work, bread, care for the sick, supervision for the children and peace in the ghet-to. Concern for the children, he says, remains at the forefront of his activities. There is no sacrifice too great when it is a ques-tion of helping the ghetto's youngest inhabitants.

After his speech, the little children make a ring and dance around him on stage to the cheers of the audience. When they are finished he gives each of them a little parcel of bread and candy.

Chapter 10

Berlin. 1941.

24 JULY

The Teilkommando which was dispatched to Slonim has carried out with the police a Grossaktion against Jews and other Communist elements. During this action about 2,000 persons were arrested because of Communist activity and looting. Of these, on the same day, 1,075 persons were liquidated. The Kommando alone liquidated another 84 persons in Slonim.

14 AUGUST

Until the final solution of the Jewish question for the entire continent is achieved, the superfluous Jewish masses can be excellently employed and used for cultivating the vast Pripet swamps, the northern Dnieper swamps as well as those of the Volga.

20 AUGUST

A member of the militia was shot dead from an ambush near Pinsk. As a reprisal, 4,500 Jews were liquidated.

29 AUGUST:

In Minsk, 615 more persons were liquidated in the course of an action in the civilian-prisoner camp there. All the executed were of racially inferior stock.

12 SEPTEMBER
Executions of Jews are understood everywhere and accepted favourably. It is surprising how calm the victims are when they are shot, both Jews and non-Jews. Fear of death seems to have been dulled by twenty years of Soviet rule.

19 SEPTEMBER
On 6 September, 1941 Kommando 4a carried out an action against the Jews in Radomyshl. There, Jews from all over the district had been assembled. This led to an overcrowding of Jewish homes. On the average, fifteen persons lived in one room. Hygienic conditions became intolerable. Every day several Jewish corpses had to be removed from the houses.

It was impossible to supply food to the Jews as well as the children. In consequence, there was an ever-increasing danger of epidemics. To put an end to these conditions, 1,107 Jewish adults were shot by Kommando 4a, and 561 juveniles by the Ukranian militia.

... As the perpetrators could not be found, 1,303 Jews, among them 875 Jewesses over twelve years, were executed ...

20 OCTOBER
A total of 537 Jews (men, women and adolescents) were apprehended and liquidated. The Ukranian population and the Wehrmacht looked upon this action with satisfaction.

25 OCTOBER
In a further action, another 812 male and female persons were given 'special treatment', all of them racially and mentally inferior elements.

27 OCTOBER

Thus, even if about 75,000 Jews have been liquidated so far – Rudolf circled the figure in red and wrote beside it 'correlate against previous figures for this Einsatzgruppe' – it has already become clear that a solution to the Jewish question will not be possible in this way. True, we have succeeded in bringing about a total solution to the Jewish problem, particularly in smaller towns and also in villages.

12 NOVEMBER

300 insane Jews from the Kiev lunatic asylum were liquidated. This represented a particularly heavy psychological burden for the members of Einsatzkommando 5 who were in charge of this operation.

137 trucks full of clothes made available as a result of the campaign against the Jews of Zhitomir and Kiev were put at the disposal of the National Socialist People's Welfare Organisation.

14 NOVEMBER

Generally, the co-operation of the peace-loving population, particularly the Byelorussian circles, can be felt. In particular, one meets with understanding of how the Jewish question is dealt with ... 10,000 Jews were processed in Slonim ...

19 NOVEMBER

The attempt by Sonderkommando 4a to take action against Nieshin, where approximately 325 Jews are living, failed three times since it was impossible to reach on roads made impassable for motor vehicles by the mud following the rain.

... According to a report by Sonderkommando 4b, there is a mental asylum in Poltava with 865 inmates; attached to it is a 1,250-acre farm. Its produce is used to feed the insane and the staff living there. The food situation in Poltava is

191

extremely critical. For example, there is no whole milk avail-
able for the three large military hospitals. Thus, the com-
mander of Sonderkommando 4b, with the approval of the
High Command of the 6th Army and the local military com-
mander, contacted the woman doctor in charge of the asylum
with the object of reaching an agreement on the execution of
at least part of the insane.

The woman doctor in charge understood quite well that
the problem should be solved in this manner. However, she
objected because the measure would cause unrest among the
population ... A way out of this difficulty was found. It was
decided that the execution of 565 incurables should be car-
ried out in the course of the next few days under the pretext
that these patients were being removed to a better asylum in
Kharkov.

... In the area of Einsatzkommando 6, the total number
of town dwellers is around 1.2 million, not including those of
smaller places. Naturally, the amount of work to be accom-
plished is proportionally high and can hardly be accom-
plished with the forces available.

The phone rang. It was Lisa.

'Can you bring home some wine? Get a couple of bottles.
Ursula's coming over for dinner and you know how we like
to stay up late.'

'Of course. Anything else you need?'

'No, I don't think so. Just you. Any idea what time it'll
be?'

'I'll try and be early. No later than seven. Guaranteed.
How's that?'

'Fine. We'll see you then. I love you.'

'I love you too. Bye.'

Chapter 11

Slonim. Late October, 1941.

Fingers interlaced under his chin, Dietrich Hick, Section Leader for Jewish Affairs, gazes out of his office window in police headquarters – formerly the Hotel Krakowsky on Schloss Street. He doesn't see what lies beyond. His mind is elsewhere.

For those in his line of business, the rules of thumb are well-known. For 1,000 or so people, you need about a third of a cubic metre each. As you got up into the 5,000 to 10,000 sort of range, that decreases. The packing density will be greater. The larger weight of bodies will press down more on the levels below them resulting in a greater compaction. Also, those in the lower levels will quite literally drown on the blood swilling around in the bottom of the hole. A quarter of a cubic metre will be sufficient in this case. You would also make the hole deeper in the latter case. The third of a cubic metre per body works with a depth of 5m. For the larger number of bodies, you would need at least another metre on top. So, 6m.

He does the calculation quickly on the notepad he keeps for his rough notes. 10,000 at ¼ cubic metre each is 2,500 cubic metres. At 5m deep, that gives 500. Say 600 to allow a bit extra – it's only a rule of thumb after all. So, he could do them in one long line – say 4m by 150. If they do their work neatly, they could get two across, head to head or head to toe.

Of course with numbers like this, he'll be lucky just to get them all shot, never mind stacked neatly. The challenge here will be to process them as soon as possible in the short winter day. Actually, that's another point while he thinks of it. No bodily examinations. They're not going to have time for that business. Sure, they'll lose some property as a result, but the alternative – darkness coming on and a great mass of Jews still to shoot – doesn't bear thinking about. Also none of this saving pretty Jewish girls to have for a few days. This time everyone gets processed.

He reads back over the memo so far.

1. The Aktion will take place three weeks from Friday – it will be 14 November.

2. They will use that spot they have found east of the village of Czepelow, across the valley. The place is remote, consisting of open space, but with plenty of surrounding woodland to shield it from prying eyes. The soil is soft and sandy.

3. It is important not to alert anybody to what is going on in case the Jews who are going to remain in the ghetto got wind of it. There are a number of villages nearby – he checks he has the names right – Zhireva, Albertin, Czepelow, Slonim itself – and it is important that the shooting will not be heard in any of these. He proposes that they round up some Jews and do some trial shooting, and have observers in each of the villages. This is a little project in itself, but he'd better spell out the details for them. Otherwise the idiots will be sure to fuck it up.

4. The trench should be – what was it again? – 150m long, 5m deep and 4m wide. He underlines the words 'deep' and 'wide'. They should round up a bunch of Jews to dig this. How many? 50 or 60, Hick suggests. Ask for volunteers for a special job and promise them some extra bread and soup. They are going to need quite a time to dig this, and they'd better be kept up there, so they will need some kind of hole to live in and they'll need guarding and some food and water.

This is another point he will have to expand on if he wants it done right. After they have finished they should become the trench's first tenants. It's a bloody obvious point, but those idiots are quite capable of taking the Jews back to the ghetto and letting them sow panic.

5. Transport will be on foot, except for the old, the sick and the children who will go in trucks. He will have to organise these. Maybe also commandeer some peasant wagons. Not that they'll need much commandeering. From what he's seen, the Poles seem to be only too happy to volunteer.

What else? Oh yes, a spot of public relations. Get one of those international Jewish conspiracy articles into the local press. Maybe in Baranovichi, that's the nearest big town. The usual stuff. The Jews have caused the war and are therefore responsible for the deaths of millions of pure Aryans. If the plans of international Jewish capital had been carried out the whole world would have been destroyed. After Germany's total victory over the Jews and the Communists, the Jews will be deported to special labour camps and their capital will be used to rebuild Europe.

Finally, point 7. Put out some rumours. a: That the Third Reich needs workers and that any Aktion that people hear mooted is just to be a roundup of men for forced labour in Germany. b: That any other rumours about ditches being dug are indeed true. However, they are only anti-tank ditches.

Good enough. That seems to have covered all the main points. Now to write out the detailed operational plan and send it all to Gebeitskomissar Erren.

Chapter 12

November, 1941.

As he enters his apartment building and climbs the stairs at the end of his six-day week, David Steinbaum feels like a badly injured mouse. There might have been a time – had he thought about it - when he might have compared himself to a stronger, more noble animal. But that was before the ghetto. Now, given the tiny range of options and possibilities open to him a mouse seems the most appropriate.

This evening, as he makes his way up the stairs – an activity which in itself makes his hunger-weakened body feel light-headed, so that he has to hesitate for several minutes on the landing before knocking on the door – the metaphor of the damaged mouse returning to its nest is vivid in his mind. He doesn't like to take the image any further. For the mouse will rest up and may recover. For David there appears to be no recovery unless the break from work tomorrow can somehow renew some energy in his weakened body. 'Lie down for a while,' they say in the ghetto. 'A few days of quiet and you'll get back to normal.' It is the cure for everything. It is the only cure available.

Anna answers his knock and he can see the marks of tears around her hollow eyes. For a moment terror lances through his heart, and his first thought is for Marek. But then he sees the youngster playing with some tin soldiers on the pillow and bedclothes. David steps in, as Anna turns away – some evenings she kisses him, some she doesn't.

'What's wrong – ?' he asks, but then, in mid-sentence he sees what it is.

Things have been rearranged in the room. The mattress, instead of lying lengthways, lies across the room, with the result that it is squeezed between the walls and turned up at one end. A string has been draped across the middle part of the room and a blanket hangs from it. The blanket has been pulled back to reveal two other people in the other half of the room. They are wearing coats and their small heap of baggage is only partially unpacked. The man and woman are middle-aged, late forties, early fifties. The man removes his cap and says 'Good evening, sir'. The woman – David assumes it is his wife – choruses the same greeting, a word or so behind her husband.

'These are our new lodgers,' says Anna, quizzically. 'Tenants?' she says half to herself. 'Well, in any case, they're here now too.'

Chapter 13

The senior staff in Rudolf's building are having a Christmas get-together in the conference room. A table is laden with so much food and drink, and of such variety, that it is hard to imagine there is a war on.

Everyone is very drunk, including Rudolf who normally would not allow himself to go so far on such occasions. Cigarette in mouth and a beer in hand, he totters out of the conference room and down the corridor to the toilet. The men's and women's toilets are beside each other and, on an impulse, Rudolf goes in through the women's door.

The outside door gives way to an inside one. He opens that to bright lights and mirrors and a faint fragrance. He has to turn a corner to find the cubicles and as he does so he bumps into Paul and a man whom Rudolf saw around the party earlier.

'Oh, excuse me – ' Rudolf begins.

In an instant a whole scenario rushes through Rudolf's mind. Paul is a homosexual. He has caught them in the act. A very public court case. Disgrace – for Paul, and by reflection on Rudolf himself. Paul in a concentration camp. Or worse.

Paul and the other man are huddled together looking at what look like postcards. From the expression on his face Rudolf can see that Paul knows what Rudolf is thinking. Paul smiles warmly and Rudolf is taken aback by this most unexpected of gestures.

'Just looking at some photographs, Herr Fest. Would you like to see them?'

'Photographs?'

'From our boys on the Eastern Front. Ulrich here knows somebody who knows somebody.'

Paul introduces Ulrich to Rudolf. They shake hands and then Ulrich hands the photographs to Rudolf. He jams his cigarette in his mouth and puts his glass down on the edge of the wash basin.

The first photograph shows a long line of women, sitting on the ground with their backs to the camera. They are undressing while a number of armed military and civilians look on. In the next one there is a long trench with bodies in it. A number of men kneel on the lip of the trench. Behind them a line of soldiers have just fired the rifles at the kneeling men. The smoke from the rifles is clearly visible in the photograph. There are several other pictures in a similar vein. A final one shows a very good-looking, dark-haired woman squatting down, her arms held in an 'X' to cover her breasts. Around her other women are undressing while in the background groups of armed soldiers look on. One grins at the camera, a cigarette hanging from his mouth. The rest are watching the women very closely and smiling.

Rudolf looks up from the photographs at the two men. Now they seem a little unsettled as though fearful of how he will respond.

'Very interesting,' says Rudolf noncommittally.

Paul says: 'Ulrich also has a movie if you'd like to see that.'

'A movie, eh?'

'Yes,' says Ulrich.

'Of our heroic boys?' asks Rudolf and now he breaks into a smile, which confirms for them the irony in his voice.

'Our heroic boys,' the two men chorus, their relief evident.

'And where can we see this piece of cinematographic art?'

'Just follow me,' says Ulrich.

Ulrich disappears, returns with a can of eight millimetre

film and leads them to a small projection room at the rear of the building. He threads the film onto the projector while Rudolf and Paul take seats. Then he switches off the lights.

The film begins with a crowd of people, mostly men but also some women, their backs to the camera. The camera looks down on them as though it were mounted on a truck. The crowd is gathered around a doorway, the top of which can just be seen. Then the crowd parts so that the doorway becomes fully visible. A woman appears in the doorway. She is perhaps in her early forties, stark naked with one arm across her breasts, the other covering her crotch. There is fear in her eyes as she looks right and left at the assembled crowd. A man by the doorway catches her by the arm that covers her breasts and pulls her out through the doorway into the crowd. Her large bobbing breasts are visible now. Several men catch her and push her away from the door through the gauntlet of the crowd. A booted kick to the buttocks sends her running off to the right of the screen. The camera follows her through the passageway that the crowd has made for her. As she goes, an officer lashes her across the buttocks with a riding crop. She runs off the screen as the camera turns back to catch another woman emerging from the doorway.

This continues for several minutes as one naked woman after another, mostly middle-aged but one or two young and attractive, are manhandled by the crowd. The youngest appears to be no more than twelve or thirteen, but she is handled as roughly as the rest.

The film cuts to a new scene. A naked woman sits on the edge of a pavement, one foot tucked under her, her other leg stretched out in the gutter. She is very attractive with high cheekbones and long thick hair. Fragments of her clothes lie on the pavement beside her. One leg of her knickers may actually still be on her leg – it's hard to tell. A group of men are gathered around her. Incredibly, rather than looking frightened, she looks defiant as though she were saying 'you men are so great – doing this to a woman'. Rudolf feels himself becoming aroused.

The film cuts again. Amidst a crowd a chubby, naked woman is spread-eagled over the top bar of a wrought iron railing. Two men stretch her arms out in front of her so that her abdomen rests on the railing while her white thighs and buttocks are to the camera. The angle is such that one of her breasts can be seen pendulous beneath her armpit. An officer with a riding crop in his left hand walks into the frame. He grins at the camera and raises the riding crop, waving it jauntily. Then standing on the far side of the woman and settling his feet like a golfer, he lashes her exposed buttocks with the whip. The men strain to hold her arms as her head of black hair jerks up every time a blow lands. Her breasts wobble every time she jolts. Rudolf's erection grinds against his trousers. He loses count of the number of times the officer lashes the woman, but at length he stops. By this time the woman's thighs and buttocks are black with blood. The officer turns to the camera, smiles broadly, holds up the riding crop and kisses its shaft. Suddenly he puts on a theatrical grimace and spits. He does this several times before pretending to get sick. Around him there are gales of laughter in the faces of the crowd. He turns again to the woman to find that the two men have let her arms go and she has collapsed onto the pavement. Two other men catch her by the arms and drag her off the screen.

The screen suddenly explodes into spattered white and the film rattles noisily off the sprockets.

Rudolf, his face flushed, is startled by the sound. The room goes dark and very quiet as the image on the wall dies. Then Ulrich rushes into the silence.

'My source can get more. He says there's much stronger stuff than this. Paul, why don't you go get some more drinks while I rewind this. I'm sure your boss would like to see it again.'

Chapter 14

There are other films, like those that Rudolf saw at the Christmas party, found from time to time. They are almost always viewed by the finders and then, when their contents are seen and realised, hurriedly destroyed.

In one such film, which has yet to be found, soldiers stand in groups, rifles hung on their shoulders. One group stands in a circle while one soldier lights the cigarettes of his compatriots using a shielded match. While many of these men are now dead, one or two are still alive, living out their old age in gentle retirement in prosperous post-war Germany or Austria.

The camera moves back from the men to reveal the scene in the foreground. Some people – both men and women – are undressing. A man with his back to the camera is removing his trousers. Two other men are bent over, their faces appearing strained, though it is unlikely to be only from their exertions. Amongst the men and in an area of ground carpetted with discarded clothes, a girl squats. She appears to be already naked. Her knees are together, arms in an X across her breasts, fingers on her shoulders. Her hair is dark, her eyes hooded by the position of her head. She stares directly at the camera, as though she is looking through it. The camera lingers on her. It is as though with the camera's lack of movement, it is trying to provoke a response from the girl. And eventually it gets one. The girl turns her head away. You can just see her eyes close before she buries her head as far as she can in her shoulder.

Satisfied, the camera moves on.

PART FIVE

Chapter 1

Lodz Ghetto.

NEW YEAR'S DAY, 1942.

*W*e *have lived through a long and terrible year in the
ghetto. Things which we have only known as concepts
have become for us a daily reality. Slavery. Public executions.
Starvation. Things which we thought had been consigned to
the dark days of human history are now with us constantly.*

*I write these words, but words are inadequate to convey
the story. Words come from a certain part of our psyche, a
part that is somehow rational, that deals with the thinking
processes. But the reality of this place could only be conveyed
by having lived it.*

*Last year I began praying again. Do I believe in God? I
don't know. I truly don't know. When we were still in normal
life, I was fashionably sure that I didn't. Now, I just don't
know. But I will do anything to try to get us through this alive.*

*Despite my best intentions, I have not written in this
diary for many weeks. I can blame only tiredness. No, it is
more than tiredness. It is weakness. Hunger weakness. There
are days when I wake and my body doesn't know how it will
get through the day. My mind has long since given up. Now
it is my body, operating on whatever energy it can eke from
the minute portions of food that we eat. We are starving to*

death. We know this. Let me tell the story of the bean. Last week our food ration contained a small quantity of some unidentifiable beans. We cooked them and unlike most ghetto food they felt nutritious. Next day I was in work when I felt the need to go to the toilet. I excreted and looking down in the toilet, noticed a full bean embedded in the stool. It's quite possible that in my rush to eat the food I failed to chew the first one or two mouthfuls properly. I am ashamed to say what I did next. I reached in, extracted the bean, rinsed it under the tap and ate it. I can still taste it in my mouth and no matter what I do the taste refuses to go away. This is what the Germans have brought us to.

We are all gaunt. I want to cry when I look at my beautiful family – Anna and Marek. What have I allowed to be done to them? At the end of November I went to the doctor. There was nothing he could give me. He had nothing. But I got permission to stay out of work for a few days. I stayed in bed and tried to sleep and get some energy back. I felt a little better after it. It was like that time earlier last year when I experimented with eating all my bread ration at one meal. I felt good after it. Full. Energetic, almost. Like I had actually eaten. I thought I had discovered the secret of living in the ghetto. But then I went so far downhill so quickly over the next few days before I got bread again that I realised I must never again put my body under such stress. Everything must be slow and steady and gradual. This way perhaps we will hold on.

We have adapted to sharing our room with two other people. They were horse owners before the war, and had a small place south of Lodz. They are always keen to talk, but neither Anna nor I are. Nor is Marek for that matter. When they first came, they were always bringing back the latest rumours, until one day Anna exploded at them. Ever since then we've all been more circumspect about what we say and I think *that's what's enabled us to manage. The woman talks to Anna mainly, while I talk to the man. I have to confess I quite like him. He is a great lover of nature. He is devastated by the loss of his land and his horses. The Germans took them. He let them, although he did think at first of killing the horses. He just couldn't bring himself to do it. He talks about his old place with such fondness that I feel I have been there myself.*

Anna has started working in one of the soup kitchens. The previous incumbent in the job died of starvation, and Anna knew somebody who knew somebody. That means that all three of us are now working because Marek got a job last summer, sorting scrap metal. It is a cruel job, especially in the winter. Our hearts break when we see his cut hands, or we notice a coarse habit he has picked up or we see him pulling his stick-like body out of the bed in the morning.

I have been writing all of this up to now because I fear having to write that which comes next. We heard the rumour first through the horse owner and his wife. Because of what had happened, they were reluctant to mention anything that even remotely resembled a rumour, but one night they seemed so unsettled we had to ask them, and they blurted it out. There were rumours that people were to be deported from the ghetto. We disregarded it because so much of what they had told us in the past had turned out to be false, but over the next few days, we heard it everywhere, and eventually I was able to check it in the ghetto administration.

It is true. There is a group called the Resettlement Commission who are already making up lists. It is being said that it is only troublemakers and people in the ghetto prison who will be deported, but this is no consolation. We fear every knock at the door now. It is the most worrying time we have had.

I have decided to stop writing this and put it away. It has all become too awful. All I seem to be doing is chronicling our slow but constant slide towards death. I have heard that there are some people who are writing diaries to record for posterity what is being done to the Jewish population of Lodz. Such an aim is laudable, noble, sacred would probably not be too strong a word for it. But I have no such grand aims. I just want us all to live, and this diary is serving increasingly as a reminder of how difficult that has become.

The ghetto, which up to now we have loathed with a passion, has suddenly become the dearest place on earth to us. They have stripped us of almost everything, but all we want is to try to live out the war and still be alive at the end. Our loathsome room has suddenly become like a palace, a haven. All we ask is to be left here and to try and get through in peace. We will work, we will starve, we will go dirty, but dear God, please don't let us be taken from here.

Chapter 2

Adolf Eichmann came to see Rudolf on the first Friday of the new year. It was just after lunch. Together, they took the stairs to the basement where there was a cafeteria. Eichmann ordered them both coffee and then went to find the lavatory. Rudolf waited, wondering what it was all about.

At a neighbouring table were two burly men, shirt sleeves rolled up, drinking coffee and smoking. Rudolf noticed that there were fresh bloodstains on one of the men's shirts, across the front where the man's chest strained against the fabric of the shirt.

'Any plans for the weekend?' asked the one without the bloodstains.

'Depends on this guy. If he talks we can wrap it up today. If not, I'll have to come in tomorrow. I'm not on duty this weekend, but you know how it goes.'

The man ground out the cigarette in an ashtray as Eichmann returned, his hands smelling of soap. He took a hurried sip of his coffee and glanced at his watch.

'As you will be aware from your statistical work, some movement of Jews is under way.'

He finished this sentence, paused and gazed at Rudolf significantly. Rudolf nodded.

'This is likely to increase over the next few months. It will also become several orders of magnitude more complicated as movements take place to and from a variety of destinations. My organisation has managed up to now, but we feel we need additional help to cope with the demands that are now to be placed upon us by the Fuhrer.

'We would like you to come and join us to deal with this increased workload. We want somebody who has a general familiarity with the current situation but somebody who is also a details person. We need somebody who can be responsible for a huge organisational effort but still not lose sight of the fact that because of some small detail the whole thing fouls up. We think you have this mixture of the strategic and the operational. Also we like your management style. Your team seem to like working with you. We've heard comments like "None of the usual hierarchical limitations", "complete access to you".

'What about Herr Doktor Korherr?' Rudolf asked. 'What does he think?'

'Between you and me, Rudolf – may I call you Rudolf – what the good doctor thinks is neither here nor there.'

Rudolf smiled. Eichmann pulled out a pack of cigarettes, shook it and flicked the packet in Rudolf's direction.

'Are you interested?'

Chapter 3

Normandy. The present.

'I kept going back to Poland and the Soviet Union. I wasn't really looking for her any more. I just wanted to go to these places. They seemed to exert a terrible hold over me. Morbid. Ghoulish, really. I went to places like Auschwitz and Majdanek. They have these photographic displays. I often wondered what I would have done if I had seen her in one of the photographs. At least I would have known, I suppose.

'I hated Stefan. Hated him for not having loved her properly during her life, and for not having taken more care of her, protected her. She was the dearest person to me. How different it might all have turned out if she had come to France.

'Then a letter came. From Poland.

> *Dear Katya,*
> *You probably don't remember me, but my name is Bronislaw Polonsky. I played the piano in a club in Warsaw before the war. You may have known me as Broni.*
> *I understand you are looking for news of the fate of Ariela Steinbaum. I may be able to help you.*
> *If you want to know more, please contact me at the above address.*
> *Very sincerely yours,*
> *Bronislaw Polonsky*

Chapter 4

Lodz Ghetto. February, 1942.

It is Anna who hears the crying first. With some difficulty she wakes David from a deep, exhausted sleep.

'What is it? Marek? Where is Marek?'

'Shhh, it's not Marek. It's a baby.'

'It's coming from across the landing,' he says.

Marek wakes, peeping out from under the bedclothes like a little animal from its nest.

'What is it?' he asks.

'We don't know. Your father's going to see what it is.'

'You'd think the mother would do something about it,' says David, sourly, pulling himself from the relative warmth of the bed into the icy, smelly air.

The crying has reached fever pitch by the time he reaches the door of the other apartment. The child shrieks hysterically, its voice alternating between terror-stricken screams to quieter crying while it gathers strength for another effort. David knocks loudly on the door, and after a cursory wait, tries the doorknob. The door swings open. Stepping inside he finds the light switch, and turns it on, conscious that he is breaking the law. The room is heavy with the smell of urine, excrement and boiled cabbage. A rumpled bed with a pail beside it and an ancient cot occupy most of the room. A woman lies on her side in the bed, her back to him.

Dishevelled blankets and sheets, crawling with lice, partially cover her. In the cot a tiny figure, wearing a soiled sleep suit, rolls violently, completely uncovered against the bitter cold that fills the apartment like a solid mass.

David picks the baby up. It looks no more than a few months old and stinks. Nevertheless, he holds it in his arms and begins to coo soothing noises to it. The crying immediately abates somewhat and David changes to a soft lullaby. As he does so he turns to the woman in the bed. As far as he can see she is fully dressed and has merely lain on the bed and pulled the blankets around her. Holding the baby in one arm, he reaches out to touch the woman's cardigan-covered shoulder.

The unyielding response tells him why the child is crying.

At the same moment, Anna appears in the doorway. David puts a finger to his lips, and continues to la-la-la softly to the child, as he carries it back to their apartment.

Enquiries fail to reveal any relatives of the dead woman. Indeed they fail to reveal anyone who had even known her. She was a strange, silent woman in life. She and the baby only arrived a month or so ago. David and Anna met her on the stairs from time to time, but she studiously ignored their greetings. Only recently had that changed when, in response to seeing them, she made a darting movement with her eyes, or a noise that sounded like a cross between an intake of breath and a giggle. They find her name and the baby girl's name – Rachel – in the Department of Vital Statistics. It turns out the father died at the turn of the year.

Anna is the one who says that they will take the infant in. It is the only thing to do, given that the alternative is an orphanage. They move the cot plus whatever baby things they can find, into Anna and David's part of the room. A search of the woman's personal belongings reveals nothing of value, except for her and the baby's ration cards and a photograph of the woman herself, smiling through lipsticked lips and wearing a straw hat. She had been very pretty. Anna pins it to the head of Rachel's cot.

For a reason that he can't explain or rationalise, David notices that having the little girl there has the effect of lifting all of their spirits considerably. The manner of her coming seems to have increased that tiny pinprick of light at the end of the tunnel. Perhaps, in one way, they will walk out of the ghetto with more than they came in with.

Their optimism lasts only until the first deportations begin. They continue through February and March. Ten. Twenty. Thirty thousand people are driven out of the ghetto. There is constant traffic on ghetto streets. Columns of people. In early morning darkness. Under the blue skies of spring. Whether in sun, in rain, in snow – capped, coated, muffled and booted. Thin faces and frames carrying suitcases, packages, home-made bundles. A man carrying a brown paper parcel and with a baby in his arms, huddled up in its cap, muffler and little coat. Many people wear their best clothes; it is still possible to gauge who might once have been well off before the ghetto. Over cobbles. Past arches. A group of teenage girls, all wearing their yellow stars, and looking like care-worn women in their forties. Those not for deportation stay well off the streets in case they get sucked into the maelstrom.

'Deportation to the east.' To work camps, some say. Polish farms. There may be food there. Either the debilitating hunger or the crippling fear of expulsion into the unknown could, by itself, be – and often is – enough to kill somebody. Together, though, they provide a terrifying cocktail, which the inhabitants of the ghetto are forced to drink to the dregs every day, only to find it refilled next day.

Chapter 5

March, 1942.

The child waiting with his parents in front of the Radogoszcz railhead in Lodz is mentally retarded. He is wearing his best clothes as though going on holiday. His parents sit protectively on either side of him. They seem to be trying to explain to him what's happening, though because they are out of earshot, it is a mime show. Now it appears as though they're trying to teach him a pronunciation. He tries several times and falters. 'Radogoszcz' could be the word, judging from their lips. Finally he gets it right. The mother touches his hair and gazes at him. Later, when the people start to move and there is shouting as the third class carriages are loaded, there is panic in his face.

Now that the 'deportation to the east' is actually under way, there is a minute lessening of dread amongst the railway car's occupants. They are still alive. Maybe what the Nazis said was true this time. Maybe it won't be so bad. Maybe it will be a farm. Maybe there *will* be work and food. Maybe in the outdoors – with the spring here that would be nice. Maybe. Maybe. Anyway, anything would be better than the ghetto. Or so they try to convince themselves.

Trees sway in the wind. There is blue sky with high white clouds moving swiftly across it. The sun comes out, warming the spring midday. But for the cars' occupants this raises new anxieties. The sun lies behind the train on the left side – to the southeast. If they were heading east the sun would be ahead, on the right.

The train begins to slow down. Several of the car's inhabitants recognise the spot. Kolo, a small town, 50km northwest of Lodz. The train slides into the small country station. A sign reads 'Platform 4'. It is one of the last normal, recognisable, sane, explicable sights they will see.

The noise of the brakes, squealing their way into Kolo station, startles a crow, perched on top of a telegraph pole. Lazily, it lifts its wings and launches itself into the air, flapping away. Even before the train stops, German police are springing onto the wooden steps of the railcars, opening the doors and returning to earth in one practised movement. The first harsh bellow of '*Juden, raus*' has already left their lips.

The train pulls past Platform 4 to the re-loading platform. Some Jews who have mistakenly thought that the train is going to stop at Platform 4, have already alighted and now they find themselves alone beside the moving train with the German police. This moment always amuses the guards – what the Jews have done could be classed as an escape, and the horror on the Jews' faces indicates that they realise this now. These first few Jews give the guards a chance to warm up, and they lay into them with truncheons, boots and fists. The first blood flows. The first people go down. A couple of guards join in kicking one of them until the train stops.

The train from Lodz stops beside a local train which runs on a narrow-gauge railway. The local train consists of twenty fifteen-ton, closed, freight cars and one passenger car. With much beating, swearing, kicking and shouting the Jews are rousted out of the Lodz train. A young boy of about twelve steps down, looking to right and left with hunted eyes. He turns back and extends a thin arm to a woman with a pack on her back and carrying a baby in her arms. The baby is

214

sleeping. She steps gingerly so as not to wake it. As soon as she reaches the ground she turns and scolds a smaller boy for not moving fast enough. He jumps from the top step. A small girl comes next, taking the steps one at a time, holding onto the safety rail until the last minute, leading with her thin right leg in sandals and white ankle socks. Finally, an even younger member of this family appears in the doorway of the carriage. However, this one refuses to move. People back up behind him. His mother pleads with him to step down but he shakes his head. She becomes first embarrassed, then anxious, then frightened. The people behind the small boy are shouting. After more fruitless negotiating she nudges one of the bigger ones to go and get him. He climbs the steps and gently starts to pull the younger ones' arm.

But now all of this has attracted the attention of one of the guards who has been standing at the other door of the carriage, dragging people down with his left arm and giving each a blow with his truncheon as they stumble to the ground. Some have fallen and these he kicks and flails with his baton until they crawl or are dragged out of range. Furiously he roars '*Schweine Juden!*' and strides towards the other end of the carriage. People scatter out of his way, though this is difficult in the narrow passageway between the two trains. The mother screams at her child but this only unnerves the child more and he grips the wall of the carriage while his older brother, standing with him on the top step, tries to coax him down. The people behind try to push past the two small figures and get onto the steps.

The policeman strides up to the door. The boy doing the coaxing looks around as if about to explain what he is trying to do. The policeman signals with his baton that the boy should step down, and the boy does this frantically, to get out of baton range. Quickly the policeman slips the baton into the brightly polished belt of his tunic, and reaches forward

215

with both arms. For an instant, the gesture has a fatherly or avuncular appearance, and in that same instant, the expression on the child's face changes to one of faintly pleasant surprise. He relinquishes his hold on the carriage and goes as though to extend his own arms.

He screams as the policeman seizes his ankles and jerks him out of the carriage doorway. He literally flies through the air. The policeman takes a step back and swings the terror-stricken child back to his left. The child's mother is frozen to the spot. It all happens so quickly she doesn't have time to respond. The policeman half swings, half throws the shrieking child forward, his body half a metre above the ground so that the back of his head crunches the steel springs of the railway coach. The shrieking stops instantly. The policeman lets the child fall from his grasp and he drops face down on the cindered earth to lie like a heap of rags between the two sets of tracks. His hair is covered in blood and the rear of his skull looks like it has collapsed. The Jews still in the carriage doorway look on in horror. The policeman pulls his truncheon again, and smashes it down on the steps of the wagon, roaring at the Jews to descend. Then, when he is happy that things are flowing again, he returns to the other end of the carriage.

The narrow-gauge railway takes the 800 or so people to the village of Chelmno. Here the unloading is repeated, except for those who died during the first unloading. The untidy crowd of people is assembled and herded towards an imposing building surrounded by a wooden board fence. There is a sentry box at a gateway through the fence. The Jews shamble along like a large crowd of tramps. There are constant blows and angry shouts. At the rear of the crowd as it moves along bodies start to appear. They lie on the ground as though they were the droppings of some phantasmal animal. But then some men are dragged from the crowd and driven back to bring up the bodies. The crowd straggles through the gateway into a courtyard. The sentries close the gate behind them.

An SS man bounds up the imposing front steps of the building, and turns to face the crowd.

'Jews,' he shouts. 'You have come here to work.'

A murmur runs through the crowd. Heads turn. Eyes meet. In hope. In relief.

'Everybody will work. But first you must take a bath and have your clothes deloused.'

A bath. That would be welcome. A *hot* bath would be an almost unimaginable luxury.

'We have trucks to take you to the baths.'

Trucks. This too is a luxury.

'Now come this way.'

The people flow up the steps of the building. A sentry at the door counts off 50 or so of them – families are kept together – and he lets them through the front door and into a long hall. Behind these he closes the door so that the rest must wait on the steps or in the yard.

In the hall, an SS man orders the people to undress. There is a door at the end of the hall, and people look towards it expectantly. They expect some sort of segregation of the men and women. The SS man shouts at them again to undress and to do it now. He also tells them that they must hand over their valuables to the Polish men with baskets who will pass among them. The Poles will take their names so that the valuables can be returned later. The men undress more quickly than the women. The SS man, seeing the hesitancy, begins to scream and lashes out at anyone within range with a leather whip. The undressing goes quicker now. A young child, only half awake, raised his arms over his head hesitant, shivering, swaying with drowsiness, while his mother removes his shirt. A blonde girl with glasses removes them and puts them into

217

a basket. The SS man watches her undress. Clothes soon carpet the wooden floor of the hall. The adults try to cover their privates, while the children are quite unselfconscious and a couple even play hide and seek amongst the adults' legs.

Now, the SS man tells them, this way to the baths. Behind him, in the long side of the hall, there is a door, and he opens this. With an angry impatience he indicates with his whip that they should come this way. The first naked bottom or two through the door he lashes to encourage the others. The rest respond accordingly, almost running in their eagerness to get past him. Parents interpose themselves between the SS man and their children as they go through the door. As soon as they are all inside the SS man follows them in, closing the door. Sometimes the Poles do this, but the SS man likes to do the first of the day himself. It shows those lazy Poles what standard he expects from them. The Jews have slowed again so he shouts and kicks the flabby arse in front of him. A lash across the thin back raises a vivid red weal.

On the walls of the staircase are signs saying 'To the Baths'. The SS man reaches the end of the stairs and roars another '*Raus!*' as they continue straight on along a passageway. His voice booms and the naked Jews pick up speed, so that they are now almost trotting. A few metres further on, the passageway turns right and now, he can see – over the bobbing heads of those immediately in front of him – that the leaders are jogging down a plank footbridge, onto the ramp and into the van. There is a further hesitation at this point, but a few further '*Raus's*, a '*Schweine Juden*' or two, plus some liberal application of the whip to bare buttocks quickly gets the entire crowd into the truck.

He strides forward and stands between the high board fences that enclose either side of the ramp so that those who come down the passageway have no other course but to go forwards down the footbridge and across the ramp. Neither can they look out to either side. The naked Jews look down at him with bovine faces. Several of them are breathless. One of the women is crying. An old man has a 'have pity' look on his face. There is no sign of the pretty blonde girl with the glasses; she has disappeared somewhere into the depths of the truck. The SS man closes the doors and padlocks them. Then he bangs loudly on them several times with the flat of his hand.

Hauptscharfuhrer Gustav Laabs sits in the cab of the truck. Laabs is glancing through a copy of *Berliner Illustrierten Zeitung*, and is smoking a cigarette. The banging confirms what Laabs has been keeping an eye on anyway through the rear view mirror – his truck has its complement of Jews. You first know that they're coming when you hear the shouts and cries coming from the cellar passage. Then you can usually see bare feet on the boards of the footbridge. Then once the shaking has died down you know that they're all aboard. The banging is the final confirmation.

Laabs jumps down from the cab and flicks the cigarette away. The lorry looks for all the world like a pantechnicon, a removal truck. It is a rectangular box mounted on the back of the lorry and painted green. The inside of the box is lined with sheet metal – zinc – and the metal floor is covered by a wooden grid like those found in a public baths. Laabs slides in under the truck and picks up a flexible metal hose. One end of the hose is connected to the truck's exhaust. The other he now couples to a fifteen-centimetre-wide nozzle underneath the floor of the truck. This nozzle connects inside the truck to a metal pipe, which lies under the wooden grid, and in which holes have been drilled. He checks that the connection is secure and then comes out from under the truck and returns to the cab.

He turns the ignition, starts the engine and guns it a few times. In less than a minute shouting and banging comes from inside the truck. Laabs gets out of the cab, reaches back inside for his magazine and walks over to a low stone wall. He sits down, lights a cigarette and checks his watch. By now, the shouting has developed into terrible screaming and animal groans. The truck rocks violently, and there is hefty banging on the rear doors.

By the time Laabs has finished two cigarettes, there is silence in the rear of the truck and the only noise is the steady throb of the engine. He closes the magazine and walks back towards the truck. Ducking under it again, he disconnects the hose and clips it back into its rest. Then he climbs into the cab. A German policeman appears a few moments later and climbs in the passenger door. Laabs releases the hand brake, puts the lorry in gear and pulls off.

The four- or five-kilometre drive to the forest takes less than ten minutes. The vans are not easy to drive, though. They are sluggish and don't turn easily. Laabs has heard that when they first started using these vans they used to try and do the gassing *while* driving the Jews to the disposal site. It was a good idea on the face of it – look at all that time saved. But the vans were too unsteady with all of the moving Jews on board, and apparently – it was before his time – there were several crashes where the van overturned and spilled out its cargo, some of which was still not dead. Now they take the slower but more certain way. Up ahead Laabs sees another one of the vans coming against him. For some reason it's already been up to the forest, which is strange because his was the first load of the day. They're late too. Somebody's going to be pissed off about that. The driver is Burmeister. He honks the horn and salutes Laabs. Laabs draws an index finger across his throat and points at Burmeister to indicate that the latter is in trouble. Burmeister grins, takes both hands off the wheel and shrugs. Laabs laughs. It's an easy-going command around here. They get the job done and that's all that counts. Burmeister will charm his way out of that like he

220

always does.

Laabs turns carefully off the road onto the rutted muddy track leading into the forest. He splashes through the deep pools of turbid water, the truck bouncing like crazy until he eventually finds the more secure track where they have spread gravel. The swaying of the truck stops and he drives through mature pine trees, the track curving and winding until he sees some figures up ahead. The trees slip back and the area opens out into a vast clearing. There are prisoners, a police officer and more guards with automatic weapons around the perimeter of the clearing. Laabs turns the van left off the track and into the clearing.

The place is for all the world like a construction site. A churned up pathway wide enough to take one of the vans, runs across the grass into the clearing and then turns right between two long pits. Prisoners can be seen working in the pits. They appear to be extending them. A tree stump lies in the path of this extension and several men are hacking away at the roots of the stump, trying to dig it out. The pits are a good 30m long, 10m wide and deeper than a man. More prisoners stand a few metres back from the police officer in a shabby huddle. There are about eight of them. Laabs drives towards where the police officer is standing and the latter guides him in. The policeman uses a gloved hand: 'come on – come on' and then as Laabs get closer and begins to slow, the policeman switches to his index finger, beckoning the van onwards. The passageway between the pits is quite narrow and with the ungainly truck and the relatively soft ground, Laabs is anxious not to let the truck's wheels drift too close to the edge. The police officer indicates 'stop' with his index finger upraised and then 'cut the engine' by drawing the finger across in front of him.

Laabs and the policeman occupying the cab hop down, and the latter goes round to remove the padlock. In the meantime, the police officer beckons to the prisoners who jog towards the van and round the back. Laabs and the two policemen take a few paces back from the truck. Laabs takes out his pack of cigarettes, offers them round and lights up all three men. They draw deeply and watch as the prisoners open the double doors gingerly. A man takes each door and the rest stand back, leaving an open space by the rear of the truck. As the doors open, naked corpses tumble out. They are still pink, but with a grey-blue tinge and their legs are covered in brown excrement and some with red blood. The corpses glisten with sweat as they drop in an untidy heap on the earth. A strong whiff of exhaust gases drifts across to the smoking men, and hangs in the air. All three draw on their cigarettes to try to replace the smell in their nostrils.

The place is remarkably peaceful. There is no birdsong, just the sound of the breeze in the treetops and through the grass. There is an air of quiet efficiency. The Germans don't even have to shout. A couple of the Jewish prisoners jump up into the back of the truck and begin to throw the remaining corpses onto the pile. Meanwhile more prisoners catch individual corpses by arms or legs and drag them to the edge of the pit. Here another Jew scans their fingers, necks and ears for any jewellery. Then he checks inside their mouths for gold teeth. Occasionally he reaches for a pliers, extracts a bloody fragment and drops it into a can. Having checked for teeth he then puts his fingers into the vaginas of women and girls checking for hidden items. He has less success here than with the teeth but he still finds things.

'That's the job to have,' remarks the policeman who accompanied Laabs.

They laugh. The prisoner checks all females – even children. Finally he turns the corpse over and checks its anus. When this is done he rolls the corpse over the edge where a waiting prisoner takes it.

There are two prisoners in the pit. Their job is to arrange the corpses face down, head to feet. Two children go into the pit. One is placed with its head against the earth wall and resting on the feet of a corpse underneath. The second child is smaller and by tucking its head between the legs of the first one, both fit no more than the length of an adult corpse. Laabs notes this tidiness approvingly. He remarks on it to the others – how every job, no matter how unappealing has its own skills that one develops and knowledge that one acquires.

'Are there many today?' asks the police officer.

'There'll be 300 anyway,' says Laabs, after a moment's thought.

'Jesus, that's five more loads. We'll be here all night.'

'Rumour is it's going to get worse. They're doing a big clear out of the ghetto in Litzmannstadt. You know the boss' aim – *ein tag, ein tausend* – one day, one thousand.'

'I don't know where we're going to put them all. We're going to have to find some place else. Either that or start burning them.'

'Any news of any leave?' asks the policeman who accompanied Laabs.

'I'm going,' says the police officer. 'This weekend.'

'Lucky bastard,' says Laabs.

'I wonder what's the second thing I'll do when I get home,' says the police officer.

It's the oldest military joke in the world, but they all laugh anyway.

The truck is empty now and it's time for Laabs and the policeman to take it back. Some Jews will hose it out and then it'll be time to go again. Laabs needs to take a piss. Most men do it on the spot or into the grave on top of the Jews, but Laabs is very particular about such things. He strolls off into the edge of the forest where the air is deeply tree-scented, relieves himself and returns.

Laabs carefully reverses the truck out. On the main road he passes Burmeister again coming in the other direction.

Back at the building in Chelmno, the next group are already undressing in the warm anteroom. Outside, in the chill of the late afternoon, about 150 people wait patiently. Dusk is starting to come on in the short day. The sky overhead is cloudy. The woman, whose child was killed by the guard at the railway siding, holds the broken body in her arms, and looks up. She can just about see the bare tops of trees above the walls that surround the courtyard. Her other children cluster around her and she can feel their small bodies pressing into hers. A flock of black birds float around the sky like fragments of black paper from a bonfire. In the villages, fires have been burning all day, but now thoughts are turning to preparing the evening meal. Yellow lights will be coming on in the villages. Home. Warmth. Food. Men on horse-drawn carts will be making their way home in the cold twilight. The wind waves the trees. It feels as if there will be a frost tonight. The murmur of a distant car or the occasional squawk of a bird are the only sounds that disturb the silence.

Chapter 6

On 2 April the resettlement is suspended. This raises spirits and optimism returns. Never mind, as David reminds himself, that they will be living the filthy life they have lived for nearly two years now. Never mind that many people have lost loved ones – gone to an unknown fate. The prevailing optimism seeks out a rosy view – they are indeed in work camps, or better still on farms. After the war, after the ghetto, they will be reunited. It is indeed heaven in comparison to the events of the last six or seven weeks.

Despite their efforts to enclose and isolate the ghetto, even the Germans, with all their power, cannot keep spring out. And so this year again there are signs of the change of season – tiny green patches of grass whose colour is so vivid it is almost painful on the eyes. Blue skies, which tempt with the promise of beaches, mountains, rivers, lakes. Warm suns on bony backs enclosed in layers of ragged clothes. Dry ground underfoot so that feet are not sodden and frozen.

Both David and Anna work, but Marek's job came to an end when a man with a family to support replaced him. As a result Marek spends most of the day in the room minding Rachel, or – now that the weather is improving a bit – playing with some other boys in the courtyard, while she watches from her pram. He doesn't mix easily. If none of this had happened, he would have tended to stick to himself and he still does. But if this means being in that awful room all day, then even shy Marek will go out. David has seen him with the other boys.

Sometimes Marek is in the thick of things, but equally often he is by himself, or isolated on the edge of the group. It upsets David to see his son like this, because David himself was like this as a boy. Of all the traits he would have wanted his son not to inherit, this would have been top of the list. How terrible then that this is the very one which has emerged.

Marek is nine but is so tall that he passes for twelve. It broke David's heart to see his son going out to work. Slave labour it may be, but for ghetto inhabitants, work – even this work – is infinitely desirable. Here again is the cruel cunning of the Germans. There are very few certainties in the ghetto, but one of them is that work offers some protection against deportation. For this reason, anyone without work – even a child or an invalid or an old person – stands out like a sore thumb. Thus, when Marek was working, when all three of them were working, they had some sense of stability. This was undermined when Marek lost his job, and this morning it collapses totally when – on his way to work – David reads a proclamation, posted on the ghetto walls, that anyone above the age of ten who is not working is to be subject to a medical examination.

For the rest of the day he cannot get the thought out of his head, and it gnaws at him and weakens him in a way that hunger never could. They could pass Marek as over ten but then he doesn't have a job. But the real question is if they are doing this for the over-tens, what of the under-tens? He knows too that Anna will have seen the proclamation, and he worries about her. All day David tries to analyse, to understand, to comprehend. Where did this proclamation – Proclamation No 374 – originate? Presumably in the German ghetto headquarters, there is some kind of master plan for the ghetto. This is the plan that determines who is deported out of the ghetto and who stays. This is the plan that decides the quantities of food, that arranges material for the factories and workshops, all the innumerable details which the Germans are so good at.

The Germans divide the population. This is one of the standard tricks they use and here they are doing it again. But the other part of the trick is that you never know the reason for the division, or which part – as a result of the division – is the 'right' part. The over-tens without jobs are next to be deported? Is this the decision? Or is it that the under-tens will go first and then the over-tens without jobs are to be next in line? Or does it depend on the results of the medical examination? Which slice of the ghetto pie is next to be devoured by the Nazi cannibals?

So somehow the decision is made – on what basis it is impossible to tell – and then the decision is passed to Chairman Rumkowski's ghetto administration who compose a proclamation. This in turn goes to the ghetto printing shop. During the early hours of the morning the announcement is posted on ghetto walls, so that people going to work can read about this latest depredation of their lives. These proclamations have immense power. While their authors think no more about them, in the ghetto these proclamations cause despair, unimaginable depths of human grief, physiological changes in people, and for some – who can no longer cope with it all – suicide. Such is the power of these yellow sheets of paper in the ghetto the Germans have made.

In due course, the medical examinations are carried out. Everyone examined is stamped on the chest with an indelible letter. There are sixteen different letters, eight for men and eight for women, though, as always, the significance of these letters is anybody's guess and the subject of endless speculation.

In May, the deportations resume, this time of the remaining Jews of Western Europe who were brought to the ghetto at the end of 1941. The harrowing scenes of separation and grief are repeated. These were the people who were told they were going east to work. They arrived looking not unlike holidaymakers, people going on a winter vacation. For several weeks they stood out from those Lodz citizens who had been in the ghetto from the outset. The newcomers had money and possessions which they could sell. Some are remembered, because, when they arrived, they asked if there were not hotels in which they could stay. No, there were no hotels. Indeed, because of these people, the ghetto schools had to be closed down, so that they could be housed. A few weeks of living like that soon sorted them out. In no time at all their western finery and possessions were gone, and they were no different from the Lodz Jews. Except that it was as though their western living had softened them. They died in droves over the winter, their death rate and suicide rate so much higher than that of the natives. We Polish Jews have lived with this fear of what the *goyim* can do to us for centuries, David ruminates. It's in our blood. The westerners had forgotten what that was like. Forgotten until now, that is.

There is a new angle to these deportations that hasn't occurred before. As they were boarding the trains, these Jews had all of their baggage and packages taken from them. They were deported in what they could stand up in. Where are they going to with not even their most meagre supplies and possessions?

On the edges of the ghetto, there are streets where the boundary of the ghetto runs along the street. In such streets the houses on one side are in the ghetto, those on the other are not, and a chain link fence separates the two. To live in these streets is to be on another plane of mortal danger. Here the German sentries will shoot without warning anyone whom *they* judge approaches too close to the wire. Sometimes, it must be said, this mandate is nothing more than an excuse for target practice. In a world of almost complete uncertainty, however, not everything is uncertain.

Approaching the wire is one of these certainties. To approach the wire is to die. In the twisted world of the ghetto, this certainty serves a useful purpose. If there are people who wish to commit suicide – and in the ghetto there are such people every day – then approaching too close to the wire is a guaranteed way of doing this. Provided the sentry is a decent shot, then it will be quick.

There is a phrase in the ghetto. 'I am going to the wire.' These are the words of somebody who has given up hope. They are words which have never been spoken in the Steinbaum household, but at the end of May, an incident occurs which causes them to be uttered for the first time.

A few kilometres southwest of Lodz is the town of Pabianice. Here, until recently, several thousand Jews worked in a ghetto employed by two German firms. On the Sabbath, 16 May, the Jews were ordered to assemble in front of the buildings where they lived. From there they were taken in groups to an athletic field in the town. They were placed in the centre of the field in a very small area, and segregated according to letters *they* had received during medical examinations. There was a small table with some German officers at it and each person in turn had to line up, approach the table and bare their chest so that their letter could be read. Some of the women especially were shy about doing this and if they were too slow, then they were struck by one of several Germans who stood to either side of the table.

Those people with the letter 'A' – *Arbeitsfahig* (fit for work) and those who possessed working papers were ordered to pass to one side, while the unfit, the aged, the sick, the children, and those marked with the letter 'B' were placed on the other side. The two groups were kept separated. Children were not allowed to go to the persons in group 'A', infants were taken from their mothers, children ran crying and screaming around the field looking for their parents. Parents pleaded with the guards to be allowed to take their children with them, but were pushed or beaten back.

They remained on that field until evening. It was a day of heavy rains and they were all drenched to the skin and parched with thirst. In the evening they were told they were leaving for the Lodz ghetto, while those unfit to work and those marked with the letter 'B', as well as the children, were loaded onto peasant wagons and taken away in a different direction, to an unknown destination.

It is Anna who tells David this story one evening after their bird-like meal, and when there is still some light left for them all to be outside before the curfew. It is a warm evening, the sky lemon from the sunset and with the promise of summer. She and David stand together on the edge of the courtyard, rocking a sleeping Rachel in her pram and watching Marek in the midst of a group of children. They are playing 'deportations', a ghetto game. Some of the boys play the Order Service men, while the rest are a family, some of whom have received deportation certificates and some haven't. Some members of the 'family' have small scraps of paper, and some don't. It is the Order Service's job to arrest those who have these papers and to march them across the courtyard to the gate. Here they all turn around and come back in again, where the roles are changed and the game played again.

Anna is sweating from hunger weakness, and wipes the cold perspiration from her brow with a cloth that was once a handkerchief. A woman who works with Anna has seen the Pabianice mothers lamenting the loss of their children. Anna sways slightly from dizziness. There is a zig-zag snake in her right eye like a black neon sign, which no amount of blinking or closing her eyes, seems to be able to remove. 'If that were to ever happen to me,' she whispers hoarsely – and David is struck by the word 'me' rather than 'us' – 'if that were ever to happen to me, I would go to the wire.'

230

Chapter 7

Berlin. May, 1942.

It was over a year since the night in Krynica when Rudolf had slept with his sister-in-law. 'Sister-in-law'. The phrase carried an aura of danger that excited him. 'Sister', with its undertones of incest, and 'law' when clearly what he had done had been unlawful – by traditional moral codes anyway.

Rudolf told Lisa he was working late and staying in town. Then he left work and went to Voss Strasse.

Ursula was just letting the last customer out when he arrived. She ushered him inside. He wandered around, looking at the various items and fingering them, while she did her cash. The lacy, filmy, satiny fabrics excited him.

'I'd love to see you in some of these things,' he said.

She continued to count some notes, then placed them in a pile, looked up and smiled.

'Just pick your favourite,' she said, and then, added after a pause, 'you'll have to buy it though. You can't wear these things once and then bring them back.'

'I'm not planning to wear it at all.' She laughed.

'Will you help me choose?'

'Just let me finish this.'

The following night, after the children had gone to bed, Lisa suggested that it was probably time to decide on holidays.

The North Sea was out this year with the war in the west, but maybe the mountains? Yes, that was fine with him.

'I was thinking,' said Lisa, 'I don't know what your reaction would be, but I was thinking of asking Ursula along with us. I think she's lonely, Rudolf. Yes, her business is successful but she doesn't seem to have many friends. She's got nobody to share things with. I was thinking that if you didn't mind, we would ask her along. She might meet somebody there, and she's easy company.'

Rudolf could hardly believe his ears, and it was all he could do to stop the wonderment from breaking out all over his face. Scarcely trusting himself to speak, he said: 'Yes, it's fine with me.'

They went in the middle two weeks of August. Ever since Lisa had proposed it, Rudolf had begun to fantasise about being in bed with both of them – two sisters.

The hotel gave them three connecting rooms with balconies which looked out onto a pine forest. Rudolf and Lisa occupied one, the kids occupied the middle one and Ursula the other. The weather was glorious. They sun-bathed, swam in a lake and played. Lisa looked pretty in a new white swimsuit she had bought in 'Ursula's Secrets', and Ursula had two, one green, one black, that she alternated. Both women turned heads by the lake, especially Ursula, with her tall, lithe figure. Rudolf found himself in a permanent state of stimulation and arousal. It was like falling in love except doubled because there were two women.

Ursula left the door into the kid's room open pretty much all the time and soon the five of them used the three rooms as if they constituted one large suite. Whenever Rudolf found himself alone with one or other of the women, he would kiss them passionately. The thrill of doing this with Ursula in her room, when Lisa might be in their room, and the kids next door, was indescribable. Every evening after Lisa had put Eva

232

and Viktor to bed, they drank and danced and talked.

A couple of days before their holiday was due to finish, Lisa took the kids off for an afternoon to buy some gifts for grandparents and friends. Rudolf declined to go along, saying he wanted to lie by the lake and finish his book. Ursula had gone into town earlier that morning, to see what shops similar to hers were doing and whether she could get any ideas from them. Lisa had been gone no more than an hour when Rudolf, engrossed in his book, felt a foot prodding him in the ribs.

'Must be an exciting book.'

He looked around and saw white shoes, tanned legs and a white dress, tied with a red belt. She looked down at him from behind sunglasses.

'Exciting enough,' he smiled.

'Do you want to come back to the hotel and read me a few pages?' she said.

They made love in her bed. Rolling apart afterwards, they lay on the tangle of sheets naked in the afternoon heat. Rudolf held his arm around her and she nestled her head in his armpit. When they had lain together for a perfunctory period of time, Rudolf said:

'We'd better get going. The others will be back.'

He went to get up but she put an arm across his chest.

'We've got plenty of time,' she said. 'I know my sister. Put her in any kind of proximity to shops and she'll be there for the day. Anyway, you can't just fuck me like that and then walk out.'

She often used the phrase during their lovemaking. Then it sounded like a prayer, an incantation. Here it sounded coarse. Not like the Ursula he knew. He made a pretence of relaxing, though now he was feeling quite anxious.

'Kiss me, Rudi. Here.' She touched her lips with her index and middle fingers.

He gave her a long, slow kiss, genuinely abandoning himself to it in the hope that this might be enough to satisfy her.

'Now here,' she said, caressing one breast and nipple with the same fingers. He complied.

She touched the other breast and nodded. He kissed it.

She rolled away from him, turning her bottom towards him. She reached an arm behind her, the same two fingers circling one cheek. Rudolf heard a sound in the corridor and almost jumped out of the bed. She glanced casually over her shoulder.

'The maid,' she said. 'Here.' She still indicated her bottom. 'Come on.'

The sound in the corridor receded. He heard a pail clanking and realised it was indeed a maid. It crossed Rudolf's mind that Ursula had decided that they should be found; that this was her way of making a play for him. She was going to end it all for him and Lisa and have him for herself.

'Come on,' she said impatiently. 'Kiss it.'

His mind raced. He could feel his heart pounding. What should he do now? He slid down in the bed and kissed her where she had indicated. As he did so, she rolled back, and slipped one thigh across the top of his head. The result was that his face now lay in her groin, inches from her vagina. Her fingers went to it, pressing and rubbing it.

'Now here,' she said in a voice that had suddenly become husky.

Rudolf kept imagining the scene if Lisa and the kids came in and found them here like this. He was ready to snap. The only thing that stopped him was that he didn't want Ursula getting the better of him like this. He kissed where she had indicated, inhaling the smells and feeling his withered penis stir into life again. As he did so she lifted her thigh across him once more, pivoted on her bottom with her legs in the air, and rolled out onto the floor.

'Better get going,' she said. 'The shoppers will be back.'

Rudolf had just put on his bathing shorts and was coming out of Ursula's room carrying his book, when he heard voices and a key in the door. He knew he didn't have enough time to cross the room. The door opened and Lisa and the kids came in, laden with parcels. Rudolf saw the happy expression on Lisa's face waver ever so slightly as she took in the scene. He held up the book.

'Ursula borrowed my book.'

He was surprised himself at how casually the lie came out. Whatever perturbation there had been in her face disappeared.

'Now, what did you buy?' Rudolf added, fully in control again.

The following morning Ursula apologised to Rudolf.

'I don't know what came over me. I must have been crazy. They could have come back at any time and then where would we have been? I think I just wanted to know what life would be like if I had you to myself, if I didn't have to keep looking over my shoulder all the time. Don't worry. It won't happen again.'

'You really had me worried there for a while,' he said.

Chapter 8

Lublin, Eastern Poland. June 1942.

Otto emerged from the showers wearing cork sandals and wrapped in a towel. Passing by the notice board, he stopped to see if there was anything of interest on it.

Command Lublin – Command Order No 60
(1) On Sunday, 7 June, Catholic services will be held by the army, once at 9AM, and again at 7:15 PM in ... that at both services there will be opportunities for receiving the sacraments.

(2) At 10 AM on Sunday, 7 June, 1942 on the playing field behind the soldiers' barracks, a soccer championship game will be played between the SS and Police Sports Club and the Wehrmacht 'Blue-White' team.'

Tomorrow. That might be worth going to.

As he sat on his bunk towelling his grey-flecked hair, he thought of Helga. He missed her a lot. In fact he missed female company. Some of the men had their wives and families with them. He had broached the idea with Helga by letter, but she would be involved in school for a few more weeks, and then there was going to be some kind of summer camp for the League of German Maidens. If the truth be known, he reckoned she was holding out for a marriage proposal. But Otto wasn't sure if he was ready for a move like that just yet.

As it turned out the day passed slowly, and he ended up doing nothing in particular. A *Wunschliste* came his way. A *Wunschliste* was a list of objects wanted by Germans and which would be taken from the Jews in a particular town or ghetto. He filled in his rank and name and looked across the top. Man's wristwatch, woman's wristwatch, pocket watch, clock, boots. He entered the numerals '1/40' under the 'women's boots' heading. He would get a pair for Helga, and he had specifically asked her size the last time he had been with her. He scanned the rest of the headings. Boots for boys and girls, women's galoshes, leather suitcase, portfolio, shopping bag, woman's handbag, wallet, change purse, raincoat, woman's coat, blanket, Afghan, man's long underwear – Jesus, who would wear a Jew's used underwear? – sport shirts, woman's umbrella, fountain pen, razor, strap, shaving brush, beauty cream, shaving soap, laundry soap. He chose a pair of men's boots for himself, '1/43', a pair of women's shoes, a wallet, a raincoat, a woman's coat and a woman's umbrella. Under the comments heading he wrote 'all goods, only if in good condition'.

In the mess that evening Otto made it his business to speak to Becker, the latest addition to his unit. The man was newly arrived from Germany. He was quite handsome, wore glasses and had a studious look about him. He seemed nervous, and stood by himself, a dead beer in his hand on the perimeter of things. His tunic was still all buttoned up.

'So, Becker, enjoying yourself?'

'They seem like a good bunch of people.'

'Once you get to know them you'll find they're the best.'

Becker's face went as though he were going to smile though none appeared. Then he lifted his glass to his lips, swilled the beer but returned all of it to the glass.

'Here let me get you a fresh beer.'

Becker blushed. Otto took the glass, cloudy with hand prints, away to the bar and returned with a foaming one.

'The work we do here is hard. The hardest. Oh, people say that because nobody is shooting at us that we are safe. But, I'll tell you Becker, I would rather fight the Red Army a hundred times over than do what we have to do.'

Becker took a gulp of his beer.

'We try to break you in as easily as possible. We will start you out on guard duty while these gentlemen' – Otto indicated with his forearm – 'do the work. It is up to you to say when you want to take a more direct part. If that is tomorrow fine, if it takes a bit longer then that's all right as well.'

'Thank you, Herr Oberscharfuhrer.'

'Now, drink up,' said Otto. 'To your new career.'

They clinked glasses before emptying them, Becker taking much longer than Otto to empty his.

Becker's journey had begun nearly two weeks earlier in Vienna. There had been all sorts of ceremonies and speeches to see them off. The Inspector of Vienna police had made a speech in which he had referred to the importance of the work that lay ahead and urged them all to fulfil their duty in enemy territory. The had sworn an oath of allegiance to the Fuhrer, uttered numerous '*Sieg Heils*' and sang '*Deutschland*' and the *Horst Wessel Lied*.

Then the Company Commander and the Battalion Commander addressed them in the barracks parade area. More '*Sieg Heils*'. A band accompanied them to the railway station. Becker remembered they played '*Alte Kameraden*' ('Old comrades') and '*Muss i denn, muss i denn, zum Stadtelein hinaus*'. He felt no sadness at leaving 'this little town'. He had spent all his life here and was glad to be going to foreign fields, to be lifting his eyes to new horizons.

They had a short job to do the next day. It began just after lunch in the garden of what had once been a convent. The location had been chosen for its privacy – there was a high wall all around the garden with a pair of high wrought iron gates out onto the road. Becker's job, along with another man, Wilhelm, was to stand guard outside the gate.

'It's easy,' said Wilhelm, cheerily. 'Just keep prying eyes away, while we enjoy the show ourselves.'

The Jews were brought by covered lorry, several of them in convoy, sweeping in through the gates. Becker and Wilhelm closed the gates again, pushing the bolt into its socket. The trench had been dug about 75 metres away on a lawn fringed with rose bushes.

'We've come to see the Jews.'

Becker spun round. Two women, one with a stubble of dark hair above her upper lip, the other with some browny-red traces of food around her mouth and on her cheeks.

'Go on, move along,' said Wilhelm, good-naturedly. 'You can't stop here.'

He winked at Becker.

'But we just want to see the Jews. We hate them as much as you do.'

'Move along,' said Becker, finding his voice. 'This is secret Reich business.'

The woman with the food stains cackled into laughter.

'Some secret,' she said, elbowing her friend. 'The dogs in the street are talking about what you people are up to.'

The first fusillade of shots echoed from inside the wall. Becker jumped, while Wilhelm involuntarily turned round. The two women took advantage of the moment of surprise to run past the sentries to the gates. They grabbed the railings and pressed their heads against the bars.

'Come on now, get out of here before we have to arrest you.'

Wilhelm sounded stern. The two women ignored him. He

signalled to Becker and the two men pushed the women away from the railings with several solid shoves of their rifle butts. Wilhelm managed to deliver a kick to the moustachioed ones rear as she waddled off.

'Now, fuck off, you old cows' he said, 'and don't come back.'

Becker looked up and down the road as another fusillade rang out. Apart from the two women, there was nobody else around. He looked through the railings in time to see the puffs of smoke over the trench diffuse into the air. Another group of Jews came forward, naked girls and women. They knelt facing the ditch. A man stood behind each one. An order was given. The shots cracked and the people leant forward as though about to be sick, before tumbling into the ditch. Becker saw that it was Otto giving the orders. Otto also walked along the edge of the ditch with a sub-machine gun firing shots into it.

When a pause came in the firing, Otto left the trench and came towards the gate.

'Ah, here comes the Oberscharfuhrer,' says Wilhelm. 'He'll be wanting to know if you'd like to give it a try?'

'Have you done it?' Becker asked Wilhelm.

'Oh sure, it's not too bad. The first day is the worst. After that you hardly think about it.'

'Everything under control here, Becker?' Otto asked from inside the gate, his hands behind his back. He had put a large carmine rose in the buttonhole of his tunic.

'Yes sir.'

Otto acknowledged the reply silently but continued to stand there.

'We moved some civilians along,' Becker threw into the silence.

Again a silent acknowledgement.

They heard more trucks. Wilhelm and Becker went to open the gates. As the first truck turned in, Otto uttered a sort of snort and turned back towards the trench. When the trucks had passed through, and they were closing the gates, Wilhelm said: 'You should have said you would do some shooting. That was why he came over. Didn't you realise?'

'It's too late now, is it?'

'For this time. It'd only throw things out if you went over now. Wait until the next lorries come.' As an afterthought, Wilhelm added, 'It's best to get it over with, you know.'

As the empty lorries were leaving, Becker asked if Wilhelm would guard the gate. Then he went inside and walked slowly over to where Otto was sitting down on the edge of the pile of excavated earth having a smoke. Becker saluted and only then did Otto look up.

'Ah, Herr Becker,' he said, surprise in his voice.

'I would like to take a turn at … here … at the shooting.'

'Of course. Let me see if we can accommodate you.'

Otto issued some commands and immediately a different man made his way to the gate.

'Now then, Becker. Behind the trench with the other marksmen. Then we will wait for your first customers.'

Trying not to look into the trench Becker skirted round to where Otto had indicated. The ground was mushy at the lip of the trench with small ponds of blood in the depressions caused by repeated sets of feet. Becker noticed some long greying hair attached to a piece of scalp.

A voice said 'here they come' and Becker saw the gates swinging back and the first truck appearing.

Otto got a couple of days off duty. There was not much he could do with them. It wasn't enough to get back to Germany. The fine summer weather turned wet, the evenings grey and green. He hung around and was first into the mess when it opened. Generally he was by himself for a couple of hours. He could hear the reason for this faintly in the distance where shooting continued each evening from between six and eight.

Chapter 9

Normandy. The present.

'Broni had been arrested as a spy when the Red Army liberated Belorussia. They had sent him east and kept him in a labour camp in the Gulag. He was there for about ten years and then they released him. He made his way back to Poland. He was still imprisoned in Russia when I found Stefan. That was why I wasn't able to find Broni. He got my address from Stefan.

'As soon as he wrote to me I went to see him. He met me at the railway station. He held a sign up so that we would recognise each other. We wouldn't have otherwise. He was in his forties but looked much older than I had expected. Much, much older. He still had the big construction worker's build and the badger haircut – except now he was a grey badger – and those impossibly stubby fingers.

'He'd stopped playing jazz – the regime regarded it as decadent. You know, there's so much about Eastern Europe that would break your heart. After all the effort and suffering those people put in – the Russians especially – to be taken over by another totalitarian regime. Anyway, his hands had been damaged in Siberia. The best he could do was to play the piano in a hotel for westerners, you know playing kitsch music.

'So if we've both met him then we both know the story?'

'Yes, but you heard it nearly 30 years ago. I only heard it a few weeks ago. Presumably it was fresher in his mind back then.'

'You're probably right. So let me tell you what he told me.'

Like the rest of Warsaw, I was woken on the first of September by the sound of aeroplanes and bombs falling. There were already great plumes of smoke above the buildings. Overhead, between the roofs, you could see the black shapes of German aircraft like crosses against the blue morning sky.

My first thought was for Ariela. I had no family – the band was the closest I had to one. You could say that at that time Stefan and I were rivals for her. But that would mean there was some kind of contest going on, and there was no contest. She was his girlfriend. I just loved her – from a distance, I guess.

I knew that her family were in Lodz and I wondered if she had already gone down there. I hadn't seen her for a while. We weren't playing just then – with all the talk of war, nobody seemed to want to listen to jazz. I had been trying to stay out of her way – it only upset me when she was around with Stefan there. I had heard rumours about the two of them going off to Paris, but there was nothing definite as far as I knew.

The word was that the Germans planned to take all the men for forced labour. That wasn't for me. I was already packed and ready to leave Warsaw. But that wasn't my main concern. My main concern was that she was Jewish.

I'm not much interested in politics but I had been in Germany when I was seventeen. A school band thing. There was some kind of anti-Jewish rally near the hotel where we were staying. The noise was like you'd hear from a football stadium. But not the kind of cheers or groans that you get at a football match. These were people baying in hatred – like a lynch mob. I went out in the street afterwards to watch people coming away from the rally. They looked changed. Kinda crazy. I knew then that if the Nazis stayed in power the Jews would be in for it. And the Nazis had ripe territory in Poland where there was a lot of anti-Jewish feeling already. We had had our own boycotts of Jewish businesses and victimisation of Jews and even small pogroms.

I knew things could only get worse when the Nazis arrived in Poland. The Russians are dogged, as I found out, but the Germans – the Germans are thorough. If they say they are going to do something, then they do it. Of course, nobody could have predicted the things that they actually did.

I knew where she lived – I had never been there but I knew her address – and I wanted to make sure she was safe. It didn't strike me that I was being particularly brave. It was only as I was going over there that the idea entered my head that she might come with me. Once that occurred to me I was hardly aware of the bombs – I began imagining the two of us on the road together travelling east. We would be a duo, me playing the piano, she singing. It was a fine fantasy.

There was no answer when I knocked on the door of her apartment. There was quite a lot of bomb damage in the area, and I thought maybe she had tried to go home, or had gone to Stefan's place or that the pair of them had already left Warsaw. Maybe they had gone to Paris. I sat down on the step and waited for a while but there was no sign of her. I had given up and was going down the stairs when I saw her, a couple of flights down, coming up against me. She appeared to be by herself and I was surprised by this.

'Broni!'

When she saw me she bounded up the last few steps and

hugged me.

'I'm so glad to see you.'

Her eyes were red from crying.

'Is Stefan not with you?' I asked. Like any jealous lover I was trying to show up my rival.

'No. I was out trying to phone my family in Lodz but I couldn't get through. I just came back to get some things. I really don't know what to do. Whether to go to Stefan's or try catching a train to Lodz.'

'Don't even think of it. The Germans will be coming from that direction. Who knows how close they are already. You'd be trying to cross a battlefield.'

'But what about my family?'

'They're all there together. They have each other. You're here by yourself.'

'Apart from Stefan. I'd better go to his place then. What are you doing?'

'Well, they say the Germans will take all the men for forced labour. I'm not staying around for that. I was going to go east – Lwow, Zhitomir, maybe Kiev.'

'Kiev's in Russia!'

'I know that! You should really think of going east yourself. Jewish people aren't exactly the Nazi's favourites.'

'I must pack and then I'll go find Stefan and see what he's doing.'

'I'll come with you, but we have to hurry. Who knows how close the Germans are.'

'But what about Russia?'

'I'll start later on today.'

She went into her bedroom and began to pack a rucksack. She left the door open and I saw that she packed a heavy coat and changed into walking boots. Then she threw a few other bits and pieces into the bag along with two photographs that stood on the table beside her bed. Then she went to the kitchen and began packing food from the cupboards.

We found Stefan late afternoon in an air raid shelter near to where he lived in Zoliborz. I was surprised he hadn't come looking for her. Always the performer, he was playing loud tunes on the sax, trying to drown out the noise of explosions outside. I told him what I had heard about forced labour. He said he would go east too until it became clear how things were settling down under German occupation. Ariela was prepared to do whatever he was doing. Once he was there her attitude towards me changed. It was almost like I wasn't there as she fussed over him. That hurt a lot.

There was still a few hours of daylight left by the time he had packed and we were ready to get on the road. We hitched a ride on a passing truck, and this took us towards the centre of town. There was a lot of damage – buildings crumpled to matchwood and rubble, craters, an overturned tram. Bombs were still falling over towards the city centre and the sky was obscured by drifting smoke. Explosions and the bells of fire trucks filled the air. We crossed the Vistula and the driver pulled up at the Wilno railway station. The truck was going to Vilna – we toyed with the idea, but decided to head due east. A kilometre or so and we were in Kamionek and on the road for Siedlce.

What were we thinking? A mixture of things, I think. Stefan was showing off. Fearless. The leader. That sort of thing. Ariela was pensive – is that the word? She was worried about her family. At first this was all she could think about. But then as we all got more caught up in our own situation she seemed to put those thoughts to the back of her mind. I was on cloud nine just to be with her. That was all I had ever wanted. Even though she hardly noticed me and he was there.

The roads were mayhem. Thousands of people, many of them Jews, trying to get out before the Nazis arrived. It was about 200 kilometres to Brest Litovsk, and it was going to take us at least a week to get there. There were German planes around, but high up. They didn't seem too concerned with us. That first evening we stopped once it was dark, and found a grassy spot just off the road. We had dinner of some bread and sausage and cheese, and then we slept covered with our coats. The weather was still mild and the night wasn't too cold. She and Stefan slept together under their coats. I stayed as far away from them as I could.

The next day Stefan wasn't half as cheery as he had been the previous day. I think he was starting to realise what he had got into. She spent the day trying to cheer him up, but he was really sour. Towards late afternoon, a German plane appeared. But he wasn't flying high like the others. Instead he swept down and came along the road flying east so that everybody had their back to him. Then he opened fire on us. They put big bullets into machine guns on planes that are meant for shooting down other planes, not for skin and bone. Everyone scattered off the road, but after he'd strafed the road another couple of times he began to do the verges. I don't know how long he kept this up. I guess it was until he'd run out of ammunition. Then he cleared off.

Even while the noise of his engine was still fading, you could see that there'd been terrible carnage. I remember there was a horse with its guts hanging out, trailing along the road. There was a man with a child in his arms. A little girl. Limp like a doll. In the grass by the side of the road were bodies, rolled off the highway like sacks of corn fallen off a lorry. People had awful, gaping wounds. There was blood everywhere.

I remember thinking at the time how different it would be if Stefan got killed and she and I were able to continue by ourselves. That's a terrible thought, I know. I think that of the three of us I was the least afraid. I didn't want to die because then I would no longer have been able to be with her. That was my only fear.

247

Everyone was too shaken to go on. Even though there was still a few hours of daylight, we pulled off the road into the shelter of a wood. I could see then that Stefan was in a bad way. He was shaking. She was trying to comfort him. It was ages before he managed to speak.

'This is madness. I'm going back. I'd rather take my chances with the Nazis than die out here. We haven't come too far. We can make some ground while there's still light and be back in Warsaw by lunchtime tomorrow.'

'Ariela can't go back,' I said.

'Why not?'

'She's Jewish. You know how the Nazis will treat her.'

'Bullshit. Once the Germans have settled in there won't be any problems. They'll want to hear good music. Alright it mightn't be jazz but there'll be a good living to be had under German occupation.'

'He's wrong, Ariela. Don't believe him.'

'But what about my family? I should be back with them. It was stupid of me to come here.'

'Ariela, he doesn't care about you or your family. He just wants to save his own skin. Look at him. Do you really think he's worried about you?'

It all came out. All the resentment I felt because she loved him and not me. I just let it all loose. She saw it too. I wanted to stop but I couldn't. Eventually, I stormed off, saying that I didn't care, and that the pair of them could please themselves. I don't know whether I was in shock myself after the strafing. I went off deeper into the woods and sat on a tree trunk not knowing what to do. I wondered whether I was really worried about her or whether I was just trying to drive a wedge between them.

I stayed there until it got dark. I realised I'd left my pack with all the food in it back with the two of them. I was suddenly very hungry and didn't want anyone else making off with it. I went back through the woods to the edge of the road. The crowd had settled down but it seemed much thinner. There was a lot of muffled weeping. Unlike the previous night there were no fires.

I found her just where I had left her. She was sitting on the ground with her knees raised and her arms resting on them, staring at the ground. There was no sign of Stefan. I asked him where he was. At first she didn't answer, but then I knelt beside her and asked again. She was crying, and she just said the one word: 'Gone.'

'What happened, Ariela? Tell me what happened.'

It took her a long time to reply.

'I asked him what if it was true what you were saying about my being Jewish. About what the Germans would do. He said he could fix it. He had friends. They could get me false papers. Or I could go into hiding … It suddenly dawned on me that he was just making it up. None of these things were true. There were no friends or false papers. He didn't care about me or what happened to me. He just wanted to save his own skin. If we'd gone back there and there had been any problem with the Germans, he'd have just walked away from me like he did tonight … I don't know why I ever got involved in any of this.'

I didn't know what to do. There was a part of me that was overjoyed. But I had never wanted to see her like this. She was devastated. And she seemed to be blaming me for her situation as much as she was Stefan.

I got some food ready but she refused to take any of it. When I tried to cover her up with her coat, she just shook it off and told me to leave her alone. I stayed awake most of that night, keeping an eye on her. She just sat like that until some time near dawn. Then she just lay down on her side and fell asleep.

For the rest of that journey she said almost nothing. She

was exhausted but every time I suggested stopping to rest, she just said, no, that we should carry on. The planes became less, the closer we got to the border, but even when one did appear, she acted as though she were oblivious to them. She would turn slowly off the road and walk with the same calm walk. I used to have to push her or drag her to get her into cover. I tried to lie beside her to protect her with my body, but she pushed me away. And that was how we made our way to Brest.

By the time we got there, all our food was gone. We were exhausted and wet from sleeping in ditches and hadn't eaten anything in a couple of days. Add to this, periodic attacks by the Nazis and we were a sorry sight. We trudged through the city wondering what to do. It was thronged with refugees, so there was no question of us being able to find work or anything like that. There was a soup kitchen and we managed to get something there. That was how we got through the next few days. We tried to save some of the bread we got with the soup, but we were still having to sleep rough, and the weather was starting to turn very cold.

We had to get out of Brest. There were too many refugees there with more flooding in all the time. There was too great a strain on the resources of the town. We had to go further east, where hopefully the number of refugees would have thinned out somewhat. At least this was what I thought – she was taking no part in the decision-making.

The next big city eastwards was Minsk, but that was 350 kilometres away. Anyway, it didn't seem to make sense to go there because that was where everybody would go once they'd caught their breath. I studied a map she had brought. There was a secondary road that led north-west out of Brest. I decided to take it and that was how, I don't know how many days later, we came to Slonim.

We had stopped the night before about 15 kilometres short of the town. There were still refugees on the road –

mainly Jews – but the number had thinned considerably. People were starting to die by then. Every day we would see bodies or what looked like makeshift graves by the side of the road. Most of us were beginning to starve, but it just showed how afraid the Jews were of the Hitlerites. It made me more confident in what I was doing.

We started out that last morning of our trek in pouring rain. It had started during the night, and so we were already wet and freezing by the time we got going. We trudged on in silence as we had done every day since Stefan had left. The trees were deeply into their autumn colours. The wind swirled leaves and rain around us. We had been going for about an hour, when I heard her say:

'Look – a bird.'

Sure enough, a black shape was blown across our path, before it flapped its wings and soared off on an air current.

'If the birds are out, that means it's going to stop raining,' she said.

It was like that moment on Columbus' voyage when he sees birds – or is it a branch floating in the water. I can't remember which. Anyway, she was right. The rain gradually eased off, and as it did, more birds started to appear. One or two at first, and then a little squadron. Finally, the rain stopped, the clouds parted and the sun came out. She hadn't said any more since we'd seen the first bird, but when we felt the warmth of the sun, she turned to me and her face broke into a smile. No words. Just a smile.

The sun became quite hot, so much so that we started to steam. We could feel ourselves drying out by the time we picked up the first houses on the edge of town. They were mostly wooden, all with neatly tended gardens filled with riotous growth. Apples, chestnuts, potatoes, a courgette plant trying to escape under a fence, flowers. We passed a house with a small orchard in the back, and there was a Jew wrapped in a white and blue prayer shawl, standing amongst the trees, his eyes closed, chanting softly. Further into the town, almost the first sound I heard was that of somebody getting piano lessons. I heard the sounds coming through an open window, and whoever it was didn't sound too bad. You can imagine a town like that is going to leave a good impression on me.

'Yes, of course, after Broni told me about it, I had to go to Slonim. It took me a couple of years to arrange it. I don't know if you can imagine what it was like in those years. The people had finished with the Germans and now they had the Russians. Nobody would talk. Everybody thought I was from the KGB or whatever they were then. I was arrested at one point by the local police and interrogated. Eventually I managed to convince them of the harmlessness of my search.

'I had a photograph with me, of her with the rest of the band. It was a promotional one that the nightclub owner got done. It was all I had. I just walked around from door to door showing it around, asking if anyone remembered them. Eventually I found somebody. A Jew who had hidden during the entire Nazi occupation. He said they had stayed with a woman who lived further up his street. The woman, who was also Jewish, had been killed by the Nazis. If they had been staying with her there was a fair chance that that was what would have happened to them too.

'There were three mass killings in Slonim. In July 1941, November 1941 and June 1942. The first and last were at Petrolevits, 5 miles from Slonim, the second Chepilovo. The Nazis killed over 21,000. I went out to these sites. I wondered whether this was where she had spent her last hours. Or was she still alive somewhere in Russia?

'It was the end of the line for me. The trail died out and with it the hope.'

Chapter 10

Days pass. For David, Anna, Marek and Rachel, an endless round of twelve hours a day, tottering home, starving while eating, and nights with filth, bedbugs, flies and cockroaches. All four of them are losing strength, dreaming, waiting, counting. Late August brings a heatwave with temperatures reaching into the forties. 30 August is the hottest day of the year. David is told that it is 45 degrees.

1 September. The third anniversary of the start of the war. Ella's birthday. Marek has made a wonderful discovery. In a corner of the courtyard, underneath a rotted pile of hay, he finds a bucket. Out of the bucket, like alien tendrils, climb the death-green shoots of potato plants. It is a rusty bucket of seed potatoes, discarded, forgotten, whose seeds, oblivious to the goings on in the ghetto, have sprouted and have been doing their best to find the light. Unfortunately, due to the dampness of their environment, the potatoes have also rotted so that the tendrils climb up out of a black, malodorous, oozing bed.

Despite all of this Marek drags the stinking bucket home and up the stairs. (The bucket is not particularly heavy – in other times he could easily have carried it.) As he does so some neighbours pass him on the stairs and look enviously at his treasure. The stench of the bucket fills the whole room. Nonetheless when Anna comes home she works her way through the rotten mess salvaging, washing whatever she salvages and managing to cook something from the result. The smell remains in the patties she makes and it is hard to get them under your nose into your mouth. But they make a small additional impact on the shrunken bellies in which they lodge.

Later that night all four of them are sick, and the rotten potatoes, along with any other food they had, is scattered over the bed, the floor and Rachel's cot.

Chapter 11

August, 1942.

Rudolf Fest likes to keep a clean desk. His only conces-
sions to this policy are a heavy brass inkwell from which
he fills his fountain pen, a black telephone and a calendar
which he uses in conjunction with a heavy gold wristwatch.

It is Monday and he is in early. From his briefcase, he
extracts some papers that he was working on over the weekend, a note pad for any thoughts he may have during the day
and his fountain pen. He unscrews it, checks that it is full of
ink, and then works briskly through the papers, transferring
them from a pile on his left to a pile on his right. He writes
on some of the documents. Many he throws in the bin. By
8:45, when his secretary comes in, he has already cleared the
left hand pile and hands her the right-hand one, in exchange
for the cup of rich black coffee.

First on the agenda every Monday is the weekly operations meeting. This morning they begin, as always, with what
used to be Poland.

'Shall we begin with the Warthegau, Erich. Let's see the
graph for Lodz.'

Erich Grunberger is Rudolf's man in charge of Poland.
The other three people seated at the circular conference table
are Karl Ebermayer, in charge of Central Europe – the Reich
itself, Czechoslovakia, Austria, Elsbet Seetzen who deals with

255

Western Europe – France, the Low Countries – and Rudolf's secretary, Viktoria, who will take minutes. Erich passes Rudolf the chart and begins to talk.

'As of 1 July there were 102,546 people in the Lodz ghetto. At 1 August there were 101,259. As you can see the figure has been steadily dropping since February. With the winter in the offing, I don't think any action is required at the moment.'

Rudolf, who has been half listening while studying the chart looks up.

'I'm not sure I'd agree, Erich. This rate of descent has been slowing steadily. Your point about winter is well taken but that's a long way off. We've been rather stubbornly over 100,000 here for the last few months. I think it's time we took a bite out of it. If only to make room for more people from the Reich, eh Karl?'

'I'd have no complaint with that. If the people and resources are available, let's do it now.'

Erich colours slightly. Despite Erich's expertise, Rudolf still likes to show him who's in charge. Trying to recover, Erich says, 'Chelmno may not be available. That's why we didn't do anything about this up to now, if you recall.'

'Yes, what was the status of that?'

'Last time we checked, they were hoping to be back in business early in September.'

Rudolf likes Erich – he is businesslike and to the point. Not like Karl, Mister Bombastic, as Rudolf privately thinks of him. Ask him the time and he'll tell you how to make a watch.

'Right, so you'll have to check that, Erich. What reduction should we be looking for?' Rudolf asks the table in general.

'25,000,' says Karl, with the voice of somebody at a gaming table.

'That won't work,' explains Erich, his methodical manner re-emerging over his annoyance. 'Lodz is the biggest work ghetto in the Reich. We can't reduce its workforce by 25 per cent, just like that.'

'But they're not all workers, are they?' asks Rudolf.

This time he didn't mean to catch Erich out. But he has genuinely overlooked this detail.

'No, I suppose not,' mutters Erich. 'But there's still the capacity at Chelmno.'

'Mmmm,' murmers Rudolf. 'Right, look, let's say this. First check to make sure that Chelmno's back in business. If it is, then let's get Lodz down to 90. No workers. Just old people, children, the sick, that sort of thing. And we'll review it again say, mid-September.'

Viktoria begins to write this down in shorthand.

Rudolf says 'Very well, what's next?'

Chapter 12

Lodz Ghetto.

The first inkling anyone has is that notices appear on ghetto walls around lunch time. 'At 3:30 in Fireman's Square, the Chairman and others will speak about the deportation.' A hot afternoon. People would normally have been queuing for their meagre rations. Trying to get through another day. Trying to draw some heat or strength or comfort from the fine weather as the sunshine made the smells of food and sweat and bodies and too many wearings rise from their clothes.

Normally. But today is not normal.

An empty stage. A crowd of about 1,500 people pressing closer to the stage. But more than that pressing to the left where the slowly sinking sun yields precious extra inches of shade. The firemen and the Order Service act as stewards pushing the crowds away from the stage and out of the shade.

It is 4:45 when the Chairman steps up onto the stage in the company of other ghetto officials. He seems to be moving with some difficulty.

'A grievous blow has struck the ghetto.'

The crowd tenses as though an electric current has passed through it.

'They are asking us to give up the best we possess – the children and the elderly.'

A monstrous wailing arises from the crowd. It moans and

sways as though in a harrowing communal madness.

'I was unworthy of having a child of my own, so I gave the best years of my life to children. I've lived and breathed with children. I never imagined that I would be forced to deliver this sacrifice to the altar with my own hands. In my old age, I must stretch out my hands and beg: brothers and sisters, hand them over to me! Fathers and mothers, give me your children!'

Rumkowski continues his speech. How he had no choice. If he hadn't consented the Germans would have done it themselves as happened in Warsaw. That he was asked for 24,000 but got the number reduced to 20,000. How 'the part that can be saved is much larger than the part that must be given away'.

It is an astounding, staggering speech. Here in this sun-drenched square with its crowd of ghosts who will never – for the rest of eternity – never sleep. Never rest in peace. Not after such a speech as this. The man's motives have been questioned. As has his sanity. But more basic questions arise. Do Jews love their children less? Or East Europeans, perhaps? How is such a speech possible?

No, it is not possible. Surely the Germans will come along. Say it was all a joke. A ghastly joke to further torment the residents of the ghetto. Even the Germans would not do this. Even for them there are lines they would not cross. And this surely is such a line.

'We all will go,' people shout. 'Mr Chairman, an only child should not be taken; children should be taken from families with several children.'

The terror in the square builds like a thunderstorm.

The work has begun long before the Chairman gave his speech, and will continue right through the nights and days ahead. From the Resettlement Commission notices are sent by messengers to the individual Order Service precincts for execution.

Chapter 13

4 September 1942.

In the west beyond the ghetto fence, the sun is setting in a smoky red haze. Its mellow light settles affectionately on the roofs and chimneys of the ghetto. It is a warm evening with some lingering vestiges of summer. Down amongst the ghetto roofs in a courtyard five children are playing. Three boys and two girls, all with tightly cropped hair. Their yellow stars are vivid in the drabness of their clothing and their surroundings. They are hunched in a circle and one of them picks at the earth with a stick. They talk softly. With long comfortable silences. There is none of the rowdiness that marked their earlier play. One of them says something and they all smile. They are tired, hungry. They are weak. They are planning what they will do tomorrow.

The sun sinks low enough to throw the courtyard into shade. It is several minutes before the children become aware of the chill in the air. When they do so they gather up various objects lying on the ground, stuff them into their pockets and stand up.

'See yah.' 'See yah.'

Marek Steinbaum moves at a conspicuously slow pace across the bare earth of the courtyard and in through the doorway to the stairs that leads to his apartment. Whatever little food there is and then to bed. He is too tired for anything else. He climbs the stairs slowly. On the landing halfway up he has to stop and sit down, until his breathing eases and the cold sweat on his body warms slightly. Then his stick-like legs in their short trousers continue the climb.

Almost as soon as he walks in the door he realises there is something wrong. There is none of the evening bustle of preparing their bird-like meal, even though Rachel gurgles cheerily in her cot. Both his parents sit at the table, looking pale as ghosts; as corpses.

'What's wrong?' he asks.

Ghetto life and working has toughened Marek. He is older, so very much older and wiser than his nine years. He says, 'Tell me, please – I'm frightened.'

His mother comes as quickly as she is able to him and holds him so tightly that she actually hurts him. She says, in a whispery, choking voice, 'We'll all be together. That's all that matters. We'll all be together.'

His father encircles each of them with an arm and holds them both. Marek realises that the three of them are crying. He shakes himself free. 'What's happened?' He says it as though he were the parent and they were the children.

'The Germans have given orders that all children under ten are to be deported from the ghetto,' David says through tears. His eyes are red, his face changed.

Marek feels the blood empty from his face, as when the contents of a sink goes down the plug hole. Now he begins to cry. 'Are they going to kill all the children?' he asks through his sobs.

'No. They are sending everybody to a big labour camp.'

'Sending children? But they won't be able to work. I could, but not the small ones. What about Rachel? They're going to kill us, aren't they? All the children.'

His father lifts imaginary water to his face, holds his hands there and then draws them slowly down his face. He inhales and snuffles back tears at the same time. Marek's mother gazes out the window at some far away object.

'Here, come sit on my lap,' his father says. 'Do you remember when you were four or five? The big dog – do you remember?'

Marek shakes his head, snuffling.

'We were out walking one day and this big dog appeared suddenly from a gate, barking and snarling. Do you remember now?'

Marek nods.

'I reached down and picked you up. You cuddled into me. And do you remember what you said?'

Marek shakes his head. There are tears just waiting to burst out through David's voice.

'You said, "When I am with you I am not worried". Do you remember that?'

Marek nods.

'So here's what we're going to do. We'll pack our things tonight and in the morning we'll get up early and go to report, the four of us. Whatever happens we'll stay together.'

After a pause to let all of this sink in, he adds, 'Alright?'

Marek snuffles and nods his head.

They are in bed before the colour has faded from the sky; Rachel is long since asleep. David usually lies in the middle, since at his own request Marek has taken to sleeping on the outside. David has a feeling that Marek is starting to teeter on the edge of puberty and that this is the reason why he now sleeps on the outside. Tonight Anna sleeps in the middle. David is aware that she embraces Marek.

Marek slips very quickly into an exhausted sleep. His father is astonished at the child's ability to leave it all behind him. David wishes that he too could find some forgetfulness in sleep, but despite his death-weariness he remains wide awake. He flirted with Zionism in his youth. If that had been real they'd be in Palestine now. If he had been more forceful, pushed harder in the embassies, they'd be free now. How could he have known? How could any of them have known? Who – in his wildest nightmares – could have imagined such a creation as the ghetto or its terrible deportations? He feels that whatever last fragments of the normal world existed have gone and he is now in a world where he is as powerless and helpless as a child.

Anna stays awake the whole night. Tears stream down her face unceasingly.

The nightmare begins with the sound of snoring, a sound like ripping cotton. Time passes before David realises that it is not snoring at all but rather truck engines. He hurries to the window, almost opaque with dirt and spiders' webs with dead flies trapped in them, and tries to see the source of the noise. But it is out of sight, no matter how much he cranes his neck to see.

Anna is beside him. 'Come on,' she says, 'we must rouse the children.'

'The children'. It is the first time either of them have ever used this phrase. His eyes meet Anna's as though she too has just realised what she has said.

Marek's hair is scattered on the pillow, his mouth slightly open. There are freckles across his cheekbones and the bridge of his nose where he got severely sunburned when he was five. He is breathing deeply and is locked in sleep, so that it seems to take forever to wake him. David sees that everything is taking too long.

The truck engines start cutting out and now there are the sounds of tailboards dropping, and boots on cobbles. David wants to go to the window but he knows that they must get moving. Marek is awake but drowsy, stretching like an animal. David hustles him out of the bed. Anna has her coat on and Rachel in her arms. Their case is by the door.

'Come on,' David says to Marek urgently, 'we *must* go.'

Eventually they are all ready, with their overcoats on. Anna gives each of them a little piece of bread, the last of their food. But even as they open the door, there are boot thuds on the stairs, reverberating up through the building. In the ghetto there is a phrase for this. It is called 'hunting for game'. David goes in front.

The men on the stairs are Order Service men.

'Down now,' they shout, 'into the courtyard! Line up in the courtyard! No one is permitted to stay inside! All doors must be left open!'

The men race past them, fanning out onto each of the floors of the building. As one of them goes by, David smells garlic of his breath. In the ghetto garlic means that somebody has eaten a good meal. The Order Service men wear caps and their Jewish star armbands have different designs depending on their rank. The ranks go from trooper all the way up to Kommandant, whose star carries a design reminiscent of the oak leaf clusters of generals.

In the centre of the courtyard, a pair of German soldiers with shouldered rifles are blowing on their hands and stamping their feet. It is chilly in the early morning. Several metres from them is a ghetto dweller. He looks like a Westerner, perhaps one of the more recent arrivals, since his grey herringbone coat still looks relatively clean and in one piece. More Order Service men mill around the exits from the building, collecting the people as they come out and funnelling them into a line. As the line begins to take shape, the commander of the Order Service unit goes to the head of the line accompanied by an assistant carrying a sheaf of papers. The line starts moving.

David, Anna with Rachel in her arms and Marek shuffle

forward. David sluggishly lifts the case and then puts it down each time. Occasionally he looks up to see the clean blue of the sky, but he finds the surrounding buildings bring on a feeling of dizziness. Children and old people are sent off to one side, the rest to the other. David scans the children and old peoples' group for any family units like his own, but doesn't see any. Some German soldiers come running into the courtyard and go into the building and thundering up the stairs, shouting, screaming, as they go.

Despite the constant worrying by the Order Service, David, Anna and Marek try to stand side by side so that they will all reach the head of the queue together. From behind them they hear screams and then some gunshots.

Now David can see – through the heads of the five or six people ahead of them – what is happening at the head of the queue. They are asked for their name, a list is checked and then a decision is made. Right or left. Occasionally, the ghetto dweller, who appears to be a doctor, is sent to the left hand group to examine a particular old person. Children are not examined. Nobody seems to change groups. Four people ahead of them now. Everyone is dealt with singly. A woman in a shawl and two men in front. Dirty necks with short bristly hair. The woman is asked to remove her shawl from her head as the list is being consulted. She does so and is then sent to the left. The process takes only fifteen or twenty seconds. The man behind her is asked his name. Is he her husband? David sees his head nodding. The Order Service commander orders the man to the right and David feels his blood run cold. A terrible shudder runs through his body. The man goes silently to the right. Now the man in front of David. He removes his cap. Name. Consult the list. The Order Service commander nods to the right. The man says 'thank you, sir', bows and scurries over to the right.

David, Marek and Anna step forward together. David is

265

bareheaded with the suitcase in his hand. Dear God, please make it happen. Ten seconds. Make it all be over and keep us together.

'We would –'

David finds his throat is coated with phlegm, so that the words hardly appear. He clears his throat and tries again.

'Name?' The Order Service man cuts across David's second effort.

'We are David Steinbaum, Anna –'

David realises he is already taking too long. He says swiftly:

'Anna, Marek and Rachel Steinbaum. We would all like to go together, please sir- '

'Nine.'

It is the man who consults the list. The word hangs in the air like the report of a gun.

'Give the boy the baby. They go to the left. You and the woman to the right. Next.'

'Please sir, we would all like to go together. We have brought our luggage.' David indicates the case which he lifts a few inches.

The Order Service commander looks anxiously over his shoulder in the direction of the two German soldiers. The interruption in the steady routine of processing the queue has attracted their attention. In a louder voice, the Order Service commander says:

'The boy and the baby to the left. You two over there.'

The German soldiers stride over, pushing in between the Order Service commander and the doctor.

'You heard what the man said, Jew.'

'But sir, we will go together. This makes it easy for everybody –'

The German kicks the case out of David's hand. It tumbles to the ground and springs open, spilling its contents.

Davis realises that Marek has been grasping his other hand. Somewhere on the edge of his consciousness, and too much for him to deal with at the moment, Anna shrieks, a shrill, loud cry that he's never heard before.

'Take them,' says the German.

Order Service men grab Marek and pull him from David's grasp. Marek screams. Then the German turns to Anna. Reaching out, he takes a step towards her. She tries to back away but the queue of people behind impede her. She tries to step out of the queue but by then the German is inches from her. His hands grip Rachel and rip her from Anna's grasp in one clean movement. He turns away.

Anna hesitates, unsure of whether to run to the still screaming Marek, or after the German carrying Rachel. She chooses the latter. But to do so she has to cross the path of the other German. As she tries to do so he hits her across the side of the head with a broad whip of his hand. She reels to the right, stumbles and falls to her knees. The German then hurls David after her, kicking the case and some of its contents after him.

'Now take your bundle of shit and get out of my fucking sight, you filthy Jew.'

'And take this bitch with you,' the German screams at David, 'or I'll blow her fucking head off.'

David notices that the crust of dirt and mud and shit across the cobbles of the courtyard is dry and that the clothes which have spilled from the suitcase are not dirtied in any way by it. He notices splashes of blood appearing on the brown surface and sees that they are coming from Anna's nose. She is on all fours and groaning. A strangled, animal-like groan. He goes to her and reaches down to lift her up. She seems to collapse into his arms, but as he pulls her up, the groaning stops and she sobs:

'Marek. Rachel. Please get my children.'

As she lifts her head, and pushes her hair back, David sees that her face is crimson and drenched with tears. Blood drips from her nose down the front of her coat and her top lip is cut so that her whole mouth and chin is bloody.

He pulls a filthy handkerchief from his pocket and gives it to her. Then he puts his arm around her and leads her over to the right hand group as she continues to sob Marek's and Rachel's names.

Marek continues to scream as an Order Service man pulls him towards the crowd of children and old people. The man's overcoat is crusty and smells of cooked food. He pushes Marek to an Order Service man guarding the left-hand group. Marek is strong and wriggles, trying to break free. The man takes Marek violently and shoves him into the group of children. 'Shut up,' says the man.

Behind the line of Order Service in their shabby overcoats, caps and armbands, everyone is silent. Marek goes silent himself, and turns round trying to see what has become of his parents. They stand together in the front of the other group. His father, tears in his eyes, has his arm around his mother. She sobs uncontrollably, gazing at Marek, holding her hand across her nose and mouth. She is no longer holding Rachel. Marek wonders what can have happened to his 'baby sister'.

The day is starting to warm up by the time the line is finished. By then both the left and right groups have swollen considerably, and Marek has been pushed somewhere into the centre of his group. Because of his height, however, he can still see across to the other group, where his parents stand, still in the front. His mother's eyes are swollen from crying and the lower half of her face is smeared with dried blood. Her hands hang by her side, a reddy brown rag in one of them. The Order Service commander and some of the other Order Service men have clustered together, glancing expectantly towards the German soldiers who are talking. At length the Germans decide that everything is ready. They break off their conversation, and indicate the gate to the Order Service.

The Order Service select the old people first, commanding them to step out of the group. They line up and are ordered towards the gate. They move at a snail's pace out under the archway. A terrible wail goes up from those left behind as the 30 or so children are lined up in threes and marched towards the gate. Looking back at the other group Marek sees shoving, jostling, pushing and the Order Service replying with kicks, fists and batons. He thinks he hears his mother's voice calling his name, but whatever he may have heard is lost in the noise and melée. He wonders again where Rachel has gone.

By the time the children reach the street the old people have already disappeared. The children go in the direction indicated by the Order Service. There are Order Service on all sides, and glancing back, Marek sees the two German soldiers at the rear. They have unslung their rifles. Shooting, dogs barking continuously, shouts and screams come from the buildings past which they march. They hear shouts in German. '*Alle Juden raus!*' Marek is puzzled by the fact that there appears to be nobody in the column that he knows. Where are his playmates, at least the two who live in the building he lived in? Did they have a hiding place? Why weren't they caught in the round-up?

Their destination is the hospital on Lagiewnicka Street. Here, outside the entrance, there is a great bustle of vehicles and people coming and going. Trucks or horse-drawn wagons drive up the ramp outside the door and unload their contents of old people or very young children. There are soldiers and Order Service everywhere. The children are led up the steps through the entrance, up a stairs and along a corridor. Every room they pass is jammed with people, all old ones or children. There is one room with tiny babies, not in cots but lying on beds, several to a bed. They are all crying. Some of them wear clothes or just nappies. Some are naked and soiled. He wonders whether that is where Rachel is. There is a faint hospital smell in the air, but the stronger smell is of excrement, not just from the baby room but pervading the corridor and every place that they pass. They are shepherded into a small room with two beds. Some of the children immediately jump on the beds announcing that this is going to be their spot. Marek goes to the furthest corner and sits down. He suddenly feels terribly tired. The linoleum floor is cold and strong smelling but he hardly notices as he lays his head down on it. He wishes he wore a cap that he could put under his head. Sounds become distant: the fighting over places, murmured conversations, the sound of footsteps in the corridor. His breathing becomes deeper, heavier. He feels that he is falling, gently like a leaf onto snow.

Biscuit-coloured sunlight is streaming through the windows of the hospital when he awakes. The room is warm. It feels like late afternoon. The sounds of the building seem to have dimmed since this morning. There is still coming and going, but it sounds more familiar, more of a routine nature. Marek stretches. He rolls over to see what is happening. His mouth tastes awful and he has stiffness pains in all his bones.

The room is not as crowded as it was when he arrived. The beds are taken up with the sprawled bodies of sleeping children. On the floor several boys sit cross legged in a circle playing some sort of game. A group of girls have a doll and are at the sink pretending to bath it. Other children sit by themselves, their backs against the wall. Marek sits up. He is hungry and remembers the piece of bread in his pocket. He'll have to find some place to eat it. If he takes it out here everyone will want some. He gets up slowly, and assembles himself into a standing position. Some of the other children look at him with sunken, inquiring eyes.

He goes to the door and looks out into the corridor. There is no guard, just some old people and children shambling along. He takes it that he can just go out, and as if to confirm this, another pair of youngsters push past him and go off down the corridor. He follows them at a distance. The door of the room that contained the babies is closed. Marek wants to venture in but he is too hungry. Food first. Then, with some strength, he will try. He reaches the stairwell and descends. In the main entrance the front is devoid of anyone except soldiers and Order Service. There is still much activity, trucks pulling up, people arriving. A German soldier carries in two babies, screaming, one under each arm as one would carry large sacks, and bounds up the stairs. Marek slips round the heavy marble and wood banister and out towards the back of the hospital. He finds the back doors open and goes down some steps into a yard bathed in sunlight.

Marek's mouth is watering at the prospect of the bread and he can restrain himself no longer. He reaches into his pocket, pulls it out covering as much of it as he can with his hand and takes a large bite which demolishes about a quarter of it. He chews surreptitiously, his back against a red-brick sun-warmed wall.

The yard is a space at the rear of the hospital used for deliveries and keeping the hospital rubbish. The place stinks from overflowing garbage bins round which squadrons of flies are buzzing. The yard may once have opened out onto a street, but now a chain link fence on stout wooden poles encloses the yard. The entire frontage of the fence is crowded with people, their hands gripping the wire as they talk to their relatives on the other side. A young man with full lips talks to a grey-haired woman in a scarf. There is a woman with dark curly hair and a pinched face, the veins standing out in her neck. She is kneeling on the far side of the fence with two children beside her, talking earnestly to a young boy who sits cross legged in the dust and rough grass on this side. He wears a cap over a shaved head and sticky-out ears. The woman passes something under the wire to him. A parcel wrapped in paper. Some food probably. The eyes of the woman and her two children are red from crying. From the back the boy on this side of the wire appears to be sitting serenely, his elbows resting on his knees, the yellow star on his jacket as though it had been stamped onto him.

'Marek! Marek!'

It is a few seconds before Marek can work out where the sound is coming from. Then beyond another boy with a cap and a couple of small girls in coats, Marek sees his parents. He runs over to the wire and worms his way past the others, pushing his hand as far as he can through the diamond patterned wire. His mother is there and takes his protruding fingers in hers. Her hand feels icy. His father reaches some fingers as far as he can through the wire and touches Marek's face, his hair.

'Have you come to take me home?'

His mother looks at him uncertainly. She shakes her head. Then she pushes a small packet wrapped in newspaper under the wire.

'We brought you some food,' she says.

Marek bursts into tears. Through the sobbing he says:

'They are going to kill me.'

'No. We have found out,' says his father. 'Listen. You must listen.'

Marek notices that his father is speaking slowly. This is unusual because normally he speaks quite quickly.

'They are taking you to a work camp,' says his father,

272

'We have heard a rumour, only this time it is confirmed. It is like a farm. You will be kept there until the end of the war. There will be plenty to eat. All those crops. Milk from the cows.'

Marek surveys his father's face uncertainly. He looks at his mother. She is nodding, nodding, nodding.

'It's true,' she says. 'It's true.'

'But the Germans have told us lies before. That's what you said.'

Marek thinks his father is going to cry.

'No, we have this – it has come down – from the Chairman, Rumkowski himself.'

'I saw where they have taken the babies. I don't know if Rachel is in there. What will happen to the babies? They are dirty and crying. Nobody's changed them.'

'They – they will go to an orphanage,' says his mother.

'And that is where Rachel will go?'

His mother nods, biting her lips repeatedly.

She strokes his hand rapidly, holding it, pulling his fingers so hard that one of the joints cracks.

'But where will you go?' he asks. 'There may be other deportations.'

'Don't worry about us,' says his father. 'You just take care of yourself and we will find you when the Germans have gone.'

Marek dissolves into tears.

'I don't want to go without you. Please get me out. Or else come with me.'

Now both his parents are crying. His mother's grip on his hand hurts him, but something stops him from taking it away. She says:

'We would love to. How we would love to. But you must go by yourself ... until we can catch up with you. Until we can find you ... you must be a man.'

There is a sudden noise behind him. Looking around him, Marek sees a group of Order Service men descending the back steps of the hospital.

'Everybody inside. Roll call. The doors must be locked.'

Marek extracts his hand from his mother's grip and wipes his eyes and snuffly nose with his sleeve.

'We will come again tomorrow,' she says, her face with a strange expression that Marek finds a bit frightening.

'Yes,' says his father. 'We'll be here first thing tomorrow.'

The Order Service are having to prise some peoples' hands away from the wire. As they draw closer Marek takes his hands away gently from his parents.

'We'll see you tomorrow,' they say almost in chorus, their hands through the fence, their faces pressed against it. Marek can see the wire biting into the white skin of his mother's small hand, into her cheek. Further along two people are trying to kiss through the wire which presses into their skin.

'I'll see you tomorrow,' he says, almost in a whisper.

The Order Service man reaches him and his hand turns Marek towards the hospital. He walks the short distance looking back over his shoulder several times. The last he sees of them is of his father's quivering hand waving and his mother's fists pressed into her mouth.

Marek walks back towards his room. On the way he passes the room where the tiny babies were. It is empty now. Filthy. Stinking. Silent. Maybe they have gone to the orphanage, like his mother said. He walks into his own room, and it is scarlet. The setting sun lights it up so that all of its occupants look like actors in a play about hell or the end of the world. Marek goes to the windowsill and leans on it. It is as though the sun is disintegrating and that tattered red remnants of it float in the sky over where it has disappeared. Everybody knows – a red sky means a fine day tomorrow.

Marek eats a little more of the bread. Even though there

is no other food in the hospital that night, and he gets very hungry, he keeps the remainder in his pocket for tomorrow and tries not to think about it. It gets very cold, and though he would rather be by himself, Marek ends up on the edge of a huddled group where the body heat means he can get some sleep. He dozes intermittently. Distantly he hears groans. Shouts. Weeping. There is the occasional moan or whimper in the room he is in.

He realises he is on his own. He must make his own decisions. Be responsible for himself. Maybe he will see his parents again but until then, there is only him. Marek Steinbaum.

He is not particularly surprised by this. He has often imagined it before, and now that it has arrived he's ready to face it. Keep safe. Get enough food to keep strong and he should be all right until the war ends.

He falls asleep and dreams. In the dream he finds his aunt Ariela and they live together in a city somewhere. His parents come to visit but now they are old like his own grandparents. He and Ella go for walks in the park. While she cooks he plays with his toys.

It is the scuttling of a mouse that wakes him. The mouse has run right over his hand and past his face. Years ago, he was terrified of mice. That was before the ghetto. The building starts to slip from its night time to its daytime noises. Coughs. Groans. Footsteps in the corridor becoming louder, going past the door and then fading. Marek goes to the toilet and finds the floor awash. The toilet bowl itself is clogged and full to the brim. Knobs of shit bob around in a thick brown soup. Marek just wants to piss. There isn't enough food in his belly to make a good shit. He pisses into the bowl which overflows further. Then he splashes back out.

There is movement in the corridor. The Order Service. The voices come first and then a few moments later he sees the men.

'All children! Out! Now! Come on! Come on!'

Everything Marek owns he has on him – there is no need for him to return to the room for anything. The children are emptied from the rooms and lined up in the corridor. Apart from the orders of the Jewish Police, everything is done in almost complete silence. There is no shouting this morning. The commands are given softly. The Order Service men almost sound like parents. When the rooms have been emptied, the column of children goes downstairs, out through the main entrance and across the forecourt where a line of trucks are waiting. They have large muddy tyres and sides of wooden planking. The tailboards are already down and some wooden packing cases have been placed on the ground as makeshift steps. Marek waits his turn and clambers in after the others. Inside the truck smells of its canvas cover. When the truck is full the canvas at the back is pulled down and tied, plunging the inside of the truck into semi-darkness.

The truck engine fires and the children stumble and fall as the lorry jolts off over the cobbles. The heavy engine growls and gears mesh as the lorry is driven across the ghetto. After a while it comes to a halt, and the engine idles. There is dead silence in the truck as people try to hear what is being said. German voices. A command. The engine is revved and the truck resumes its journey.

'We must have left the ghetto by now,' says the boy next to Marek. He is small, wizened almost, with alert, rat-like eyes.

'How do you know?'

The boy touches the side of his nose with his finger. Then he closes his eyes and leans his head back, cocking one ear. The occupants of the truck sway and tumble as the truck speeds along. Eventually, with a last series of jolts, the truck veers to one side, glides through an arc, stops, is ground into reverse and then backs up and is halted. The engine is switched off.

The canvas flap is thrown up to reveal a railway track with a string of freight cars. The doors on them have been slid back and over on the left children are boarding them. A series of plank ramps have been put in place at the doors and the children walk up these reminding Marek of when he played at tight-rope walking. Again loads of Jewish Police and some Germans on the edges of all the activity. The children begin jumping down from the rear of the lorry. They are formed up in fives this time and marched to where the latest boxcar is being filled. They line up behind two Order Service men with their hands behind their backs and wait while the group ahead of them enter the car.

Marek realises how hungry he is as a wave of sweating breaks over him. He feels suddenly weak and lightheaded, and thinks he is going to faint. It is a sensation he has felt many times over the last few years and he knows that it will pass. He waits patiently, closing his eyes and feeling the sun on the back of his neck and head, trying to draw some energy from its rays. Maybe tonight there will be rest and a full belly.

The interior of the boxcar smells faintly of resin and strongly of shit. It is already half full and starting to get very hot. When the car is packed full of standing children the door is slid shut and they hear it being locked.

'I'm frightened. I'm frightened of all these people.'

It is a girl's voice. She is very much shorter than Marek and squeezed in beside him. She has untidy brown hair and big cracked lips. Her eyes are wide and round and appear close to tears. She wears only a thin, faded sleeveless dress in which her arms look stick-like.

'There's nothing to be frightened of,' he says. 'We're going to a farm where there'll be plenty of food.'

'No. They're going to kill us. They're going to kill all the

Jews. That's what my father said.'

Outside Marek can hear more doors being slammed shut. The boxcar jolts. A train whistle sounds. With a distant whoosh of steam the car jolts again and then begins to move forward slowly.

'Did you get separated from your parents too?' Marek asks, not wanting to think about what she said.

She shakes her head. Her eyes become pool-like with tears.

'No, they both died last year.'

'What's your name?'

'Sara.'

'Mine's Marek.'

'How old are you?' he asks.

'Ten.'

Marek is surprised. He thought she looked about six she was so small and skinny.

'What about you?' she asks, wiping her nose with the back of her arm.

'Nine and a half. I'll be ten in December. '

'You look a lot older,' she says, gazing up at him.

'I have a little bit of food,' he says. 'Would you like some?'

She nods, the sadness in her eyes unaltered by the mention of food. He removes the packet of bread from his pocket and as unobtrusively as he can divides it into two, catching the crumbs in the wrapping. It is not the easiest thing to do with the train now gathering speed. Sara chews amazingly slowly at the hard crust.

'Maybe we can be together when we get to the farm,' she says.

'Unless they separate the boys from the girls,' he says, and as he says it, he hopes that they won't.

It becomes oppressively hot in the boxcar, even though a

breath of air drifts in through the gaps in the slats. Many of the children in the boxcar have to go to the toilet during the journey. There is nothing they can use, no bucket or anything so that they go wherever they can. The carriage stinks. Several of the children are crying for water. Marek and Sara try to forget about their thirst by talking about where they lived in the ghetto and about life before the war. Marek gets the impression that her parents were rich.

The train begins to slow. Children at the walls struggle to look out while everyone else asks what they can see. Nothing much. The countryside. A station up ahead. The train comes to a stop. Immediately there are shouts and sliding sounds followed by a thud of doors being swung open. Daylight bursts into Marek's boxcar.

'I'll go first,' he says.

Reaching behind him through the crowd, he finds Sara's hand – it is tiny – and encloses it in his own. Then he leads her to the front where he finds there is a drop. There are no ramps or wooden crates this time. He also notices that there are no Order Service. This time it is only Germans. Germans with guns and Germans with dogs on leads. He bends his knees, jumps, lands. The impact rattles the bones in his legs. Turning round he finds Sara standing above him on the lip of the boxcar. He reaches up and she jumps down. As she drops, Marek catches a glimpse of worm-white thighs and grey knickers. Malnourished as she is, she is still too heavy, he is too small and the drop is too great for him to catch her properly. They tumble into the dirt but get up quickly to avoid being trampled on by the people who continue to flow out of the boxcar. He catches her hand again and they follow the crowd of children walking away from the freight cars towards the station buildings. They go through the small single-storey building and out the front where another column of trucks are drawn up. The sunshine is warm and there is a soft breeze. Marek helps Sara up into the truck and then clambers up after her.

The trucks come to a stop after about fifteen minutes, and everyone is ordered out. There is no shouting or screaming or hitting like there was during roundups in the ghetto. There are Germans everywhere in lots of different uniforms. The children are herded into a group and marched towards a large building with a wooden fence around it. Marek holds Sara's hand. They have been talking non-stop since they found themselves beside one another in the boxcar. They shuffle past the sentry box at the gateway through the board fence. Once inside they find themselves pushed forward by the crowd behind them.

On the top steps are a group of Germans. They talk amongst themselves for a few moments, and then open the doors behind them. One of the Germans smiles and beckons with gloved fingers to the children in front. Slowly at first, hesitantly, they begin to climb the steps. After a number have been counted up, the door is closed behind them. The Germans says 'Wait please children. It'll just be a few moments' in a kindly voice.

Marek and Sara are close to the front, so it doesn't take long before they are climbing the steps. As they pass by the German who has been doing the directing, Marek says to him in German:

'Where are we going?'

'Just for a bath, little one. Just for a bath.'

Marek turns to Sara and hisses, 'Do you speak German?'

'No,' she whispers back.

'I asked him what we were doing. He said we were going for a bath.'

'I couldn't believe you spoke to him. I would never do that with a German.'

'It was nothing,' says Marek, with a casual flip of his hand.

It is only when they go inside the door that Marek realises how warm the sun had been outside. In here it is cooler, as though sunlight never reaches this part of this place. After the huge crowds they have been mixed with over the last few days, the small group of children in here seems almost intimate. Apart from the two Germans, there are four civilians in jackets waiting along one wall.

'You must undress,' says a German. 'And then we will take you to the showers. Fold your clothes and leave them where you can find them afterwards'.

Marek and Sara do as they are told. He steals several glances at her. She seems to be less embarrassed about it than he is. She has no hair on her body but has small mounds of breasts. She is incredibly thin. Marek takes off his underpants and shields his thing with his hands.

'Will you take my hand again Marek, please?'

He hesitates.

'Please,' she says. And then she smiles. It is the first smile he has seen her make since he met her. Her eyes lose the empty look they had and are full of brightness. It reminds him of his aunt.

'Just until we're out of this place,' she adds.

He wipes his hand on his hip and takes her hand. She too holds her other hand over her crotch. Then together, they make their way towards the door at the end of the room which the German has opened. Through the door there is a descending staircase with signs on the wall saying 'To the Baths'. They go down the stairs and along a passageway. Then they turn right.

'What can you see Marek?' Sara asks as they shuffle slowly along.

'A big truck. That's where we're going.'

'Why are we going in this truck?' Sara asks. 'Why didn't they take us in the other truck?'

281

Marek hardly hears her question because he is suddenly overcome by a feeling of great fear. It is as though some shadowy devil had jumped down from the ceiling onto his back. It is like the sensation he had when he walked into their room on Friday night – only much, much worse. They are pushed forward to the entrance to the truck. They seem to be going faster.

'I'm frightened, Marek. I want to go back.'

Marek looks back. The last of the children have entered this stretch of the corridor, but behind them are two Germans. They are still hastening the children along with their soft voices.

'Hurry up now, children. You don't want to be late.'

Marek realises he is in a trap. His first day on his own, and he has ended up here.

'We can't get out,' he says to Sara.

His parents were wrong. There is no farm here. They reach a plank footbridge. This leads onto a ramp which slopes downwards and then they are into the back of the truck. The other children crowd in behind them.

In the crush Marek and Sara wriggle round so that they are turned towards the rear of the truck. There is a tiny patch of blue sky visible over the roof of the building. The German who begins to shut the doors has black hair, a red nose, and looks like he hasn't shaved. Marek notices that the floor of the truck has a slatted wooden grid on it like they had in the swimming pool he went to during his last holiday. As far as he can remember the grid *was* in the shower. But where are the showers here? There are no shower sprinklers.

'Enjoy your shower, children,' he says, as he closed the second door and his face disappears. The interior of the truck is plunged into darkness.

Marek feels a surge towards the doors. There is the sound of them being locked and then a hand banging on them. Now the silence breaks out into cries, screams, shrieks.

It is hot inside the truck and the bodies give off a strong smell of shit. Sara has begun to cry and taking his hand away from his crotch Marek puts his arms around her and presses her gently to him. Her face only comes up to the hollow of his shoulder. She buries it there for a moment but then he feels her lift it. He feels tears slide down his cheeks.

There is some thumping that seems to come from underneath the truck and the uproar goes quiet as people try to hear what is happening. By the time the sound has died down though, this noise has stopped. Then, the truck rocks as though somebody has gotten into the cab.

Sara's wild hair tickles Marek's face. He can feel her body warm against his. He holds her more tightly. He can feel her feet, her thighs, her belly, her breasts like little apples. The wooden grid hurts the soles of his feet.

The truck's engine is started. People brace themselves for the truck to pull off.

But it doesn't move.

Instead Marek smells a strong car smell coming from underneath his feet. He feels some kind of warm air swirling round his legs and wafting up his body. If it weren't for the smell, the sensation would be quite nice. But now the smell starts to get stronger. Sara coughs. He coughs himself. He tries to move away from the smell but it is everywhere. And anyway he couldn't move even if he wanted to – they are packed in too tightly. People start to scream. Howl. Bang with their small fists on the doors of the truck. There is no air. He can't breathe. As the pandemonium in the truck increases he tries to hold onto Sara but she is pulling, trying to break free. Now the mouthfuls he is gasping are all poisonous – there is no air at all in them. His head feels like it is going to explode. The rapid inhaling and exhaling of his lungs feels as though it is tearing them apart. His legs sag and even in the crush he finds room enough to fall. Others fall on top of him. He is in terrible, terrible pain. 'Mama, mama,' he tries to scream through corrupted lungs. His body feels contorted as though the weight of all the falling bodies is snapping it apart. He feels no more.

Ever since he was a child, David Steinbaum never liked Sundays. Grey. He remembers them all as being grey. 'Catholic Sundays' he called them, as though the Catholics had decreed that Sunday should be a day where nobody would do or enjoy anything. This is such a Sunday. Anna sits at the table, hands folded on the surface in front of her, looking at the wall. She wears the shapeless dress she wore yesterday morning, the front still spattered with puddles of dried blood.

Twelve words keep running around in his head.

'The boy and the baby to the left. You two over there.'

If he had spoken quicker. If they had tried something else.

Friday night. Can it really only have been Friday night? Less than 48 hours ago. Friday night when they decided they would all go together. They had decided long ago that hiding was no good. You hid, but if they found you, that was it. There was no second chance. This way had seemed like the best way forward. But this evening, on the stairs, David had caught a glimpse of one of Marek's friends. Younger and smaller than Marek. He would have been a certainty to have been taken but here he is walking around the place as large as life. They should have hidden.

After the selection, when Marek and Rachel had disappeared, David had gone everywhere, tried everyone he knew to see if he could get the decision changed. But there were vast crowds at all the ghetto offices and nobody was dealing with any changes. At least nobody David could get access to. He and Anna had expected to see Marek this morning. They were up early, despite the roundups still taking place on the ghetto streets. But all roads leading to where he was being kept were closed off. He and Anna heard the lorries being driven away. But they couldn't get anywhere near them.

Where did the lorries go? What would the Germans do with children, some of them babies, and old people? David would like to think that the Germans are not capable of his worst imaginings, but he knows that they are. Marek's resourceful. Maybe he escaped. But at the thought of this David's eyes sting into weeping. Marek is not resourceful. He is cautious. Uncertain. A follower not a leader. Careful. He will not have escaped. And my God, is David serious? He and Anna deliver Marek into the beast's hands and then expect him – a child – to do something about it.

They agreed yesterday, after he was taken, that they would try to see him and tell him the story of the farm. It is a rumour that began to circulate through the ghetto when the deportations of the elderly first started.

Nobody believes it.

Not when they have seen the vast mountains of baggage and clothing in the storehouses of the ghetto. Both David and Anna agreed that it was better to tell him this.

But how could it be?

Deliver their son up to be murdered and then tell him not to worry? That everything will be all right.

Anna has hardly spoken a word to David over the last two days. Radiating from her he can feel the unasked question. Why didn't he do something?

He has no answer. Their rations – in ghetto terms quite a decent amount now that Marek is gone – lie uneaten on the table. David has tried to get Anna to eat a little or take some water. She pushes it away. She pushes him away.

They didn't even have the sense to build a hiding place. All he needed was a rudimentary knowledge of carpentry. A night class. A subject David could have done in school instead of history or physics.

He is back at where he began. Like a broken-down horse moving around in a circle.

David has contemplated suicide. It is a thought that has been rarely out of his mind over the last two days. That he has not done so is for no other reason than that he has to take care of Anna. If she were gone, he would have no hesitation.

And in a few days, maybe he will broach the subject with her.

Being this high up, David can see sky over the ghetto. It is filled now with a sickly light. Great cream-coloured clouds billow upwards like mounds of whipped ice cream. The sky is electric with the onset of rain and the promise of thunder. The evening light has the effect of drawing shapes and colours in sharp relief. The bright ochre of individual bricks, the slight imperfections in the apparently straight line of a rooftop or wall, the ornate arc of a street lamp holder. White walls or chimneys which take on the same colour as the sky so that they look like pieces of iced cakes. Red bricks show through the cracked white plaster of a wall. A wisp of grey chimney smoke hangs in the calm air as though it had been painted against the sky.

Later the rain comes, and with the onset of twilight comes thunder and lightning. For a few minutes the rain is torrential, setting nerves on edge as it rattles into gutters, sloshes and gurgles down drain pipes and washes along ghetto pavements and streets looking for a channel, a duct, a sewer. The rain turns the thin, crisp cake of the courtyard into a soft dough and bathes away the splashes of Anna's blood. By morning sky, earth and buildings are washed clean and the ghetto is ready to begin another day.

Chapter 14

September, 1942.

David is working at his desk when he becomes aware of some activity by the door. Somebody looks in, then somebody else. Then a group of people. Then Biterman, the supervisor, threads his way through the clutter of desks towards David.

David knows what it is even before Biterman opens his mouth.

'It's Anna,' says David. It is a statement, not a question.

She has been shot, says Biterman. They have taken her to the hospital. He offers to accompany David, but he says no. He'd rather be by himself.

David goes to the door, and takes his coat from the line of hooks outside. The yellow patches are the only brightness in the shabby collection of rags. He goes downstairs slowly, buttoning the two remaining buttons on the coat.

It is less than a fortnight since Marek was taken away. In that time, Anna has hardly spoken. She has stopped eating, and David, rather then letting the food rot, has eaten it himself. Though she still goes to work every day, Anna is wasting before his very eyes. This morning he watched her trudge away from their building and she moved so slowly it seemed to take her forever to reach the corner. She is only 37 but she moves like a woman of 70.

One night, out of the blue, she said, 'I'm not going to die, you know. I want to live. To find out if Marek is still alive. And Rachel. And whether they are or not, I want to avenge myself on the Germans who did this.'

At the time he took it as a sign of hope. Now he realises it was perhaps a last protest.

At the hospital the doctor tells him that she was shot near the wire. She is dead, he tells David. There's really no point … Better to remember her as she was …

No, David would like to see her.

The doctor shrugs and leads him down a corridor into a room. Here there are several bodies on tables, covered with filthy, blood-encrusted sheets. The doctor pulls back one of the sheets.

There is blood all over her chest, bright against the indeterminate colour of her clothes, and another bullet wound just at her cheek bone. This is a neat wound, with some bruising, and a small bloody entrance wound. Her eyes are half closed, the pupils dead. Her once lustrous hair is lifeless, like the fibres of a brush. Her wide lips and almost undamaged features give a faintly peaceful and childlike expression. Her long neck is blue and cold to his fingertips.

David kisses her on the lips and touches her unmarred cheek. Then he caresses her hair, remembering the time he first touched it. No tears come into his eyes. It is as though he emptied himself of tears after Marek. Or maybe he was crying for Anna too, knowing that it would come to this. He closes her eyes completely, and draws his shaking hand and fingertips slowly along her cheek again. Then, he turns and walks away.

—— Part Six ——

Chapter 1

Berlin. September, 1943.

Rudolf snatched an hour with Ursula. The weather was still warm enough that they arranged to meet in the Tiergarten. Despite the damage caused by British and American bombing raids, you could still find places to sit. They hadn't managed to get away together since her birthday, but Rudolf was hoping in the days that lay ahead that he would get at least a couple of nights in town with her.

As she approached he thought she looked tired, not her usual radiant self.

'I've been thinking,' she said, after they had eaten, and sat watching the people around them. 'You know the way I was talking about my biological clock.'

He turned to look at her, concerned that this subject was coming up again; it had first come up the night they went out to celebrate her thirty-seventh birthday. She wore sunglasses and was looking straight ahead.

'I'd like to have a child. Ideally, I'd like to have a husband too,' she said, turning to face him. Her mouth was smiling, but he couldn't see her eyes behind the lenses of the glasses. He went to speak but she held up her index finger to stop him.

'Don't worry, I'm not going to mess things up for either of

us. It's a child that I really want. I think I could give it a good home. While I'm not wealthy, I don't think it'd want for anything. I know a woman who would mind it during the day while I ran the shop. All that side of it is organised. Now, all I need is a father. I've heard about places you can go – they're run by the SS – where – well, basically they'll impregnate you.'

She took the glasses off, a wry smile on her face.

'As you can imagine the prospect of some bull-necked SS man sweating and pumping over me has about as much attraction as a pork sandwich to a Jew. I'd like you to be the father, Rudi. Oh, I'd make up some story about the father being killed at the front or something like that, so nobody need ever know.'

Rudolf felt deeply flattered and alarmed simultaneously.

'You could have just done it,' he said. 'Why ask me?'

'Because I respect you too much. What would you think if I suddenly announced I was pregnant? That either I was trying to ruin your marriage or I was sleeping with someone else. How would you have felt in either case? I had another idea, though, and I toyed with this for a long time. Lisa knows how I want a child. I was going to ask her permission to use you as the father.'

Rudolf felt his eyes widening in astonishment.

'She'd never agree,' he said.

'Perhaps you're right. But you have no idea how close sisters can be. In the end, though, I decided it wasn't worth the risk of losing her.'

She went silent. Rudolf was relieved.

'What would you do if I said no?' he asked.

'I haven't given it much thought,' she said. 'Would you? Say no, I mean?'

As he hesitated, Rudolf realised that his affair was about to move to a new and much more dangerous plane. There would be no going back from this. The affair was one thing.

If it ever came to it, he could deny all knowledge that it had happened. Where was the evidence? The proof? If he did this, the proof would be living, breathing, walking around. It would come to his house, play with his children. What if it fell in love with one of his kids? Yes, this was crossing the Rubicon. But he loved her. In a different way from Lisa it was true, but love, nonetheless.

'No one must ever know,' he said. 'The birth certificate must say "father unknown".'

'Of course,' she said. 'Of course.'

'I'd be honoured to,' he said, smiling and taking her hand.

'Let's make it tonight, she said.

That afternoon, he called at the shop as she was closing. He waited while she counted the cash and did a few bits of paperwork.

'Business good as ever?' he asked.

'It dropped off a bit after Stalingrad, but I think it's pretty much recovered. I must tell you – I came across a good deal this afternoon. This fellow came in. He was wearing civilian clothes but he had the cut of a military man about him. He had a suitcase with him, and when he opened it, it turned out to be full of lingerie. High quality stuff. Really top class. The funny thing was – well, actually, there were two funny things about it. The first was that it wasn't quite new. But it was as near as makes no difference. Somebody like me would have spotted it but customers wouldn't. Not if it was packaged up nicely and faintly scented. The other funny thing was the price. It was about twenty per cent what you normally pay for these things.'

'And did you buy it?'

'I bought the lot. And said I'd take any more he could get.'

'He told me there was plenty more where that came from. I didn't ask any questions. He's going to ensure I have a regular supply.'

Chapter 2

Slonim. September, 1939.

'Any ideas?' asked Broni, as they trudged towards what appeared to be the centre of town.

'Yes, I think so,' said Ariela. Her eyes were hollow from lack of proper sleep and her face was dirty. He noticed the tiny cracks in her lips.

'We wouldn't be here if it wasn't for me ... and I'm only here because I'm a Jew ... so let's make my Jewishness pay for itself. Let's go find the synagogue.'

In the courtyard of the Great Synagogue, the Jewish community of Slonim had established a reception area and soup kitchen for the refugees that continued to stream in from Poland. As Ariela and Broni approached it, they saw a large crowd milling outside.

'Seems like everyone else had the same idea,' said Broni.

'Never mind,' she said brightly. 'Let's see what we can do.'

They joined the queue. When they reached the top, they found a man with white hair and a frizzy grey beard sitting at a small desk. His eyes nestled within pouches of skin. Ariela spoke in Yiddish.

'My name is Ariela Steinbaum. I was wondering if you could help us find a place to stay. We have no money but we can work. We will do anything.'

'Miss Steinbaum. And your friend' – he nodded in Broni's direction – 'you are welcome to Slonim.' In a slow, gentle movement of his arms he indicated the horde of people milling around. 'As you can see there are many like you here today. The population of our small town has nearly doubled in the last few days. However, we will try to help. The first thing is to give you some food and find you a place to stay. I will write your name down and that of your friend. Then we will consult our lists. It may take a while. You will have to wait but we have some soup and bread. It's around the back. Just follow the smell.'

He smiled warmly, lowered his head and began writing.

'My friend is not Jewish.'

The man looked up again, this time at Broni. A moment of silence.

'If he is your friend we must take care of him.'

'He's a wonderful pianist,' she said.

The man looked from one of them to the other. 'Ah, a pianist. We will have need of music in the time to come.'

They devoured the single bowl of soup and chunk of bread they were given.

'I wonder how my family are doing,' she said. 'I fear for them with the Germans.'

He tried to change the subject, to brighten her up.

'Would they have an organ in a synagogue? I could do with touching a keyboard. Did I tell you I was once caught playing jazz on a church organ?'

'Really?' She laughed, showing her regular white teeth.

'Miss Steinbaum?'

They looked up. The woman who stood in front of them was tall, almost painfully thin, in her twenties. A headscarf held back dark hair. She wore a dress of the same material as the headscarf and wooden clogs.

'The elder says you will come with me. You and your

293

friend. Please.'

She gestured with her hand. Long bony fingers and a sun-weathered complexion.

They got up, gathered their packs, and followed the woman away from the synagogue. She was silent as she walked along talking long, nervous strides.

'Is where you live far from here?' Ariela asked.

'Not too far. Up the hill. My apartment is not big, you understand. I have only one bedroom and a kitchen.'

'We are sorry to impose on you like this. My friend and I are most grateful to you. We will work or do whatever we can.'

'Whatever. The elders give us a little money if we take in people. This helps.'

Broni couldn't tell whether she was resentful or just shy.

'What's your name?' Ariela asked.

The woman turned and smiled a little. 'Paula. My name is Paula.'

Ariela extended her hand. 'I am Ariela and this is Broni.'

Paula took the proffered hand uncertainly. It was as though shaking hands was something she rarely did. 'You are married?'

Ariela laughed.

'No, no, we're not married. We're just friends.'

Now Paula smiled. 'Then the sleeping arrangements are going to be a bit of a puzzle,' she said.

'What day is it?' asked Ariela.

Paula sounded surprised. 'Why it is Friday,' she said, 'the eve of Sabbath, *Erev Shabbes*.'

To get to the apartment they went under an archway, into a courtyard, in a doorway and up some stairs. The plain wooden door was unlocked. Inside, the two rooms had white chalky walls, and a single window from the bedroom looked out onto the street.

'I will make some tea,' said Paula.

'Do you live by yourself?' asked Ariela.

Paula was bent over, stoking the fire in the tiled stove. She shut the door, put away the poker and looked up, pushing back a stray hair with her forearm. 'I do now.' She straightened and pushed the kettle onto the centre of the stove. 'I had a husband. We were married only a few weeks. He worked on a farm just outside town. He was killed in an accident there.'

'I am so sorry,' said Ariela.

After a meal of tea, bread and dried fish, Paula said, 'I must continue my preparations for Shabbes. It will be nice to have somebody else here for it. Please – if you would like to wash, or have a sleep. Make yourself at home.'

'I would so much like to sleep in a bed for a few hours,' said Ariela.

'Then you must do it. There is hot water in the kettle for you to wash.'

In the end Ariela took the bed, and Broni the floor. She offered the bed but he would have none of it. Broni fell into a deep sleep, and by the time he woke it was dark beyond the window. He lay there for a while trying to remember where he was. Outside in the street he could hear Yiddish voices. They paused for a while under the window chattering, then some goodbyes were said and he heard a group of people moving away. Broni sat up. Ariela's bed was empty and the blankets had been folded back into position. He rubbed his eyes and went outside into the other room.

The two women and the room had undergone a transformation. A gleaming white table cloth had been spread on the table, and on it stood a seven-branched candlestick with three unlit candles. Beside the candlestick stood an opened bottle of wine, a goblet which looked like it was made of silver, and the caramel-coloured noses of two loaves of bread peeped out from under an embroidered towel. The room glowed in the soft yellow light of candles which were scattered around the room. Sweet food smells filled the small space.

The kerchief on Paula's head was gone, and her rich dark hair was tied up behind her head. She wore a black silk dress with a round neckline, and flat-heeled shoes of soft leather. She had put on a little makeup – bright red lipstick and some powder which made her face look pale. She wore a string of pearls round her neck. Ariela too had changed, into the skirt he had first seen her wear at her audition, and a white blouse. She wore the same colour lipstick as Paula.

'You're just in time, Broni – we're just about to celebrate the Sabbath.'

'Do you know I'm not Jewish?' Broni asked.

'Yes, I know,' said Paula. 'But you are welcome to join us, if you would like. You will be our *oyrekh*, our guest for the Sabbath meal. The Sabbath is better for this. When my husband died, my friends and neighbours would ask me if I would come to them for *Shabbes*, but I have always stayed here. This was our home, myself and my husband. I carry out the ceremonies a little differently since there is no man in the house, but the rabbi says this is good. We are meant to speak only Hebrew at the beginning of the Sabbath meal, but I'm sure it is alright if Ariela tells you what's happening.'

'I've been to the synagogue, Broni. I went with Paula while you were asleep. It was beautiful.'

Paula opened the stove door and lit a twig, which she took from a chipped cup on the back of the stove. Then she lit the three candles, repeating something softly in Hebrew. Ariela translated the words into Polish for Broni.

'Blessed art Thou, oh Lord our God, King of the Universe, who hast hallowed us by His Commandments and commanded us to kindle the Sabbath light.'

Shaking the twig to extinguish it, Paula moved her arms over the candles in a gesture of embrace as though drawing the rising flames towards herself. Then she covered her eyes with her hands and Ariela and Broni followed suit. In the darkness dancing with the afterglow of the candle flame, Broni thought that he didn't know what he believed in, but he was thankful to be safe and here with her. He wished that they would be together always.

'*Gut Shabbes,*' Broni heard Paula say.

He opened his eyes.

'*Gut Shabbes,*' said Ariela.

Broni repeated the blessing uncertainly. Both women smiled at him.

'I will say the next prayer for you both,' said Paula. 'Even though I know you are only friends, you are good friends. "A woman of worth – who can find her? For her price is far above rubies. The heart of her husband trusteth in her ..."

Next, Paula poured wine into the goblet, filling it to the brim. Lifting the goblet in both hands, she held it to her chest and recited another prayer in Hebrew. Having finished, Paula took a sip from the cup and then passed it to Ariela. Ariela said the same prayer and passed the goblet to Broni. Unable to say any prayer, he sipped silently and handed the cup back to Paula.

There was a small table beside the larger one on which were set a jug of water and a bowl. Each of them took turns to wash their hands, Broni noticing that both Paula and Ariela poured water over their hands three times and recited another prayer.

'Now,' said Paula, gesturing with the open palm of her hand, 'let us eat.'

Paula lifted the napkin from the loaves of braided bread, lifted them together for a moment, and then set them down again. She took a knife, and passing it over one of them, cut the other in half, before cutting slices for each of the three of them. They took the light slices, and breaking a little piece off, dipped them in the little dish of salt that stood beside the bread.

They ate slowly. There was fish in a spicy gravy, amber-coloured chicken soup in which thin noodles and golden globules of fat floated, and boiled chicken. Ariela and Broni talked of what had happened since they had left Warsaw. Ariela made only the briefest mention of Stefan, saying that there had been a third person with them originally, but that he had turned back very soon after they started. Paula talked about Slonim – she worked in the Jewish guest house as a waitress and chamber maid. They took breaks between each course and sipped the wine. The candles burned lower.

After the meal, Paula sang some peaceful tunes, which she said were *zmiros*. Ariela sang one or two soft jazz melodies. Eventually, Broni extinguished what remained of the candles and they made their way into the bedroom. Ariela and Paula shared the bed, Broni slept on the floor.

Next morning, Paula was gone early.

'My mother came from a little town like this,' said Ariela over breakfast. 'Being here makes me feel close to her, to all my family. I was never so aware of what it meant to be Jewish as I was last night. Being in the synagogue, and then having *Shabbes*, all the crazy things that happened over the last few weeks – the War, Stefan, being here – last night seemed to make sense of all of it. I don't know what will happen to us, but I feel confident now that we can survive all of this and get back to a normal life.'

She reached across the table and placed her hand on top of his.

'It's all thanks to you, Broni. You've saved my life. You've been the dearest friend, and I've been a bitch towards you. I'm sorry. I hope I can make it up to you.'

Briefly, Broni wondered whether he should say anything,

but thought better of it. It wasn't the right time. And after all, now they had plenty of time.

On 17 September they joined the building's other tenants to hear the Soviet Prime Minister Molotov say on the radio that the Red Army was on its way to 'liberate' Belorussia and the western Ukraine. A few days later Russian tanks entered Slonim. Girls danced in the street with Red Army soldiers. Amongst the Jewish community there was, if not joy, at least relief. While there might still be anti-Semitism – Soviet now, instead of Polish – at least it gave a sense of protection from the Germans just across the border.

Things changed under the Soviet regime. The shops emptied. Queues for everything, but especially food, became the norm. Almost overnight, the town seemed to become drabber. There were soldiers on the streets and talk of informers and arrests by the NKVD and deportations to Siberia. The Jews kept their heads down.

Broni and Ariela found bits of work here and there and this helped to keep body and soul together as autumn came down into the Szczara valley. The chill sunny mornings when a few white clouds might be seen swimming in the river soon gave way to the colder, rainier, sleetier days of October and November. Leaning over the parapet of the Long Bridge, gazing into the rain-swollen river which carried fallen leaves and branches away Ariela said: 'Paula told me that the Jewish Hassidim used to go to the river to cast their sins in.' To their right, away in the distance, the Great Synagogue looked down on the town.

One snow-clad night, Ariela suggested they go for a walk. She and Broni wrapped up, put on boots and set off. Ariela wanted to get into the countryside. It didn't take long.

A strong wind soughed in the pine trees and a half moon lit up the landscape. Blowsy clouds sat around the rim of the horizon on all sides and climbed halfway up the sky. Above them the night was clear and the stars shone in it like embedded diamonds. The moon irradiated the grey clouds so that they stood out in sharp contrast to the grey-blue of the clear sky.

'What's going to happen to us, Broni?'

Broni's heart leapt at her use of the word 'us'.

'I don't know. Sit the war out here. Go home when it's over? I don't know.'

'It would be so much easier if I knew my family was safe. You've heard the rumours about what they're doing to the Jews in Poland. My parents are too old for that. My brother and his wife have a seven-year-old child ...'

Broni longed to put his arm around her. Instead he said:

'How do you feel about Stefan now? Now ... now that you've had a few months.'

'I'm over it. It's behind me.'

Broni said, 'Don't they say that you only love once and that's first love? Wasn't he your first love?'

Her eyes smiled – a scarf covered the lower part of her face.

'I don't believe that - about first love, I mean.'

They walked on in silence.

'What about you, Broni? How do you feel?'

'I'm really glad I'm with you.'

Broni wondered what to say next. While he was still trying different phrases in his mind, she said, 'We'd better go. Look at those clouds. And the wind seems to have risen. I think there's a storm brewing.'

By the time they got back, there was wind, squalls of wet snowflakes and a sky full of immense clouds. They went to bed with the wind rattling the window and doors as it swept in through any slit or gap it could find. Broni woke some time before dawn and had to go to the single toilet at the rear of the house that served all of the building's occupants. By then everything was quiet. The gusts had abated to a business-like wind. Looking out the window he saw that the trees were engaged in nothing more than some energetic swaying. A full moon shone on the garden illuminating everything with amazing clarity. The night had been like a baby: earlier unhappy, crying, its face transformed by pain or sadness, but now it slept a calm and innocent sleep.

The harvest of 1940 brought lots of work and plenty of food. They worked in the fields and turned nut brown. Their hands became hard. Ariela sang as she worked.

'Isn't it high time you got yourself a new boyfriend?' he said one day as they lay in a sun-baked wheat field, waiting for the foreman to call the end of the lunch break. They were on their backs side by side.

'From around here? A Russian? A yokel?'

'Shhh, they'll hear you.'

She laughed.

He wanted so much to touch her. Instead he pushed her shoulder playfully. He was conscious of the material of her blouse and her arm beneath it.

Their second winter came and went. Snow fell, settled, melted, swelling the rivers. Ariela and Broni took over the care of Paula's small vegetable plot and as spring lengthened into summer, the regular, varying rows of green started to appear. It was here that Broni – anxiously searching - found Ariela standing early one Sunday morning, her legs from the knees down obscured by foliage, the remainder of her body bathed in sunlight. She was dressed like Paula. Her sleeves were pulled up above her elbows and her hands hung dirty. She smiled when she saw him. The whiteness of her teeth made him realise how tanned her face was.

'I've got some bad news.'

'Is it my family?'

He shook his head.

'No. How would we have heard anything? No. It's the Germans … They invaded the Soviet Union this morning.'

The three of them sat in Paula's kitchen holding cups of tea. Ariela encircled hers tightly with her fingers. Broni noticed a tremor in her hands so that the disc of liquid on the surface swung like the needle of a compass. Eventually she put the cup down, her hand still shaking so that it did a tiny tap dance on the table. Broni felt like screaming. The conversation was going round in circles. How could these two women – these two *Jews* – be in any doubt about what to do?

'We *must* leave. We *have* to go east.'

'It'll be different this time,' said Ariela. 'This isn't the Polish army. The Red Army will stop them. Surely.'

'Just like it did in the last war,' said Broni, sarcastically. 'I don't think so.'

'But Broni, these people have taken us in. Paula has. We can't just leave like this.'

'You must come too, Paula. God in heaven, I'm no Jew but I've heard enough about the Germans to know that *I* wouldn't want to fall into their clutches.'

'I can't leave, Broni. This is my home, my relations, my friends,' said Paula.

'They should all be getting out.'

'There are old people. Children. They can't just go on the road.'

Broni threw up his hands in exasperation.

'You've heard the stories from Poland.'

'Stories,' said Paula. 'The older people remember the last time the Germans were here. They said they were a million times better than the Russians.'

'Things are different this time. These are Hitlerites.'

Ariela said, 'We'll stay for today anyway. We'll listen to the radio and try to find out what's going on.'

During the day long columns of military equipment passed westwards through the town. The radio announced that the Soviet air force was pulverising Berlin and that the German army had been beaten back scores of kilometres. The news cheered the women up but Broni was morose and went to bed early.

He was up at first light and went into town to see if he could find out anything. He was back within an hour, breathless.

'The Germans are attacking the Derewianczycy airport. I went down to the river. On the Baranovici highway bridge, going east. Remember all that equipment we saw passing through the town yesterday. Well, I saw it going in the other direction. They're retreating. There's your precious Red Army for you. Now will you listen?'

'Maybe Broni's right,' said Ariela. 'Maybe we should try to round up your family and leave.'

Paula shook her head.

'It's not possible. They wouldn't come. It would take too long. You should go' – she smiled – 'you've done this before. You're experienced refugees.'

Nobody laughed at the joke. Broni looked at Ariela. He sought a decision in her face. When she went to speak, no sound came and she had to clear her throat and try again.

'These people have been good to us, Broni. When we came here neither of us was Jewish really. We can't run out on them after what they've done for us. You've been a wonderful friend, more than I could have deserved. But now it's time for you to do what is best for you. And I don't think hanging around with Jews is. You should leave. Go back to Poland or go deeper into Russia.'

She paused. Her eyes were glistening. Her voice had shrunken to a whisper.

'Something will work out.'

Chapter 3

It is the vague hope that his son or sister might be alive that stops David from following Anna, though for Marek he has almost no hope. There are too many rumours in the ghetto. Too many fragments which when added together give only one possible picture. The Germans are killing all the Jews that they can find. In the case of Marek, David finds life a suitable punishment for failing the child. Death would be too easy a way out. This way David can suffer every day for what he allowed to happen to his son.

David also assumes his parents are dead. If not the Germans would have brought them into the ghetto. David has checked at the various ghetto offices and there is no record of them.

That leaves Ella. If she got trapped in the ghetto in Warsaw then, by all accounts, there's no hope for her. But if she managed to escape, if she went East, if she managed to stay ahead of the Germans, or to hide from them, then she might have made it. It's a lot of 'ifs', but it puts a time limit on his punishment. When he finds out what happened to her, one way or the other, he will end it.

Now that he has no real reason to live, the filth, the lice, the bedbugs, the starvation, none of this causes him any real hardship. He almost welcomes them as a form of punishment. Now he longs only to die and to be with Marek, Anna and Rachel, or – as he believes more likely – let him disappear, as they have done.

He has never really believed in an afterlife. That's the funny thing. He never believed much in religion at all. He was no Jew. That's what's so stupid. *He was not a Jew.* He was busily trying to leave all that stuff behind him. The mumbo jumbo, the ancient leather and tassles, the dusty books, the ancient smell of Judaism. He had rationalised things to a point where he believed that you were born, you had your few years in the light, and then you returned to darkness. How terrible that several of his few years – and almost all of Marek's – had been in a darkness unimaginably worse than the comfortable pre-dawn of the womb and dusk of the grave.

Chapter 4

Berlin. June, 1944.

U rsula's baby boy was born with no complications. Thankfully he had his mother's looks. By now Allied bombing raids had become so widespread over Germany and particularly Berlin that she was in no rush to stay in a large public building, even if it was a hospital. Three days later, she and the baby, whom she called Karl, left the hospital and went to stay with Lisa and Rudolf.

The arrangement suited everybody. Rudolf was immensely busy at work what with a vast number of Jews to be processed in Hungary; he left early, worked late and every weekend. He was glad that the women had each other. Ursula was glad of the support and help in the weeks after the birth. Lisa was delighted to have a baby around again. Ursula's story was that Karl's father was a Wehrmacht officer whom she had met at a party. It had been a one-night stand. Shortly afterwards he had been killed on the Eastern Front.

July passed. Rudolf's organisation hummed. Swollen to a group of nearly 50 people, it juggled camp and ghetto capacities, availability and capacities of rolling stock, availability, strength and location of police and SS detachments. In the morning he was usually in by 7:00 but there were already people in place from the day shift and often the night shift stayed an extra few hours if there was a job that

306

needed finishing. This had been one of his guiding principles that he had drummed into them from day one. Finishing. Making sure it was all over. Confirming that the last details had fallen into place.

'Nothing will get you into trouble quicker here than leaving something undone,' he told every new recruit, all of whom he interviewed personally. 'Do it once and I'll be unhappy. Do it twice and you won't get a third chance.'

By the end of July Ursula was starting to talk about returning to work. This was when Lisa proposed that she would mind Karl. It was the perfect solution.

The Monday operations meeting began with the familiar formula, almost like an invocation: 'Poland first?'

'Lodz. Erich, what's the latest on Chelmno?'

'Yes, well you'll recall they suspended operations on 15 July. We got something in overnight that said Chelmno isn't going to re-open. They're blaming the advance of the Russians and the nearness of the Eastern Front.'

'So what now?' asked Rudolf.

'We're checking with Auschwitz when they'll have some capacity. As of the middle of July they're pretty much finished with the transports from Hungary, but they've got lots of bits and pieces to deal with after such a sustained effort. Hoss is saying early August. He's promised us an exact date later today.'

'Very well, the sooner we know the sooner we can get ready to empty Lodz. Anything else?'

Erich shook his head.

'This is an important one, Erich. It's the last big concentration of Jews in a ghetto. Completing this will mark a major milestone for us.'

Despite the workload Rudolf took an hour off in the sunshine of the Tiergarten for lunch. He needed to clear his head. A lot of things had been swilling around in his mind, but it was the mention of the nearness of the Russian front that prompted his excursion.

It was treasonous to say so, and could earn you a slow and painful death, but it didn't take a genius to see that his country was going to lose the war. That led immediately to the question of who would occupy a defeated Germany. If it were the Russians they would do – with some justification, he reasoned – what the Germans had done to their country. Rudolf had read the reports. He was under no illusions what would happen if the Russians were first into Berlin. With the British and the Americans it would be different. They were pragmatic. They knew life had to go on. He was a professional manager, statistician and logistician. He could get things done. In the reconstruction that would follow a German defeat, there had to be a place for people like him.

That was his career. Now what about his family? Or rather the women in his life. He had hoped that once the baby was born, everything would return to normal. Lisa at home with the now, three children. He and Ursula resuming their careers and their affair. In a German defeat all of this would change.

The obvious answer was to tell Lisa about the affair and possibly – he wasn't sure about this yet and needed to think it through – the baby. But it was more than that. He needed not just to tell her but to get her to agree that from now on the family would consist of him, herself and her sister and their three children. If he could do that and pull it off then a whole pile of complications, mainly stemming from his relationship with Ursula, disappeared. Lisa would mind the children. He and Ursula would work. The children loved having Ursula around so they'd be happy. In fact that was it – they all loved each other. He loved the two women. The children loved their mother and their aunt. Lisa and her sister loved each other. The new arrangement would put all of that on a practical footing.

He toyed with another thought. In which of the women's beds would he sleep? Some nights in one, some nights in the other? With both of them together? He might get his three in a bed after all? Him, his wife and her sister sharing a bed. Having sex together? An orgy? With a bit of incest thrown in? Was he mad?

He thought about it during his walk back to the office and it hovered in the back of his mind for the rest of the afternoon. He would sleep on it, of course. If it's potentially fatal, sleep on it, was a maxim he had used from his earliest days. Just before he went home Paul looked in on Rudolf.

'Lodz is on again from 7 August. We just heard from Hoss.'

'Very good,' said Rudolf.

'Erich and some of his people are staying back to get the ball rolling.'

'Excellent. Thanks, Paul.'

Chapter 5

Lodz Ghetto. August, 1944.

The mist lies sullenly around the ghetto. However, as the morning advances and the sun rises higher, it flees as though frightened. The stage is quickly cleared for what is going to be a gorgeous day.

As David turns the corner the rail sheds came into view. In other times the sight of the station might have meant – had meant – excitement, joy, a relative returning from America or the beginning of a journey. Now, the sooty buildings, the steel water tower with the ladder up the side, a square red-brick chimney and some arc lights that seem to have been left on by mistake, have no such happy associations. Overhead, swallows swoop joyously in the morning light that is gold like vessels in a synagogue.

It is the final clearing out of the ghetto. While others approach it with terror far greater than any of the previous deportations, David joins it tranquil and composed. He will be glad to leave the ghetto. Even in its awfulness it has too many happy associations. He wants to leave Lodz and irrespective of where he goes, he never wants to come here again. One sunny August morning, in a group of 5,000 people, he goes through the streets of the ghetto and then along the railway tracks to the railhead.

His destination is Auschwitz-Birkenau.

Chapter 6

Normandy. The present.

'Why did she decide to stay? Broni said he thought it was perhaps a kind of family loyalty. Slonim had become like a home to her. They had taken her in. She felt some kind of responsibility to it. To Paula. Let me tell you very quickly the rest of what he told me.'

The first Germans came in past the Jewish cemetery and then downhill along Ruzany Street into the city. They were coming from Bialystok. They had already done terrible things there, and their blood was up. These were the ones that afterwards we came to call the 'good' Germans. You have to understand that the word is used in an ironic sense. They were good only in the sense that the ones who came after – the SS, SD, the Gestapo – these were so savage. During those first few days, we had a little food so we stayed indoors with the doors locked and the windows shuttered. We waited to see what would happen. In Slonim during those first couple of weeks it was particularly bad. Many people were killed. Many Jews were killed or dragged off some place and not seen again.

We wondered what to do that day the Nazis came. There were the three of us and a bunch of Paula's neighbours crowded together in a cellar. They were all Jews and they were terrified. There was nothing they could do. They were trapped. Outside in the street some vehicles drove past making the building vibrate. We heard the sound of running boots. Shouts. Gunfire. I remember a huge shudder pass through Ariela's body.

In the days that followed, things did return to a sort of normality. People had to go on living their lives, to eat, to sleep. Things quietened down a little, even though the streets were much more dangerous for Jews. The Germans issued the usual anti-Jewish laws. Jews couldn't walk on the footpath, Jews couldn't go to the market, Jews had to doff their caps to a Nazi officer. The signs went up. 'For Germans only'. 'For Aryans only'. Of course, there was the law about having to wear the yellow patch on their chests and on their back. When she went to get hers, she tried to persuade me again that I should leave. I wanted to wear a patch too but she talked me out of that.

Things ran like this for a week or two and it seemed like we might be getting back into some kind of routine. Then came the first mass disappearance. The Germans took away about 1,200 people, mainly men, in trucks. They called them the 'intellectuals', but really what they were was anyone with any kind of education, or position in the community, or anyone who just stood out. That was always the thing with the Nazis. How could you merge with the crowd? If you could do that you might survive.

I'll never forget the fear and grieving that night. But then there was the terror of what would happen next. There were rumours circulating that the men had been shot but the Germans denied this. Why would they kill useful Jewish labour, they said?

I got a gig in a local hotel frequented by the Nazis, playing there several nights a week. It wasn't the sentimental stuff that they liked. Murderers always seem to have a sentimental streak. The pay was pretty lousy but there was always food left over at the end of the night. And it was like I had a family to feed. At least that's the way I thought of it. I was very dubious about playing for the Nazis. I never felt right about it at the time. Later, when the Russians came, they weren't so understanding either. And there were always people around prepared to say you'd collaborated. To this day, I don't know if I did the right thing or not.

Ariela had a job by then too. The Nazis gave out different colour passes. They were like postcards with a German insignia and signed by some German higher-up. Skilled workers were one category, labourers were the second. The third consisted of the elderly, the sick, invalids and very young children. The categorisation scheme was clear to everybody. Useful, less useful, useless. For a while she worked in the Jewish hospital. It wasn't a real hospital. The Nazis had made all the real hospitals 'For Aryans only' so that the Jews had to improvise one for themselves. Then she went to work in a bakery. The baker himself had been one of the disappeared, and so his son took over. I think he was sweet on her and that was the only reason he hired a woman. Although by then many of the men had been taken for forced labour so very few able-bodied were left around. She started to develop that reverential tone about bread that good bakers have. She would lecture us on the quality or otherwise of a particular loaf, though by then most of it was shit. We used to tease her about it. After the war she said, if she didn't make it as a singer, she would become a baker.

I don't mean it to sound like a quiet and happy time. It wasn't – except in comparison to what came after. It was a time of permanent stress and danger and fear. Rumours circulated constantly. There were shootings. People disappeared. We were constantly hungry – really, we were slowly starving. We worked different days, the three of us. Paula worked a normal day. Ariela went out to work around the time I came home. She was normally finished around four in the afternoon. It was usually the sound of her singing while she worked downstairs in the kitchen that woke me. I would get up and we would have a couple of hours together before I went out to the hotel. Between the three of us we covered the clock. But when one of us went off we never knew whether we would see the others when we returned later. We used to hug each other when we left and returned. We never knew if that might be our last sight of each other.

She told me she liked those early morning starts even though as the autumn came on it became colder and colder and harder and harder to get out of bed. She liked to see the stars on her way to work. It was a bonus in the day, she said, if she saw them. She would come home in the evening, pale from the flour dust.

And that was how it was. When I look back on that time, I see that we were living on the edge. Well, when I say 'we', I mean the Jews, really. They carried on about their daily lives – there's Ariela getting up every day to go to the bakery to practise her new skill – and all the while the machinery was being put in place to end it all.

So many times I wanted to tell her how I felt. But I never got the courage. Or when I did, the conversation didn't go as I had expected and I lost direction when she didn't give me the kind of message I was looking for. I was afraid that if I said anything, it would ruin our relationship. I was happier with the friendship and the uncertainty than knowing for sure and poisoning our friendship in the process.

I'll … I'll never know how she felt about me. We never … we never talked about it.

Some time that autumn we were expelled from Paula's house and forced to move closer to the river – or the canal, I'm not quite sure which. That area anyway. We were only there a few weeks when it looked like we would be moved again. The Nazis created a new category of worker and a new pass; a yellow one this time. These were for skilled workers. She could have got one. But it would have meant the three of us being split up, because they moved all of the people who had these passes onto the island between the canal and the Sczara. I wanted her to go. Both Paula and I did. But she felt it would be better if we were all together.

Once this last set of passes was issued, things changed. There was a different atmosphere around the place. You could feel fear in the air everywhere you went. All kinds of rumours were circulating. The Nazis had dug these trenches outside the city. We all knew about them. And there were these truckloads of Lithuanian soldiers or police arriving in the city. It was said they would only be looking for men to go for forced labour. But if that was true what were the trenches for? We didn't know whether to stay put, to run or to hide.

It happened on a Friday. People going to work were turned back to their houses. '*Nach Hause!*' – Go Home! – the Nazis were saying. '*Nach Hause, Schweine Juden!*' Then all hell broke loose.

Chapter 7

30 August 1944.

Paul looked in just as Rudolf was getting ready to go home.

'Just thought you'd like to know that we're finished in Lodz.'

'The ghetto's empty?'

Paul nodded. 'Except for the clean up squad. Less than 1,000. To all intents and purposes it's *Judenrein,* free of Jews. The last ghetto in Europe. It's an historic day.'

'An historic day, indeed, Rudolf mused. 'Very good, Paul. Thank you. Oh Paul.'

Paul was halfway out the door and dived back in energetically. 'Yes?'

'You'll update the maps?'

Paul nodded. 'Of course.'

The maps were an invention of Rudolf's. There was one of all of Europe, and then a series covering different regions. For example there was one covering the Baltic Countries and another for Poland. Each map showed ghettos and their populations. If a territory was now free of Jews this was indicated by the word '*Judenfrei*'. The second item was the number of Jews evacuated in that territory. This was indicated by a coffin, drawn to scale, and with a number beside it.

Rudolf forgot about the maps as Paul closed the door. Rudolf intended to talk to Ursula and Lisa tonight and tell

316

them what he planned to do. He got his opportunity with Ursula just after dinner when she took Karl out for a walk. Rudolf went with her. Once they were out Rudolf explained his analysis – of the war and everything.

'I want to tell Lisa – about us, I mean. That way we'll be able to normalise the relationship between us all.'

That word 'normalise'. It was a word from statistics.

He was relieved at how calmly Ursula received the news. He hadn't been at all sure what her reaction would be.

'What about the baby? Will you tell her about Karl?'

'I wondered about that,' said Rudolf. 'I think not. Maybe one shock at a time.'

'Maybe it won't be much of a shock. Lisa's broadminded.'

When they got back Ursula said she was tired and went to bed. Rudolf sat down with Lisa. As before he described the situation that would prevail in Germany if the war was lost. He spoke of their leaving Berlin and going west towards the Americas; how he proposed that the six of them go as a family unit. Lisa seemed relatively relaxed and philosophical about the idea.

'I'll be sad to leave the apartment, but you're right – things would be much, much worse with the Russians. Especially for Aryan women.'

'There's something else I have to tell you,' said Rudolf.

Lisa looked at him unblinking. 'Yes?'

Rudolf thought he detected a faint smile around her lips.

'I've been … Ursula and I … we've been … we've slept together – ' He could find no more to say. The words hung in the air.

Lisa said nothing for several seconds.

Rudolf started to feel uncomfortable. Phrases formed in his head. 'It was only because she was lonely,' 'I didn't mean to –'

Lisa smiled. 'I know,' she said.

'You know?'

She nodded, amusement on her face.

'How do you know?'

317

'Guess.'

'You found something … you suspected … you saw … we said something?'

Lisa shook her head. 'Guess again.'

Ursula? The only other possibility began to dawn slowly in Rudolf's head. Lisa put words to his thoughts.

'Yes, Ursula told me. She's my big sister, you know. We have no secrets.'

'But … when?'

'Christmas. 1940, it must have been.' Her voice took on a dreamy quality.

'My goodness, it's so long ago now. So much has happened.'

'But, that was before we'd even … before it even started.'

'I know. Remember she came to stay with us for Christmas. She and I stayed up late one night and she got to saying about how lonely she was. Well, not so much lonely, but what she called "skin hungry". She said that she envied me because I could get sex on a regular basis. You know how she cared for me when I was a child. I love her more than anyone in the world.'

Rudolf wondered if Lisa would qualify this statement or make some mention of him, but she continued without doing so.

'I'm not being quite accurate when I say that she told me. She didn't tell me. She didn't ask my permission. I suggested it.'

Rudolf was flabbergasted.

'You *suggested* it?'

Lisa nodded. 'I had two reasons, I suppose. One was the one I've just mentioned. But the other was that you were drifting away from us. We became a real family when the five of us were together – you, me, Ursula and the children. I thought that this might bring us all closer together in the long run. I suggested she try it once as an experiment – '

'An experiment?'

' – and see if it had any effect good, bad or indifferent. It seemed to work. We were all together more. Ursula was happy – she just needed some sex on a regular basis. You were happy to give it to her. We saw more of you. Nobody lost out. On that basis, I was happy to let it continue.'

'But what about you and me?'

'We're still married. We still make love. What's wrong?'

Rudolf could find nothing to say.

'I love my sister, Rudolf. If she's unhappy, I'm unhappy. If this was all she wanted it was a small thing.'

'She didn't tell me. I … I didn't know.'

Lisa burst out laughing. 'Isn't that my line? I'm the one who should be annoyed. You're the one who was having the affair.'

'I'm going to wake Ursula now. We need to talk about this.'

The expression of amusement suddenly fell from Lisa's face.

'Don't be so damn stupid, Rudolf. Look at you. You're like a schoolboy who's had his catapult stolen. Snap out of it, for God's sake. If the Russians are coming we'd better start making plans.'

'And the baby?' He had blurted out the words before realising what he was doing.

Lisa sounded like a teacher who had lost all patience with a particularly dense student.

'That was Ursula's suggestion. I know my sister. Sometimes better than she knows herself. All along I knew it wasn't really skin hunger – or sex. Maybe that was part of it, but what she really only ever wanted was the same thing I've only ever wanted. Love. A family. Companionship. If she couldn't find a man she really wanted to be with, then she'd make her own. That's what Karl will be – her companion for the rest of her life.'

Rudolf threw his hands in the air. 'This is insane.'

'Jesus Christ. You're pathetic, Rudolf. With your job and your self-importance. I can't imagine what I ever saw in you.'

And with that Lisa stormed out of the room.

────── PART SEVEN ──────

Chapter 1

Rudolf, Lisa, Ursula and the children left Berlin the evening of Friday, 23 March 1945. By then it was evident to everyone that the Russians would be first into the capital.

Rudolf had been making his preparations steadily since last summer. He and Ursula had gradually withdrawn all their savings from the bank – gradually, because these were the kinds of things the Gestapo checked. As well as German currency, they also had gold coins procured through his Gestapo contacts. He knew he was running huge risks by doing this, but he had been studying the gradually shrinking fronts for months now, and he reckoned that insofar as it was humanly possible, he had got his timing right.

Last year he had learned to drive. He had bought a *Volkswagen* and the six of them squeezed into it with some difficulty. They packed it full of as much as they could take – primarily food – and drove southwestwards, towards Frankfurt. Rudolf's RSHA identity papers ensured that he was able to pass unhindered into what was increasingly a battle zone. Refugees began to appear. He saw scenes which he had last seen on newsreels five years ago – only then they had been of France and Belgium and Holland. They managed to reach Frankfurt and lay low for a few days. Money

– especially gold – could buy anything by then. He, Lisa and the children got new identity papers, where they all kept their christian names, but changed their surname to Furst. It wasn't the kind of comprehensive change that Rudolf would have liked, but it required the least amount of explanation to the children. Lisa's showed her having the same maiden name, and so Ursula was able to leave her identity unchanged. They were in Frankfurt on 29 March when Patton's divisions entered the city.

Rudolf found himself watching the khaki-clad Americans with a sense of relief. At least now the war would pass eastwards and leave them behind. They had a few more months of precarious living ahead of them, but he reckoned they had enough money to get them through. Let things settle a bit and then it would be time to go to the Americans asking for a job.

On the personal front, things had been strange since he had told Lisa about Ursula. Or rather since Lisa had told him about Ursula. He and Lisa continued to share a bed as before, but Ursula seemed preoccupied with her baby. Since August she and Rudolf had not made love once. It was awkward, of course. How could they? Where could they? When Lisa knew everything.

Rudolf approached the Americans on 1 May, the day after Hitler committed suicide. He had been responsible for a civilian section, he told them. Dealing with logistics, supplies, planning – but for civilians, especially refugees. He understood that they were still running a war. He could take away a lot of the problems they were having dealing with the vastly swollen civilian population. He'd lost everything when his apartment had suffered a direct hit. He's been lucky to save his family – his wife, children, sister-in-law and her nine-month-old baby. Did he detect a wisp of guilt on their faces. Had he supported the regime? No, he wasn't really political. All he had ever wanted was to do his job to the best of his ability.

They hired him. A week later the war ended. Shortly after that they had found him a reasonable place to live. The six of them had enough food, there was money coming in again. The Americans were happy with him. He did as he had promised – acting as a buffer between them and the local population.

'We like you, Rudi,' one gum-chewing officer told him. 'You take the pain away. The pain of being an occupying power. Jeez, I'd rather fight a war any day.'

Soon Rudolf had built up a staff. As the year wore on he and his extended family were moved to a more substantial house. They had a maid, something they had never had before. By the time winter started to approach, the children were back in school, and Ursula was looking around for a likely spot to open a first shop. She had a new plan now. Not exclusive any longer. That was too much like hard work. And anyway, the ones with the money – the Americans – would soon be leaving. No, instead a chain of shops, upmarket but within the reach of the middle to upper-middle classes. She would start with one shop and the economy would just be starting to recover when she would be ready to open more.

Christmas came. It snowed. The six of them went to church and even as they walked through the piles of rubble, past gutted shells of buildings, Rudolf had a Janus-like feeling of looking both into the past and the future. For Christmas dinner they had roast goose, potatoes, green beans, red cabbage and canned fruit for dessert. There were cigars and wine, all courtesy of the American commissary. There were some small gifts for the children though nothing like on the pre-war scale. By the time the children had gone to bed, everyone was in high spirits, with Lisa especially hovering just this side of drunkenness. At that point Rudolf produced a bottle of champagne he had managed to get his hands on.

'Bravo,' they cheered, and the three of them hugged, both

women kissing him simultaneously, one on each cheek.

They turned on the radio, tuned it to the Armed Forces Network and began to dance. It was jazz against a crackly background. Rudolf realised he hadn't heard jazz since the 1930s. That was one thing the Nazis had had all wrong – banning jazz. It was wonderful music. The three of them danced together. Both women's faces were flushed. Lisa danced with her eyes closed. Rudolf smiled at Ursula and she beamed back at him.

They stopped and without saying a word the three of them came closer together, embraced and began to move almost in slow motion to the music. Their heads, heavy with alcohol, half fell forward so that Rudolf could smell the women's two separate perfumes.

Lisa's eyes were open now and she looked at him. They were watery and appeared to be not quite focused. Rudolf slid his arms further around the two womens' backs and eased them closer to him and to each other. Lisa turned to her sister, smiled and leant over to kiss her. Ursula responded. Rudolf pretended to be drunker than he was.

'Let's go to the bedroom,' he whispered.

Nobody said anything but the three of them began to sway towards the bedroom.

'I love you,' he said, his eyes meeting theirs in turn.

With a hand behind each of their heads he pulled them closer to him so that all three sets of lips touched. He realised he was able to differentiate between two different types of lipstick, and found this amazing. The two sisters kissed again. Rudolf watched their breasts pressing together. Time for the big roll of the dice.

'Undress each other,' he breathed.

Rudolf felt Lisa stiffen. The dreamy look dropped from her face. By what appeared to be almost a manual effort, focus came back into her eyes. Lisa stopped dancing as did

Ursula. In the stillness which followed it was as though some-body had turned the music up. Lisa began to extricate herself from Rudolf's embrace. He resisted.

'Let me go,' she said. Her eyes were flaming now, focused directly on him, boring through him. She seemed to be sud-denly stone cold sober.

'Lisa, I –'

He glanced at Ursula, realising that his arm was already slipping from her, as though of its own accord. There was nothing in Ursula's eyes that he could read. No solace, reas-surance. No message as to what he should do.

'Let me go, you bastard,' Lisa said, and ducking under his arm, she half ran out of the room.

'Maybe it's time we all went to bed,' said Ursula, avoid-ing his eyes.

With that she pushed back her hair which straggled over her cheeks, and went after her sister. On the radio the slow music had stopped. In its place were streaming, jaunty drums, clarinets and rolling piano. Rudolf strode to the radio and jabbed the 'off' button savagely.

A knocking sound tunnelled its way down through the layers of alcohol fug into Rudolf's brain. 'Open the door', some far away voice said. Shouted. 'Open the door.' It was German but spoken with an American accent. His sleep-encrusted eyes flipped open. His mouth tasted vile. He found he was on the sofa, still in his clothes, with a single blanket tangled around him. More knocking. 'Open the door or we'll break it down.'

Rudolf pulled himself slowly to a sitting position. The movement of his body seemed to momentarily leave his brain behind to catch up. He got to his feet. The knocking became more like a crashing, as though they were indeed trying to break the door down. Where was Lisa? Why hadn't she answered it?

'I'm coming,' he shouted. 'I'm coming.'

There were four American soldiers at the door, three wearing Military Police armbands and helmets, the fourth, standing in front, an officer.

'Rudolf Fest?'

'No, my name is Furst. F-U-R- .'

'Rudolf Fest, I have a warrant for your arrest on suspicion of war crimes. You must come with me.'

'War crimes? What the hell are you talking about? I work for you people. That's not my name. Here, let me get my papers.'

'We know all about who you are, Herr Fest.'

The soldiers pinioned Rudolf by his arms.

'Who are your superiors? Do you know who I am? I'm an important member of the Frankfurt ... I report to General – '

The officer stepped forward, and jammed his face right into Rudolf's. He spoke in English.

'Listen pal, I know exactly who you fucking are. I know exactly what you're an important fucking member of. And I don't care jack shit if you report to fucking General Eisenhower himself. You're coming with me.'

'Let me get my shoes.'

Lisa emerged from the bedroom, wrapping a dressing gown around her. Behind her, Rudolf saw Ursula and the children.

'What's happening?' Lisa asked. 'Who are these people?'

'They've mistaken me for somebody else,' said Rudolf, as the soldiers pressed him into the sofa. One of them unclipped the cover on his holster and pulled a truncheon from his belt while Rudolf pulled on his shoes. As he was about to tie the laces, the soldier with the truncheon said 'Leave them'. His colleague then squatted down and tied the laces together.

'OK, let's go.'

Lisa was silent as Rudolf half-shuffled, and was half-dragged from the apartment.

Chapter 2

In Birkenau David is not selected for death but rather to work. Every new incident, every reality that unfolds in this place, he follows as though it were happening to somebody else. Afterwards he thinks that it may be this as much as anything that sees him through

There is a moment within days of his arrival when an SS man orders him to push a loaded wheelbarrow. When David goes to pick up the handles of the wheelbarrow he finds he cannot lift it, cannot shift it at all. In that moment he knows he is going to die. Furious, the SS man kicks him savagely on the hip, but rather than shooting him, storms away. David remembers another incident. An inmate, totally distracted and enthralled by a flock of birds, wondering what had brought them there, no doubt envying them their lives. Then he is shot by an SS man.

Roll call. Interminable. In the deep blue evening sky, a glistening cradle moon hangs low in the sky, with Venus shimmering above it like a diamond.

David spends until just after Christmas in Auschwitz. Then he is moved to Belsen. By now he is moving in a sort of slow dream, where very little impinges on his consciousness. His mind is like a malfunctioning camera which takes an occasional photograph on the film, but leaves most of the rest of the roll blank. He arrives at Belsen in the depths of the European winter. Arc lights, frosted ground, freezing fog so that up ahead buildings are only discernible for a short distance and after that everything disappears into a murk. He sees female SS guards in greatcoats, solidly constructed boots and hats; their hair, faces and backs of their knees the only bits showing. He remembers spring. One of the female guards has blonde hair. He notices how it is held back and tied up with hair clips and a blue ribbon. Her neck is thin, pink, feminine, criss-crossed with stray wisps of hair.

He is there when the British liberate the camp.

David first knows for certain that he is alive when he has his first shower: up until then the nurses have washed him. The hot water caresses his body. There is perfumed soap. He remembers how he longed for this, a lifetime ago in the ghetto.

He marks his journey to recovery by the food he eats. First it is some sort of porridge or gruel. Then there is soup. But not the watery obscenity that used to pass for soup in the ghetto or in Birkenau – hot water with the odd fragment of mouldy vegetable. This soup is so thick that his spoon floats on the surface. There are chunks of sausage in it with a deep, explosive taste. When he can sit up and get out of bed, he finds himself eating white bread. With butter. It is six years since he has seen this commodity, freshly baked, scented. Then one morning on his breakfast tray he catches a smell that is fruity and acid; a smell that is faintly familiar, but strange at the same time.

An orange. He is still marvelling over it, rolling it in his hands, smelling it, putting off the moment when he will bite into it, when the nurse returns to take his tray. She's American – from the South she tells him, but not the Deep South. The phrases mean little to him. She is blonde, pretty when she smiles. She smiles now.

'I guess y'haven't seen one of those in a while, David.'

'No,' he smiles, shaking his head.

When she has gone an idea drifts into David's head. After he has recovered his strength, after he has found out about Ariela, he will go to Palestine and grow oranges.

Chapter 3

Rudolf was released early in 1946. All the time he was in custody, he stuck to his story that they had the wrong man. Yes, he had worked in that office but not in the senior role they thought. There had been two of them there with similar names, the director – Herr *Fest* – and Rudolf, whose surname was *Furst*. There was often confusion over the two names and memos going astray, Rudolf joked, to interrogators who were anything but amused.

They had ample evidence against him, though none of it, he was proud to say, was from his office's own filing system. Somebody – Rudolf wondered whether it had been Paul – had done an excellent job in destroying the entire contents of the vast set of files they had created. Other departments hadn't been so careful, however, and there were enough references and trails that led back to Rudolf.

He had known this was always a risk, and hoped that the change of identity and location would be enough. He had also reckoned that the Allies would have had their hands full chasing after the people who had actually done the killing. After all, he wasn't a murderer. He had never held a gun in his life. He had merely shuffled papers and held meetings.

Despite the evidence they let him go. From what he could see they had to be pragmatic. Life had to go on. The country still had to run. The country had to be rebuilt for Christ's sake, and he was one of the people with the skills to help rebuild and run it.

He stayed with the story of his having been in a lowly

position in the department and filled out his denazification questionnaire accordingly. When he came before his panel, he managed to convince them that he was a category 3, lesser offender, escaping the category 1, major offender and category 2, offender, classifications. For a while they had even hovered on category 4, follower. His job was restored and though his voting rights were restricted and a special deduction from his income put in place, he was back at his desk by the end of March 1946. Four years later in October, 1950, the Bundestag, which by then had taken responsibility for denazification, voted to lift even these sanctions from anyone to whom they had been applied. By then, however, Rudolf was in private industry, Marshall Plan money was flowing into the country and his career was looking bright.

Lisa visited him regularly while he was in custody, but as soon as he was released she told him she was divorcing him. He talked to Ursula. Could he see her? No, she didn't think so. There was Karl, her new business and Lisa and the children were also going to need a lot of support.

Rudolf packed his things in a suitcase he got from Ursula – brown leather with tan straps and reinforcement on the corners. It was one in which she had received a consignment of that cheap underwear.

The two women and three children lived together for several years after that until Ursula's business had become established. Then, in the early 1950s, they moved back to Berlin where Ursula bought them adjacent apartments. Rudolf only saw his children very rarely after that – mainly during business trips to Berlin where he would see them for a few hours before flying off some place or returning to Frankfurt.

Chapter 4

Otto surrendered to the British early in May. His activities with the Einsatzgruppen had finished at the end of 1942 and he spent the rest of the war fighting, first on the Eastern Front, then in the west in the long, slow retreat that began on the Normandy beaches. He was wounded in Russia and again in Normandy, before being evacuated to the rear. By then his dreams of a small holding in the east had long faded, and all he wanted to do was to survive the war and be with Helga.

He slipped completely through the hands of any would-be war crimes investigators, and returned to find that Helga had been killed in a daylight bombing raid. American bombs paid for with Jewish capital. He found some work, but couldn't settle. He drifted in and out of jobs. It was like a re-run of his life after the First War. Though he had a craving for women, he never had a steady woman friend after that. He found himself constantly mentally undressing women and feeling the urge to grab one from a crowd. Powdered, perfumed, well-dressed women pushing past him made him especially angry and he felt impulses at times which he found almost impossible to control.

He was initially pleased at the resurgence of neo-Nazi groups in the 1980s and 1990s and he involved himself through the Old Comrades, but the movement never became much more than a crank thing as far as he could see. He still met with a few of the Old Comrades who were left and they reminisced about those days in 1941 and 1942. 'The best days of our lives – when we were strong and our enemies quailed before us.'

Otto received a pension from the state and a new apartment. While neither was lavish they were sufficient to his needs. In 1995 he was still healthy, alert, though becoming somewhat less so and living in Berlin.

Chapter 5

Warsaw. Early September. The present.

A taxi drops David Steinbaum at the Warszawa Wschodnia railway station, and soon he is on the late afternoon train to Lodz. A lot has changed since the last time he made this journey, but even so, he still catches sight of things – a building or a landscape or a scene – that bring a rush of memories. He is glad he is alone in the compartment.

The train deposits him at the Lodz Fabryczna station and it is a short taxi ride from there to the Savoy Hotel. When it was built, it was the most modern and luxurious hotel in Poland. There is even a novel written about it – by Joseph Roth. David had the book – written in German – in his collection before the war. He often wonders what happened to his books.

The Savoy could no longer be described as luxurious, but it is clean and functional. He eats a pleasant meal in the restaurant that evening, and enjoys some good Polish beer. A three-piece band plays pop songs. He imagines Ariela fronting such a band, but then decides she would have regarded the music as rubbish. He is in bed by 9:00 for an early start the next day.

Despite his age, despite the rigours he has endured, David is fit and active. He eats a good breakfast, and then surreptitiously makes some sandwiches using ham and cheese taken from the buffet. The urge to hoard food is something he has never shaken off. At a grocery shop near the hotel he buys a couple of bottles of water and with these in his pack, and a camera slung from his neck, he walks out to the waiting taxi.

In the honey-coloured light of early morning, the driver speeds up Zgierska Street and drops David at the junction with Julianowska. The weather is glorious – a clear sky and the promise of a hot day. David is reminded of how beautiful the land of his birth can be in autumn. In a few moments he is standing outside the house where he was born. The satellite dish is new but, other than that, the place is not too different from the way he remembers it. Maybe it seems smaller. Window boxes of red flowers cascade from the balcony just as they did when his father tended the garden. The lawn in the back garden is bathed in sunlight, and David is reminded of a photograph of himself and Ariela sitting on the lawn. It was taken when she was three, and the two of them are sitting on a rug, squinting against the sun and laughing.

He enters the gate and rings the doorbell, hearing it sound somewhere in the rear of the building. The doorbell has a new sound. However, there is no answer, and all the blinds are down. He tries again, but to no avail. Stepping back onto the pavement, he takes some pictures and walks back towards the city. Tomorrow, he will locate the house where he and Anna and Marek lived – the one before the ghetto. He will find that Poles live in it now. There, when he knocks on the door, it will be opened, but when he explains who he is and what he wants, they won't let him in. Just before they close the door on him, he will notice the floor that Anna was sanding when the war broke out. She never got to finish it and whoever tried after her didn't do it properly. It is a half-hearted job. Not at all the standard she would have wanted.

When David was in the ghetto, he used to wish that when

333

it was all over, the whole place would be knocked down. He wanted to see it bulldozed, erased, and something new and clean built in its place. This is what happened to the Warsaw ghetto – the Germans saw to that. However, what David finds as he enters the area that is still called Baluty, is that many of the buildings of the former Lodz ghetto still stand and are inhabited. A lot of Marysin is vacant, and there's plenty of Communist 'architecture', but much of what is there looks terribly familiar.

And almost every sight comes laden with memories. A sunlit archway framing a steel frame. The frame is for hanging rugs and carpets so that they can be beaten clean. He remembers that a sound he once mistook for somebody beating a rug was actually a German soldier whipping an old Jew.

David has done a lot of research for this trip. It was always his way whenever he travelled with Anna and Marek. As a result, he has a number of books with him. Amongst them are *The Chronicle of the Lodz Ghetto* and a book of photographs taken in the ghetto. One of the photographs is entitled 'Lunch break for women working at cleaning feathers in the Church of the Holy Virgin'. The feathers were taken from the bedding of Jewish families from Lodz and its vicinity who perished in the Chelmno death camp. He walks into the grounds of the Church of the Holy Virgin on Zgierska Street. Here, under a drain pipe, he finds the spot where the two women sat more than 50 years ago, eating their soup. They wore headscarves, their feet were wrapped in rags and the soup was little more than foul tasting hot water. Yet, the photograph shows that it was a sunny day, just like today, and the warmth of the bricks on their back and the sun on their faces must have been a tiny pleasure. He stands there for a long time looking from the photograph in the book to the vacant spot and back again. He feels a tremendous sense of desolation. Who were they? Where are they gone?

Somebody is airing bedding in the sunshine. The clean white pillows and sheets stick out of a fourth-storey window. It used to be a familiar sight in the ghetto, except the bedding was always filthy or bloodstained. If you were lucky, the bloodstains had been caused by bedbugs. Such upper-storey windows also had another use. In those days, people jumped from them.

David wanders into the hallway of an apartment block. Flaking plaster revealing the red bricks underneath. Heavy wooden doors. Ornate wrought iron banisters. Windows almost opaque with dirt. Stone steps worn by generations. In the ghetto days, families who could find no other accommodation, literally lived on these stairways.

On Spacerowa Street, David finds a neat little house with yellow window frames, and a tiny patch of greenery in front beneath the windows. Yellow flowers grow in profusion. A white blouse on a coat hanger hangs from one of the windows, drying in the hot sun. A clean red car, and the vivid blue sky complete the splashes of colour. David reads the diary entry for 5 September 1942, written by somebody who lived across the street from this charming house.

'The house across from us (8 Spacerowa Street) was sealed off, and after an hour and a half three children were brought out of it. The screams, struggling, cries of the mothers and of everyone on the street were indescribable.'

David reaches the spot that was known in ghetto days as Fire Brigade Square. It is a park now – shady with trees, the grass almost gone after a summer's use. There are families and groups of children from the houses that surround the square, a dog or two, old men, a grandfather with his grandchildren, little flocks of birds, the sound of distant traffic. Children call to each other. Here he stops to eat his sandwich, and quickly birds begin to land close by, scrapping over the

335

crumbs. The opening words of Rumkowski's speech come back to David: 'A grievous blow has struck the ghetto ...' 'A grievous blow has struck the ghetto'. He cannot get them out of his head. 'A grievous blow has struck the ghetto ...' Quickly, he finishes his sandwich, gets up and moves on.

In the afternoon, he takes the long walk from south-west to north-east, through the grassy spaces of Marysin. It is an achingly beautiful day. He finds the long cobbled path that leads up to the main gate of the Jewish Cemetery. Its imposing archway of ragged red brick speaks of a time when Jews formed a third of the population of Lodz. It's hard to imagine there ever could have been such a time. The gates are locked, but an arrow points to the right. He follows the ornate wall around, and having paid some money, enters the cemetery through a small side door.

The first thing he notices are a number of evenly-spaced holes like grassed-over shell craters lying just inside the wall. He is puzzled for a second, but then remembers having read somewhere that the Nazis left some open graves when they fled from Lodz as the Russians approached. These graves were intended for the last of the Lodz Jews, who – having cleaned up the deserted ghetto after the deportation of most its populace – were then to have been shot themselves. Despite the heat, David feels an icy chill pass through his body.

Photographs of the cemetery from the time of the ghetto show tombstones in every direction. These days, it's all overgrown with bushes and trees. He walks down to where the ghetto dwellers are buried – the so-called 'ghetto field'. Here, where butterflies flit through the shoulder high grass, here – in a common grave – is where Anna lies. David remembers that on the day she was buried, he tried to fix the location of the spot by counting the number of pillars from the main gate and then pacing from there to the grave. He repeats this

336

process today, but it's hard to know if he is exactly right – the skyline has changed so much.

He takes off his pack, and stands there in trousers and shirt sleeves and dusty boots. His eyes smart and he feels tears start to flow. He tries to wipe them away but he only succeeds in smearing them down his cheeks and dampening his fingers. He breathes her name. Images flash through his mind. The night they met. Their last holiday. How she longed to move to the country. To have a garden. This kind of weather today is Anna weather.

It is early evening when he makes his way back towards the hotel. His feet ache. The westering sun send shafts of yellow dusty light through archways, warming old cobbles and walls still pock-marked with bullet holes.

Chapter 6

Normandy. The present.

'No. I never remarried. I think I have been alone from the day we shut our house and went into the ghetto.'

'Every year, when the orange harvest is over, I load my revolver and go deep into the orange groves. There I want to kill myself. I really want to. I want to leave all of this behind me. But year after year, I fail to do it. You see, I love living ... life ... being alive ... this world. Sunshine, food, drink, birds, a river, deep sleep – not that I get much of it. It's like we were deprived of these things for so long that now, my longing for them cannot be satisfied.

'It was while I was there last year, standing amongst the orange trees, with the gun in my hand, that I thought I would make this trip to Europe. I haven't been back here since the War. I thought that if I returned, then maybe it would bring some kind of closure to my life. Then maybe next year I could do a proper job in the orange groves.'

'I flew to Warsaw. That was where I found Broni. Ella had told me about him. He gave me your address. From Warsaw I went back to Lodz. My parents' house is still there. So too is the house that we lived in – Anna and Marek and I. I couldn't find the place we had lived in in the ghetto. That had been demolished.'

'After that I went into the country. It was September, the

same month Ella had first gone to Warsaw. The harvest was still in progress. Potatoes were being gathered in, wagon loads of them on the road, bonfires of withered potato stalks smoking in the fields, the flat countryside with the clumps of trees showing where farmhouses were. I found where my parents' house had been. The Germans burnt it. There were just the foundations and a few sections of low wall. They killed my parents. I don't know how. And I have no idea what happened to the bodies. I asked around the neighbours. Some of them remembered me. They weren't able to help. We had had a helper. One of the neighbours told me that he buried my parents' bodies. He died and the location of their graves died with him.

'Next I went to Chelmno. That was where they killed Marek. His body would have been buried, but then later dug up and burnt, his ashes scattered. Where is my son? Where is he, my beautiful boy? I wonder constantly about this. I am a scientist by training and so I can tell you the scientific answer. If they burnt him then some of him became gasses which diffused into the air. Those molecules are somewhere around the planet. But the rest of him, his ashes, the pieces of bone that they put through the bone grinder, they are scattered around that clearing, the fragments of my son. My beautiful, beautiful son.

'I returned to Warsaw by train from Lodz. In doing that I realised I was beginning to retrace the journey that Ella made. She and Broni walked to Belarus. I took the train from Warsaw to Brest Litovsk and then another train to Baranovici. There I hired a taxi and we drove to Slonim.

'Slonim was pretty much razed during the First World War. You see photographs of it during the 1920s and 1930s as it was being rebuilt and it looks prosperous with fine buildings, like almost any small town in say, France. The Slonim I saw looked like it had given up hope. Maybe the combination of losing 25,000 of its Jews plus the Communist regime proved too much for it.'

'The Great Synagogue there is one of the oldest in Eastern Europe, built in the seventeenth century. It's falling down now – held up with rickety wooden scaffolding. Even so, it's still an imposing building and almost possible to imagine it vibrant with Jewish life. The street where Ella had lived has been demolished and it was very hard to get any sense of her there. I imagine her in peasant dress and headscarf bringing in the harvest. You know, like you see in those Communist propaganda films. It's about as far away from what she wanted to do ... from what she was, as anything you could imagine.'

'Finally, I went out to Chepilovo. It's a tank training ground for the Belarus army now. There were a couple of soldiers in a hut at the gate. Once I gave them some cigarettes they were happy to let me in. It's a windswept place – at least it was the day I was there – wooded, with rough grass and sandy soil and lots of wild flowers. It's a lonely place. Terribly lonely. There was a memorial erected in the 1960s to what happened. It's in ruins now, knocked down by who knows what people. Anti-semitism, even when there are no longer any Jews.

'I stayed there for hours. Thinking about my beautiful sister. Trying to imagine her last few hours. Trying to feel her presence. There is nowhere on earth that I can bring her close to me. Sometimes, it is like she never existed.

'Thank you again, from the bottom of my heart. You have been more than generous – with your time, with your memories, with your hospitality.'

'It was good to meet you at last. She told me so much about you.' Katya smiled.

'That's funny now, isn't it? Because I always thought she

went her own way.'

'She did. But her family – why, you were the reason why she didn't come to France with me. She told me that you were the person who had had the biggest influence of anybody on her life.'

'Me? But how was that? What did she mean? Did she explain?'

'She told me that what she learned from you was perseverance. Doggedly going after what you wanted and never giving up.'

'I never thought of myself like that.'

'You survived the camps, didn't you?'

'Survival? Yes. But at what price? For what? For what? I've lived three different lives but I only ever wanted one of them.'

'I must go. I'll miss my train. I don't know how likely it is, but if you're ever in Israel –'

'Next year in Jerusalem?'

'Something like that.'

'You'd never know. I still haven't quite lost the travelling bug. I'd like to see Masada.'

'Ah yes, Masada. Goodbye Katya.'

'Good bye David. Goodbye.'

Chapter 7

Slonim. 14 November, 1941. 3AM.

The condensation has frozen to ice on the inside of the windows in the tiny house which Paula, Broni and Ariela share with eleven others. In one of its squalid rooms, Ariela lies on the double mattress with Broni and Paula. Despite the cold, she is fast asleep and dreaming.

In her dream, a large summer party is taking place at her parents' country house. With the exception of Stefan, everyone she might possibly know is there. Sophia and Rebecca have come all the way from Paris. Broni is there with Paula, who has made the journey from Slonim. David, Anna and Marek, her parents and heaps of aunts, uncles and cousins make up the guests. The weather is glorious and the party takes place outside. Ariela is not with anybody, but is aware that she will shortly be leaving for Paris. Whether this is known to anybody else is not clear, but there seems to be an assumption in the dream that everybody is, or will be, happy with the notion.

Dawn. All of the room's occupants are wearing heavy coats, gloves, mufflers, scarves – anything that has not already been taken by the Germans. In the unlit kitchen, the older occupants sit at the table, praying. Above the murmuring of the prayers, the sounds from outside come all the more amplified. A heavy lorry revving its engine as it roars past makes the small pile of chipped plates on the window sill vibrates with its passage. There are sounds of gunshots, not too far away. German voices shouting. Dogs barking. Running feet. Screaming. High pitched. Shrill. Terror stricken. The combination of the cold and fear makes Ariela shiver violently. She sits on the floor, knees up, hands clasped around her shins. Beside her sit Paula and Broni whose faces have a corpse-like pallor. From time to time Ariela catches her breath as she tries to hear what's going on outside.

She feels guilty about Broni. There is no need for him to be here. He has acted like a faithful guard dog ever since they left Warsaw, but she shouldn't have allowed him to do that. She should have seen something like this coming. Yet, she never did. She had always imagined that one day they would just pack up and make their way back to Warsaw. When she thinks about it now, it was insane.

The kitchen is at the rear of the house. It is almost as if they hope that the Germans, finding the front room empty, won't look here. It is a vain hope. Several of the women scream as they hear the first kicking and thudding of rifle butts on the front door. Ariela finds that she has screamed too, and can feel her underwear damp where a spurt of urine has dribbled into the fabric of the gusset. Her mouth is dry as sand and an icy sweat lathers her body – her shoulders, armpits, belly – her heart is pounding. There is a strange feeling in her stomach, and she retches, but nothing happens and the sick sensation remains. The front door gives way and the floor shakes as feet pound into the hall. The kitchen door is blown open with such force that its upper half comes away from its hinges. It sways, the screws that held the hinges like broken teeth.

The first man in the door is very tall, with tightly cropped hair and a broad, spade-shaped face. His features are Slavic. Despite the cold he is dressed in a grey tunic and trousers and

343

his face is flushed. He is panting. His boots seem enormous on the floorboards.

The second man is also big. He has a greasy, swarthy complexion and looks like he hasn't shaved. His black hair is oily looking. He too has been running and his face is almost purple with the exertion. Both men carry rifles and their little forage caps seem impossibly small for their large, bull-like heads and necks.

Behind these men, whom she assumes to be Lithuanians, comes a German. He is by far the smallest of the three and wears a green greatcoat with two rows of buttons down the front. His belt and ammunition pouches are strapped on over his coat. He has a thin, V-shaped face with a sort of permanent smirk on his lips. It is there even when he doesn't intend to smile.

'*Raus Juden, raus!*' The roar of their voices fills the kitchen. The German carries a Luger and jerks his head towards the door.

The people at the table sit as though frozen. It may be that only a few seconds pass, but it is as if the Jews are disobeying the German order. 'Move,' Ariela screams silently, 'otherwise they'll shoot us all.' The Lithuanian with the cropped hair roars something and kicks the chair out from under one of the men. He tumbles to the floor and the Lithuanian kicks him violently. The man struggles to his feet, and crouching, runs towards the door. The German pistol whips him with the Luger as he runs through the doorway. Stumbling and falling, Ariela sees him disappear out the front door.

She, Paula and Broni stand up. Ariela notices that a faint wintery sun has emerged outside. The bricks of the window surround turn carmine in its light. Her eyes register rooftops, birds and the bare tops of trees unmoving in the calm air.

The people are literally being beaten out of the house and

344

they go through the doorway like parachutists leaving a plane. Of the group that were at the table, Mira, an old woman with a black shawl over her head, is last through. She is unsteady and as she crosses the threshold, the German lands a tremendous kick on her back, just below where the V of her shawl ends. Mira crumples as though her body had somehow disappeared from inside her clothes. She lies in a heap like a grave-mound. One of the Lithuanians goes to get her to her feet, but the German holds him back with his left arm. With his other he places the barrel of the Luger onto her head and fires once. The heap jolts. Bits of fabric and hair fly through the air. Other, shell-like fragments clatter against the wall and onto the floor with the spent cartridge case. Splashes of blood and grey mush appear on the wall.

'*Raus, schweine Juden!*

The soldiers overturn the furniture as though it is match-wood. Paula runs towards the door, trying to avoid the objects now strewn around the place and Mira's body. In the midst of all of this pandemonium, Ariela points at Broni as he struggles to get past the Lithuanians and the overturned chair. She screams in German.

'He is not Jewish. He is Aryan. *Volkdeutsch*. Aryan. Only Jews go for forced labour.'

Paula has disappeared out the door. The two Lithuanians looked at each other and then at the German. They stop shouting. Broni stops midway across the room. Ariela hears a bird singing in the tiny yard behind the house.

'Check for yourselves, if you don't believe me,' she says, in a quieter voice.

The man with the Luger hesitates. The pistol is pointing in their direction. Slowly he traverses it from Broni to Ariela and as he does so his eyes meet each of theirs in turn. His eyes are appraising, mocking, pitying. The Lithuanians look at the German who indicates with a nod that they should check.

They, in turn, point their rifles at Broni's groin, indicating with the barrels that he should take his trousers down. He is half turned to Ariela and she sees him fumble with his belt and then his pants drop around his knees. He lifts up his shirt. His bottom is starkly white in comparison to his back.

'You can hardly see that cock,' says the German. 'Fetch it up here so we can see it.'

One of the Lithuanians takes a step forward and Ariela sees Broni shudder as the barrel of the rifle is prodded between his legs. He recoils, turning somewhat so that Ariela can see that the Lithuanian has draped Broni's penis across the top of the barrel of his weapon, and is displaying it to his colleagues. It is so shrunken that it looks like a slug crawling along the grey steel.

'The whore is right,' muses the German. 'A good Christian cock.'

He spits onto the floor. The Lithuanians look again at the German for guidance.

'Of course we should shoot the bastard for fucking dirty Jewish sows.'

The Lithuanian with his rifle in Broni's groin goes to execute the order.

Then the German says '*Nein*, I guess it's his lucky day. Forget him. Bring the bitch.'

Visibly disappointed, the Lithuanian withdraws the rifle. Then, in one smooth movement, he up-ends the weapon, bringing the stock crashing into Broni's face. Ariela's hands go to her mouth and she screams. There is the sound of bones cracking and Broni groans before crashing to the floor, where the Lithuanian kicks him again in the face with his boot. There is blood on the floor and – when the man withdraws his leg – on his boot as well.

'Now,' screams the German with renewed energy. 'Come on, you Jewish cunt.'

Stepping forward, the German catches Ariela by the hair, and wrenches her towards him. Then he strides out the door and along the hall, dragging her along with him. Crouching, she clutches at his hand and tries to remove it. Her hair feels like it's going to be ripped out. At the front door, the German relaxes his hold. Then he slaps her hard on the back of her head, so that she stumbles and knocks against the door jamb. She feels something sharp hit the top of her skull and knows immediately that whatever it is has punctured the skin and that there is bleeding. A kick from behind sends her reeling dizzily out of the doorway into the street.

The cobbles that Ariela stumbles onto are wet and muddy. Her knees and shins are skinned as she falls. Dizzily, she gets to her feet. There is no sign of Paula. The sun has become obscured by a layer of grey, driving cloud. The noise is much greater now. Shouting. Terrible screams. Gunshots. Motors can be heard running over towards the marketplace. She touches her head and her hand comes away sticky with blood. In her coat pocket, she has a piece of cloth she uses as a handkerchief, and with a shaking hand she half mops, half smears the wound. She becomes aware that she is swaying as though she were drunk. She needs to sit down. She feels like she's going to faint.

A great crowd is moving on the street. Men, women, children, old people, infants in mothers' arms, a woman pushing a pram. Many of the people have their hands up or on their heads like prisoners of war. The crowd flows towards the marketplace. Somebody appears beside Ariela. It is a man with a small moustache, a beard that runs along his jaw line and an eagle-beaked nose. His clothes smell and when he opens his mouth to speak, his breath is rancid. But she feels an arm around her and when she almost relaxes against it, it is strong and supports her.

'Come, girl. We must go to the market. They will shoot

you if you stay here.'

The words 'they will shoot you if you stay here' register in her brain. They become the only words there and she repeats them over and over to herself. They will shoot her. Somebody will shoot her. What has she ever done to cause somebody to want to shoot her? She joins the press of people moving up from the river towards the market square. She looks around to talk to the man but he has disappeared. As she makes her way along more people spill out of houses and flow in from side streets. Gunshots and screams reverberate constantly from the houses and yards.

What is going on? What is all this for? Even though the houses and streets are more than familiar to Ariela, she feels as though she's seeing them for the first time. It's like the day she first arrived in Slonim, a place that in her wildest dreams she had never expected to visit. In fact, what with the gunshots and the screams, what passes through her head is that this is like some kind of movie; a crowd scene in which she has somehow been caught up.

In the market square there are already large numbers of people. They are sitting on one side of the square on the wet cobbles. Children are crying. Germans and Lithuanians armed with rifles, stand at regular intervals facing them. A knot of four Germans stand to one side in a little group, hands held behind their back in some kind of conference. Two of them wear officers' caps.

Ariela sees a fleet of seven or eight trucks drive into the square. The trucks turn in a circle and then, one reverses towards the sitting Jews while the remainder wait with their engines running. Two of the soldiers step aside as the driver revs the truck and then drives it back at high speed. The people sitting on the ground behind it scatter as the truck almost careers onto them. A cloud of diesel fumes envelope the people and they start coughing. The truck has sprayed them with muddy water, and driven over some of their bundles, crushing them into soggy masses.

The driver jumps out grinning and walks round to the two guards who are laughing. One of them helps him lower the tailboard, and the guards begin to pick out whom they want to put onto the truck. They start with old people. One soldier points and waves people forward while his colleague prods them towards the truck with his rifle. The first man to come forward is old and very fragile. He has a walking stick and totters through the sitting mass of people, who part as best they can to let him through. At the rear of the truck the man is at a loss how to board it. He reaches with a hand. Lifts a foot. Hesitates. Looks round, confusion and fear on his face. The German with the rifle nods to the driver, who is cupping his hands around a match to light a cigarette. The driver flips away the match, jabs the cigarette into his mouth and approaches the rear of the truck. Now the old man becomes totally fearful and makes more frantic efforts to work out a way to mount the truck. There is an amused look on the driver's face. He places his left hand on the man's shoulder and with his right he holds it up, palm outwards, to indicate stop. Then, the cigarette still dangling from his mouth, he disappears round the side of the truck. The old man stands stock still as though frozen to the spot. The driver reappears. He carries a wooden box and places this at the rear of the truck. Then, taking the old man's hand, as though he were a dance partner, he gently helps the man to put one foot onto the box. The other foot follows. Meanwhile, the driver pulls himself up into the rear of the truck and the old man, now understanding how the technique will work, extends his arms to the driver, the walking stick dangling from one hand.

The old man is small so that he goes up on tiptoes to extend his reach. The driver half bends as though to stretch

349

down to him but then suddenly stands up and kicks the man in the face as if kicking off a football match. The crowd screams as the man literally flies through the air, hurtling backwards and landing amongst them, where he lies silently. The driver throws away his cigarette, and stands at the back of the truck, legs akimbo, the tips of his boots extending over the edge.

'Now,' he roars in German, 'hurry up, you stinking Jews.'

Helped up by their fellows, the selected old people begin to scramble on board. Ariela joins a group squatting, about 40 metres from where the trucks are.

A car rolls into the marketplace and stops. The car's driver gets out and clicks to attention, opening the door for an SS officer. An officer who has been standing in the centre of the square strides over to the SS man, stops and salutes. The soldiers who have been in conference break up. The SS officer has greying hair, a sharp nose and chin, carefully shaved face and fine teeth. His uniform is immaculate and his boots are gleaming. He looks like an ambassador or a successful businessman. He smiles as he strolls down the line of people in the bare space between the guards and the crowd. At about the mid point of his traverse he stops. He turns to face the crowd, thinks for a moment and then says:

'Jews! You are all going to Leszno. That is why you have been allowed to bring along your valuables, food, extra clothing. Nothing will happen to you. There are trucks for the old people and the children. The rest of you will march there.'

With that he turns to the other officer and nods.

Ariela keeps looking around trying to find Paula, but without success. Unable to squat any further – her legs are starting to cramp – Ariela wraps her coat under her as best she can and sits on the cobbles of the marketplace. The act of doing so seems to have a settling effect on her mind.

Are they really going to Leszno? Even though a voice keeps telling her that it's a lie, it *could* be true. But if it's not, then all this shooting means that the alternative must be much, much worse. What about escape? Get to the edge of the crowd and slip out of the square. No, not here. The Germans have the place all sealed up. It would be certain death.

Further down the square people are being ordered to their feet. The crowd gradually rises like a wave breaking down the square. There must be thousands of people, and now they start to flow out of the square towards Skrobive Street. Eventually the wave reaches where Ariela is. She is counted into a group of six and told to follow the six in front. There is not much shouting or violence now – more an air of bored efficiency.

At the exit from the square, the trucks have been reversed into position so that their stumpy bonnets point towards where Ariela is. She is still 60 or 70 metres away when she realises that these trucks are also being filled – with children. A rumour runs through the crowd that it is to save little ones the walk, and to save hunger-weakened mothers from having to carry toddlers. There is much commotion and a large number of guards at the trucks. Ariela can see whips being raised. There is wailing, then screaming and then a gunshot. One. Then another a while later. And another. But the commotion continues. Guards near to Ariela start to urge people along, hitting those on the outside of the column with the rifles. Some guards have shouldered their rifles and use short whips instead.

There are some women just ahead of Ariela who have children, one an infant wrapped in a blanket, another leading a young girl by the hand. Ariela sees them becoming agitated and talking anxiously to their neighbours. The woman with the infant tries to hide it under her coat but the package is too bulky. By now they have come very near to the trucks. The Germans have set up a sort of funnel of soldiers on either side of the moving column, with the result that people have to pass through the funnel in single file. The neck of the funnel occurs just beside a reversed lorry. Here some soldiers are separating children and babies from their parents.

They enter the funnel and there is some jostling as they approach its neck. Amidst the bobbing heads, she can no longer see the woman with the infant. But suddenly, Ariela recognises the blanket in which the child was wrapped. A tall SS man has the bundle which he must have plucked from the woman. There is shouting, jostling, whip arms raised. Then the SS man half-turns and tosses the bundle to a Jew standing in the rear of truck. There is panic on the man's face but he succeeds in catching the bundle cleanly. He goes into the dark interior of the truck where he can vaguely be seen laying the bundle down delicately.

Not all the infants have been so lucky. Several bundles with small limbs protruding lie untidily on the cobbles at the rear of the truck. There is blood everywhere – on the cobbles, on the heaps of rags, on the infants' bodies. Ariela sees a young boy – he can't be much more than five – led off and pointed at the rear of the truck. He hesitates and looks back, calling 'Mama, Mama'. Eventually a German pushes him so that he stumbles onto the heap of infants' bodies and has to climb across it before being pulled up onto the truck. Ariela finds she is holding her hands together as though she were praying. A violent shaking runs from her hands through her arms and up to her shoulders so that the whole upper part of her body is wracked with trembling. She reaches the narrowest part of the funnel and is waved straight through.

Beyond the funnel, the soldiers spread out again. They chivvy people into sixes and channel them out of the square into Skrobive Street. The street is almost deserted as the long column of people flows along it. They walk in the centre of the street, between the pavements, as though in some sort of ceremonial procession. Ariela is hungry and weak. She has not eaten since last night and even then it was only a crust. Her feet hurt and she has a terrible headache from the blow she received. A cold wind sweeps the shambling procession as it finds its own rhythm.

Inside a window Ariela sees a boy smiling. She notices a cheap ornament, a plant with bright red flowers. The ramshackle alleyways of Slonim. There is an occasional onlooker or a fearful face glimpsed at a partly-drawn curtain. An old woman on the sidewalk watches the procession and crosses herself. Her lips are moving as though in prayer. The column is silent except for the quiet sobbing of the people whose children have been taken. Maybe they are going to Leszno. Ariela prays silently that it is so.

They are still in the town when a halt occurs and the people are ordered to sit on the ground on one side of the street. Soon afterwards another column of people appears coming from the direction of Skrobive, a village outside Slonim. This column passes and those seated notice that there are still children and babies in the passing column. As soon as they have passed, the march resumes for the seated column.

They are now on the highway to Baranovici, leading eastwards and crossing the bridge over the Szczara. Beyond this a luxuriant avenue of old willows lines the road which climbs to the Albertin pine forest. Ariela has fond memories of this walk. The first summer after she arrived in Slonim, she and Broni used to come out this way and walk to the woods at Chepilovo. They had several picnics there. The trees provided welcome shade. With a soft breeze blowing through them and birds singing in their branches, the place held a distillation of the sounds of summer.

The procession trudges slowly up the hill. Suddenly, Ariela hears a short, faint crackling sound. It is like summer lightning. The first time she hears it, it is so faint, that she isn't sure whether she just imagined it. Then, it comes again, a sound like a piece of fabric being ripped. It sounds so much like this that she looks around wondering who in the crowd is doing that and why. She sees nothing and then in a minute or so, the sound comes again. It's in the distance – up the hill and away to the right. Once more she hears it, and then as a terrible wail goes up from the crowd, she realises what it is. Repeated volleys of rifle fire.

The column wavers. The guards act as though they have anticipated this moment, and urge the people on with increased ferocity. A woman ahead of Ariela faints. Ariela sees the woman sag and then collapse to the ground. The crowd stumbles until she is lifted under her arms and carried forward. Feverish praying now fills the air. It is punctuated with the hysterical screams of a man somewhere up ahead. These continue for a short while until they are silenced by the loud report of a gunshot.

Suddenly, she sees two figures break away from the right-hand side of the column. Hunched down, like people sheltering from a downpour, they sprint for the bushes on the edge of the roadway. A fusillade of rifle shots smacks bloody holes in their backs, and they are knocked head first into the foliage. There is no Leszno now.

Ariela looks around, but there are soldiers everywhere and clear lines on either side of the column. One of the guards spots her and roars. She hastily turns back, hoping she won't hear his boots coming towards her. Her breathing becomes very rapid. It is like she has been thrown into freezing water. She is having difficulty catching her breath. Her headache throbs at her temples, feeling like a leaden hood above her eyes. Panic grips her. Her vision wavers. She cannot see properly, so that even if she wanted to flee she wouldn't be able to. Her heart is pounding in her chest. She starts to sway and holds the top of her head to try to steady herself.

If only she could faint and wake later to find all of this gone. She must run. Get away. Escape into the bushes. She begins to jostle her way to the edge of the crowd. People clear out of the way to let her through. She is at the edge. Only a few footsteps – four, five, maybe six – and she will be safe. She blinks repeatedly to try to clear her eyes. Now, her mind says, go. Go. Go on. Go on.

'Don't,' a voice says. 'Wait. Wait until we get into the woods.'

Because of various delays, the shooting begins at Chepilovo just after 10am on 14 November. In accordance with Hick's plan, a single trench has been dug. It is 4m wide, 5m deep and 150m long. The shooting party consists of four squads of ten men each, spread evenly along the length of the trench. The method is to take groups of 40 at a time, then channel them into four groups of ten for processing at each of the shooting locations. Allowing 1-2 minutes to set each group of 40 up, to get them into position on the edge of the ditch, shoot them, and tumble any bodies that fell the wrong way into the ditch, he calculates they should do about 1,600 in an hour. With six hours of daylight that should enable them to do the whole 10,000 before nightfall. It is an aggressive schedule. If darkness comes and they aren't finished, there will definitely be escapes whether they hold them here for the night or march them back to the town. And Christ, who wants to spend the night out here? Still, he'll just have to wait and see how it goes. At least these Germans are experienced at this sort of thing, whatever about the Lithuanians. That experience has already paid off. There was some foul-up with the column coming from Skrobive. Somebody forgot to take the babies, so that the people arrived in Slonim with babies still in tow. Nothing is more liable to slow up a shooting schedule than mothers with babies. Thus, it was a genuine

355

piece of inspiration when Otto somebody-or-other, one of the NCOs, suggested they deal with the babies as they were passing over the Baranovici bridge. Sure enough, by positioning a few men there, they were able to relieve the mothers of the babies and throw them into the river. That now means that the entire column is coming to the shooting area, free of this particular encumbrance. Some babies are always smuggled through but this time it'll be a lot less.

The first family is brought forward. Parents, both in their forties, the wife younger. Four children, three girls and a boy of about seventeen. The eldest girl appears to be about nineteen. The youngest, an infant, perhaps two or three, is carried by the mother. They are urged forward with plenty of shouting and blows from the guards. It's always good to start out like this. Despite the violence, the father takes the son's hand. The other two daughters hold hands.

In the first 40 shot are a bank manager and his wife. They married in Warsaw and spent a short honeymoon there in a luxury hotel. There is a photograph of them on the balcony of the hotel, she sitting, he behind her leaning proprietorially on the railing of the balcony. Ever since, he has carried the photograph in his wallet. When the victims undress to go forward to the trenches, a Lithuanian auxiliary searches the pockets of the clothes they leave behind. He finds many such photographs, but they are irritants, since what he is really looking for is money. He is a tidy-minded man though, so he creates a number of different piles for the various things he finds. There is one for photographs and the photograph of the bank manager and his wife is the one that begins that pile.

Another 40 are led to the pit. A woman with a three-year-old girl. As they approach, the woman tries to carry the girl, but she screams and wriggles, and eventually slips out of her mother's arms. The woman catches the child's hand, hoping to gather her daughter up again, but the girl pulls her hand away. A German close by tells the mother to leave her, and sure enough the little girl trots along contentedly beside the mother. A man who knows children. The people already at the edge of the pit are kneeling. The mother makes yet another attempt to catch the child's hand, but again the child squeals and tears her hand away. Now, at the edge of the pit, a German pushes her to her knees with his rifle. Her child watches her closely and does the same.

The people are prodded forward with gun barrels. Here is a woman who worked in a grocer's shop beside the Szczara. For no reason that she can explain, a memory comes into her head of a February evening several years ago. She can't fix the exact year, except that it was before the war and she remembers that spring came early. The day had been mild. Warm. Brilliantly sunny. So calm that the surface of the river had been like a mirror. That evening, the setting sun had turned the sky pink. A brazen, deep, radiant pink which had taken ages to fade from the sky.

She went to the door and leant against the doorpost. From there she gazed into the river at upside down Slonim: The inverted bridge and buildings – a fantasy Slonim, peaceful, prosperous, happy, with none of the sadness of the real town; and the pink sky so that the glass of the river was a colour of indescribable beauty in the oncoming cool of evening.

These thoughts threaten to break up, to spin away in pieces from her, but she grapples to hold onto them as she is directed towards the edge of the pit.

There is another woman in the group who is in her eighties. She had aunts and uncles who remembered Napoleon's invasion of Russia. Born into a Jewish family – she has always been something of a non-conformist. She is a vegetarian – something to which she attributes her long and healthy life to date. Her garden, but especially her roses, are well known throughout Jewish Slonim. Often vulgar – she will say things about a particular variety of rose such as 'No good up against a wall, got to have this one in bed' – she roars invective at her executioners as they lead her forward. The Germans and Lithuanians are amused and laugh. As the group is marshalled at the pit, and the Lithuanians withdraw out of the way of the shooters, one of them says good-humouredly to the shivering, naked, women, 'Now ladies, the doctor will be with you shortly'.

In the next group is a woman with a baby, which some-how, she has managed to hide up until now. She hugs the small naked body to shield it from the cold as best she can. The baby is crying. With tears in her eyes, the mother sings to it softly, tickling its tummy and armpits. The baby stops crying and begins cooing delightedly, wriggling its legs and waving its tiny feet in the air. At the pit, the woman transfers the baby from its cradled position and holds it in front of her, hugging it to her, its back to the pit. Her tears form small pools on the top of the baby's head with its faint growth of dark hair.

Another 40 men, women and children are brought to the pit.

And then another 40. It is always the same, the guards notice: the women are much more conscious of the shame of being naked. The men seem to find undressing in front of neighbours the most embarrassing thing. And then another 40.

And so the first hour passes.

Just after eleven the four shooting squads are relieved and go to a spot behind the trenches where a fire smokes. Here there is fresh coffee and cigarettes, and clouds of breath hang gauze-like in the chilly air. The handful of soldiers who already cluster there wear greatcoats, hats and mufflers, but the shooters are in tunics with the top buttons open. They are sweating despite the cold. They flex their fingers to release the stiffness in them.

The shooters take cups of steaming coffee, laced with

vodka, in their hands and blow on the surface. 'Anyone have any chocolate?' one asks. There is a general shaking of heads. 'Shit, some chocolate would have been nice.'

The new shooting squads shoot their first 40. The bursts of gunfire die away and the bodies tumble in that slow-motion way that they have. The next crowd of Jews are prodded into place.

Onto the pile of photographs goes a school class photograph. A group of teachers sit solemnly in the front with hands on their knees or folded. The Lithuanian notices that the children all seem to be carrying sticks or maybe they are actually toy guns. The children seem to be only four or five but in their jackets and caps they are like a small Yid army. He didn't realise they began training their soldiers so young. Jesus, these Jews. The Lithuanian doesn't know that the photograph was taken on Lag ba'Omer, the Jewish spring festival commemorating the revolt led by Bar Kokhba against the Romans. It is traditional for children to carry bows and arrows or toy guns on this holiday.

Another 40 men, women and children are shot.

Hick is unhappy. They are running behind schedule. He decides they will work through lunch time.

In the next group, a watchmaker, almost blind from too many years dealing with small parts and intricate mechanisms in the weak daylight that came in through his single north-facing window. His oil-ingrained fingers are long, delicate, feminine. A nine-year-old boy approaches, still wearing a cap, which one of the Lithuanians pulls from him savagely and throws into the pit. He cuffs the boy so hard around the head that the boy loses his balance and topples into the pit and onto the still-warm, blood-washed corpses. He tries to stand up but dives when he hears the burst of machine-gun fire. Before he can stand up again, he is caught by the weight of falling bodies.

A group of 40 men, women and children and another group of 40 men, women and children.

The Lithuanian SD soldier counting off the groups of 40 is puzzled. There were meant to be no babies. Alright, so an occasional one gets through. But the question is, do babes in arms count or not? He checks with his commanding officer who checks with Hick. Yes, comes the reply, of course babies count as an extra one. Jesus, thinks Hick, can these people do nothing for themselves?

Another group of 40 men, women and children. A woman whose independent spirit, rebellious nature, her 'modern' ways and her insistence on standing alone had been the bane of her family's life.

Lunch time comes and goes and the men grumble at not having a chance for a break. Hick fumes. The slide in the schedule has been stopped, but they have not made up any time. He wonders if he should increase the group size to 50, but decides not to for the moment. To do that he would need at least one more squad of ten shooters and that would mess up the hour-on hour-off rota he's got going. No, best to leave it for the moment.

The guards bring on another 40 men, women and children. And another 40.

In the next group: the proprietress of an inn. Her 29-year-old unmarried daughter. Two girls together, teenagers or in their early twenties, arms folded across their breasts and linking a third woman in the middle. The third woman also has her arms folded and her head down as though ashamed of her nakedness. The guards are somewhat gentler now – if only due to tiredness. Provided the people move quickly, they confine themselves to regular verbal goading. The Jews' bare feet tread gingerly across the rough, frozen ground. Another woman by herself, older, arms folded covering her breasts. A small boy of nine or ten. An old woman by herself. 'Get along there, mother,' the guard says, touching her, not roughly, across her withered buttocks with the barrel of his rifle. A very old man, supported by a middle-aged woman. Two girls in their early teens, sisters, twins perhaps; the same hair and features manifest in two different faces, one fat and handsome, the other thin and pretty. A fat woman – incredible after all this time in the ghetto. Must have been fucking someone in the *Judenrat*. Four women, arms covering their breasts, pressing close together one behind the other, as though the closeness of their bodies will give them some sort of protection. A little girl, very pretty, with luxuriant dark hair. A tall, big-boned woman, with a figure ruined from child bearing, clasping a child to her breast, her fingers splayed across the infant's bald, pink skull. A smaller woman who looks up to the taller woman as though for guidance. A fine-figured girl with her dark hair tied in a pigtail. A man with a naked child sitting on his forearm, the child's arm around the father's neck; child and father whispering as though exchanging a secret. A blonde woman. The Germans wonder at how Aryan she looks. A swarthy-looking man. An emaciated looking woman, shivering violently. A woman who stops to vomit, and while she is still in the act is prodded sharply forwards by the guards. The vomit spills down her front onto her arms and breasts, and – when she pulls her arms away in an attempt to regain her balance – onto her pubic area, where it coats the bushy hairs. A man, white knuckles, clenched fists holding onto a handkerchief, held to his mouth, crying hysterically. A woman with her hair pushed back behind her ears and a sleeping infant in her arms. The child is big, so big that she can hardly carry him and retain her balance. The guard is about to push her but realises that if he does she will probably fall and delay the whole business even further. It crosses his mind that he should shoot her but then he would probably have to drag her to the pit. She has moved out of his range by the time he decides to do nothing. A woman with emaciated, conical breasts. A woman with long silky hair, again with a tall, skinny child in her arms A girl of six or seven by herself being shepherded along by the man behind her. A girl with short, bobbed hair. An alcoholic, regarded as proud and snobbish by his neighbours, still trying to exude an air of haughtiness, although naked. Two sisters, beautiful, tall, statuesque. A woman with deep green eyes, pouting lips and an immensely weary look on her face. A schoolteacher, her thick hair tied back with a ribbon.

And another 40.

And another 40. A woman comes forward screaming. She refuses to stand or walk and is carried and dragged by two men, urged on by a German with a whip. When she gets to the edge of the pit and sees its contents she redoubles her screaming and lurches backwards, dragging the two men with her. The woman falls to the ground, half-toppling the other two. The German lashes at all three and the two men who had been doing the carrying, stumble to their feet. The only place they can go to get out of the range of the whiplashes is back to the edge of the pit. They do so and are quickly brought under control by a Lithuanian. The woman lies on her back on the muddy, shit-covered ground, writhing and screaming. The German lets the whip fall from his hand and it dangles from his wrist by a leather thong. Then he reaches into his open holster and extracts his pistol. He clamps the heel of his boot onto the woman's upper arm and squashes the toe onto her breast. He notices how erect her nipples are in the cold. There is a flash of some kind of recognition in her eyes. Then he shoots her once in the face.

And another 40.

One of the guards never ceases to be amazed by the astonishing variety of women's breasts. Small one. Pointed ones. Droopy ones like spaniel's ears. Droopy ones that would look fine if supported in a bra. Fine big ones. Tiny ones – ones that he'd almost have bigger himself. It is unusual, he reflects, to find a pair that without any support or anything, are just perfect. In a sense he feels that this has been his work for the last few months – to find such breasts. That's why he is always annoyed if they separate the sexes and he gets stuck in the men's part. Of course, when he does find such a pair, which he occasionally does, it's such a pity, because he knows he'll have no chance to enjoy them.

The whole procedure is humming along now like a well-oiled mechanism. It begins back down towards Slonim where people are still queued up along the road in groups of 500. These groups are brought to the shooting ground one by one. After that people are fed, 40 at a time, towards the trench. Hick knows that this is the part of the day when the most work gets done. The system is at its most efficient now. In another couple of hours his men will begin to tire. But for the moment they are working to optimum capacity.

Getting the total number of people processed right is important. The guard doing the tally counts out the groups of forty, waving them through lazily with his hand.

'*Eins, zwei, drei, vier, funf, sechs, sieben, acht, neun, zehn, elf, zwoif, dreizehn, vierzehn, funfzehn, sechszehn, siebzehn, achtzehn, neuneun, zwanzig.*' A man with a bow tie. '*Einundzwanzig, zweiundzwanzig, dreiundzwanzig, vierundzwanzig, funfundzwanzig, sechsundzwanzig, siebenundzwanzig, achtundzwanzig, neinundzwanzig, dreisig, einund dreisig, zweiund dreisig, dreiund dreisig, vierund dreisig, funfund driebig, sechsund dreisig, siebenund dreisig, achtund dreisig, neunund dreisig, vierzig.*'

In the gap between two groups the guard is struck yet again by how many Jews there are in the world. He never realised it until he came here to Russia. Wherever their outfit goes, endless streams of them. Can it really be that they will succeed in getting rid of *all* of them? It hardly seems possible.

'*Eins, zwei, drei, vier, funf, sechs, sieben, acht, neun, zehn, elf, zwoif, dreizehn, vierzehn, funfzehn, sechszehn, siebzehn, achtzehn, neuneun, zwanzig, einundzwanzig, zweiundzwanzig, dreiundzwanzig, vierundzwanzig, funfundzwanzig, sechsundzwanzig, siebenundzwanzig.*' A youth on a wooden crutch. Has he come all the way from the town like this? Why didn't somebody shoot him and put him out of his misery way back? He looks half dead already. It's a long way to have hopped, thinks the guard, and smiles at the thought. '*Achtundzwanzig, neinundzwanzig, dreisig, einund dreisig, zweiund dreisig, dreiund dreisig, vierund dreisig, funfund driebig.*' A man carrying a child in his arms. Lots of children got through. The Jews are infinitely inventive. *Sechsund dreisig, siebenund dreisig, achtund dreisig, neunund dreisig, vierzig.*'

The guard hesitates and his hand stops moving. He is blocking a man carrying a dog. A small dirty white dog with a sharp face and pointy ears. These fucking Jews. Can't they understand anything? They were given clear instructions about what they could and couldn't bring. He wonders if he should let the dog through. If it gets loose it could cause all kinds of problems. But what will he do with it? A dog would be nice but where is he to put it while he counts through these thousands of Jews? Best to let this one go. There'll be other dogs. Besides it's a Jewish dog. The guys up at the undressing can deal with it. Anyway, it'll give the lucky bastards a nasty little surprise for once. The guard waves the man on. The man smiles a weak, grateful smile as the guard says '*neinundzwanzig, dreisig, einund dreisig, zweiund dreisig, dreiund dreisig, vierund dreisig, funfund driebig, sechsund dreisig, siebenund dreisig, achtund dreisig, neunund dreisig, vierzig.*'

Each time the guard counts 40 through he marks a stroke on a small pad. When he gets to ten, he draws a line through the ten strokes. 400. Later on, his figures will be checked against the number of yellow stars unstitched from the Jews' clothes. But it usually takes a few days before that figure comes to hand. They will have a fairly good idea this evening, a number that won't be too inaccurate. He could do with a break. Looking out towards the road though, he sees an endless sea of faces. He'll just have to keep going until a relief comes.

'Eins, zwei, drei, vier, funf, sechs, sieben, acht, neun, zehn, elf, zwoif, dreizehn, vierzehn, funfzehn, sechszehn, siebzehn, achtzehn, neuneun, zwanzig, einundzwanzig, zweiundzwanzig, dreiundzwanzig, vierundzwanzig, funfundzwanzig, sechsundzwanzig, siebenundzwanzig, achtundzwanzig.' Though he has no way of knowing it, the man counts through Paula. Then come three children together. A boy and what looks like his baby sister. A young girl with big sad eyes and the same big nose and pouty lips. Some of these Jewish kids are very good-looking.

His brain exhausted, the guard continues to count monotonously.

Word reaches Hick that they have moved into the last 2,000. It is good news because the light is starting to fail. He relieves the shooters and starts to move around from one man to the next. 'Not much more to go now.' 'We'll soon have you back in billets with a warm meal inside you.' 'Just a few hundred more.' 'Another hour or so.' 'Keep it up – we're nearly there.' He recognises the man who made the suggestion about the babies on Baranovici Bridge. 'Your men are doing good work, Otto.'

And another 40 are led to the pit.

It is late afternoon when the group of 500 in which Ariela finds herself gets the order to move. By then the colour has gone from the sky. They are just on the edge of Chepilovo woods, where the churned up track through the woods, leaves the main road. A cold wind is blowing. Despite all the people, it is a lonely place under this November sky. All day she has gradually moved up the hill from Slonim, the sound of the shooting becoming louder and louder. It is now quite close in the woods off to their right. Every time the guns go off she shudders. Some people scream. There is a strong smell of excrement – mounds of it lie on the road like cattle droppings on a country path.

The man who stopped Ariela breaking away from the crowd and being shot is in his late thirties or early forties. He has solid features and bright blue eyes. It turns out that he was a soldier in the Polish Army. He tells her that they have almost no possibility of escape, but whatever chance they do have will be when they are amongst the trees. Even though his skin is pale and sweaty with fear, the businesslike way he says all of this has a calming effect on her. Her vision clears. In fact she can suddenly see things in great detail almost as if they were magnified. He stays beside her as they stop-start their way up the hill. There is nothing to do but wait and try to keep her courage intact. She realises she must stay clear headed and aware. Whenever the monstrous feeling of complete and utter helplessness tries to overwhelm her, with an immense effort she locks it back into a corner of her mind. Even as she does this it starts to ooze out again.

She understands now why it's said that your whole life flashes before you just before you die. It is not a rapid survey of a life, to see how well or how badly it was lived. Rather it is an attempt to understand how you came to be at this particular point. What could she have done differently? Where could she have made different choices? How could she have avoided this place and time? If she were here at this spot a week ago, or in a few days time, nothing would happen to her. But because she happens to be here today she will die. It seems an impossibly high price to pay for such a small coincidence. Ten, twenty, 50 times, she replays the events that brought her to this point.

A track has been beaten into the woods, broken down by the passage of thousands of feet. The pathway is slippery with mud and strewn with shoes, boots and cast off bundles. Soldiers with rifles stand every few yards. It looks as if there is no chance of escape. Some have tried. They lie by the side of the path, or even in the failing light they can be seen in the gloom amongst the trees. Another halt is called. There is no apparent reason. People around Ariela are praying, mumbling the words fervidly. They seem no longer aware of their surroundings; they look with eyes that don't see.

'We'll have to do it here,' her companion says, his face marble-coloured, like a corpse. 'The further in we go, the less chance we'll have. When we get moving again … down here … when I give the word, just run like crazy. Run to the left. All right? To the left.'

She nods. Her eyes are full of tears. She clutches her upper arms in her hands. She is shaking violently.

The crowd of people around them gradually resolves itself into a single file line, which begins to move briskly over the uneven ground. The Polish soldier is behind Ariela. Between the darkness caused by the trees and that of the failing day, it is impossible to see what lies up ahead. They pass guards, who stand with impassive, bored faces. Between gaps in the rifle volleys she can hear the wind in the trees, feel the first spots of rain or snow on her skin. She keeps glancing to the left trying to see where she might go. She waits for the word. She passes several likely spots, but still the man behind her says nothing. Why hasn't he given it? Up ahead – she hears it before she can see who's doing it – there is somebody counting. The voice is soft, a murmur. It sounds tired.

'*Neinundzwanzig, dreisig, einund dreisig, zweiund dreisig, dreiund dreisig.*'

She looks behind her at the soldier. To her horror, she sees that his face has changed utterly. His nostrils are widely dilated, and his breathing is gasping and convulsive. He paws at his throat, eyeballs bulging so that they are white in the shadows. His eyes look right through her.

'You fool,' she screams. 'We've left it too late.' 'Too late. We've left it too late.' In response, a nearby soldier pushes her on with the butt of his weapon, so that she stumbles forward and arrives at the man doing the counting. He has a rifle on his shoulder and is waving people through like a steward at a football match.

'Vierund dreisig, funfund dreisig, sechsund dreisig, siebenund dreisig, achtund dreisig, neunund dreisig, vierzig.'

The person in front of Ariela goes through and a gloved and overcoated arm comes down in front of her. It is careful not to touch her. As she watches the people who have gone through, disappear round a bend on the track, she starts to surrender herself completely to panic. She's going to die. She's going to die. There is another burst of rifle fire brutally close. There is silence for a moment as the shots die away. Then, a symphony of screams and groans and shrieks. The German lifts his arm. He is young, baby-faced with thin lips pursed tightly together. Show him you're beautiful. The thought escapes into her head from a fuzz of terror. She forces a smile onto her lips. 'Sir,' she says, 'please –' He looks at her like she's not there and gestures with his head. When she doesn't move, he catches her upper arm and shoves her forward. *'Eins,'* he says irritably, beginning the count again.

Urged on by more soldiers, she hurries along the track, the low ferns brushing her leg. It feels like a tunnel. She becomes less and less aware of the ground, the treetops, the lowering sky. She weeps. She is going to die. In the next few minutes she is going to die. Up ahead, at the end of this tunnel of trees. There she will die. Her life, which has hardly started, will end. Just at the end, the path turns to the right in a dogleg bend. A guard stands at the knee of the bend. Turning the corner, she realises that she has entered a sort of clearing, because the sky is somewhat brighter. Here, more guards hold rifles at the ready and utter '*raus, raus*' in tired voices. One of them swings a whip at her as she passes, but it is done lazily, in an offhand sort of way, and she barely feels its touch. Everything seems to be happening so quickly.

The depths of the forest stretch off to her left while on her right sparse trees have now given way to an unexpected sight. An immense pile of clothes rises up like an ancient burial mound. Beyond that the ground rises slightly so that it is impossible to see what lies up ahead. A line of soldiers, heavily clothed, stands at the end of the pile of clothes. They have rifles on their shoulders. However, it is an unarmed man who approaches her, meets her eye and tugs at her coat. He smiles and says something unintelligible.

She doesn't understand. But then he pulls her coat so violently that it is half torn from her shoulders. He makes some other sounds and gesticulates at the pile of clothes on the ground. Some other people have arrived and started to take their clothes off. Ariela's legs feel wobbly, like she is going to collapse. She's is going to die naked. She removes her coat, and the man rips it from her grasp. Then he goes over to issue orders to some newcomers.

She turns away from the guards and takes off her cardigan. The cold grasps at her skin through her thin blouse. In the blur of her brain, the familiar movements of undressing feel so out of place here. She unlaces her boots and takes them off. Then she undoes the catch on her skirt and pushes it down, stepping out of it. It is so cold. Standing on her skirt, she peels down the heavy black woollen stockings with their elastic garters. The bottom of her blouse comes down over her underpants, but now she takes this off so that she is left in only her underwear. She hears laughter. Reaching behind she undoes her brassiere and tries to peel it off without uncovering her breasts. At this point she stops, but the man returns, roaring again, and reaching over to pull at the band of her pants. Shivering violently, she takes down her knickers and steps out of them. She presses her thighs tightly together. Despite the cold she is coated in sweat.

There are lots of other people around her now, standing and undressing. She crosses her arms, with her hands on her shoulders, and squats down, trying to hide her pubic hair. Looking up she notices a German with a camera. He points it straight at her and she hears it click. He murmurs something to one of the guards who roughly bundles a group of women into a row. The cameraman photographs them and moves on. Ariela sees a man who points a cine camera at her. She turns away.

'Raus, Juden. Raus.'

The familiar shout comes from somewhere on the edge of her consciousness. She stands up as something stings across her shoulder and snakes down onto her breast like a whiplash of molten steel. It draws a thin line of blood. She is unaware of whether or not she cries out, but she begins to jog, partially because of the cold, partially because of the urging behind her. She holds one hand across her pubes and with her other arm she tries to cover her bobbing breasts. The ground slopes uphill for some metres and then runs out onto the remainder of the wide, flat clearing.

She is dimly aware of the grey sky overhead. Against that background the tops of the trees are blurry in the oncoming twilight. At the base of the trees is a table with soldiers clustered around. A bright yellow fire is burning, and some of the soldiers are silhouetted in its light. The smell of burning pine is blown on the wind. She is close enough that she can distinguish the occasional face, ruddy in the firelight. Out in the clearing where it is brighter, more soldiers stand in a rough line between where she is and the trees. They stand several metres apart, waving people on. She can see naked figures ahead of her bobbing along and she jogs along after them. She feels the sandy soil and the frozen grass swishing through her toes. She stands on something that feels as though it has punctured her skin. The pain hardly registers.

The icy turf is replaced by loose earth. She can feel it between her toes, mixed with occasional sharp pebbles under her feet. She is panting and her heart is racing. The ground rises slightly and feels muddy. She is at the edge of a pit.

The pit stretches off on either side. In the gloom, she cannot see where either piece ends. The sides of the trench slope for a metre or so before going vertically downwards. The earth she stands on and the earth sloping down into the trench is soggy, sodden with blood. She can see little rivulets of it running down into the trench like tiny canals. There is other matter on the earth. Mushy, warm, spongy, it oozes up through her toes. It is shades of grey and red; butcher shop colours. The ground is slippery.

The trench itself is packed with bodies. She registers a person lying on their back, hands joined in supplication, mouth open as though in prayer. A teenager in a foetal position. A child, its mother's arm still clasping it around the back of the knee. An arm seeming to climb up the wall of the trench as though its owner would climb out. A body with its buttocks in the air as though it had ducked its head under water. Two women, face down, one with her arm across the other's shoulders like friends. A little girl on her side as though she had fallen awkwardly from a tree. A face destroyed, with just a mess of blood and bone where it used to be. A woman lying, her legs splayed, one leg straight, the other bent. A child, lying on its back, its little fingers curled as though holding something, a bullet hole near its mouth. A woman whose upper body is raised slightly, her arms and head thrown back, so that the pose looks almost like one of seduction. A baby thrown by itself like a doll. A man's head as though buried in another man's bottom. A woman lying on her back, silent, unmarked, her head to one side as though in gentle repose.

The bodies have fallen every which way and some lie draped across others. Individual bodies in a long carpet of interlocked, bloodstained, nude corpses that stretches off on either side. Heads, arms, legs at all kinds of crazy angles. People frozen in the positions in which they fell. They are twitching, stretching. Hands raised or covering eyes. There is blood everywhere. People try to move limbs. There are groans. Muffled screams. There is a sort of frozen violence in what she sees. A German with a pistol stands on the lip of the trench, occasionally firing into it. Ariela recoils and stumbles backwards several steps. 'I'm going to die,' she wails, in an animal-like wail. 'I'm going to die.'

'If you have babies,' says a bored voice, 'hold them in front of you'.

'Babies in front' the voice repeats in several languages.

Soldiers appear and start to form the people into a rough line. A gloved hand grasps her, pulls her across the sand towards a particular spot, and then stops her there. There is wailing. Crying. Screams. 'No, no.' 'Please sir. Sir, please.' Somebody is saying the *Shema Yisroel*. The smell of excrement is very strong.

Ariela is clothed in a shroud of terror, anticipating the bullets that will shatter her body. Somewhere in the last few minutes, she knew she should have tried to escape, but that thought now seems impossibly far off. It recedes into the distance, fading away, away for all time, out of her reach. On either side of her are naked people. Glancing over her shoulder she sees an orderly line of soldiers with rifles. There seems to be one soldier for each Jew. She could run now, run or jump into the pit before they shoot. A command is shouted.

She holds her head back over one shoulder. Straining it back as far as it will go. Eyes in turn stretch to try to see what is happening. She feels her thighs suddenly warm as her bowels let go. Run. Run. At least don't give them the satisfaction of having you die they way they wanted. Fluid washes onto her feet and the ground underneath them becomes warmly slimy. Or jump. Jump into the pit ahead of the rifle shot. She crouches and turns to face the front. The air suddenly flashes bright. She feels a sledge hammer blow in the back of her head. Terrible pain invades her brain, her eyes, her chest, her lungs. Her body becomes pain. She falls forwards. Rolling down the sloping piece of the trench. There is wet mud in her face and eyes. The tumbling drives the pain into her like spikes. She falls onto something. Wet. Flesh. Bone. She smells and tastes the iron tang of blood. Then there is nothing.

The guard lights a match and sets fire to the pile of photographs. Two girls, sisters, posing in front of a tree. People at a beach, waving. Schoolchildren in a classroom. Babies – in prams, baths, in photographer's studios. A couple walking hand in hand in woods. Groups posing on the bank of the river – or it could be the canal – with one of the numerous bridges in the background. Everyone seems to be in their best clothes – coats, suits and ties on the men, the women in long skirts or dresses with their hair tied up. An excursion, some people wearing jackets and ties, to a hilltop. The two photographs that Ariela used to keep by her bedside. The last one is of two women out for a walk – one with a coat and hat, the other in a sweater, cap and skirt and pushing a bike. There are bare trees and long shadows.

Chapter 8

In the pitch darkness five candles and a hundred times as many mirrors create countless fingers of flame. The Children's Memorial at Yad Vashem in Jerusalem. The flames symbolise the souls of children who perished in the Shoah. After the blinding morning sunlight, the underground interior is womb-like.

A voice speaks the names quietly and without emotion.

'Marek Steinbaum. Aged nine.'

Where does a sound go when it dies?

Aftermath

The cart driver who drove Ariela and her parents to the station on that sunny Sunday was not Jewish and survived the war. The baby-faced Chassid who smiled at Ariela was murdered in Treblinka. Of his colleagues that day on the bench not one survived the war. One ended up in Odessa and was there on 23 October 1941 when, with 19,000 other Jews, he was taken to the square at the harbour. The square was surrounded by a wooden fence. Here they were sprayed with gasoline and burnt alive. The railway official retired from the railway service during the wave of government sponsored anti-semitism in 1968. He was not Jewish. Of the twenty Polish soldiers, over half were killed during the war or died in captivity. One is alive today, as is the young Pole who helped Ariela with her luggage, and the man beside the window with whom she changed places. The taxi driver was killed during the bombing of Warsaw on 1 September 1939. The man with the chair whom the taxi driver swerved to avoid was killed by the Germans in a random shooting. The hotel owner and his wife died in Treblinka during the emptying of the Warsaw ghetto in the summer of 1942. All the other people at dinner that night were Jewish and died during the *Shoah*.

The porter in David's office survived the war. The people in the embassies whom David and Anna met all went on to pursue successful diplomatic careers.

Ariela's schoolfriends, Sophia and Rebecca, together with their families, were rounded up on 16 July 1942. They were amongst 7,000 people crowded into the Vel d'Hiver sports arena in Paris and left there for days with no food, water or sanitation. Some time later they were shipped to Auschwitz. Both girls were the only members of their families to be selected for slave labour and both died in that camp before it was liberated in 1945.

The Austrian refugee that Ariela and Katya met in Prague died of starvation in Theresienstadt. The Jewish girl in the department store, who helped Ariela to choose her clothes, was deported to Treblinka during the great deportation of 1942 and gassed there.

Heinrich Katz, who was in the SS with Otto in 1939, was killed at Stalingrad. The Jewish family they terrorised on that night in November was deported to Riga in Latvia exactly three years later. When the train arrived, they were marched from the train to a wooded area near the Rumbuli railway station, undressed and shot into pits.

Rottenfuhrer Bauer, Private Fritsch and Private Eberle all survived the war, though Bauer left his legs behind at the Battle of Kursk. The two women and the eldest daughter were shot by Otto's unit the night they cooked the meal. The two remaining orphaned children were shot some weeks later by Einsatzgruppen members.

Of the two Polish policemen, one survived the war. The other was killed fighting for the Polish underground, the Armia Krajowa. The woman from whom Otto confiscated the telephone died of starvation on a street in the Lodz ghetto. Her child died in a gas van at Chelmno. The old man whom David saw hustled off a tram was shot a few minutes later in a back street in Lodz.

Paul, Rudolf's assistant, spent the years immediately following the Second World War unemployed and subject to war crimes investigations. Eventually, at the beginning of the 1950s, he went into private industry where he carved out a successful career for himself.

The Jews who were deported to the ghetto in Ozorkow were all subsequently deported to Chelmno where they were gassed.

Of the people who attended the conference at which Rudolf

spoke, other members of Rudolf's staff, Eva Frank, Otto's colleagues Erwin, Bucholz and Probst, Becker, Wilhelm, his lieutenant, the police officers who participated in the executions, the SS man at Chelmno, Ulrich who had the photographs and movie, the two burly men in the coffee shop of Gestapo headquarters, the SS guard who ordered David to push the wheelbarrow, the female SS guard with the blonde hair, the SS doctors and staff at Auschwitz, some were killed during the war; the remainder returned to civilian or professional life. Several of the police officers returned to the post-war police service.

There were approximately 233,000 Jews living in Lodz on the eve of the Second World War. When Lodz was liberated by the Red Army on 19 January 1945, there were about 800 in the city left alive. Those dead included Chaim Rumkowski who was deported to Auschwitz in 1944, along with the rest of his family.

Hans Biebow, head of the German Lodz Ghetto administration, was tried in a Polish court after the war. He was later hanged.

Dietrich Hick disappeared during the Second World War, being last heard of on 18 September 1944.

Gebeitskommisar Gerhardt Erren was tried in Germany in 1973. On 26 June 1974, aged 73, he was found guilty and sentenced to life imprisonment.

Arthur Nebe, who addressed Otto's *Einsatzgruppe,* was executed by the Nazis on 3 April 1945 on a charge of 'treason'. Sturmbannfuhrer Rolf-Heinz Hoppner was never charged with any offence. Adolf Eichmann was hanged for war crimes in Israel on 1 June 1962.

Hauptscharfuhrer Gustav Laabs was sentenced to fifteen years imprisonment in Bonn in 1963. He died in prison.

Walter Burmeister was sentenced to thirteen years imprisonment as accessory to the murder of more than 150,000 people.

The American nurse whom David met returned to her home town of Staunton, Virginia, where she is happily married and in her late seventies. David Steinbaum is still alive in Israel.

Author's Note

With a book like this whose subject is the *Shoah*, it seems to me terribly important – indeed mandatory – that the reader is clear which parts are fiction and which are not. All of the characters, with the exception of named Nazis, Heinrich Himmler, Adolf Eichmann, Gustav Laabs, Burmeister, Dietrich Hick, Arthur Nebe, Sturmbannfuhrer Rolf-Heinz Hoppner are fictitious. The historic events and places described – the Lodz ghetto, Chelmno, Slonim and the November massacre there – are all real, however, and the descriptions of them are based on contemporary accounts and documents.

Becker's itinerary in Part V Chapter 11 is based on a similar one to be found in the book *Those Were The Days* by Ernst Klee, Willi Dressen and Volker Riess. The letter in Part 4 Chapter 6 is taken verbatim from the same book.

Rudolf Fest is a fictional character, but the Statistics department in which he initially works was real, as was his boss Dr Korherr. The conference he goes to is imaginary but is based on other similar conferences. The logistical department within Eichmann's Section IV B 4 to which he is transferred is imaginary – no trace of such a department has been found. However, such a department would have to have existed [see *Harvest of Hate*, Leon Poliakov, Holocaust Library, 1979, pp. 145], and I have tried to imagine what it must have been like.

The operational announcements are based on material in

Hitler's Willing Executioners [Daniel Goldhagen, Little Brown, 1996] and the Einsatzgruppen reports are real and taken from *The Einsatzgruppen Reports* [Yitzhak Arad, Shmuel Krakowski, Shmuel Spector, Holocaust Library, 1989]. The actual dates of the former have been modified slightly to fit in with the chronology of the narrative. The phrase '*10,000 Jews were processed in Slonim ...*' was inserted by me into the entry for 14 November on the basis that such a report of the actual event would have appeared somewhere.

Forgotten

You wanton, quiet memory that haunts me all the while
In order to remind me of her whom love I send.
Perhaps when you caress me sweetly, I will smile,
You are my confidante today, my very dearest friend.

You sweet remembrance, tell a fairy tale
About my girl who's lost and gone, you see.
Tell, tell the one about the golden grail
And call the swallow, bring her back to me.

Fly somewhere back to her and ask her, soft and low,
If she thinks of me sometimes with love,
If she is well and ask her too before you go
If I am still her dearest, precious dove.

And hurry back, don't lose your way,
So I can think of other things,
But you were too lovely, perhaps, to stay.
I loved you once. Goodbye, my love!

Zdenek Ohrenstein

Zdenek Ohrenstein was deported to the Terezin ghetto on 24 October 1942 at the age of thirteen. From there he was sent to Auschwitz. He survived the war and died in Prague on 4 November 1990.